The King and Prince

The King and Prince

Tom Morris

A Journey of Risk

Book Four

Walid and the Mysteries of Phi

Wisdom/Work
Published by Wisdom Work
TomVMorris.com

Published 2017

ISBN 9780999352441

Printed in the United States of America

Set in Adobe Garamond Pro
Designed by Abigail Chiaramonte
Cover Concept by Sara Morris

To Grayson Teague Morris:
I hope you enjoy reading this story at least half
as much as I enjoyed writing it!

Contents

I

Some Unexpected Action

Egypt: Many years ago.

The twentieth century had been around for only three and a half decades. Many things had changed in the world with this new era. More had not. And as at all other times and in most other places, a peaceful day could quickly turn into something quite different.

Danger often announces its approach, even if just in a whisper. But if you're not listening, you might not hear it coming. That's why even the worst circumstances and most dire threats can sometimes take people by surprise, despite any cautionary signs they might have provided in advance.

Hoda El-Bay, her daughter Kissa, and Kissa's best friend Hasina were all sitting on the bare wooden floor of a moderately spacious room above a tailor and seamstress shop about three blocks from the El-Bay home, a space accessed by an external staircase that reached up the side of the plain and modest building. Hoda and the proprietors of the shop were old friends, and the two owners had offered her this empty space for what had been described to them as some special exercise and workout times she would have with the girls. They held other sessions in the palace, but it was good to have a space set apart like this, as well. They could have more privacy away from their normal environment.

It was a short walk to the shop, typically three or four days a week, and a nice time to enjoy some fresh air along the way after hours of schoolwork inside the palace classroom. Best of all, they could do their most intense Phi training sessions here in total seclusion, without any unexpected interruptions or prying eyes. The business downstairs was booming, and because of that, the owners rarely had a chance even to say hello during their normal hours of operation. Plus, Hoda had explained at the very start that their sessions would require completely undisturbed quiet.

The shop was about to close for the day. The three members of Phi had just sat down after their big workout to relax and talk quietly about the main elements of the day's session. They could hear the two shopkeepers outside the store laughing loudly and saying goodbye to a customer and then closing up and leaving for the night just a few moments later. It was approaching that almost twilight time between very late afternoon and early evening, and they were all due to go home for dinner soon.

The girls had been having an unusually hard workout with Hoda on this particular day. They had started with some easy yoga and other stretching exercises, had moved on to more aerobic warm-ups, and then they had done an hour and a half of specific weapons practice, rehearsing and drilling some difficult things they had been working on for weeks. After that, they had gone through a few simple cool down exercises. They were now in a general discussion about body strength, weapons, and the nature of hand-to-hand fighting.

Hoda said, "It's important to remember that the concept of a weapon is a functional idea."

"What do you mean?" Kissa asked right away.

"A weapon is essentially a tool with a suitable range of uses, and this means that almost anything that's available with the right properties and at the right time can function as a weapon. Remember when your friends Set and Jabari were kidnapped?"

"Sure," both girls answered.

Hasina said, "Set found a gun and Jabari picked up an ordinary screwdriver to use to defend themselves."

"Yes. Exactly," Hoda responded. "Both could be used as weapons, and both were. A weapon doesn't have to be designed or made to be such, or even generally recognized for that potential. It doesn't need to be a standard knife, or sword, or gun, or anything else that might come to mind when people hear the word. It's anything that can be used to extend your defensive or offensive power in a context of physical threat or attack."

The girls nodded. Kissa said, "That makes sense."

Hoda continued. "Whenever you're in a situation of possible threat, you need to be aware of anything in your environment that could be used as a tool of defense. And in fact, that's a good general practice in any case. A creatively defensive mindset will quickly see potential weapons all around, where the ordinary untrained eye sees none."

Hasina said, "You mean that something like a brick or a stick, or a long hairpin could be a weapon."

"Yes."

"Or even a vase, or a rope, or a pot of hot tea," Kissa added.

"Definitely. Even an empty pot, or a scarf, a belt or a book, or a door—anything that you can use to delay, deflect, or defeat an adversary. You need an opportunistic mindset to see the defensive or offensive potential in the things around you. When you do, you become a person who is almost never unarmed—or, at least, not for long. Look for a weapon and you'll find one."

Kissa said, "It seems like what you're calling an opportunistic mindset can be helpful way beyond times of physical conflict."

"You're absolutely right," Hoda replied. "With any goal in mind, the opportunistic mindset naturally finds tools that can help to accomplish that goal, or at least move you in its direction—tools that others with a similar goal might miss if they're not properly focused and thinking openly, flexibly, and creatively."

The conversation continued on in this vein for a few more minutes. The girls were relaxed and deep in thought, taking in all that their teacher was sharing with them from her personal experience. In the middle of it all, Hoda had just said something funny and the sudden loud laughter from the girls covered the noise of faintly creaking wooden steps outside the door of the room, a sound that they otherwise most likely would have heard. But it was without any detected warning that a big man flung open the door and stepped through the doorway, holding in his hand a large knife. He looked as surprised as they all were.

"Well, look at what we've got here," he said. "Three lovely ladies all alone."

At the first sound of his voice, Hoda slowly stood up and turned around to face the door. Following her lead, Kissa and Hasina rose as well, with an army of butterflies in their stomachs, fluttering and flying about frantically.

"What do you want?" Hoda asked the man in a calm but firm tone. Her face held no expression.

"Oh, you'll find out soon enough, I think. Yes, you will."

"We're having a private meeting here."

"Well, that's nice, but it's not so private anymore."

"I need to ask you to leave us in peace."

"Oh. No. I'm sorry. That's not happening. I think it's my lucky day. You're a real bunch of top-of-the-line beauties. All of you are a real prize—yes, indeed." The man was sliding a finger slowly along the side of the blade of his knife now as he spoke. Then he said, "Where are your men?"

"There are no men here," Hoda answered and surprised both the girls and the interloper.

Without taking his gaze off Hoda, the man turned his head slightly and barked out in a louder voice, "Boys, come up here now!" A scrambling on the staircase outside the door announced the arrival of more intruders. There were two other men, both of them shorter, thinner, and younger than the man who had called them, but also strong and rough in appearance.

All three of the strangers were wearing rumpled, torn, and badly soiled clothes. The big one now wiped the back of his hand over his mouth and grinned in a distinctly malevolent way, while he said to Hoda, and maybe also the others, "We came here just to take some cash from the shop down there, but it looks like we're in for a lot more than a little extra money tonight."

"You should rethink your plans," she said, softly.

The older man ignored her words, and the shortest of them said slowly, "Bandar, we hit the jackpot here. Look at these three, like something from a movie. And there's one for each of us."

"You need to leave," Hoda said again.

The large man said, "I don't think we need to do anything we don't want to do. Like I said, it's our lucky day. Maybe it's yours, too." He paused. "Why don't you boys close the door? I think we might need a little time here alone and private with our new friends. I don't want anybody to hear us up here and interrupt our time together. We can have a real party. And, you know what? I bet three fine females like these might also have some extra cash they'd be willing to share with us—and I wouldn't be surprised at all to come across some nice, expensive jewelry here, by the look of these three. But first of all, Ahmed, I should award you the smallest little lady over here."

"She's gorgeous."

"Yes, you're right. I may have to take her back in a little while for myself, but she's yours for now."

"What about me?" The other man said.

"Tasir, you get the beauty in the middle. The older one's mine, just mine." By that point, all three men clearly had knives in their hands. The older man was gripping the handle of a longer, curved blade. The two others had shorter, but still very intimidating, weapons. And their expressions could not have been more menacing.

Throughout all of this, since her firm suggestion, Hoda had been preparing herself, silently listening and observing the men, taking in everything she could about the situation. So had Kissa and Hasina. They were all using what Masoon called "The Triple Double" for dealing with trouble—prepare, perceive; anticipate, avoid; concentrate, and control.

As the older man had been talking and staring right at Hoda, apparently unable to take his eyes off her, Hasina had been moving slowly and very gradually backward and to her right, inching toward a nearby table. The two younger men noticed but thought nothing of it, since, as far as they could see, she had nowhere to go. There was no escape available. And there were some rolled up mats on the table that blocked any view of what Hasina had in mind. Hoda was the closest to the door, and she was having her customary effect on any man who caught sight of her. The other two were nearly as mesmerized as the one who was apparently their leader, and they kept returning their attention to her.

Hoda herself was looking intently from one face to the next, always gazing into their eyes as they looked back at hers, and mentally commanding them to restore eye-to-eye contact whenever their glance wandered to take in the rest of her appearance, or anything else in the room. They were all in one way or another magnetically locked in on her and a bit mesmerized. She was now breathing slowly. And her lips suddenly parted as if in preparation for speaking, while she gently began to raise her hands in a gesture that could appear to be a first bodily preparation for imploring these men to please stop and reconsider and have mercy on them. But appearances are notoriously unreliable guides.

Before anyone could register what was going on, the older man yelled, "Ow!" and grabbed his head with his left hand just as Hoda sprang forward to kick the knife out of his other hand and, spinning, lunged again with a second vicious kick that sent him sprawling into the wall and the door behind him. As he shouted out in more pain and his two companions, caught totally off guard, quickly looked over at him, dazed and puzzled, to see what was happening, Hasina had picked up two long items from the table next to her and, yelling to her best friend, threw her one of them, a razor sharp sword that they had just been using in their practice session.

When the older man slammed backward into the wall and his younger companions had looked over at him in shock, the girls sprang into action. In the moment that it took the two of them to glance back at the girls, Kissa and Hasina now stood facing them in a slightly crouched posture with their swords held out in front of them, ready for anything. Each of the girls was mentally saying to herself, “Calm, stay calm—now concentrate and control.”

“What the?” Ahmed had time to say before Hasina, the one he had just been given as his own, swung her blade so quickly and carefully that she instantly disarmed him without touching any part of his body, removing the knife from his hand with a quick flick from the tip of her sword, and sending it flying across the room. At nearly the same time, Kissa was doing roughly the same thing to a completely stunned Tasir, who shouted in pain and began to back up, rubbing his hand, as the blade he had held bounced noisily off the side wall of the room, a good ten or twelve feet away. He had moved just as she swung and so had taken a deep cut across a part of his hand.

“Down on your knees!” Hasina yelled out as she had been taught. Adrenalin was coursing through her body at this point, but all her practice had taken over and she was doing exactly what she had repeated many times in their sessions. As she and Kissa now held the points of their swords toward the assailants who had meant them such harm, the older man on the floor, unnoticed at this moment by the two of them, quickly pulled out a small concealed handgun and raised it directly toward Kissa. From across the room, Hoda had just grabbed her own practice sword off the table a split second before this infuriated, half-crazed man pulled the trigger, unleashing an overwhelming explosion that tore at their ears in this otherwise empty and enclosed space, shocking everyone else.

Two things of great importance happened in an extremely brief span of time. Kissa, having overheard an earlier sound of movement from the big man's direction, had turned quickly at the last moment, caught a glimpse of his revolver and, in a move worthy of a world class gymnast, had twisted her body around and downward in such a way that the otherwise lethal bullet missed her completely and tore into the wall just past her. Hoda, noticing the man's finger as it pulled on the trigger, quickly threw the sword in her hand with all her might across the room where, flying straight and true to its aim, it pierced his gut and penetrated deep into his body, ripping away his life within the next few seconds. But, before she could see the result of her throw, she had witnessed Kissa's move, dashed across the room, picked up a knife off the floor, checked on her daughter's safety, and now stood confronting the other two men.

"No! No!" The two younger men were shouting out at the same time, as they looked at her in shock. One added, "Please!"

Hoda said, "Faces on the floor, hands in front of you! Obey and live. Disobey and die!"

The two men immediately lay flat with arms and hands outstretched as they had been told. The youngest pleaded, "Don't kill us." And just as soon as he said that, he felt the sharp point of a sword in his lower back, hard against his clothes. One threatening move and he knew he would be skewered. The other man felt the same thing, but the point of the sword touching him was on the back of his neck, at the base of his skull. Kissa was seriously ready to end for good the danger that this one posed. Murder had already been attempted, and they had been well taught to meet the level of danger they faced with an appropriate degree of countervailing force, as necessary.

Kissa was breathing deeply. She said, "You're both so close to death, I hope you can taste it," and she pushed ever so slightly on her sword so that the point of her blade would barely pierce skin and draw a little blood but, at this moment, nothing more.

"Ow! Ow! No, please! We're sorry! We mean you no harm."

"It's easy for you to say that now, isn't it?" Hasina replied.

At this point, Hoda had grabbed some rope from the corner of the room, something they had used in practice the previous week, and she was quickly tying the two men, hands and feet, cutting the rope in lengths with the knife in her hand. She moved quickly and efficiently, almost as if she did this every day.

"Stay still, cooperate, and you'll live to see tomorrow," she said softly while she worked. "But the least resistant move from either of you will be the last move of your life."

"We're still. We won't move." Tasir had fear in his voice, and that terrified Ahmed even more. Tasir was his older brother and was always strong, and even arrogant. But now, he spoke from what sounded like nothing but the worst sort of fright and alarm.

Just then, the nob on the door turned and someone tried to open it, but the older man's lifeless body blocked access. The door banged against him a second time, harder, and a third time, harder still, pushing forward an inch or two, but the heavy bulk of the inert body prevented its opening. Hoda had turned at the first sound of this, with the knife still in her hand, and she quietly positioned herself up against the wall right beside the doorframe, to be unseen at first by any other intruder who might force his way into the room. She knew how to stop anyone in his tracks at his very first movement into the room. Speed would be necessary because she understood that, whoever this was, he likely had heard the gun shot already and now even saw a body on the floor, and would come in prepared for a fight. But if her angle of attack was perfect and her lunge was fast, there would be nothing an adversary could do in self-defense, and she knew this with complete and total confidence.

What she didn't anticipate was that this new arrival would have the strength to kick down the door, which he immediately did, and it fell from its old hinges into the room. The shock and sound of it forced her back a few inches, as she suddenly heard a loud voice call out.

Not far away, King Ali was sitting in his usual seat at an unusually early dinner with Walid and Mafulla. He put down his fork and said, "I almost forgot to tell you something interesting, a piece of news that could be quite illuminating for us all."

"What's is it, Your Majesty?" Walid spontaneously asked.

"There's an old man who worked in the palace long ago. Our friend Bancom met him last week. From what he told me, Bancom was sitting at a café in town where he often has breakfast, and he overheard this man at a nearby table telling some funny stories and a few dramatic tales from decades past, all featuring the basement of the palace."

"Really?" Walid said.

"Yes. The man who was speaking apparently once had the title, Director of Palace Storage."

"No way." Mafulla said.

"Yes, indeed. I've had Bancom track him down since then and invite him to come by to see us the day after tomorrow for dinner. I think there's a chance he might be able to help clear up some mysteries lurking in and around this place."

"Wow. That would be so great," Mafulla said. He was obviously excited by the news and went on: "Maybe he can tell us about all the Fibonacci numbers and golden ratio stuff in the storage rooms, and in the tunnel, and in a few other places."

"That's exactly what I was thinking," the king said.

"That Fibonacci stuff is so strange," Mafulla replied. "I mean, just look at my hands."

"What about your hands?" Walid asked.

Mafulla held both his hands up over his plate, with his fingers spread out wide, and continued by saying, "Before I was born, there were no Mafulla hands—zero. Then, I came into the world with one hand on my right, and one hand on my left, adding up to exactly two hands. Each hand in turn has fingers consisting of three segments separated by knuckles, and there are five such fingers on each hand." He stared at his left hand and pointed with his right.

"Ok. So?" Walid laughed and said this with a smile on his face. He knew he was going to hear something interesting in reply. Maffie never let him down. The king was also slightly smiling in anticipation, even though he knew what was coming, as the intellectually handy Mafulla Adi responded with enthusiasm and began to explain.

"So—what we handily have are the numbers zero, one, one, two, three, and five, and they're the first sequential Fibonacci numbers."

"Oh, man," Walid replied with a smile.

"No, no. It's important. These numbers structure the most basic realities of my hands. I mean, as you know, of course, they're all over nature—describing seashell spirals and flower petal numbers and the swirls of galaxies and … many other things, and they're in our bodies, and so is their cousin, Phi, the golden ratio. And of course, none of that has anything to do with human free choice. All of it comes from somewhere that's way beyond our capacity for choice. And, yet, we've also kept coming across these same numbers since we moved into the palace—I mean, since you took power, Your Majesty, and you and the prince so graciously invited me to the world's longest sleepover here, which, of course, I love—and the occurrences of these numbers in the palace and around town clearly originated in ways that do involve human free choice."

"Indeed," The king said.

And Mafulla continued. "Just think about the boxes in the basement storage rooms being numbered by the sequence, and all the locks we've gotten through with a part of Phi, 1.618, as the source of the digits in the combination, or permutation, that opened the locks. And of course, there was the safety deposit box at the bank where we got The Stone of Giza and the box was number 1618, and there was that street name and the number of the building where Idi Falma was operating in the warehouse district and our friends were held hostage—1618 Golden Street. And then, of course, there's the weirdest thing of all, maybe."

"Which is what?" Walid asked.

"A hybrid of human free action and what goes way beyond that: Your birthday, of course," Mafulla said, before he had even thought about the fact that he was saying it in front of the king, a fact he was now reminded of by the look of complete surprise on Walid's face.

"Oh," Mafulla said, looking at Walid and then at the king. "Oh, Gee. Ok, I should explain." Now, looking at the king, he said, "I noticed months ago and pointed out to Walid that his birthday is a proper set of Fibonacci numbers. And he said it's most likely just a coincidence that doesn't really mean anything at all. And I thought, maybe so, but then again, maybe it does—you can't be sure. And he sort of, I think, really didn't want me to go around talking about it. And I don't, I don't at all, but I mentioned it just now because, well, you know, it's just us here and we feel free to tell you pretty much anything and everything, at this point, Your Majesty, as you have yourself wished and even asked. And I really, really don't go around ever saying anything about this, I double and triple promise—which are both, of course, good Fibonacci promises—but, there you go."

"There's no need to worry. I know all about Walid's birthday."

"You do?"

"Yes. I was there. He was a nice looking baby. I saw him right after they gave him a little bath and wrapped him in a blanket."

"Oh, Ok. But, I mean, you also know about the date and everything? It has occurred to you that this is not just any sequence of numbers?"

"Well, of course. Walid's date of birth, 8-13-21, in that standard, shortened form of month, day, and year identification within our century, is indeed a sequence of Fibonacci numbers. And it's a sequence in perfect order. And, furthermore, you may not have realized that prior to his birth, there were 0 children in that 1 house, and so he was the number 1 and only child of 2 parents, whose birth created a nuclear family of 3, sharing a home with what at the time was an extended family including me and my mother, Walid's grandmother, or exactly 5 people in all, total. With those facts running up to and through his birth, you have then the full beginning of the infinite Fibonacci series as it is most completely given by classic mathematicians, the series of: 0,1,1,2,3,5,8,13, and 21. To get this series, as you know, we begin at the absolute starting point of 0 and make the first natural whole addition of 1. And then after that, each subsequent number that has two numbers before it is the sum of those two. So after the beginning of 0 and 1, we get as the next number their sum, and thus 1 is repeated. Then the subsequent number is the sum of 1 plus 1, or 2. Then there come the numbers, 3, 5, 8, 13, and 21. And all of those, of course, comprise a complete Fibonacci segment of the famous series that never ends. And that segment corresponds to a lot of Walid's family history up to and including his date of birth."

"Wow. I didn't know all that about the series and the family and birth."

"The series is mysterious and quite interesting in all of its many applications."

"Yes, Your Majesty—I totally agree. I mean, I remember all about its construction from our first discussion of it. I just didn't know all that about Walid and his family and how it mapped onto the series."

"I'd never thought about it like that, either," the prince said.

The king, who was enjoying this, continued. "And then, as you may have realized, you can add Walid's current age of 13 to the year of his birth, 21, and you get the next number in the series, 34, a number that's quite significant because, in this century, it was in the 34th year that we laid the final foundations for our political revolution that will eventually make him king. And we arrived here mere months ago in that 34th year, shortly after Walid turned 13. Plus, and you wouldn't know this, but he's apparently the 55th member of our family in known history to live and serve in the palace of our kingdom in some royal capacity, if the history books are right and our family journals are complete. And, of course, 34 and 55 are the next Fibonacci numbers, as I'm sure you know. But then, again, who's counting?" The king laughed and took a sip of tea. And then he added, "And, by the way, 34 added to 55 gives us the next Fibonacci number, 89, which was the number of the mystery box that contained the hidden objects, The Book of Phi and Ring of Phi, and that got your crime solving adventures together started—without which, I'm sure you'd agree, there would likely be no Golden Viper and Windstorm.

Walid and Mafulla were both just staring at him, mouths open.

"If I didn't know first hand that you had just enjoyed a big meal with abundant juice to drink, I would think that, with your mouths so wide open, you both look like a couple of hungry and thirsty camels."

"Oh, sorry," Walid said. "I'm just amazed by all this."

Mafulla said, "Does it have any … significance?"

"Yes, I'm sure it does," the king replied.

"What does it all mean?" Walid now asked.

The king looked at him with great kindness and said, "You seem to be specially marked, I think it's safe to say."

"But, for what?"

"For a remarkable life, perhaps? Or, it could be for a special destiny, for an unusual role in the world."

"But, what does that mean?"

"No one is yet sure. I've always been convinced that you're here on the earth for a special reason, that you have a unique mission, important work that you're to do, and a distinctive, far-reaching impact that you're here to make."

"But, isn't that true of everybody? I mean, each of us? You've been teaching me that every one of us has something like a royal birthright, a special place in the realm of the spirit, an irreplaceable mission that we can either embrace or avoid. How am I, then, any different?"

"It's true that everyone is marked, by their very birth into this world, and set apart for a mission of good, a mission that too many refuse in their avid pursuit of other things, or else in an easy, lethargic pursuit of nothing. Each of us is, by birth and nature, unique, special, and set apart. But some of us are set apart in quite unusual ways, and not in every case in ways of our own choosing, at least initially. But we must eventually decide and opt to embrace the mission that we sense we have, or else we'll drift through life and never find the thread we were here to follow. There's something about your mission here that none of us fully understands yet, but that's been announced, we might say, by the special circumstances of your birth in our small out-of-the-way village, as esoteric and hidden from the general public as those circumstances might be."

Walid said, "But it's not exactly like I was born in a stable and laid in a manger under a special star with shepherds and angels all around. Although, I do know there were at least a couple of wise men present on that day."

"Ha!" Mafulla laughed loudly.

"No, you're right. It wasn't like that." The king chuckled. "And, fortunately for us all, you most likely don't have a mission that demanding awaiting you, by any means."

"But, right now, you can't tell me anything more about all those numbers and their meaning, if any, for my life?"

"Not at the present time. There are things yet to be revealed."

Walid remembered the few special times he had heard his uncle say those words, and they always foreshadowed something of great importance that would soon happen or be discovered. The king didn't talk like that lightly, but always with special care and conscious intention.

Walid took a deep breath and said, "Ok, then. I'm a guy who can live with a little mystery."

Mafulla spoke up. "You're a man of mystery, my friend, and I am just pleased to be your slightly enigmatic side-kick."

"Enigmatic?"

"Look it up."

Walid laughed and said, "Fortunately, I don't have to. I just like the fact that you're being mysterious about the word 'enigmatic.' That seems nicely appropriate."

"Yes. I work hard to be a puzzle wrapped up inside a conundrum, and 'Riddle' should be my middle name—although, admittedly, many may just see me as odd. But don't worry. I will eventually get … even." And of course, Mafulla's eyebrows shot up on that last word.

Walid couldn't help but laugh. And the king also enjoyed hearing this silliness. He said, "There's nothing like a little Mafoolery to tie a bow on the day."

Walid said, "Yes, indeed."

And, in response, Mafulla just grinned and did his full famous double eyebrow jump.

2

New Things on the Horizon

"Freeze in place and stay where you are! No one moves!" The very loud voice of a man boomed out from right beyond the doorway.

Hasina could hear her heartbeat in her ears. A slight shiver ran up her arms. She was ready for almost anything at this point, and somehow at the same time she realized that she wasn't afraid. Kissa was feeling the same, and then her first moment of shock quickly gave way to a sense of peace—of everything being all right.

"Palace Guards!" Those were the next words they heard, from a different voice, and then into the room came Omari and Paki, guns drawn and ready for use, instantly sweeping right and left to take in the entire space and everything in it.

"Oh!" Paki exclaimed.

"Oh, my!" Hoda said, as she relaxed and stepped out from where she had been concealed against the wall. "What a nice surprise for a change! It's good to see you two! We've had quite a time here. We could use some help to get a couple of malefactors to jail."

Omari said, "Hoda! Kissa! Hasina! What happened? Are you Ok?"

"Yes," Hoda answered. "We're all fine. These men were here at first to rob the shop below us, but then they crept up the stairs to where we were in our regular exercise and training session, and when they saw us, they immediately began to have other malicious thoughts that were made clear with unwelcome words and actions. Their intimated intentions couldn't have been worse."

"Is this man dead?" Omari looked at the older man who was lying motionless on the floor.

"Yes, I'm sad to say that he's gone. His body alone remains and will need to be moved."

"How did it happen?" Omari bent down to him and slowly pulled the sharp sword from the man's torso.

"I relieved him of a large knife, and kicked him into the door and down to the floor. When I was reaching over for the practice sword like the ones the girls had just used to remove weapons from the two younger men, he suddenly pulled out a gun and shot at Kissa before I could stop him."

"Oh, no!"

"Yes."

Omari turned to Kissa. "Are you Ok?"

"Yeah. I dodged it."

Both Paki and Omari looked especially impressed. Hoda continued: "And then, I did manage to stop him from any further attempts at such harm. These other two were at that point easy to tie up. I think the charges of assault with a deadly weapon and attempted murder, added to attempted robbery, should do the trick."

"We didn't do anything!" Tasir grumbled out from the floor. "I should have cut your throat for what you did to Bandar!"

"Quiet!" Omari shouted, as Paki moved over and squatted down and placed the end of the barrel of his gun on the man's face.

Holding the hard steel tip of the weapon up against the man's right cheek, Paki pushed it gently forward, cocked the hammer back, and said in a low voice, "You will not speak again, or your next words might be your last."

"Wait," Omari said, looking back at Hoda. "Did you say that the girls disarmed these two?"

"Yes."

Kissa explained, "We've practiced a lot."

"Very nice," Omari said. "Was this your first time with a real opponent?"

"Yes," Hasina quickly replied.

"Me, too," Kissa admitted as well.

"Were you nervous?"

Hasina answered. "Only at first, and then I knew we could do whatever we had to. We've had great training. If these guys had put up a fight, they would have ended up like the older one. I was ready and I knew Kissa was. I mean, in some ways, it's really different from practice, but once you focus, what you've practiced takes over."

"Good," Omari said. "That's the way it's supposed to be."

"Very good," Paki echoed.

Omari put his index finger to his lips in a way that all three ladies could see, but the criminals could not, and he then said, "You know, we should take both these guys to jail, but it would be a lot easier if we had just one to carry."

"Yes, I agree with you completely," Paki said. And then he added, "But what can we do?

"A gunshot to the head at this point would make too much noise, especially with no door on the room anymore, and it could attract unwanted attention. So, maybe you should put your gun away. My special position in the military gives me the legal right to do whatever I see fit while we're still in a field of conflict, which is really what this has become. But I wouldn't want to have to explain to strangers or a regular city policeman all the details. So, no gun shots."

Paki replied, "I agree. We'd need to explain far too much. And we don't have the time." He had an intuitive feel for what Omari was doing now, and wanted to help out in any way he could.

Omari then said, "Look, Hoda, I haven't used a sword in this way in years, but I was expertly trained long ago and still remember how to be most effective with one. And I have to say, these are sharp."

"Wait. You've taken a life with a sword before?" Paki asked.

"Yes, unfortunately, my friend, far too many times in the past. So, actually, what's one more? It's good to stay in practice. And it's always right to rid the world of dangerous vermin."

"Wait," the younger man said.

Paki ignored him. "I feel the same. So, which one of them will it be?"

"I don't know. One of them has spoken disrespectfully. But maybe we should let the ladies decide." At that, Omari reached out to both girls and they handed over their swords, which he clanged together, and then he swished one blade down the length of the other one, making a distinctive sound that could not be confused with anything else.

Both the subdued criminals had begun to breathe more heavily, but were otherwise silent again as they listened to all this. The younger one was clearly covered in sweat and began to groan softly. Omari put the point of a sword on each of their necks and said, "Ok, ladies, I would like you to choose. Who lives a bit longer, and who goes now?"

"No! Please!"

"No! Have mercy on us!" Both men broke their silence with cringing pleas, first the younger man, then the slightly older one, equally desperate to fend off an end they had not anticipated on this evening.

Omari said, "Roll over and face your fate." He shoved one of them over with his foot, onto his back, and then he did the same with the other. He looked at the face of the older one, and then stared into the eyes of the younger man. "I want both of you to know in this moment, first hand, from real experience, what it feels like to be under a credible threat of immediate death, and to be helpless in the face of that threat. I'm sure you've put other people through the experience, and it's not a pleasant one, as I know you'd agree. I want you to feel every moment of the situation you're now in before it's brought to a proper conclusion."

"But it wasn't our idea." The younger of the men spoke with stark fear in his voice.

Omari paused for effect and stared at each of them. Then he said, "I think I'll now use one of these swords to do away with … neither of you, at the moment."

"Are you sure?" Paki asked.

"Yes, for now. But a judge may decide differently at some time later. We'll see."

Paki smiled and said, "The quality of mercy is not strained."

Omari looked back and replied, "It droppeth as the gentle rain from heaven upon the place beneath."

Hasina said, "What?"

"Shakespeare," Hoda explained. "The Merchant of Venice, Act Four, Scene One." She looked back at Paki. "And we're the ones twice blessed today, by you two," she playfully concluded as an allusion to the next lines of the play being quoted.

Omari began to walk away from them at this point, but suddenly turned back and said, "Regardless of our current mercy, new things are on the horizon for both of you that you didn't anticipate today. And I promise they won't be enjoyable in any way." He paused. "And, by the way, you should know one thing. I'm not like you at all. I live within the law and uphold it and give our legal system the chance to do what it thinks best. But then again, our particular system says it's good for me to be able to defend myself as vigorously as I deem necessary. So, if you speak inappropriately again or disobey us now, or make any resistant move, you might not get to the jail or the judge after all. And I'll only be praised and commended for dealing with you decisively. Cooperation in every way is thus your only good option."

Both men were covered with sweat at this point from the visceral shock of the quick game Omari had just played with them, and were now silent again, mortified that they had been toyed with, and yet mostly just numb and shaken and angry and humbled at the same time—and grateful to be still alive.

Omari then said to Hoda, "We do need to get these two camel droppings to the palace jail and find out what we can about them. Paki and I can take them in. Why don't you ladies go home now? You can help us fill out the legal forms tomorrow, describing everything that happened here tonight. Once we get to the palace, we'll send someone for the body of the older one and have the room cleaned up and the door repaired right away. The owners need not be distressed by knowing that anything so alarming happened here this evening."

"Thank you, Omari. We're already much later than usual for getting home."

"Yeah, thanks," Kissa and Hasina said, at about the same time.

"You're welcome. You shouldn't have to bother yourselves with any more of this unpleasantness tonight."

Hoda said, "Before we go, though, I have to ask. How is it that you two are here with us at all?"

"Oh," Omari said, "Paki and I were walking to his apartment nearby to have dinner together, and about a block from here we heard the gun shot. We rushed over, saw the light on in this room, and crept up the stairs to intervene in whatever was going on. As you know, this is not a neighborhood where gunfire is to be expected."

"I'm glad you were nearby," Hoda said. "We could have handled these men ourselves, I assure you, but it would have been more difficult for us to get them to jail and locked away this evening. And others would have worried about where we were. So, I do appreciate your taking over for us now, both of you."

"It's our pleasure," Paki said.

"Yes, we're happy to help," Omari added. "And if we ever get into trouble, we now know who to call."

"Girl power," Kissa replied, right away.

Hoda laughed and said, "Yes. But, I just realized: What about your own dinner?" She was clearly concerned about these friends.

"Well, I think we'll get a snack back at the palace and still have plenty of time later for a good meal," Omari replied.

"Yes, my sister's fixing something for us tonight, and she's a very good cook," Paki said. "We'll still be back in plenty of time. We're often at work far beyond now. So don't worry about us."

Hours later, in the king's private quarters at the palace, things were winding down. After an evening of talk with Walid and Mafulla that was completely uninterrupted by royal business—which was unusual these days—the king finally looked down at his rose gold rectangular Reverso watch with its shimmering black face and announced, "My friends, I believe it's time for us to part. I wouldn't want to keep you up too late. I know you like to review your school work before bed."

"Yes, Uncle, I think we're both a little tired tonight. It was a big day."

"It promises to be a big day again tomorrow," the king said.

"Why?" Walid asked. "What's going on tomorrow?"

"There's a new ambassador here from Tunisia. He and his family have just moved to town. We're putting on some ceremonies to welcome him and introduce him and his son, who is about your age, I think, to some of the officials here in the palace as well as to a few of their fellow diplomats from several other countries. I'd love for the two of you to be present for at least one of the events that we have planned—a big reception tomorrow evening."

"Good. I'd like to meet them both," Walid said.

"Me, too," Mafulla agreed and then he smiled. "I may need to size up the new guy, and make sure he's no competition for me."

"His father's quite handsome. You never know," the king said as a joke.

"Oh. Well, we'll see, then," Mafulla replied. "The kid may be a junior movie star in appearance, but that doesn't mean anything in the real charm department. If there's nobody home behind the pretty face, he can't possibly pose any genuine threat to my lofty place in the hearts of the kingdom's lovelies."

"If Hasina could only hear you now." Walid smiled.

"Hey, I can't help it that I'm a natural charmer. I don't try to go around breaking hearts. It's just a fact we have to deal with."

"Is that right?"

"It is, indeed. And, of course, the beautiful Hasina knows she has no rivals in my heart. She's completely secure, and well aware of her solid place in my affections. I'm sure she has no jealousy at all toward all those many, many other young ladies who can't help but pine away for me, day and night."

That made Walid laugh and the king chuckle. "Enough!" The king said, "The two of you must leave now so that I can get my beauty rest, too—otherwise, how can I ever compete with Mafulla?"

With a waving of his hand, he shooed them up off their chairs, across the room, and then out the door. As the boys walked down the long hall toward their rooms, Mafulla said, "The king can be pretty funny."

"Yeah," Walid replied. "He really can."

"I think I'm having a good effect on him—you know, loosening him up a bit, inspiring his wit."

"A grateful kingdom will certainly appreciate your efforts."

"Yes, once they can take the full measure of his mirth." Mafulla said. And then he seemed to be in thought for a second before asking, "Have you previously heard anything about this new kid in town?"

"The ambassador's son?"

"Yeah."

"No, nothing until now."

"I wonder if he'll be in our class."

"Not likely. There's a school nearby for the children of ambassadors and prominent foreign businessmen who have offices here in the capital. I guess he'll be a student there."

"Oh, yeah, that's true. I forgot. But it'll still be good to meet another guy our age."

"I think so, too."

"Now, on a completely different topic: Do you feel super weird about all the Fibonacci stuff? You know, with your birthday and everything?"

"Well."

"First, I should say that I'm really sorry for mentioning it. I was just on a roll earlier and didn't stop to think. I didn't mean to say what I did. It was all spontaneous."

"Yeah, I knew."

"But I'm glad, too, because of all the stuff the king said in response that I had no idea about. I just don't want you to think I can't be trusted with, you know, private information."

"Don't worry about it. We can tell the king anything, and I guess we should, especially stuff that bothers us or puzzles us."

"Yeah, I know, you're right. But, what about all that stuff he said? How did you react? How do you feel now?"

"I'm not sure. It was all pretty general and sort of vague."

"Except for all the many non-vague ridiculous specifics."

"Ok, except for those."

"It means something to me that at least he's noticed all those things and thought about it, and so I'm not personally crazy in thinking that something strange is going on with your birthday and stuff."

"Yeah, apparently not, I guess. But otherwise, I always think it's safest to go with the personal craziness hypothesis. I mean, just where you're concerned, of course."

"Ha. But then, again: No-Ha. Seriously, my friend, let's face it. There's something extremely odd going on. I mean, some of the Fibonacci stuff and Phi stuff is natural, like I said, and beyond anyone's control or free choice—ratios in nature and the like. And some of it's clearly a result of somebody's deliberate intentions. And then there's the birthday stuff, which is ... what? It can't all be contrived, and be the simple result of human free choice. It has to be something beyond that. You could have been born a day or a week earlier or later, and with a natural birth, no one can determine exactly when it happens, not to mention all that other background stuff about your family."

"The king's really clever. He could have just been spinning it out for us, making it up, so to speak, on the spot, like a jazz guy. Maybe he was just playing with it. All that other stuff—the family stuff—could be nothing more than a silly coincidence."

"Do you hear yourself? Really? You've suddenly become Captain Coincidence, after all that we've experienced?"

"Ok. Ok."

"Coincidence is thin soup, philosophically—too thin for the situation."

"I get what you're saying."

"The stuff happened like he said. And the problem is that I don't think it could have been contrived by anybody here below, so to speak."

"Yeah, well."

"But then, again, all the Fibonacci birth and life business can't be just a result of nature. It's not like there are some laws of biology or physics or anything that pop out one baby into just that circumstance, and on exactly that date, and with all the other stuff. But then, since it couldn't all be intentionally devised by any or all of the participants either, what we're left with is just weirdness on a major, major, level."

Walid sighed out loud. "I know you think I'm some sort of a strange, mystical freak now."

"No, no, no, not at all. You, my friend, are a completely normal, garden-variety freak. It's just all the other stuff that's super freaky."

"You think we'll ever figure it all out?"

"You know what your uncle said, that there are things yet to be revealed."

"Yeah, and whenever he says that now, I get a little concerned because in the very recent past, it's meant that there was some huge discovery or revelation or change coming."

"Yeah, I know." Mafulla remarked, "You've said so before. But don't worry. I'm ready for something big, GV. And you are, too."

"Thank you, Stormie. That's reassuring."

"You're welcome. And, by the way, The Golden Viper is now definitely and abundantly confirmed as the right crime fighter name for you in more than one way."

"What do you mean?

"When we picked it, it was in honor of The Golden Palace here, which is our base of operations and, in my mind at least, also in honor of your birthday numbers, which at the time we still thought might be a coincidence—or, at least, you did. But maybe now you can finally contemplate the possible fact that you, my friend, are ultimately much more golden than the palace, in all the right Phi and Fibonacci ways, and maybe even in spooky ways yet to be revealed, after all."

"Well, Storm, I don't know. But I guess we'll find out soon enough."

"Maybe sooner than we think."

"Yeah, maybe. I sort of have a feeling. It seems like there could be some new things on the horizon."

"I'm getting that, too."

"But the biggest feeling I have right now is a strong sensation that I'm going to fall asleep standing up if I don't go into my room immediately and get to bed. I'll review my work in the morning. I think I'm ready to just pass out, in the meantime."

"Yeah, I actually feel the same way, too." Mafulla yawned.

"See you tomorrow morning then, maybe a little early."

"Ok. Goodnight, GV."

"Night, Storm."

The boys went into their respective rooms and each of them was asleep within ten minutes, tops. It was a dark and windy night. Gusts boomed against the windows periodically, but the boys somehow slept soundly through it all. Even the king managed to secure every bit of the beauty sleep that he needed, as well. But after a time, he dreamed in a particular way that we all sometimes do when there are noises in our rooms, or otherwise around us, that we hear and manage to process enough in our unconscious minds to be able to incorporate them instantly into the content and flow of a dream.

The gusting of the wind became in the king's dream the first sign and warning of a massive storm on the way. He was outside on a roof and gazing at a distant display of natural violence blasting up the sand. He could tell that this particular storm was going to be big, and even possibly without precedent. People would be pushed and stretched and challenged to their limits by it. It would threaten to overturn and destroy much that was of great value in the kingdom and in the lives of those living and working in the palace. It would come quickly, like a desert tempest, but then perhaps not pass by quite as fast.

Afterwards, there was another dream quick on the heels of the first one where, instead of a big storm coming, there was some other sort of massive disturbance. At first, it seemed to be just another desert sandstorm on the way, with the sky growing dark at mid day. But then it became clear that the horizon this time was being eclipsed with sand kicked up into the air by countless horses and riders and carts and wagons and modern military vehicles traveling together toward the capital city. An army was on the move, and it was headed right for the center of power, for the palace, and for the people of the palace the king himself had put in harm's way when he chose them for special service because of their talents and goodness and character.

And this dream went beyond what the king could at first see. Farouk al-Khoum and his brother Faraj were sitting together at a distance behind the stormy invasion force to watch their plans unfold. With them, there was an open box, and in the box there could be seen a book, a ring, and a stone.

Earlier that same evening, on their walk to the El-Bay home, Hoda had invited Hasina to spend the night with Kissa, and they stopped by Hasina's house to ask the permission of her mother, Layla, and they also filled her in on what they had all just been through. Layla took the news well and was very proud of the two girls. She also felt, as a result, even more appreciative than ever for the work Hoda had been doing with them. She had joined in their training sessions as often as she could, but in the current cycle of things, the girls were learning some specific skills that Hoda had a particular aptitude for teaching, and Layla's afternoons were mostly taken by some important volunteer work she was doing in the city.

The girls gave a blow-by-blow account of everything that had happened, and Layla then took them through a big "alternative scenario" discussion. What if things had gone differently? What would they have done? She posed plenty of questions. What if all the men had been carrying guns, and not just one of them? What if the two younger men had been more prone to fight? What if the gunshot had wounded Kissa and rendered her unable to do her part? What if the consequences of the shot had been worse than that, for either Kissa, or, in another scenario, for Hasina or even Hoda, as an alternative? Layla and then Hoda both steered the girls through what their most appropriate responses could have been to each of these more difficult scenarios, and they did so as Layla brought out some food she had already cooked up for the evening.

By the time Hoda got the girls home to the El-Bay house, it was already a little after eight o' clock. Khalid had gone to the palace earlier in the evening to eat in the kitchen with their older twin boys who both served as assistant chefs there. They had enjoyed some time together afterwards as well, so that, as delayed as the ladies were in returning home, they still got back before Khalid did. And Hoda thought to herself that it was good he'd not been there to worry about the three of them being so unusually late after their exercise session. He would likely have been concerned.

When Khalid walked in the front door, Kissa and Hasina were back in Kissa's room and Hoda was at a small table, going through the day's mail. She heard him at the door, and as he came in said, "My favorite husband! Welcome home. How was dinner with the boys?"

Khalid smiled and said, "Oh, thanks for asking, my favorite wife. It was great. We had a fine time. They've both become excellent cooks, as you know, but tonight they took it to a new level altogether. The lamb that Baqid prepared was so succulent, and … there are just no words for the tenderness and rich flavor of it. And, my goodness, the sauces they made! Then, Shumar presented us with the most heavenly dessert. I wish you could have been there."

"I do, too. But this was important guy-time for the men in my life. I'm glad that you enjoyed yourself so much. I'm sure they did, too."

"Did you and Kissa have a good dinner?"

"Yes, we actually ate at Layla's. And Hasina is here to stay over for the night with Kissa. You know how the girls are. Now and then, they like to stretch out their day and talk about it all. They're in Kissa's room now, just chattering on and feeding Shibby her dinner."

"Very nice. The girls do love to talk. And that's good. It's always helpful to review the day before bed. And I'm glad they've got Shibby back there with them. The poor dog has to be alone so much of the time. And she really enjoys the companionship of the girls."

"They do love her," Hoda replied. "I'm just so happy that we have the neighbors next door who are always at home during the day and can let her out to exercise a bit in the early afternoon."

"Yes, that makes a big difference. Otherwise, she might chew open a hole in the door. I know how strong willed all my girls can be."

"Very funny. I chew only on the problem of what to do with such a creatively humorous husband."

"Just pat me on the head like a good dog."

"I can do that. Bend over here. Good boy."

Khalid got his playful head pat, and looked down at the table where all the mail was laid out and said, "Do I see the corner of an official palace envelope there under some other things?"

"Oh, I believe you're right. I hadn't noticed. I wonder what this is." Hoda pulled it out of the pile.

"It looks like a formal invitation of some sort."

"Yes, it does. Let me get it open." She picked up a letter opener and slit through the side of the envelope, and then slipped out a large printed card. After scanning it for a second, she said, "Oh, my. There's a new ambassador from Tunisia, and the palace is putting on a reception in his honor tomorrow evening, early. We've all been invited."

"All of us?"

"Yes, the entire family."

"But the boys will likely be cooking for it."

"That's true. Well, at least Kissa can go with the two of us."

"That'll be nice. I know she'll enjoy the pageantry—and the chance to get all dressed up."

"Yes, I'm sure you're right. And, you know, it occurs to me that this has never happened before."

"What?"

"We've never been invited as a family to such an important formal occasion—to a reception for a major new diplomat."

"Hmm. I think you're right. This is a first."

Hoda smiled. "There could be something new on the horizon for the El-Bay family."

"This may be true."

"Who knows what?"

"Yes, who knows?"

3

The Question of Happiness

Walid woke up an hour earlier than usual and got all his review work done in preparation for class before walking down to the breakfast room. Mafulla was already there, and just that minute had poured his tea and sat down to eat.

"Hey, Storm. Ready for today's class?" Walid asked this as he walked into the room and ambled over to the service table against the wall to pick up a small plate.

"Hey. Yeah, I think so, GV. I really enjoyed the essay Khalid assigned on happiness. It's actually, I don't know, made me happy."

"Ha! Well, that's somehow appropriate, I'd say."

"Yep. And I've been going over it in my head ever since I first read it."

"I liked it, too. It made me think. So, how do you generally rate on the happiness scale?"

"Ok, let's see." Mafulla pondered for a moment. "First of all, there's the question of contentment."

"Correct. Now, define it." Walid was going to test him before Khalid had a chance to do so.

"No problem. It's the ability to accept the present moment as being what it is, in such a way as to be free from any strong form of regret, resentment, bitterness, frustration, panic, fear, irritation, or lingering anger."

"Good answer." Walid looked impressed. But he had a quick follow-up. "Do you have to like everything that's going on in order to accept it?"

"No, not at all. You just have to let go of your negative feelings about anything you don't like—you release any bad energy inside that you may have because of it."

"Very good again."

"Thank you, professor. And I think I do pretty well on this particular component of happiness, don't you?"

"Yeah, I don't see you as ever being all balled up in negativity about the present moment, or anything else, actually. You're pretty free of sour feelings and bad attitudes in general."

"Thank you. I guess I'm pretty good at relinquishing the regrettable. And you are, too, by the way—we're just alike in this regard."

"I agree. That's how it seems to me."

"So I think each of us gets a score of 10." Mafulla grinned.

"Make mine a 9," Walid said as he reached for a piece of fruit.

"Why?"

"Well, I have to admit that I do tend to get a little agitated now and then."

"Like when?"

"I often wish I was talking to Kissa, or that you and I were out doing something fun when I'm just in my room reading an assignment that's not as interesting as this one was. And I'm not always content with the small bits of time that Kissa and I manage to get these days just to hang out and talk. I have to be honest about that. Plus, I can sometimes get a little frustrated that I have so many questions that are, as of yet, without answers."

"Oh. Ok. I see what you're saying. You're probably right. And I'm that way about Hasina, too, and maybe a few other things, when I really think about it. But that's fine. We each get a 9."

"Or maybe, to be completely realistic, an 8," Walid said.

"You're a tough grader, worse than Khalid. But, all right, I can support a lofty standard here."

"So give me an 8 and I'll be content."

"Good one. Clever. Maybe you get an 8, but no lower. I insist. And, you know, you're really no worse about this than I am."

"Are you sure?"

"I'm pretty sure. And an 8 is still very good."

"Yeah, it's nothing to be ashamed of."

"True, because, at least in part, the shame would drive us way below the 8 on this one."

"Good point."

"A score of 8 is in a sense pretty high."

"Yes."

"It's way above a 2 or a 3."

"It is."

"I mean, it's not like we're absolute gurus yet, masters of all our emotions. So, I suppose I can follow your lead here and agree that we each get a score of exactly 8."

"Well."

"But if you keep insisting on a lower score than me, that will sort of prove you deserve one, don't you think?"

"Good point. Ok."

"Thank you. An 8 it is."

"So, what about the next category?" Walid poured some tea and took a sip and said, "Hot."

"Yeah, Ok. It's fulfillment—defined as: the progressive realization of our potential in relationships, work, and the rest of life, accompanied by a feeling that we're growing, however quickly or slowly, in the right direction for who we are."

"Wow, you got that in detail, too, right on the money," Walid said, looking impressed.

"Thank you."

"Now, in my opinion," Walid reflected, "this one's really interesting."

"In what way?"

"I mean … the state of contentment, mental and emotional contentment, is one hundred percent purely psychological and subjective. It's all in your head or your heart."

"True."

"It's just about what's going on inside me, as a feeling subject of experience. It really has nothing to do with the specific objective circumstances I'm in, but only looks at my emotional reactions to those particular circumstances, whatever they are."

"Correct." Mafulla buttered some pita as he listened.

"Fulfillment, though, is different. It's about an objective process in the world and then, second, about a subjective reflection of that process."

"Yeah, it has both sides. And you're right—the subjective is supposed to inwardly mirror the objective."

Walid then reached for some of the pita and said, "What do you mean it's supposed to? Doesn't it just simply do so? I mean: the feeling of fulfillment follows along with being fulfilled, right?"

"Most of the time."

"Explain your hesitation."

"My qualification of the claim."

"Ok, explain your qualification."

"Well, in theory, a feeling of fulfillment tracks the real thing. But consider a young guy surrounded by a bunch of people who think he should be a certain way, and maybe he's developing along the path they like and that they're insisting on, and because of their praise and approval over his compliance, he feels a sense of fulfillment, but it's a false feeling, a delusion, a counterfeit of the real thing."

"How could a real feeling be at the same time a false feeling?"

"It's truly a feeling that the guy has, but it's not true to what's really going on. In the scenario I've just sketched, the guy's not actually developing all his proper talents in a way that's right for him, and so he lacks the real, objective side of fulfillment. And if he feels good, then it's about something that's maybe not actually good. It's an illusion."

"Oh."

"In this scenario, his feelings are a result of the pressure, the pushing and the praising that comes from his friends, or family members, or somebody. He thinks he feels good about what he's becoming—or he does feel good about it, but he's really just enjoying the praise that results from conforming to the pressure and going with the flow."

"I think I see what you mean."

"And maybe it could go the other way too. Maybe you could actually be developing yourself in all the right ways, but something psychologically gets in the way and emotionally blocks you from seeing this and enjoying it to the max by feeling fulfilled. Again, maybe people are saying you should do something else and their constant urging keeps you from feeling what you ought to feel."

"Ok, I get it now." Walid looked impressed at his friend's reasoning.

Mafulla waved his butter knife in the air and said, "But these situations aren't the norm. The norm is that the objective and subjective mostly track together. And yet, your personal fulfillment grade could go up or down in any of these ways."

"Understood. And so," the prince asked his best friend, "how do you grade yourself on this overall category of fulfillment?"

Mafulla took a deep breath and let it out. "I'm very tempted to say 10 again, but I can already anticipate possible objections to that lofty score. Still, I could never have imagined my life now and all that it involves, even a year ago."

"Isn't that the truth? Me, too, for sure."

"Yeah. I bet. And I'm learning more than I've ever learned."

"Ditto."

"I've got better friends than I've ever had."

"Me, too."

"I'm getting stronger than I would ever have thought possible, and so—yeah, I'm at least a 9 on this one. And, excuse me if I'm overstepping here, but you're surely the same."

Walid was eating hummus on some warm, fresh baked pita bread that was nicely crisp around the edges, and between bites he said, "I totally agree on this one."

"What?"

"I think you're likely right about yourself, and I'd have to say the same stuff about my own development. I can't imagine more progress in the direction of my personal potential than I've been experiencing since we got to the palace. I mean, the desert crossing to get here really jump-started the process, for sure, but since we've been here, it's all been impressively fast, pretty constant, and super-great."

Mafulla said, "Apart from all the criminals and revolutionaries."

"Yeah, apart from them. But at the same time, in part, I guess, strangely because of them."

"True. They have tested us and made us grow."

"They have."

"And even Masoon, who doesn't ever show any degree of enthusiasm inappropriately—even he's been saying that we're progressing a lot faster than anyone he's trained before now."

"Yeah, who would have guessed that we'd be finished with our Level Two Phi Training at this point and already be into Level Three? I think it's supposed to take years, normally, and we've managed to get this far in just months."

Mafulla stretched both arms out and said, "Despite the fact that I'm sore almost all the time, it's pretty great—the physical progress we've made. And we're lots stronger on the inside. Plus, look at all the other stuff that's going on. It's not like we're monks in isolation just to do Phi training. We're living life. We're having fun. We're being stretched in all sorts of ways."

"True. So, let's be both humble and bold and give each other a solid 9 on fulfillment."

"Good. 9 it is. Although I would be most fulfilled with a 10."

"But if such a score would fulfill you more that you already are, then you do need to give yourself the 9."

"Ok, Ok. Clever. It's a 9. No problem. Although I wish they had a 9.5, which would be much more accurate."

"A 9 is fine."

"Yeah. I suppose. And it gives us something to shoot for, still."

"Good point."

"Now, the article clearly defined what it called deep satisfaction as just contentment plus fulfillment. So it looks like we're pretty deeply satisfied guys."

"That sounds right to me."

"And then, there was that one extra condition."

"The love thing."

"Yeah, the love thing. But the writer called the overall condition enjoyment, and then defined enjoyment as encompassing both pleasure and love."

"That's right, he did. He asked the questions: Do you take good pleasure in what you do? Do you have love in your life—both as a feeling and as a caring commitment?"

Mafulla then went on to say, "Knowing at this point that you want to save a score of 10 for that perfect individual we'll probably never meet and who might not even exist, and who, certainly, neither of us may ever be, what do you say about this one? It's got to be 9."

"Well, slow down. We're supposed to sum up all the levels of our lives—the physical, intellectual, and spiritual levels, and those different areas of our day-to-day existence like family, friends, school, work, and play. Was there anything else?"

"I don't remember anything else, but I think that food would be a nice category."

"Ha! Well, then. That helps, for sure. So, what do you say, with all that stuff in mind?"

Mafulla narrowed his eyes and looked almost comically adversarial. "I say: 9, again—a clear and obvious 9. Prove me wrong."

Walid laughed and said, "On this one, I can't. I have to admit that I think you're right, at least mostly, and maybe you're even underestimating us here."

"Wait, I may grow faint. You're thinking of a higher score?"

"Yeah. I'm not kidding. We're the kings of enjoyment. Our lives are chock full of pleasure and love. Sure, we've been through some tough times, but that's universal. Everybody gets hit with a bunch of truly hard stuff—although, maybe not kidnappings and shootings and explosions."

"Probably not. But remember, I even enjoyed one aspect of being blown up."

"I wouldn't go around telling people that, if I were you."

"Yeah. Good point."

"So, overall, we find ways to enjoy whatever we're doing, in so far as it's possible. And, as a result, our cups run over with good things. So: maybe here, we deserve the ever-elusive 10."

"I can't actually believe I'm hearing this. Are you all right? Has a fever come over you? Do you need to lie down and rest for a second?"

Walid laughed and Mafulla continued, "But no, forget I even thought of suggesting that. If it's a fever in your brain that's made you come to this conclusion, then let's just leave the fever alone. Enjoy the inner warmth it brings. I'll simply agree wholeheartedly while I can, amazing as it is that I'm not simply speechless."

"You're never simply speechless."

"And it's something about me that you enjoy almost as much as I do. So, we'll say that, on this particular condition, we're each getting a 10. It's a deal. Say no more."

"And so our total score is?"

"Ok. Give me a second. Ah. A robust 27, my friend." Mafulla wiggled his eyebrows with pride.

Walid's eyebrows went up as well. He responded, "Wow, the article said that, in terms of a total score, anything over 15 is good, meaning, at least moderately happy."

"So, to put it simply, translating the math, it would seem that we're both pretty much absolutely giddy with bliss and wellbeing."

"Yeah, giddy would be a good word for it." Walid laughed.

"Excellent. And I do believe this proves the accuracy of both the article and the scoring scale, along with, of course, our personal estimations, even though we were at times a bit hard on ourselves."

"So, you're happy, though, overall, with the results?"

"Thrilled. I'm content, fulfilled, and simply in love with the grade. Our exalted score is immensely pleasurable to me in both an intellectual and existential capacity. I have a case of the warm-fuzzies now beyond anything you can imagine—unless, as an equally happy man, you're feeling them, too."

Walid chuckled again and said, "Close enough. So … it's off to class for the happy two of us?"

"Yes. Giddily and gladly!"

"Ha!"

Hoda and Khalid had decided to have both their classes read the same material on happiness. Hoda started her class by leading her students through all the categories that Walid and Mafulla had discussed during breakfast, and they also did the scoring exercise. Their teacher had passed out small pieces of paper for each girl to write down her total score, but without her name attached. And then the girls put the papers, folded, into a small basket. Hoda stirred up the papers, picked them out, one by one, and read the scores aloud: "25, 24, 18, 21, 23, 20, 23. What does this say about our class?"

Ara spoke up. "According to the author's scale in the article, we're a pretty happy bunch."

"That's right. And notice something else: There's a span, but not a huge difference among the scores. And, if we took the test a week from now, or a month from now, or a year into the future, we'd likely get different numbers, but still a span. And it would, to some extent, depend on whether people felt like they were having a good day or a bad day. Even temporary feelings can affect in subtle ways how we score ourselves on happiness, overall."

"So, next time," Kissa said, "Maybe you should give us some really nice cookies and tea before the scoring."

"Or new shoes," Kit suggested.

"Funny!" Hasina laughed.

"But, Ok, to be serious, there's something I don't understand," Kit revealed with a bit of a puzzled look.

"What's that?" Hoda asked as she walked over toward her desk.

"Suppose I was having a bad day and scored myself a few points lower overall. Maybe I was a little sad that day. But still, my total score would count as at least moderately or substantially happy."

"Ok."

"So. According to the score and to me, I'd be a happy person feeling sad. Is it really possible to be happy and sad at the same time?"

"What do you think?"

"Well, I always thought that happy and sad were opposites, like up and down, black and white, short and tall, good and bad."

"Can something be good and bad at the same time?"

"Well," Bakat interjected, "my brother tried to cook dinner the other night, and what he made was apparently good for the dog but pretty bad for the rest of us." Several of the girls smiled and even laughed at that, like they really knew what she was talking about.

Hoda then asked, "Can something be black and white?"

Ara said, "Sure, like a Keffiyeh, the checkered headscarf that some of the men wear."

"Good. So ... is it possible to be happy and sad at the same time?" Hoda was directing them back to the interesting question that had been asked by Kit.

"Well," Kissa said, "if happiness is all about contentment and fulfillment and enjoyment, I would say yes."

"Why?"

"I guess you could accept the present, be involved in an objective process of realizing your potential and feel that ongoing reality, and basically be a person who enjoyed anything around you that could be enjoyed, while at a particular time you might also have a temporary feeling of sadness about something bad, or disappointing, or even tragic that had just happened."

"How could this be?" Hoda wanted to make sure that everyone understood the precise point here.

"Well, according to what we read, being happy isn't about just having great, pleasant, positive feelings, and nothing else."

"That's correct."

"Happiness is really a complex thing involving both subjective and objective elements. But in what we read, they're not spelled out in such a way that they eliminate the possibility of something negative. And sadness is a negative feeling that could still slip into the consciousness of a basically happy person, at least for a while, and as a legitimate, real, heartfelt response to a particular situation."

"Wow, you just said a lot." Hasina exclaimed with real admiration. "And, I think it all sounds right."

"What do the rest of you think?" Hoda asked.

"It seems really insightful," Bakat said.

"I agree," Khata added. And there was some more nodding of heads around the room.

Hoda added, "A basically happy person could also grieve the loss of a pet, or of a friend, or family member. But that wouldn't keep her from being a fundamentally happy soul."

"That's wild, but it seems right," Hasina said. "Grief and also happiness. Strange."

"You surely wouldn't describe yourself as feeling happy when your dog just died, or your grandmother just passed away," Kissa said. "I mean, I can't even imagine it."

"No, but as long as a happy life is about more than the feelings of the moment or even over a relatively short stretch of time, such an individual, someone experiencing that, could still qualify as a basically happy person," Hoda clarified.

"Can a happy person be angry?" It was Kit again asking the question.

"Well, obviously, not all the time," Bakat said. "But sure, for a short time, in response to a specific situation—I don't see why not. I mean, for the same reasons Kissa just gave about sadness. You can be a generally happy person and if somebody does something bad to you, unjust, unfair, or hurtful—or to someone you care about, or to an innocent person that you know about—then you can accept that it's happened while still feeling appropriate negative emotions about it, can't you? I mean: there are some things that it would be wrong not to be angry about. Right? But you could still be a basically happy person, as long as you sought to control the anger and not let it wipe out your appreciation of the good stuff in your life."

Kissa spoke up again and said, "I agree. I think that a basically happy person can have angry feelings now and then, but not at all often, and maybe she could even show some angry behavior, but that would be rare and not likely to be extreme."

"Why?" Khata asked.

"Well, what I'm sure a happy person couldn't have would be a generally angry disposition, a habit or tendency toward anger and angry behavior.

"But why?"

"That would just seem incompatible with the contentment condition and also the overall enjoyment condition."

"Oh. Ok. I get it."

"Because of that, I don't see how a happy person could have anything like a short fuse. A basically happy person is going to be able to take a lot before they snap. I mean, if they ever do."

"You're both right," Hoda said. "A happy person can experience anger on occasion, but doesn't allow it to grow and fester inside her. She likely knows how powerful this negative emotion is, and how it can take over a mind and heart. She learns when to act on it, to right some wrong, and when conversely to cut it off and put it away. And she's not prone to this emotion most of the time. The truly happy person could not ever be characterized generally by the unfortunate quality of irascibility."

"Whoa. Hold up. Irascibility?" Cabar asked the question, but a few others had also never heard the word.

Hoda explained, "That means a strong tendency or disposition to experience anger, to feel it, and to act it out. The word's more typically used in adjective form to describe a person who often feels and acts in an angry way. We have a lot of terms for a person like that: 'thin-skinned' and 'touchy' come to mind right away. Such a person seems to be always looking for a reason to get mad and blow up. That's the sort of personality said to be irascible."

"Why would anyone go around looking for a reason or excuse to blow up in anger?" Cabar was getting into the topic now, as well.

Hoda answered her: "Some people seem to feel a lot of worry or disappointment or sadness, or resentment about things in their lives, and these are difficult feelings to experience. Many would rather feel anger than endure any such passive negativity. So they lash out. They yell. They throw something. And it's cathartic."

"What's that?"

"It feels cleansing. It releases inner pressure."

"Oh."

"The anger or angry behavior seems to replace, or cover up, the other feeling that was more difficult to live with."

"Ok. I get that. I know someone who seems to do that a lot." Cabar paused and added, "Nobody in this class, though."

Hoda smiled and continued. "Most happy people understand that anger tends to come from two sources—fear or frustration.

When they feel anger welling up in them, they ask themselves, 'What am I afraid of?' or 'What's frustrating me now, and what can I do about it in a positive way?' They don't let themselves stay in the negative emotional state that, in itself, would likely accomplish nothing good."

"That makes a lot of sense," Cabar said.

"Yeah, it does," Bakat added.

Then Kit said, "That really helps. And I bet a happy person couldn't be a sourpuss either—one of those negative, mean people who just goes around criticizing everything and not really liking anything, a person who may not actually be angry, but maybe more like bitter and grumpy and down on the world."

Hoda smiled and said, "Correct. The quality of contentment rules out both irascibility and habitual sourness."

Cabar said, "Interesting."

Khata then said, "How can you get an angry person or a sour person to be happier?" She asked it like she might have someone particular in mind.

"That's hard," Ara said.

"It certainly can be difficult to help such a person overcome whatever might be riling them up, or dampening their spirit and holding them back," Hoda said.

"Yeah. You have to just love that person," Kissa said. "That's about all you can do. You can't really talk a person out of their most common attitudes or emotions—at least, not usually. All you can do is try to be understanding, and maybe sow some good seeds of positive emotion in them. And then fertilize those seeds, which means acting with love and kindness, compassion and understanding, and not being afraid to be your normal happy self around them, while still being sensitive, but setting a good example of an alternative and better kind of life."

"That's a wise approach," Khata said.

"Oh, I just realized something," Ara suddenly said.

"What?" Hoda asked.

"Despite any appearances to the contrary, you can't be a truly happy slacker, a really lazy person who accomplishes nothing, but looks content, and even seems to be enjoying their laziness."

"Why not?" Bakat asked.

"It violates the fulfillment condition."

"But what if a guy was like that, and was indeed fulfilling his individual potential?" Kissa asked.

"What sort of potential?" Hasina said.

"Um, maybe the potential to be a world-class slackadaisical slugamuffin," Kissa said and made everyone laugh.

"A slackadaisical slugamuffin?" Hasina repeated.

"Yeah, you know, a slacker, who's lackadaisical, meaning just lamely lazy, even listless, completely unenthusiastic, and who moves like a slug, and ends up being a couch muffin."

"My older brother," Bakat said.

The girls laughed together and for a while were all a-buzz with this new category. They were amazed at how many of them knew, or even had in their immediate families, some seriously slackadaisical slugamuffins—mainly, of course, boys, and most of them brothers, but with an occasional cousin or uncle coming to mind.

Hoda said, "You girls are on the cusp of an important realization here. You're clearly not slackadaisical slugamuffins. In fact, I'd say that you're the very opposite. You're intellectually engaged to the point here that you're digging up some genuinely vital aspects of happiness." She smiled as she said this.

"What do you mean?" Kissa asked.

"Happiness is indeed supposed to be more than a psychological term. It's really more like a moral category. This is something that the best philosophers have understood since at least the time of the ancient Greeks. And if that's right, then a wicked or corrupt person can't be truly happy. And a lazy, do-nothing person can't be, either."

"Can you say some more about this?" Hasina asked.

"Sure. Suppose some man, let's call him Abdul, has the potential to be a habitual liar and even a mass murderer. Let's grant him contentment, which some would argue is impossible if he has any shred of a moral conscience at all, but let's not take a stand on that for the moment. We'll just suppose, for the sake of argument, that Abdul is a content person. He accepts the present moment as being what it is. Could he also be fulfilled? Could he be experiencing a progressive realization of his potential just by lying more and getting better at killing people? Suppose he has an astonishing potential to be a world-class liar, and that he has a huge capacity for terminal violence. Could he indulge all the worst in him and by doing so satisfy the definition of fulfillment, to the point that he really enjoys what he does and ends up being a genuinely happy person, and perhaps even the world's most deeply happy hit-man?"

"Wow. That just seems wrong," Kissa said. "The whole idea of a deeply happy hit-man seems really twisted."

"I agree," Hasina said. "Well, I mean, a totally perverse hit-man could enjoy his work, I guess, in a strange and really warped way. And I suppose that if he was really demented, he could even get super giddy about it all, but that's not the same thing as being truly happy. It can't be."

Kissa said, "Maybe what's meant by 'potential' in the definition of fulfillment is something like 'higher potential' or 'highest potential' … and not anything like the possibility or capacity for bad or evil or even laziness, or anything like that."

Kit jumped in and said, "I guess everybody has the potential, in the sense of the possibility, to be a failure or a mediocrity, or a nasty grump, and a progressive realization of that potential probably wouldn't bring you happiness at all, but maybe the opposite."

"Correct," Hoda commented. "Movement toward that sort of potential would not be, in the deepest or highest or moral sense, progress at all, and so could not literally be progressive in the relevant way here. Perhaps it would be regressive—involving corruption, or decay, or getting worse. When you're fairly young, you can either begin climbing the high hill of your proper potential, or you can begin sliding into the valley of corruption and waste, with a failure to measure up to your proper spiritual inheritance—the royalty of the spirit that we all sometimes speak of. So, I do think the author of our article was using the word 'progressive' in a moral sense, and maybe even the word 'potential' in that sense as well, to indicate the higher functions and possibilities latent within us, and not at all the lesser or lower alternative options."

"That sounds right to me, now that you've said it." Kissa looked very satisfied at this explanation.

Some of the other girls were nodding in agreement. Bakat said, "This is hard stuff to get a grip on. And I never would have guessed that. I mean—it's not as simple as it seems on the surface."

"Yeah," Ara agreed, "but a little hard thinking really pays off."

"That's often the way it is when we philosophize carefully about something," Hoda explained. "We have to think about things with precision and in detail, which initially feels hard. But if we keep at it and don't give up, it mostly gets easier and it does pay off."

Then their teacher walked back over to her desk and said, "Let me cap this off with something else to think about. Can a completely superficial person be deeply and genuinely happy?"

There was thoughtful silence for a moment and Khata said, "I don't think so."

"Why not?"

"Well, superficial people can fake being happy by being all bouncy and bubbly and stuff, but that's likely all it is—fake happiness, and not the real thing. It's like counterfeit money. It's not authentic, even though it could look real at a quick glance. Superficial is all about just skimming the surface of life."

Hasina said, "Yeah. And if happiness is tied up with potential in a moral way, then maybe that means digging down and experiencing more than just the sparkly surfaces of life."

"So, perhaps," Hoda suggested, "living deeply and well is most conducive to deep and true happiness."

"I bet that's right." Kit looked impressed.

Hoda continued. "Some experiences of sadness, then, and even some degrees of suffering may not just be fundamentally compatible with happiness, but may actually be necessary for ultimately attaining and experiencing the deepest forms of happiness."

Ara said, "That's a new idea."

Khata added, "Yeah, really."

Then Ara nodded and continued, "I'd never thought of that before. It seems like a paradox, but still … maybe true."

Hoda nodded as well and then commented further, "Life is full of such paradox. And if I'm right about this one, then we shouldn't be afraid to suffer, or to experience negative emotions when they're proper to our circumstances—emotions like sadness, or disappointment, or heartbreak, or even deep grief. These things can come into the life of a basically, overall, genuinely happy person and they may actually prepare us, develop us, or grow us into deeper people who can then drink more fully and profoundly of the great good that life has to offer. And if that's true, we should never fear what the world can bring to us. It's only in grappling with the toughest stuff of life that we become the kind of people who can be what Aristotle said we all seek to be, and that is: happy."

"Wow." Two of the girls said this at the same time.

"Just like the author of our article said, happiness is not guaranteed by money, power, status, fame, comfort, or luxury, and as I would want to add, it's not necessarily postponed or prevented by suffering."

"This is deep," Kissa said.

"Yes, it is."

"But I have a question."

"Sure," Hoda responded. "Ask it."

"If experiencing bad stuff can help develop us into people who more deeply appreciate the good stuff, then what would prevent a person from thinking that's it's Ok to bring bad stuff intentionally into another person's life, simply because it can ultimately have a good effect? And that could make people think it's often Ok to harm others."

Hoda replied, "This is an interesting version of the old question: Do the ends always justify the means? Or to put it another way, if something seems bad to do, in itself, but on a particular occasion it might have good consequences, do those results transform its moral status from bad to good? In this particular case, would it then be perfectly fine to do harmful things to people to cause sadness, heartbreak, and other forms of suffering just because those negative experiences might deepen them and make them stronger and better people in the long run, and then in that way set them up for an ultimately deeper happiness?"

"Yeah, that's the question."

"What do you say, class?"

"No. It wouldn't be Ok, or right at all," Khata said.

"I say no, too." Ara said.

"Me, too." Cabar said.

"It would be awful," Bakat added.

"Yeah, I agree," Kit and Hasina both said. And Kissa nodded.

Hoda smiled. "You're all unanimous. And you're all right. The answer is no."

"Ok, that's what I think, too, but why?" Kissa really wanted to dig under the surface agreement of intuitions here and get a feel for what made the right answer right. Fortunately, Hoda had thought about this enough to have some light to shed on it.

She took a deep but gentle breath and then said, "The answer here, I think, has more than one component. Here's a first part. Setting aside any legal considerations of justice and punishment, and also the circumstances of mild parental discipline of a child involving, say, modest and sensible deprivations of a certain sort meant to train and educate the child away from inappropriate or dangerous behavior, we can make what is otherwise a very broad generalization. Outside such conditions, no human being is in a good position to claim or know that suffering of a certain kind, at a certain point, and undergone by a certain person to a certain degree, will in fact be able to have good, and only good, long term consequences—or at least positive results sufficient to go beyond and justify any negatives. To assume otherwise is irresponsible and wrong."

She continued, "And we can accept for our reasoning here the common view that suffering, or any form of pain, considered just in itself, is intrinsically bad and not something to be directly pursued or valued in itself, but rather a negative to be avoided whenever reasonably possible. I'm not suggesting otherwise in my view that good can come of suffering. The deep perspective we're exploring now just says that at least when pain avoidance is impossible, when life does bring you a form of suffering that can't be avoided, then you can be assured that it's typically up to you how you react to it, how you respond, and whether you turn the experience into something that deepens and improves you, or not."

The girls were clearly concentrating on all this, and Hoda went on. "In normal circumstances, we rightly try to help people avoid suffering of any kind, and especially of any intense kind. We would be wrong ever to intentionally inflict it, 'for their own good,' as some people say—in part, precisely because we can't be in a position to predict with accuracy that it will indeed be for good in the end, since this is most often up to the other person's free will and chosen response. And even if we could predict a good result, we can't be sure that this would be a result that couldn't better be attained in another way. We're not ever in a position of perfect knowledge in that regard."

Kissa was really into the ideas at this point, and said, "But suppose we could be reasonably sure, like in the case of a person who was already really good and really strong, and almost a spiritual alchemist—I think that's the right word—who had a long history of overcoming bad things and turning them into good results.

This is a person strongly likely to turn any bad experience into something good. It would just be weird if it's only the best people like this that anyone could be justified in inflicting suffering on, because only in their case would we be in a good position to think, and be fairly confident, that the pain would be wisely used for spiritual enrichment."

Hoda nodded and smiled. "Kissa, you've touched on an important point. It's not just a matter of reliable prediction. There's more to the story. The moral status of inflicting pain on others is much deeper than this one matter alone. You can search all the world's wisdom literature and all the great religions in their most enlightened expressions and find something important. We're never told by the best sages and saints to go inflict suffering on others, in order that good may possibly result for them. We're always told the exact opposite—to remove or alleviate suffering whenever we can. Why? Perhaps it's in part because inflicting suffering on any sentient being, any being capable of experience, whether human or non-human, degrades us, regardless of what the other person does with the suffering. And seeking to eliminate suffering ennobles us."

"Oh. That could be an important aspect of all this," Kissa said.

"Yes. We need to engage in conduct that will elevate us and ennoble us, not degrade us. Any action we perform, anything we do, creates in us the small seed of a habit. A habit of inflicting pain or grief in even the most carefully calculated way can create an inner tendency and a callousness, a degradation of our sensibilities that's bad for us and ultimately bad for those around us in addition. So it's not just the effect on the other person that the specific suffering would have, but also the effect on us that matters, as well."

"That sounds right. And it's deep," Hasina commented.

"Yeah, it seems really profound," Khata added.

"And there's another element, implicit in what I just said: the effect on the overall social fabric."

"What do you mean?" Kissa asked.

"We're essentially social beings, all of us. We can't survive and flourish alone, in isolation. We need each other. We need to live and work in a community of positive relationships. Anything that enhances the social fabric is good. Anything that tears away at it and unravels it is bad. All the world's great religions and major cultures have in one way or another promulgated some form of what we often call The Golden Rule: Treat others the way you would want to be treated if you were in their place. Do unto others as you would have them do unto you. None of us naturally wants others to treat us badly. So we shouldn't treat them badly. No one of us in a healthy frame of mind wants others to inflict real suffering on us so that, possibly, spiritual good can result. So we shouldn't do that to them. Acting in a contrary way would undermine the qualities of empathy, compassion, and trust that any healthy community is built on."

The girls were hanging on every word at this point. "Does that make any sense?"

"Yes. Yes it does," Kissa said. "Thanks. You've given us a lot to think about."

"Good. And without inflicting any real suffering, I hope. Also, I should assure you that there's a lot more that can be said about all of this. But I think that's enough for us today."

"It's a lot, for sure," Hasina said.

"So. Go now and enjoy yourselves and experience a happy day in the most fun sort of way. You even have my permission to be a bit superficial and giddy this afternoon if you like—but only for a little while. Remember, with giddiness and superficiality in particular, a little bit goes a long way. There are always depths calling out to you as well. Be prepared to answer that call at the proper time. And I'll see you all tomorrow, at the proper time."

4

Going to a Big Party

There was often something a little odd about the timing of the short trips that Walid and Mafulla frequently made out of the palace and off palace grounds. But on the surface, at least initially, nothing would seem strange at all. They might be going out for school supplies, or to visit the marketplace, or to run an errand for one of Walid's parents. And then after a few minutes, they'd suddenly see a small child wandering into a busy street while his mother was distracted in conversation with a friend or a vendor on the sidewalk. They'd pluck the tot from imminent danger and quickly deliver him safe and dazed back to the grateful parent. Or they'd be going down a side street and happen to witness a horse throw its rider, and they'd be the only people around who could help the man and get the animal back. In many situations, they were the finders of lost items. In short, they were often at the right place at the right time to help avert a disaster, solve a problem, or meet a need. And they now also had quite a reputation for anonymously stopping crime throughout the city—at least, in their alternate guises as The Golden Viper and Windstorm.

The legend of the Viper and the Storm had become one of the biggest topics of conversation in Egypt. The most popular show on the radio had for some time now featured fictional exploits of the two masked men. And speculation on the street was wild about the true identities of these famous crime fighters. Walid and Mafulla had even been forced to curtail some of their wanderings around the capital city while wearing the lightly colored sand masks that had become so popular on windy days, and that they had long donned for the relative anonymity that allowed them to be on the loose without palace security. The sight of the two of them walking side by side in their masks had begun to attract too much attention and too many comments from people on the street. "Hey, are you guys the Viper and the Storm?" When kids yelled this out, especially, they had learned to reply, "Yes!" because then the kids would think for a second and say, "If you were the real ones, you wouldn't say that." And of course that's why, since they were the real ones, they did say that. The truth can often have strangely nice consequences.

When they did walk around with sand masks, they often even heard lame jokes, like a man shouting, "Hey, if you're the guys who stop crime—my wife's cooking is a terrible crime. Please come stop it!" So, when they went out these days, they found it generally better to go unmasked, regardless of the wind and sand situation. Sometimes, they'd wear hats or traditional head coverings, and other times they'd use long scarves wrapped around the lower parts of their faces to obscure Walid's identity, as an alternative measure of precaution. And they never went out "on patrol" anymore, looking for trouble to stop. But, still, they had almost come to expect that some adventure would lie in wait for them nearly every time they ventured down the street.

Today would be no different. On this particular afternoon, they had decided right after school to walk about eight blocks to the king's favorite tailor shop to pick up a few things that had been altered for them in preparation for the evening's palace reception in honor of the new ambassador. The neighborhood was a wealthy area of private homes and nice shops in close proximity. Many diplomats and prominent businessmen lived on and around the particular street they were walking down on their way to see the tailor. It seemed to be only by accident that Walid happened to glance down a side street and notice a man on a ladder behind some ornamental shrubbery outside a second floor window at one home, mostly hidden from view. He appeared to be taking items from other hands that were reaching out from inside the house, through the window.

"Maffie, quick, let's get back up against this building and behind the bushes," Walid said in a low voice.

"What's going on?"

"Put on your mask and your wristband."

"Why?"

"I think I see a house robbery going on."

"Where?"

"Down the street at the second home there's a man on a ladder."

"Ok," Mafulla replied. He quickly pulled out the sand mask he still always carried when they were off palace grounds and pulled it on over his face, as did Walid. They also reversed their watchcases. Click. Click. And they both quickly covered their watches with cloth wristbands as the prince led his friend back around the side of the building they were up against, heads bowed low into the scarves they also had on today, so that no one who might come by on the street would notice the masks.

"This is so weird," Mafulla whispered.

"Why?" Walid turned to look at him.

"Well, this morning, you told me about the first time you ever saw a ladder and climbed it and fell off the lowest rung on your way back down, and how you dreamed about it last night."

"Oh. Yeah, I did."

"I know. You've never talked about ladders before."

"I guess you're right. And I've never had that dream before."

"And here's a guy on a ladder."

"Yeah. That is a little strange."

"It's just weird. Did you have an inkling at some level deep down that this was going to happen?"

"No clue. But maybe so—who knows? Come on," Walid said and motioned for Mafulla to follow him.

There were a lot of thick high bushes around the house and most nearby homes, and that was probably why the thieves thought they could rob one here in the middle of the day and not be seen. Plus, most of the surrounding residences were empty at this hour, with the men out working and many of the ladies either at their own jobs or doing charitable work around town, or visiting friends, and some of them would be getting their children from school or going out to shop in preparation for the family dinner.

Walid and Mafulla were now at the edge of the house that was hiding them and were up against a large shrub. At this point, the prince could just see the man on the ladder descending down to the ground and placing several gold and silver items into a large bag lying there. Then he quickly and silently climbed back up.

"What's the plan?" Mafulla whispered.

"I'm not sure yet," Walid admitted. "We have to be able to get them both, and one guy's still inside in a room upstairs. If we grab Ladder Man, the other one might take off and escape through some other window or door that we can't see from here. We need to wait to be able to grab them both."

A car motor could be heard in the distance behind them coming down the street. It slowed when it neared the spot where The Golden Viper and Windstorm now crouched in muffled conversation. The boys compressed themselves a bit more into the bushes and closer to the side of the house where they were hiding. The car rolled slowly past them and turned down the side street where the apparent criminal activity was taking place. It pulled right up to the house with the ladder and stopped. The driver, who seemed to be alone, slid over to his passenger side and opened the front door. The man up on the ladder began his descent again and, when he was about halfway down, another pair of feet and legs carefully got onto one of the top rungs. Now after going down a couple of them, the thief who had been inside the house stopped and closed the window behind him.

While all this was happening, Walid whispered something to Mafulla and his best friend crouched lower and moved quickly out from the shrubs. He dashed down the lane and hid beside the car, creeping up to the driver's door. When he got to the door, he reached silently through its open window and pulled the car key out of the ignition.

The driver, now standing right beside the passenger door and looking at the house, jumped at the sound and turned his head quickly. "What the? Hey!" He yelled out as the car engine shut off, and ducked down to look inside and see what was going on. But he hardly caught a glimpse of Mafulla, who had moved so quickly as to seem like nothing more than a flashing blur, disappearing out from the open window of the car and sliding down toward the ground.

The driver, who was seriously overweight, ran as quickly as he could around the front of the car and, breathing hard, looked all around, confused as to what had just happened. He was surprised that he could see no one at that point. He began to walk cautiously toward the back of the car and just as he got to the corner of the trunk, Mafulla stood up and threw the keys as hard as he could across the street and far into a neighboring yard. The man was shocked and outraged and yelled, "You little … punk!" But before he could get the last word out, a well-placed and vicious kick took him down and wrapped him in pain as he writhed on the ground. Mafulla didn't wait to see this reaction, but instantly bolted toward the bottom of the ladder where he knew Walid was already in action.

By then, the prince had pulled the first guy to the ground and after a bit of a struggle had rendered him unconscious within about five or six seconds. Mafulla instinctively joined him under the ladder, knowing exactly what was next.

It was a fairly long ladder at full extension, as it had been reaching up to the second floor of an elegant home whose high ceilings on the first level provided the entire building with an impressive verticality. Given the small stature of the man still perched near the top, and the closeness with which the ladder had been placed against the house to minimize its visibility from a distance, the two masked crime fighters had no problem in pushing it away from the wall. Walid wished to himself that he could have just stood and watched the great fall that resulted, but he knew he had more work to do. He anticipated the exact spot where the inside man would tumble from the ladder, and was waiting for him so that he could complete the damage that the ground instantly did to one of his legs. Mafulla, for his part, had now run back to the car where he knew the driver would likely be recovering enough to pull himself back up. And that was something he put a stop to right away, first returning the man painfully to the ground, and then grabbing him from behind in a highly effective sleeper hold of his own.

Fortunately, some landscapers had recently staked and tied down a few young trees that had just been planted on the near side of the next-door neighbor's yard, because of a spate of high winds they had been having in recent days. Walid was able to untie a long length of rope from one of the trees and Mafulla instantly got to work on another one, which they then used to bind the men, hands and feet, one at a time in a prioritized sequence, so as to allow for the least possible amount of trouble.

The hardest part was then dragging the tied-up men to the waiting car. Another automobile, a smaller one, and a donkey cart rumbling down the street had both slowed down, their drivers having witnessed at least some of the action. "What's going on?" The driver of the cart called out.

"We need the police!" Walid yelled in reply. "These men are

thieves! They've taken things from this house!" He pointed to the window that had been used.

"Are you guys the Viper and Storm?" The driver of the car shouted from his open window.

"Yes! Please, help us and find some city police! Quickly!"

"I'm happy to help! There are two, not far from here," the man called out and turned his car around in the street, accelerating back to where he had seen a couple of uniformed officers several blocks away on foot patrol.

Walid and Mafulla quickly wrestled the heavy unconscious man into the front seat of what had been meant as the getaway car, and got a skinnier guy into the back. Then they finally placed the shortest of the men into the trunk with the bag of stolen goods—mostly jewels, silver, and some small antiques. It was much more difficult than they had imagined to lift and position all three unconscious bodies safely in the vehicle, but their workouts with Masoon had made it possible. They slammed down the trunk and went around to close the passenger door of the car after finding a piece of paper and a pencil in the glove box. Walid wrote a note: "Thieves who broke into this house with a ladder. Goods are in trunk with man #3. Please arrest."

"Oh! Write that the car keys are across the street to the left of the front steps of that big house."

Walid wrote all that quickly and signed it, "The Golden Viper and Windstorm," and secured the note under the wiper blade on the front windshield. A minute or so before the policemen arrived, they ran up the street, ducked around a neighboring house, took off their masks and wristbands, reversed their watchcases, and walked casually down a different nearby street, making their way back to the main avenue and toward the shop they were intending to visit.

"Wow, that was unexpected," Mafulla spoke first, after catching his breath.

"Yeah, I'll never get over the fact that whenever we leave the palace, it's almost like stuff is waiting for us out here."

"Destiny keeps tabs on us, my friend."

"I guess so. It sure looks like it."

"By the way, GV, are you Ok? Is that a limp going on?"

"Yeah, but I'm good. I can walk it off. I just twisted my ankle a little. It'll be back to normal in a minute."

"What happened?"

"Getting that first guy off the ladder was easy, but making him takc a nap was a harder than I expected. He was a pretty tough character."

"Yeah?"

"He fought hard and almost hit me in the face, but I dodged it."

"Oh."

"I just turned my ankle in the process. And I think his fingernails got me on my arm, pretty good. Otherwise, I'm fine. How about you?"

"I'm Ok. I got a little winded, though, from running back and forth to that big guy, the driver. I mean, who knew that it was going to turn into a two-against-three situation, and get spread out like that? Bad guy management had to become a real focus."

"Yeah. It was a little busier than I anticipated. But I'm glad we stopped those guys before they could get away."

"Me too. And it was close. Can you imagine coming home after a hard day's work and all your most expensive jewelry and stuff is just gone? There ought to be a law."

Walid replied, "Well, actually, there is."

"Oh, yeah, and that's why we do what we do."

"In one sense, yeah. But, even if there weren't any laws, I think I'd still want to do this."

"I totally agree. I'm all about protecting the weak, taking down bad guys, keeping order in the world, and of course building our legend for the edification of future generations."

"Yeah, all that. Hey, there's the shop. Let's grab our stuff and try to get back to the palace without any further complicating action. I'd hate to get our diplomatic duds dirtied due to the doings of different dastardly desperado dudes."

"Hey, that was some pretty good alliteration—impressively improvised—and a good point, too, GV. Let's concentrate on some calm, gentle, and peaceful getting-home thoughts."

A few hours later, not far away at Kissa's house, the El-Bay family was busy dressing for the big event. Hoda walked into her daughter's room and said, "Are you almost ready? We'll need to be going in a little while."

"Oh! I lost track of the time."

"The king's driver is due here soon and probably has others to pick up as well."

"Ok, just a second." Kissa finished checking herself in the mirror and turned around toward Hoda and said, "Mom, you look amazing!"

"Thanks, and so do you, young lady. Khalid may just pass out when he gets a look at us."

"Ha! I'd like to see that!"

Hoda walked over and picked up a brush and started to fix a little something in the back of Kissa's hair. She said, "I hear the new ambassador has a son about your age."

"Yeah, Kit's pretty excited about it. She told me he's supposed to be very nice looking and really sophisticated. And, you know, she doesn't have anyone special in her life right now."

"Well, she's still young. There's plenty of time for that."

"I think she's hoping the time will be right tonight, or soon."

"I see. Is she coming to the reception?"

"I would imagine so. I'd even bet on it, but I actually don't know. I just heard she wants to meet the new guy soon. Maybe, if she's not there, I might have a chance to talk to him and tell him about her, and then introduce the two of them on some other occasion."

"That would be nice."

Khalid appeared in the door. "There you are!"

"Hi Dad! What do you think?" Both ladies turned to face him.

"Someone get the smelling salts! I think I'm going to pass out."

"See? I told you," Hoda said, and laughed.

"Oh, Dad, you're so silly."

"No, I mean it."

"Just breathe slowly and deeply and you'll be fine, unless of course you want me to get you a bag to breathe into."

"Maybe a bag to put over my head. Compared to you two, no one should have to look at me—although, of course, I do benefit from the surprising juxtaposition."

"What?"

"When people see me next to your mother, they automatically assume I must have something going for me beyond mere physical appearance, and they typically figure I must be a genius of the highest order, wealthy to an extreme, and a major wit, to boot."

"Maybe you do need those smelling salts," Hoda suggested and Kissa laughed.

"No, no. I'm Ok now. I think I've steadied myself just holding on to the doorframe here. I'll be completely fine once my eyes adjust to being nearly blinded by all the beauty here in the room."

"Ha!"

Khalid then made a few more jokes, and the girls both laughed appropriately at them, regardless of their varying quality. From Khalid, however, the level of the humor factor was always pretty good—or at least, when he was in a jokey mood like this. The Oxford and Yale years continued to pay off in a linguistic mastery that made wit come easily and especially, for some reason, really bad puns, which were, ironically, often oddly good if you had cultivated the quirky sensibility required to appreciate such things. Hoda and Kissa both loved the fact that they never knew what he'd come up with next.

The girls did know that Khalid was even more excited than they were about meeting the new ambassador, since apparently they had both been at Oxford at about the same time. He couldn't recall meeting a Tunisian while he was there, but he was still keen to explore the connection.

The palace car arrived for them promptly as scheduled and the family had a short ride over to the main entrance of the palace, one they almost never used. This evening, under a colorful sunset and in the first creeping of twilight, there were dozens of lanterns already ablaze on tall poles, and soldiers in their finest dress uniforms lined the long walkway. A palace band composed mostly of brass and percussion instruments was set up a short distance away. They were already playing some lively tunes in the background to increase the sense of festivity all around as several diplomatic cars awaited their turn along the palace drive, prepared to pull up to the central greeting area where soldiers in palace uniforms would open the doors for their important passengers.

Inside the main entry of the palace itself, a guard announced the names of arriving guests. "Khalid and Hoda El-Bay, with their daughter, Kissa El-Bay." A gathered congregation of staff, guards, and recently welcomed guests lightly applauded as they turned from their various conversations to look toward the new arrivals. Formally dressed men were inviting small groups every few minutes to come farther into the palace and enter the main ballroom, where names were once again announced and an orchestra played as drinks and nibbles were taken around on ornate silver trays.

"There must already be a hundred people here tonight, or more," Khalid remarked to Hoda.

"It looks like even more to me," she said.

"Mom, there's Hasina! May I go over and say hello?"

"Yes, certainly," Hoda answered with a smile. "Just don't wander off too far, in case we'd like to make some introductions."

"Ok, no problem." Kissa walked across the room to see her

friend, and as she passed clusters of guests along the way, many of the men and women who caught sight of her allowed gazes of surprise and delight to linger for more than a moment. It was remarkable how poised and even glamorous she could look, for a girl of her age. One of the guests who noticed her at that moment with particular interest was the highly anticipated teenage son of the dignitary being honored this evening, a young man named Karim Sassi. He had been standing near a refreshment table, holding a cup of tea, and the instant he saw Kissa, he began walking in her general direction.

"Hassi! Hi!" Kissa said to her best friend. "Look at you!"

"Hi, honey girl! You look amazing! Where's your family?"

"We just got here. Mom and Dad are still over near the door. Is Layla here?"

"She wouldn't miss it for anything. She said it's the first time we've been invited to a big deal formal reception at the palace, and she must have spent three hours getting ready to leave the house."

"Wow! I bet she looks great!"

"Yeah. She does."

"Where is she?"

"Over by the big refreshments table along the far wall, talking with Rumi and Bhati."

"Oh! I see! Very elegant indeed! That's a great dress, and her hair looks awesome."

"Yeah, she dresses up nicely."

"You do, too."

"Thanks! So do you, Miss Glamour!"

"Ha!"

"I couldn't help but notice the total energy-shift in the room that was caused by you just walking over here."

"Oh, stop, you silly thing! Have you seen Walid and Mafulla?"

"Not yet, and by your question, I gather you haven't either."

"No. They're probably still on the way down. You know them.

They could have seen somebody in distress who needed saving before they could get all the way to the ballroom."

Hasina laughed. "You're right. The boys are always on duty."

"Too bad it's not a masked ball, or they'd likely be here already."

"Ha! So true."

A new voice full of confidence and smooth warmth suddenly interrupted their conversation. "Excuse me, beautiful ladies. I hope you don't mind my approaching you like this, but I'm new in town and to the palace, fresh in from the capital of Tunisia, and I don't know a single soul here yet."

"Oh, hi. And thanks for the compliment," Kissa replied to the young man who had just walked up. "You say you're from Tunisia?"

"Yes, and I just arrived in town."

"You're certainly not the new ambassador," Hasina said. "You seem a little young for the role."

"You're as perceptive as you are lovely and, of course, you're absolutely right."

"Ah," Hasina said, "I thank you."

The boy smiled brightly. "I'm fifteen, which is old enough for the top football club in my country, but indeed a bit young yet for the diplomatic service. My father's the new ambassador, The Honorable, as they say, Omar Sassi."

"He is?" Kissa said. "Well, it's nice to meet you. I'm Kissa El-Bay."

"She's honorable, too," Hasina said.

"Oh! I'm sure. I'm Karim Sassi, at your service, my dear and gorgeous lady," he said as he bent forward and, seeing that Kissa had extended her hand, he surprised her by taking it and kissing it, lingering a bit on the contact.

The other lady present then said, "And I'm Hasina, Kissa's extremely charming best friend."

"Ha!" Karim laughed and said, "You most certainly are." He reached out for her hand and repeated his motions, muttering,

"Charmed, indeed," but he brushed her fingers with his lips a bit more quickly, as he clearly had his eye set on Kissa.

"Oh, my," Hasina said in a whimsical tone, conveying multiple levels of commentary at once.

"And, if I may be so bold as to ask, what are your respective and surely exalted roles in the kingdom of Egypt?"

"We're both students here in the palace," Hasina answered.

Kissa added, "My mom and dad are teachers in the palace school. And my dad may actually have gone to college with your father at Oxford."

"Oh, really?"

"Yes, I believe they might have been there at about the same time. Dad studied philosophy, politics, and economics, but philosophy was, and is, his first love—I mean, other than my mom and the rest of the family."

"Are they here?"

"Mom and Dad are over there, near the door. Mom's the lady in the golden dress."

"Oh, my goodness." Karim paused a bit longer than might have been expected in his look toward the door. "I hope you won't mind my saying this, but your mother looks like a goddess on a day-trip from heaven. And, you know what they say—like mother, like daughter."

"Karim, you say the sweetest things. But, please, not about me. You'll make me blush."

"Well, unless it's just an effect I happen to have, you must spend a lot of your time blushing. But don't worry, it suits you."

Then looking over at Hasina, he said, "I saw you two angels, or young goddesses-in-training, over here and I couldn't help but join you. My feet simply began moving in your direction. Please forgive my enthusiasm. I hope I haven't been too forward."

Hasina replied, "No, no, not at all. We're honored to be meeting you and your feet so early on in your time here."

Karim laughed. "You do have a quick wit."

"Thanks. I practice a lot."

"Oh?"

"Yeah. I need something so that I can keep up with my more senior goddess friend here."

"There you go again! Delightful!"

Kissa then turned to ask Hasina, "Would you like something to drink?"

Karim said, "Oh! I'm so sorry. I've been standing here like a mesmerized oaf with a cup of tea in my hand. Please allow me to get both you ladies something to drink—tea, or punch, or fruit juice?"

"Oh, that would be nice. I'd love some juice," Hasina said.

"Same for me, if it's no trouble," Kissa added.

"It's my honor. I'll be right back. Please don't go away. I couldn't bear your disappearance." Karim smiled again like he knew the effect it would have, and then he turned and walked rapidly across the room, almost gliding and slipping around people with a sort of elegant flow that bespoke his life as the upper crust son of a top diplomat.

"Well, he's hitting on you, big time," Hasina said to Kissa, as soon as he was out of earshot.

"Oh, no, not at all."

"No to you, junior goddess. He obviously is. He's super keen on you, for sure," Hasina responded. "And, on one level, I guess, you should be flattered. I mean, look at him, Mr. Tall and Perfect Features, with the whole Hollywood Star quality going on. Just check out the hair, the clothes, the posture, and the charm factor. And it's all for you."

"Hush."

"No, I saw it. You got the full-on, long, lingering hand kiss. I got the briefest hand brush with the lips. I think he saw you walk across the room to meet me, and he was magnetically pulled to you."

"Stop it."

"I'm sure half the room felt the same El-Bay magnetism, but he's the one who broke free to get to you as quickly as he could. You have to give him credit for initiative. The boy is helplessly in love at first sight."

"Silly, silly girl. Stop that nonsense right now."

"Ok, angel daughter, golden goddess-in-training, no problem."

To that, Kissa, made a face, stuck out her tongue, and got Hasina to laugh hard.

Just then, Walid and Mafulla came through the far door of the ballroom, from inside the private areas of the palace. First thing, they saw Hamid standing and talking to Masoon and walked over to them, but for a moment they held back a few feet, not wanting to interrupt. Just then, Hamid finished a sentence and Masoon nodded in agreement, right before noticing the boys.

"Walid! Mafulla! Say hello to the kingdom's most heroic wounded bird!" Masoon smiled broadly and nodded to his old friend, Hamid. "Or, perhaps, I should say, wounded rhinoceros, given the thickness of his hide."

"Hi, Hamid," Mafulla said. "Good to see you, man." Hamid did a quick, smiling semi-bow in response.

"Hi to you both," Walid said. He then added, "Hamid, my friend and valiant protector, how are you feeling?"

"Better each day, Prince. And how are you?"

"I have the smallest mark on my side and an occasional sensitivity, but just enough to launch an elaborate story starring you, of course, whenever I'm asked about it."

"It's quite a story," Hamid said.

"Yes it is, and especially since the bad guys lost, and good prevailed in the end."

"That's the most important ending for any satisfying tale, and one for which, in this case, I have a special fondness."

"Me, too. And I'm glad to see you tonight. It's been at least a week or more. I was asking the king about you just yesterday."

"I've been doing all my rehabilitation work religiously, and I'm mending as fast as humanly possible. I wouldn't want to tangle with you or Mafulla any time soon, or my friend Masoon here, of course, but give me another month and you'd better watch out."

"Ha! I'm watching out already, just to be safe," Walid said.

"Me, too," Mafulla echoed his friend. "But Hamid," he added, "how about we negotiate something like a lifelong truce—no tangling allowed—so that we can just cheer on your recovery a hundred percent and not be looking over our shoulders with anxious fear and trembling in a week or two?"

Hamid chortled and said, "Ouch. Don't make me laugh. But Ok, it's a good idea you suggest—so, a long and happy truce it is."

During all this, Walid had just caught sight of Kissa and Hasina across the room. But as soon as he noticed them, he saw a tall boy he didn't recognize, and who was apparently bringing the two of them drinks with a big smile on his face. The prince could see the girls smiling back and laughing at something the guy said. Hasina then clearly said something else, touched Kissa on her shoulder, and left the two of them, walking over to where her mother was in a long conversation with Walid's parents, Rumi and Bhati, as well as with Reela Adi, Mafulla's uncle, near the bar.

Mafulla was talking to Hamid about some sort of medical thing, but Walid was now too distracted and curious, and even a little bit concerned, to pay attention. He said, "Gentlemen, please excuse me for a second," and began to walk toward where Hasina was standing near his parents, but he was also keeping Kissa in view every few seconds. She was laughing again, and she looked so beautiful, and he wondered what this apparently older boy was saying to her, and who he is, and why he's over there, talking to her all by himself.

Hasina saw him coming and intercepted him before he could get to the group near the refreshments table. She smiled with what looked like, for the first time ever, a partly fake look that she was putting on for a reason and, taking his arm lightly, said, "Walid, it's so good to see you, and it's about time."

"Hi, back, and it's good to see you, but what do you mean?"

"Would you please come over here to the punch bowl for a second?"

"Ok. Sure." They walked a few steps and Walid said, "Who's that guy talking to Kissa—the one who brought you both drinks a minute ago? Is he the new guy I've heard about?"

"Yeah. He's the son of the new ambassador, Omar Sassi, the man from Tunisia we're welcoming to town tonight. The son's name is Karim Sassi."

"What's he talking to Kissa about that's so funny?"

"Ok, first promise you won't get mad."

"Sure, I mean, I promise. But why should I get mad?"

"You shouldn't, but you might."

"What's he saying to Kissa?"

Hasina looked around and said in a near whisper, "I think we need a touch more privacy. Let's get a little farther away from everyone."

"Why? What's going on?"

"Just a minute. Come with me."

"Ok. But."

Hasina took Walid's arm without another word and directed him off to the side. She said, "And promise me, seriously, no immediate reaction of any kind."

"What do you mean?"

"Promise."

"Ok. Ok. But what's up?"

Hasina looked around and held up her index finger as if to request a moment more before responding. This was just too mysterious.

5

The Ambassador's Son

Hasina had directed Walid about twenty feet away from the punch table, toward a wall where no one else was standing. He finally couldn't take the pressure any more from all the mystery, and so he said, "Hasina. Come on. Tell me now. What's going on?" He looked at her very seriously and emphasized each word.

"Well, Ok, that's what I wanted to talk to you about. The guy over there with Kissa, the ambassador's son, he's fifteen years old and I'm thinking almost sixteen. He's just arrived here in town and he's really hitting on her, big time."

"Hitting on her?"

"Yeah. Making a serious move. He saw her walk across the room and came over toward her like a bullet to a bulls-eye. And now, he's chatting her up pretty intensely, hoping, I'm sure, to win her lifelong, undying affections on the spot, or at least to begin the process well."

"He is?"

"Yes sir, he is. But don't worry about it. She's cool. He's giving her a big bunch of your-mother-is-a-goddess-and-so-are-you hooey."

"Yeah, well, it's not exactly hooey, is it, sister divine?"

"Hey, the fact that it's true doesn't excuse a new boy for saying it right up front and laying it on thick, like the fact that he's thinking it or even noticing it is so great and such a big deal and everything. I mean, look, I was there, seeing and hearing it all. He's practically starting his own Kissa goddess-girl religion right here in the ballroom. But it's a strange religion, because I think that, really, he's hoping she'll be the one to bow down and worship him."

"That's pretty bold for a new guy in town."

"Yeah it is."

"And for someone who's known her for, what, five minutes?"

"Ten or more, maybe."

"This has been going on for ten minutes?"

"Yeah, or maybe a little longer—maybe fifteen."

"Really? And he's giving her and Hoda all these compliments?"

"Yeah."

"Wait. How does he even know who Kissa's mother is?"

"When he came up and introduced himself, she told Karim that their dads may have gone to school together and he asked if her parents were here and she pointed them out."

"Where are they?"

"They're right over there, at the door. Hoda's the one glowing in gold, of course, like any standard, ageless, dreamy goddess mother."

Walid glanced over and looked back at Hasina. "Ok. I hadn't seen her earlier because of the crowd. But I saw you and Kissa laughing, and then Kissa laughing by herself at something the guy was saying."

"Well, he can be pretty funny, in his own really over-the-top way," Hasina explained. "But she's just being polite to a guest of honor. She's definitely not going for his little game. I think if you'll just walk over and say hello and introduce yourself, you can break it up and bring her some needed relief all at once, and you can still be really nice about it."

"You think so?"

"Yeah. You should be totally cool about it all."

"Well."

And then Hasina pointed a finger at him and whispered up close, "You're The Golden Viper, not to mention you-know-what."

"Ha."

"Oh and also, by the way, you happen to be the prince—heir to the throne of a much bigger kingdom than he's even from."

"True."

"Remember it. Believe it. Act on it."

"Ok."

"And plus, by the way, none of that's even necessary at all in the first place, is it?"

"What?"

"I mean this is Kissa we're talking about, our Kissa, someone whose heart is not available for random suitors or highest bidders."

"Well, sure, I mean, yeah."

"Somebody needs saving, GV. And it's not you. So. Go, get her, boy."

"Ok. And by the way, you look really, super beautiful yourself this evening, and I'm not hitting on you at all. I wouldn't risk the instant, unrelenting wrath of our esteemed man among men, Mr. Mafulla."

"Thank you, kind sir. I know you'd never do anything to hurt his Mafeelings."

"You're funny."

"So are you."

"Thanks."

Hasina pushed him a bit and said, "Now, go save your Kissa, and I'll find our mutual Mafulla, or to be more lady-like, I'll just position myself in the room a little better for him to be able to find me."

"Good form, and thank you," Walid said, as he turned and made his way across the room, excusing himself around people and by people, most of whom curtsied or bowed as he passed. Mumbled greetings of "Prince" and "Your Highness" followed him across the room, rippling like small waves toward the far shore of his best female friend.

"Walid! Come here!" Kissa said with a big smile. He walked up, forcing a smile himself and a nod toward the stranger, his unexpected adversary, and then he stood next to Kissa, pretty close and over to the side of the guest, as she reached up to grab his arm, a gesture clearly noted by the ambassador's son. And then she began the introductions, looking at Walid and smiling broadly.

"Your Highness, Prince Walid, I'd like to present to you Mr. Karim Sassi, son of the new ambassador from Tunisia." She turned and then said, "Karim, I'm pleased to introduce The Prince of Egypt, His Royal Highness, Walid Shabeezar, heir to the throne."

Karim knew enough of high court manners to do a short bow and say, "It's a great honor to meet you, Your Highness."

"A pleasure," Walid said. "Welcome to town. I hope you're already enjoying your time in our fair city."

"Yes, especially tonight," Karim said.

"Well, that's good to hear," Walid replied with a jolly tone of real genuineness that surprised him as it came out of his mouth. Then he added, "I don't mean to interrupt what I'm sure is the brightest of bright spots already in the evening, but I need to steal my best dear friend from you for a bit. I hope you won't mind the chance to mingle further and meet others in the room I'm sure are quite eager to make your acquaintance."

"Great idea," Kissa said. "Everyone will be delighted to meet you."

"Thank you. That's very kind of you to say. Well, it's indeed been an unexpected and extraordinary pleasure," Karim said and looked at Kissa, as Walid took her arm and with a big smile and nod of his head to the young man led her away, toward a part of the room where he could speak with her without any threat of imminent interruption.

Within a few steps, the prince nearly whispered as they walked, "Our guest is so very observant, perceptive, and astute."

"What do you mean?"

"You are such a goddess this evening, in fact, even more divine than that—more like a super goddess, what all merely normal, ordinary goddesses of yore and lore have been aspiring to, lo these many vast eternities past."

"Oh, stop it."

"No, no! The bounty of your beauty and the glow of your great gorgeousness have simply reached an indescribable pinnacle of perfection that the vast majority of humanity will never have the good fortune to see. Or, to put it in a more customary way, you look quite lovely tonight."

"And it's nice to see you, too, my immensely handsome and super, super silly friend," Kissa said with a smile and mysterious look on her face. "But how did you know what Karim had been saying to me?"

"Ah. I have my sources."

"So what else did Hassi tell you?"

"That I needed to save you as soon as possible from that insistent, over-the-top, lovesick newbie."

"Ha."

"So, consider yourself saved."

"He was actually almost charming, in a really embarrassing way, if you could bring yourself to ignore all the completely obvious manipulation going on."

"I can imagine."

"You're sure you can keep him away now?"

"I have an army. He doesn't. Game over."

"I actually have an even better idea."

"Better than an entire army?"

"Yes. A force much better than an army."

"What?"

"Our friend, Kit."

"Kit?"

"Kitty-Cat Kit. She wants to meet him."

"Why?"

"Oh, other than the standard movie star looks and the obviously sparkling intellect, wrapped together with the utter attentiveness to any object of his affection, I really can't think of a reason at all."

"You're very funny tonight. Extra hilarious. Even more humorous than usual," he said, a little irked and uncomfortable at the moment, to his own surprise and despite his best intentions.

"Thank you," Kissa responded, in a playfully happy tone that masked her realization of his reaction and marked the path that she would use to reassure him as she went on: "I'm just saying that she's heard things about him, and she saw his picture in the paper and said she really, really, really wants to meet him. And there's nothing better to get a boy's mind off one girl than another girl almost throwing her super cute self at him."

"Do you actually think he's that good looking?"

"No, not at all. He's Ok, I guess, in a richly clichéd way, but a bit thin to my taste. The face is almost too angular and chiseled, don't you think? And the hair is seriously overdone. I mean, really? Plus, it's more than a little difficult to get past some aspects of the attitude. A bloated ego isn't a very attractive accessory for anyone. In fact, it detracts terribly. I prefer my men a little different."

"Like what?"

"You."

"Really?"

"Yes."

"That's the sweetest thing anyone's ever said to me."

"If we put you in a fabulous wig and a great dress, Karim could probably say something sweeter."

"You're a nut."

"I'm just kidding. But I want you to know that, as nice as it was on one level to hear the many compliments pouring forth from our guest, I do realize that, when they come out so fast and smooth, something's going on beyond the realm of clear-eyed, good-hearted, objective, altruistic praise."

Walid laughed. And she went on to nearly whisper "Plus, where compliments are concerned, I prefer to hear them from you, not anyone else."

"You mean it?"

"Yes."

"Well then, I'm really glad I didn't knock his lights out."

"Oh, good. I am too, you kind and gentle man. It would have been an exceedingly odd gesture of welcome from an official host."

"I was pretty jealous. I admit it."

"You were?"

"Yes."

"Well, you should be a lot more confident, but that's still about the sweetest thing I've heard."

"Good. After a session with Mister Smooth and Sweet, I'm relieved to hear you say that."

"Should we go talk to people now?"

"Ok, but first, I should reiterate and emphasize the fact that you're by far the most beautiful girl or woman I've ever seen, no close second. And I mean it. I'm not just saying that to be competitive."

"Thanks. I knew you were mimicking the Tunisian a minute ago. But that's really nice of you to say or even think. You know, people tend to say that about mom all the time."

"She's super stunning, too, no question about it of course. But, you have a special something, an extra and delightful quality I can't find words for. And if I try to say any more, I'll just be embarrassing myself and you, and I'll start sounding again like some Tunisian turkey—not to mention any names."

Kissa laughed. "Ok, that's funny, and cute. And sweet. Thanks."

"You're welcome. It's from the heart."

"I know. I can feel it."

"Good."

Just then, Mafulla came up like a windstorm and with a big frown across his entire countenance. "Where is this turkey?"

"I just now used the exact same word. Are we psychic?"

"Like twins. Even more."

Walid laughed as Mafulla said, "Just point him out and your worries are over: One fewer guest to share the hummus. One less person crowding the capital city and breathing the air that the rest of us could use to better purpose."

"It's Ok, man. It's under control." Walid laughed again.

"Well, when Hasina told me about it, I couldn't believe it. This kid obviously does not know who he's dealing with here."

"I can tell you who he's dealing with right now—look over at the punch bowl."

Mafulla turned and looked and said, "What?"

"Yeah, the ever lovely Hasina."

"And … she's by herself now, with no deflector shield? I totally can't believe it! Does this guy have a deep-lying death wish?"

"No, just very good taste."

"Hey, if he wants some punch, I'll give him the punch of a lifetime."

"Calm down, Storm-boy. Hasina's not exactly a fan. She told me what he was up to with Kissa a few minutes ago and sent me in to do a rescue. She knows what this guy is."

Kissa said, "Problem solved! Look to the right—just in the nick of time: There's Kit, walking over toward Hassi and Karim. I didn't know whether she was coming tonight. This will take care of everything. Problem solved."

Mafulla looked puzzled. "What do you mean?"

"She's been wanting to meet the Tunisian, and will distract him mightily from any other thought."

"I'm still going over," Mafulla said.

"She wants you to. She told me," Walid emphasized. "She was hoping you'd find her soon. That's why she positioned herself more prominently in the room, she said—so that you could see her."

"Well, all right, then. But still, have potential medical help available for the Top Tunisian Target in the room, if needed. It's a good thing Hamid's here, and your dad, to back him up."

"Be cool, no Mafool. Ok, my man?" Walid said with a big smile. "Just remember, you're a nearly official representative of the kingdom and a host of the guy and his dad tonight. Be nice and play it smooth. Everything's going to be fine. You've already won. Just chill."

"I like that. I've already won. Ok, I can do it," Mafulla sighed and gave Walid and Kissa a smile. "They call me 'Mr. Smooth,' you know."

Walid said, "Who does?"

"People. Many people. When you're not around."

"Well, I never heard that from anyone."

"Never mind. Here goes. Wish him luck," Mafulla said as he turned to walk toward Hasina and her new admirer. But first he paused and turned back and added, "You know, I can handle trouble so well that it doesn't even realize it's been handled."

"So go handle it, and now!" Kissa said and laughed.

What the prince and his trusty sidekick did not know was that there was much greater trouble on the way from Tunisia than just one Young Turk from Tunis. And it would be coming soon.

Farouk al-Khoum and his brother Faraj had quietly been building up a small mercenary army throughout the north of Africa ever since they had left Egypt. They were employing former soldiers from Algeria, Libya, Morocco and Tunisia, as well as making special deals with current military leaders from some of those nearby nations, arranging finances and favors that would allow them to use military equipment and men off the record, in two cases without the approval or even the knowledge of their own sovereign governments. The vast fortune that Farouk had accumulated through his extensive array of profitable business endeavors, added to the network of corrupt and highly placed individuals across the region who owed him favors, created a sum total effect from all his years of deal-making that was now doing its work for him as he planned his next moves. A lifetime of extreme ambition beyond all bounds was about to come to its inevitable culmination.

At the same time, Ari Falma, the former overlord of crime throughout most of Egypt, was also busy working with a few top members of the previous regime to help them prepare for their own intended takeover of the kingdom—with absolutely no knowledge of the rival al-Khoum plans. There was word in the air that some rich and powerful men in north Africa had big political aims, perhaps involving a revolution somewhere, but there were no available details concerning what country they might have in mind. Falma was so focused on this new quest that it never occurred to him he might have serious competition. Of course, he knew Farouk. The older al-Khoum brother had hired him in the past to steal some important items from the Egyptian palace, a task at which Falma had failed. But the notorious criminal had no idea of the purpose for that attempted theft. He thought of Farouk as a dangerous and successful businessman, and not as a political revolutionary, and so never suspected his true aims.

The al-Khoum brothers, on their part, were so contemptuous of Falma that they had not even sought to keep tabs on him since he initially fled Cairo, fearing the wrath of Farouk. They were simply disgusted with him and viewed him as useless. They had no idea where the man was living these days or what he was doing. And they didn't care. So they had no thought that he might be pursuing the same goal of control over Egypt that they were also ultimately planning to achieve.

As a result, and with no inkling of trouble ahead, two groups who each wanted to take over the kingdom of Egypt were getting ready to collide, unless by some chance they eventually decided to collude. There was no way of knowing with any certainty who would prevail, but the underground arms merchants in the region who realized what was going on were betting on the brothers al-Khoum, even though they still gladly sold to Falma and his senior partners whatever they wanted, and were more than pleased to pocket the profits.

Farouk had studied carefully The Book of Phi that Faraj had taken from the palace in a bold move that involved a poisoning, along with dire threats to the royal family. And at this point, he thought he knew the number of currently active members of the powerful secret society living and working throughout Egypt—their identities, their histories, and their strengths and weaknesses. He had made elaborate notes, not even suspecting that the entire book in his possession was nothing more than an expert forgery, contrived precisely to mislead him and provide false information. Like a beautiful oasis mirage in the desert, it lured him forward with false hope and an unjustified sense of security. But it also built his confidence tremendously, which is normally, in itself, an advantage for any warrior. In many other ways, his strength was undeniable and even formidable. No ruse against him would easily work.

On this particular day, the brothers were the guests of a very wealthy man in Tunis, the capital city of Tunisia. Farouk was seated on a large, golden, brocade sofa in an ostentatious library toward the front of the mansion. Faraj was in a blue chair positioned at an angle to him. They were awaiting the arrival of their host, who had been held up by a top-level government meeting nearby that was running late.

"May I bring you gentlemen some tea and pastries?" The butler of the house asked.

Farouk responded, "Yes, that would be good. It will help us to pass the time while we … continue to wait."

The butler nodded silently and left the room. As soon as he was out of earshot, Faraj said, "Do you think we're going to get what we want and need today?"

"Yes. I do."

"Are you prepared to elaborate further?"

"I'm not absolutely sure, but I think he'll come through for us."

Faraj said, "You know, with my connections, we're fine even if he doesn't."

Farouk frowned. "Yes, you've been saying that and I appreciate your confidence, but I've worked hard to put this fellow in a position where he owes me a great deal, and now is the time for him to begin to pay off the debt."

"Whatever you say, brother, but I wish you would leave this side of things to me. I'm the one with the military training and experience, after all."

"We're not here today to dig trenches, clean weapons, or dodge bullets, but to make what is, in effect, a business deal."

"Well, it's military in nature."

"Look, this is my territory, and you need to respect that. If we get the green light today, due to all the elaborate preparation I've done with this man and his son in the past, we'll be just one or two steps away from our goal."

"Perhaps," Faraj said.

Farouk simply stared at him in response. The ticking of the tall clock standing near them suddenly seemed loud. Otherwise, they were enveloped in silence. Farouk was thinking to himself how much easier this would all be without dealing with his brother's ego. Faraj was inwardly angry about what he considered Farouk's dismissive and overbearing arrogance. But he didn't want to say anything more. The less said at this stage, the better. Faraj knew that their intentions diverged, and Farouk didn't seem to be at all aware of that yet, despite his intuitive ability to read people. The great intensity of his desires in this case was blocking his otherwise acute perceptiveness.

Farouk thought he was using Faraj as an ally in attaining his own goals. Faraj felt exactly the same way about Farouk, but differed only in having an absolutely unshakable certitude that he himself was the one who was right. Farouk didn't spend much time thinking about his brother, but the younger al-Khoum was nearly obsessed with pondering his older sibling. In the younger man's ambitious mind, Farouk was much less a brother and more a stepping-stone that he both needed and resented. But then, when Farouk did think about it at all, he would have considered his bother in much the same way, yet with the resentment replaced by mere disdain.

Power had corrupted both the al-Khoums. But Farouk had enjoyed much more of it at this point in their lives, and so at some level, he understood it better and knew its limits. Faraj had never had the full taste of it that he desired, and so he could still be more strongly lured, and even unhinged, by the empty promises it made. His craving for it exceeded even his brother's level of desire, as strong as it was. And, as a result, this younger man was the one most likely to say, at some point a little farther down the road, "Am I my brother's keeper?"

The butler had come back into the room with the promised tea and pastries on a silver tray and, as he put them down said, "The master has returned just now and should be in to see you, soon. He again apologizes for his unexpected tardiness."

"That will be fine," Farouk said, and inwardly smiled. Anything that affected the interpersonal dynamics today in such a way as to give him additional leverage of any kind, even the apparently unavoidable delay experienced by his host, was a welcome gift that he knew he could use. That's why Farouk was always on time or early to any important meeting. It's also why he dressed well, and even brought an item of interest, like a book or another sort of small gift, when he was visiting someone from whom he wanted something—anything to change the balance of the situation, even if ever so slightly, and turn the tables just a touch more in his favor. People respond on a subconscious level to all such little gestures, and Farouk knew this well. What, coming from another person, would be simply a small kindness was, from him, always a form of self interested artful manipulation, but it was normally so subtle as to be masterful, and quite effective.

The man who was about ready to enter the room would fall into Farouk's trap, as nearly everyone else did, and soon grant him almost everything he had come to ask. And this would present a massive problem for the current king and prince of Egypt.

6

Surprising Information

Mafulla knocked on the door.

A tired sounding voice said, "Enter … if you really have to."

The visitor pushed the door open and slowly walked in. "Hey, my man—nice greeting. Friendly. Inviting."

"Ugh. Hey, yourself. This is a little early, isn't it?" Walid yawned and rubbed his eyes.

"Yep, I woke up really early, especially given how late we stayed up last night, but I couldn't get back to sleep, and now I'm hungry."

"When did you wake up?"

"I don't know—but crazy early. It was still completely dark out. And yet my mind was totally racing with thoughts and questions about Phi and the Fibonacci numbers everywhere around us, and your birthday, and my role in things."

"Yeah?"

"Yeah, and it was like all of this stuff circled around and around and finally just got all balled up into one big question and I kept thinking and thinking—why, why, why—and suddenly, it dawned on me."

"What? You figured it all out?" Walid rose up in bed on his elbow.

"No, I mean, the sun rose. It was dawn."

"Oh, geez. You got me all excited for a lame joke."

"Actually, I thought it was a pretty good one. But, anyway, I realized at the first light of dawn how long I'd been tossing and turning, and that I needed to just get up and go eat. I'm really, really hungry. Wondering must burn lots of calories."

"I think Aristotle was pretty fit and trim."

"Yeah, the guy who said philosophy begins in wonder, and soon gives rise to hunger."

"You added that part."

"Ok, true. Nothing gets by you these days. So, anyway, how are you feeling on this fine morning?"

Walid yawned and said, "I'm mostly still just sleepy, except for the momentary rapid pulse you gave me at the thought that you had figured out all the mysteries that have been weighing on us."

"Look, it's only a few minutes before we usually eat. We should go down and get something now."

"You think the food's out yet?"

"Sure, Kular gets on it early. And I think we both need some coffee and biscuits and some of the kitchen's best jam. It's no mystery how good that is every morning."

"Well, if you put it that way," Walid said, as he rolled out of the bed. "Give me a minute and I'll walk down with you."

"Good. I hate to eat alone. It's tragic. No one's around to hear my best jokes."

"Yeah. Well, I'm afraid I have been."

"Have been what?"

"Around to hear your best jokes."

"Oh. Ok. I see what you're implying in a very convoluted way. And I think I must reply: Hardee-har—at least before taking issue with your nearly opaque suggestion. My humor is clearly and always utterly topnotch."

"It's for sure my favorite part of breakfast, aside from the food and drink, of course, and the room decor and the view and the comfort of the chairs," Walid said in a voice of almost no inflection at all.

"Hey, it's free entertainment," Mafulla said.

"And well worth the cost," Walid replied.

As the prince then walked into his adjoining bathroom, Mafulla said to him, in a louder voice, "Could you believe Karim the Dream, the Tunisian Tornado, last night?"

Walid answered from a distance, "No. It could be that he's a pretty good guy, but he seems a little overly obsessed with the ladies."

"Yeah, the total opposite of me."

At that, Walid appeared at the door again. "Now, that's a good joke, I have to say. When do you not have femininity on your mind?"

"What? Clearly, the situation is the exact opposite—in my case, it's the ladies who are obsessed with me."

"You crack me up. And that's saying something for this early. I'd actually laugh if my body wasn't still dormant at the moment."

"Quit complaining about the time. The kingdom's active duty soldiers have been up for hours—and a bunch of palace guards."

"True."

"And grocers. And people cooking at cafes that serve early breakfast. And probably some taxi drivers and lots of other people, like guys who work at the dock."

"Good. At least, if I ever want a cab ride this time of day to a breakfast café, and want to sit down and eat with some grocers, soldiers, and palace guards, and then go visit a few dock workers, just for a chat, they'll all be up already and easily available."

"Stop kidding around and get dressed."

"Yeah, yeah."

"You know what I'm saying. Half the city is already going about its day while you're in your pajamas and grousing about getting up so early— here in the royal palace and with a breakfast waiting for you that's fit for a king, or at least a prince and a duke, or an earl or something."

Walid yawned a super big yawn and said, "Ok, Ok, let me put on something half decent for walking down the hall."

"No problem. But while you do, let me ask you something."

"Sure, what is it?"

"What do you know about Tunisia?"

"Not much."

"Me, either."

"They're a country or so over, west of us. They've got a beach on the Mediterranean Sea. I remember reading somewhere that we've had pretty good relations with them through the years."

"Why did we get a new ambassador from there?"

"I think the old one just wore out."

"Funny. Your brain's rousing itself. What really happened?"

"I don't know. He was actually pretty old. I remember him. I think he retired or something."

"I just get a really strange feeling about it all."

"What sort of feeling?"

"I don't know, and that's what worries me."

"Ok. I'm not sure that makes any sense."

"You know my feelings. I'm just not feeling great about the new ambassador or his son."

"Well, I do know what you mean about the son."

"Like father, like son."

"Ok, but what does that imply in this context?"

"I have no idea. I just said it because it's an old proverb or something, and maybe it has an application here."

"Like what?"

"Well, we know we don't really like or trust the son. So, why should we trust the father?"

"Ok, but his dad's not going to hit on Kissa or Hasina."

"No, hummus head, that's not what I mean. Boy, maybe you

should go back to sleep. I mean: the lack of proper conduct, and a clear absence of boundaries on the part of the son—all together, it says something about how the kid was raised and what he saw, growing up. He's all about what he wants, regardless of the context. He shows up and right away tries to get what he wants. And what I'm saying is that his dad is likely the same."

"That makes some degree of sense, actually."

"Thanks."

"Oh, and clever insult, by the way: Hummus head—nicely evocative of … mushiness. Very original and appropriate to the circumstances."

"Thank you. I do my best. You can probably tell by it how hungry I am. But I'm just saying I think we should be cautious with the new guys in town—both of them."

"That sounds right to me. Ok, I'm ready. Let's go down and get some of that jam you were tempting me with before the hummus talk."

As Walid walked toward the door, Mafulla said, "Your hair is kind of sticking up funny in the back."

Walid replied, "Who cares? Who's going to see us this early?"

"Good point—both in regard to what you just said and what your hair is doing right now. Up, up and away."

"Funny." The boys both left the room and walked down the hall to where they normally had breakfast. But this morning, the door was closed, not open like it so often was.

"This is different," Walid said, and grabbed the knob. "Maybe we're too early." He turned it and pushed the door inward, and could not have been more surprised.

"Whoa! Hey. What's going on?"

"Oh, hi." Kissa said.

"Hi," Hasina added.

Walid felt almost dizzy. He looked back at an equally stunned Mafulla, then at the girls again and, while suddenly rubbing the top and back of his head and doing his best to push the reportedly wayward hair down, said, "Ok, this is one of the best surprises ever, but what's up?"

"Your hair, just now, and it was a surprise, too," Kissa said.

"You sound like Mafulla."

"Thank you." She looked at Mafulla and grinned. "We just wanted to have breakfast with our favorite young men in the world. And there's nothing so very surprising about that."

"Nothing, nothing at all! It's just that this is something truly delightful that has never happened before."

"We've been in this room with you before."

"Yes. I remember it like it was yesterday. But you've never hosted us like this, never been waiting for us behind closed doors."

"Well, there's a first time for everything—as, for example, your hair's impressive elevation, before you pushed it down just now."

"Ugh, Maffie warned me. Did it look that bad?"

"No, just startled, like it was also surprised to see me. Here, bend over and I'll press it down for you a little more with some water on my hand." Kissa poured a little from a glass into her palm while Walid leaned in her direction.

"Ok, really," Mafulla said, as he looked at Hasina. "In addition to emergency hair care, what's the story here?" Both girls just smiled.

"I'll explain," Kissa said, wiping her now wet hands on a napkin. "After the stuff at the party last night, we wanted to have breakfast with you two, first, to make sure you know that there's nothing to worry about, Ok? The newly arrived Too-Nice-ian is not on the radar, and never got on the radar, and could not possibly have, despite his best efforts.

Walid had just laughed. And so had Mafulla, who then said, "Oh! The Too-Nice-ian! That gave me shivers, it's so good." He had a huge grin. "It wins the day, and much more. I should just pack my cleverness bags and retire now."

"Yeah, I'm super impressed," the prince added.

Kissa explained, "Well, Hassi had said that he was from the

capital city of his country, the town of Too-Nice, and I just improvised from there, so it's really her little wordplay."

"You're both geniuses of the highest order," Walid announced. And they all smiled.

Kissa said, "Also, we wanted to tell you about something that happened the day before yesterday."

"What was that?" Walid asked.

Hasina said, "In a minute. But, first, we talked to Kular early this morning, and got him to pick up some special treats for you."

"How early? I thought this was early."

"Yeah, we figured. We got here soon enough to keep any lazy boys from knowing what we were doing."

"Ha!" Mafulla laughed spontaneously and said, "I'd laugh even more but that would take too much energy."

"Silly." Hasina turned and pointed. "I'm pleased to say that you'll find, under the napkin on the side table over there, some really amazing pastries and treats that aren't normally available."

Mafulla walked over and whipped off the white napkin under discussion and over the food, and stopped in astonishment. "Oh, wow, look at this. Jeepers. We don't get this stuff when you're not around. You two must have some serious pull."

"We do," Hasina replied. "So grab a plate and enjoy the feast."

The boys did exactly as they were told and piled their plates full of good things. Then they poured hot black coffee into the cups that they ordinarily used for tea.

Kissa looked at the steaming brew for a moment and said, "Well, it seems you two may be in need of a little extra assistance this morning with your process of waking up."

Walid replied, "You sort of already took care of that, just by being here, but Maffie mentioned coffee to me in my room a few minutes ago and it planted the seed of a need."

"The seed of a need, yes indeed," Mafulla mumbled with his mouth nearly full and his right index finger wagging in the air.

Kissa grinned. "Well, I figured that coffee would go well with the special pastries Kular had the kitchen prepare, so I made sure to have a good supply of the best here for you."

"You figured right. And thank you."

"You're very welcome. So, we'll make our own plates now and tell you all about our recent adventure."

"What adventure?"

"That's what we're going to fill you in on, and I think you'll be pleased and proud of us both."

"I can't wait to hear."

"Well, it starts off sounding bad—like a lot of your adventures."

"Really?"

"Yeah."

"Well, Ok then, let's hear it."

Kissa finished filling her plate and took it over to an empty seat. As Hasina followed her, she began the tale. "We were doing Phi training with my mom the day before yesterday, late in the afternoon—you know, in the room over that shop I told you about."

"Yeah, sure," Walid said. Mafulla nodded his head with his mouth full of food.

"The shop had closed for the day, the owners left, and it was just the three of us upstairs."

"Ok."

"Hoda was telling us some stuff and said something funny and we were all laughing and we didn't hear some people on the stairs."

"The stairs to the room—the ones outside?"

"Yeah. And then, all of a sudden, this man appeared in the door, a pretty big guy, and he had a large knife in his hand."

"Oh, no," Walid and Mafulla both said.

"Yeah, it was a real 'Oh-no situation' right from the start."

"What did the guy do?" Walid asked, as he put down his pastry.

"He was dirty and mean and he said he had come to rob the store but saw our light on upstairs and decided to check it out. And then he started saying we were all real beauties, and he made some ugly threats, and two younger guys showed up, and all of them made it clear they had some really bad intentions—or at least, they all hinted at that pretty obviously. And these were evil looking guys."

"Oh, man," Mafulla said, obviously concerned. "What in the world happened?"

"The other two younger men seemed like really bad characters, and they had knives out, too. Fortunately, the older man, the first to come in the door, was staring at mom—well, really, they all were, at first; she's the ultimate diversion, as you know—and Hassi slowly crept backwards toward the table where our gear was."

Hasina said, "We had just been practicing with short swords, so I knew exactly what I was going to do. And just as I began to drift back to the table, Hoda did this awesome move and kicked the knife out of the old guy's hand. And then she kicked him into the closed door and he collapsed to the ground. And while the other two were totally shocked at seeing all that happen, I picked up our practice swords. And when the guys looked back at Hoda—I guess to see what she'd do next—I tossed a sword to Kissa. And before they knew what was happening, we had disarmed them both and had them frozen, still, at sword point and afraid to move."

"Really?" Mafulla said. "What did you do?"

"We ordered them to their knees and they dropped," Kissa replied.

"They did?"

"Yeah. It was almost too easy."

Hasina said to her friend, "You forgot the part about the guy shooting at you and trying to kill you."

"What?" Walid exclaimed.

"Oh, yeah, that."

"Somebody shot at you?"

"Yeah. When we had disarmed the two younger guys, the older man must have gotten really frustrated, because he pulled out a hidden gun and shot at me, but I heard the rustling of his clothes when he grabbed it, and I did this wild avoidance move and he missed."

"And Hoda saw what was happening," Hasina added, "and as the guy was pulling the trigger, she had the other sword in her hand and threw it across the room into his stomach, and he died right there."

"No way."

"Yeah. It's too bad that was the only way. Then she scooped up one of the loose knives on the floor and joined us, covering the two guys who were still alive. She made them lie still and tied them up while we held our swords on them both. And, Walid, you'll love this—Kissa had to get all Phi on one of the guys and pushed her blade into his skin so that she drew blood, and she talked really tough to him and he was totally petrified."

"And then somebody broke the door down," Kissa said.

"What?" Now it was Mafulla's turn to exclaim.

"Yeah," Hasina said, "and so, of course, we thought there were more bad guys on the way, friends of these jerks, but it didn't really scare us. We were ready for anything by then. And, also, at that point, we were sort of tired of just disarming these idiots and were ready to go all Hoda on whoever showed up next."

"Man," Mafulla said, mouth open.

"But it was Omari and Paki," Kissa said.

"No way!" Walid and Mafulla said this at the same time.

"Yeah, really. They'd been walking by and heard the gunshot. And they were all super Phi, and Omari pretended like he was going to kill one of the bad guys, just to let them know what it felt like to be threatened and to be helpless, but he and Paki took them off to jail and told us to go home and try to relax."

"Amazing," Walid said.

"Just incredible," Mafulla added. "I'm nearly speechless."

"Why didn't you tell us all this right after it happened?" Walid said.

"We didn't have time. We went over to Hassi's and ate dinner and then had a busy day, and there was the reception. And, you know, there were other things going on, so we planned this breakfast visit to bring you up to date on it all. And we wanted to let you know that, whenever you need us as your crime fighting backup team, we can do more than the cool mind stuff—which, by the way, Hoda also used on the old guy, zapping his brain and giving him one of those terrible head pains right before she first kicked him."

"Oh, wow."

"So, that's the full story. The first real battle, and the home team easily won." Kissa picked up her napkin and put it in her lap.

"I had no idea," Walid said.

"Unbelievable," Mafulla added, and he was actually forgetting to eat.

"Eat, eat! I didn't mean to spoil your appetites," Kissa said.

Walid picked up some fruit and explained, "It's just that … we had no clue you were getting that kind of physical Phi training already, and at that level, in addition to all the psychic stuff."

"Yep, we get the whole package, just like you guys."

"And Hoda can do all that?"

"Yeah, totally, and she doesn't even break a nail, or a sweat. And so can Layla," Kissa said. "And really, they can both do a whole lot more than take down a bad guy or two. They can get totally scary."

"I had no idea."

"Neither did I," Mafulla added. "You guys are two tough chicks, for sure. And we thought you needed us to save you from Mr. Too-Nice. He was the one who was going to need saving."

"Definitely," Hasina said, and laughed.

"And there's one more thing," Kissa added.

"What?"

"When we were about to leave last night, Mafulla, I saw your Uncle Reela talking to the king, and it looked like they were having a very serious conversation, all by themselves. You guys should probably find out what that was all about."

"Oh. Ok. You think it was about our guest of honor?"

"That's what I suspect," Kissa said.

"Maffie has a strange feeling about the two of them—the father and the son."

"Walid's right," Mafulla said as he cut up an apricot to put it on a biscuit. "I've got an odd, unsettled sense about both of them and I can't quite say what exactly worries me."

"Actually, I'm feeling the same way," Hasina responded, nodding her understanding.

"Me, too," Kissa added. "You know how I am about people. I got a weird sensation right away, as soon as Karim came up to me. And everything he said and did just confirmed that … ickiness. And, honestly, I have a feeling the problem is way bigger than just a normal, garden-variety ick-factor. I think it goes deep."

"Well, he was on my bad list the second I saw him," Walid said. "But of course, that was because of what I saw him doing in the ballroom. Maybe I would have been like you three and had other bad feelings about him, but what I was already feeling probably just covered over anything else I otherwise could have sensed. I've got to be more careful about emotion like that getting out of control and in my way."

"Yeah, you know what the king says about emotion," Mafulla reminded him.

Walid nodded and said, "Either we control it, or it controls us."

"Exactly."

"I'm just glad the three of you were able to feel deeper things about the guy. We all need that sort of clear-headed discernment with people. Otherwise, we get blindsided."

"You're right," Mafulla said. "It's a really good thing you have us around."

"I just wish I could have been calm enough at the time to be able to size up the guy myself."

"Nobody's perfect," Hasina said.

"Well, almost nobody," Mafulla replied. "That's for sure. But, you know, modesty forbids that I say more."

"You're too funny," Hasina grinned.

"No. He's almost funny," Walid said.

"What do you mean?" Mafulla objected.

"There's of course a big difference. But, you know, friendship forbids that I say more."

"Ha!"

Just then, Kular came into the room with an additional plate of biscuits. "Hi, Kular," everyone said.

"Hello. Hello, all, and greetings again, ladies. I'm so sorry to interrupt, but these cheese and spice biscuits are fresh from the oven and I thought you might want one or two. Oh, and Walid and Mafulla, when breakfast is over, the king wants you to stop in at his office. He has some new information to share with you."

"Ok, Kular. Thanks. And thanks for the biscuits!" Walid said with a smile. The butler, in response, just did a big bow.

As Kular then slipped back out of the room, Mafulla said, "I wonder what the king wants to tell us."

Kissa said, "Maybe it's about the conversation he had with Reela."

"Yeah," Walid replied. "I bet you're right."

They all helped themselves to some of the fresh, hot biscuits and the prince said, "Look, how about we all meet right after school in the palace garden over near the little fountain where there are a couple of benches, and we'll let you know what's up."

"That place where you and Mafulla often laze around after school?"

"Yep."

"Well, I think my friend means both yes and no," Mafulla interjected."

"Ok?"

"It's just that I believe you may have mischaracterized the location inadvertently, even though you have the right one in mind."

"Really?"

"Yes. It's the very special place where Walid and I regularly do our most profound thinking in the sun or the shade, whichever is most appropriate, given the temperature."

"I've heard that the two of you have been seen in philosophical positions that at least outwardly mimic napping," Kissa replied.

"And lazing, definitely lazing around," Hasina added.

"Ah, how easily people misunderstand the bodily postures necessary for attaining the mental rigors and depths of profundity," Mafulla responded. "Total concentration often requires a relaxed demeanor, and even a reclined outward position and a shutting of the eyes, in order to concentrate a suitable focus of the mind."

"Ok, Professor Adi. We'll gladly meet you at the … place of profound concentration. That sounds good," Kissa said with a smile.

"Yeah, there's nothing planned for right after school," Hasina added, "and we could always use a closer encounter with profundity."

Mafulla just smiled and did his double eyebrow jump. None of the four could even begin to imagine what would happen during their short time in the garden after school, or how terribly dangerous it would turn out to be.

7

A Sunny Afternoon

Class seemed to fly by for the boys. There was a short stretch of Greek translation, some history, a little math, and a discussion of the promise and perils of democracy as a political reality, a topic that Khalid said they would return to soon.

Walid and Mafulla were so focused on the meeting they'd had with the king before class and on the upcoming afternoon with the girls, it was a struggle to think very much about anything else. And yet, they both had pretty good self-control. So, they did what they could to take part in all the discussions Khalid launched. But as soon as he dismissed them for the day, they almost ran to Kular's small kitchen prep area for some snacks to take outside, and then left the palace with a picnic basket and a good selection of treats.

When they turned the corner close to their usual hangout spot near a small fountain, they could already see Kissa and Hasina walking up from the other direction, having come from the part of the palace that housed their classroom. "Nice timing," Mafulla called out to them.

"We have some goodies," Walid also called out.

"Goodie for goodies! We're hungry!" Kissa said back.

As the girls walked up, Walid set down their basket and began to take out the various snacks and put them onto some small plates up on one of the benches, along with the cups that Mafulla had just then filled with cold juice.

"Well, this is very nice," Hasina commented. "I had no idea we'd be having a catered event."

"We try," Mafulla replied with a grin.

"And by the looks of it, you succeed," she said.

He bent down and put on the ground what looked like a large rolled up cloth of some sort that he'd been carrying. Then Walid gestured toward one of the two benches and said, "You ladies can perch here and we'll sit on the ground."

"No, no, if Mafulla has a blanket for the grass that's big enough, we can all sit on the ground," Kissa said. "It'll be better for talking and, I have to be honest, stealing bits of your snacks. You know, we ladies never put enough on our plates, and we hate to ask for seconds, so it's good to be closer to your food."

"Oh, Ok, great!" Walid said, as Mafulla reached over to the large rolled up cloth he had just set down, something that could be used either as a table dressing or a picnic blanket. He then unrolled it and straightened it out over the grass, lofting it into place, and finally smoothing it down.

"I love it that there's grass here," Kissa said. "It's so soft."

"Yeah, with so much sand everywhere, it is nice to have a little greenery to relax on. It is soft. That's part of why Walid and I come here pretty often," Mafulla explained. "It's good for … thinking. Also, it's sort of out of the main area, and so it's normally quiet here."

Hasina said, "I like the way the sand comes up to right behind the benches, but under them and in this whole area, there's this nice carpet of well-maintained lawn. The grounds guys must have to work hard to keep it in such good shape."

"I'm sure they do," Walid said. "But they normally do their work in the mornings, so we don't often see them in the afternoon." He reached over and picked up two plates and said, "Here, have a snack."

Kissa thanked him, as did Hasina, and as they reached for the plates, Kissa said, "I have to hear what you learned from the king." She had a serious look on her face.

"It's not good," Walid replied.

"More than a little troubling," Mafulla said and shook his head, while he reached for a cup. "Here, have some juice."

"Thanks."

Walid began his report by saying, "So here's what we know. Mafulla's uncle Reela heard from a couple of old friends that Farouk al-Khoum and his bother Faraj have been seen in Tunisia, of all places, and in the capital city, Tunis."

"No!" Kissa said.

"No way," Hasina added.

"Yeah. And they've apparently been in meetings with one or two members of the government there, men who've built up sizable fortunes in private business endeavors over the last few years. Reela's contacts think they may have done some deals with Farouk in that time, and they might owe him big for their personal wealth."

"What would Farouk be doing in these meetings?" Kissa asked.

"Reela thinks he's angling for the use of some military supplies and men, off the record and outside of official channels, for his plans against us. The regime in Tunisia has always been friendly with Egypt, so he's keeping this very hush-hush and private. But people talk, and word can still get out as to what's going on—or at least some of it. And that's how Reela got wind of this."

"Do we know what Farouk's planning?"

"He's likely preparing for an attack and a revolution of some sort or other—here, of course. There's no indication yet that he's raised a major army or anything. But he may be putting together smaller groups of mercenaries to fight his battles for him, and then trying to get them well equipped by these guys who owe him for past favors. We don't know exactly what he has in mind, though. It's still all pretty vague and murky."

Kissa replied, "This is scary."

Hasina said, "Yeah, it is,"

Then Kissa continued, "It's like, being here at the palace, we're living in the center bulls-eye of an archery target, and we're watching a guy pick up a bow and choose an arrow." She was good with imagery like this to capture the essence of a situation and make it vivid.

"Yeah, and we can't wait until the arrow's flying through the air before we do something about it," Walid replied.

"That's right," Mafulla said.

"So, what's the story about the new ambassador and his son? Are they involved in all this?" Hasina asked as she reached for some of the cool fruit juice that Mafulla had now put down near her.

"Well, that's still a mystery," Walid answered. "No one knows yet whether the new guy's legitimate, a true representative of his government, and so is friendly to us, or is maybe just a plant, channeling information to Farouk and Faraj."

"More like a weed," Mafulla said.

"Walid, who's the man coming our way?" Kissa happened to see someone in work clothes walking down the path that she and Hasina had just taken to the spot where they now sat.

"Oh, that's one of the gardeners, a man named Nazeem Alfid. Maffie and I often talk to him when we're out here in the gardens. He knows a lot about this place and its history."

"Yeah, he's an encyclopedia of information," Mafulla said.

"Nazeem!" Walid called out and waved.

"Oh, hello, Your Highness. Hello, Mafulla, and a very good day to you, young ladies."

"Nazeem, would you come over for a second?" Walid motioned.

"Certainly." The man increased his pace.

Walid waited for a moment as the gardener drew near and

then said, "I want to introduce you to Kissa El-Bay, whose parents teach here in the palace school. And this is her best friend, Hasina. They're both good friends of ours."

"It's very nice to meet you." Nazeem did a little bow.

"Likewise," Hasina said.

"It's a pleasure to make your acquaintance," Kissa seconded.

"I didn't mean to disturb you, but I have to do a little work nearby for just a few minutes, if that's all right, and then I'll be gone."

"You won't disturb us a bit," Kissa responded. "Walid and Mafulla say that they've learned a lot from you about the history of the palace and these grounds."

"Oh, that's very kind of them. They're quick learners who ask good questions. I've worked in the palace gardens long enough to hear almost all the lore about the place, and I love it. It feels good to see young people like you enjoying the grounds that I work so hard to help preserve and beautify, day-to-day. Otherwise, a few other gardeners and palace guards would be the only people to benefit from all this delightful landscaping."

"We love the way everything looks out here," Hasina said. "We really appreciate your hard work."

"Thank you so much," Nazeem replied. "Your kind words are most welcome. You do me honor. Now, I should leave you young people to your food and talk, and move around to the other side of these shrubs to do my scheduled duties."

"Let us know if we're in the way, and we can move," Walid said.

"No, no. You're fine where you are, Prince. I don't need access to this area at all. But do let me know if there's anything I can do for you while I'm out here. I'll be able to hear you easily if you should choose to call on me. But I'll also be far enough away that your conversations will be suitably private, as well. And sometimes, I whistle while I work, without even thinking about it. So, if you hear whistling, it's likely me."

"Thanks, Nazeem," Walid said.

"Yeah, thanks, man," Mafulla added.

The gardener nodded and did a small bow in the direction of Walid, then another one toward Mafulla, and took his tools—a shovel and a hoe—and walked around some high, well-manicured bushes where he then continued on down the path to a point a short distance from them. The four friends picked up their conversation, speculated a bit more about the recent events in Tunisia and their assessment of the ambassador's son, and then they began to drift on to other topics about Phi and self-defense and the range of what the girls were learning from Hoda in their training sessions. Kissa pushed the basket back toward the side of the bench so that she could have a little more room and didn't see what was already beside the bench.

The gentle shove of the basket and the small movement it made was all it took for the deadly snake to react as if it was being attacked. It coiled up instantly, ready to strike. Walid heard the raspy noise of its scales rubbing against each other as it moved, and he right away recognized the nature of the sound from a discussion he once had with his uncle in the desert.

"Don't move, Kissa. Don't move at all, anyone," Walid said in a low but urgent tone of voice. He was sitting maybe three or four feet away. Mafulla was at about the same distance from Kissa, and Hasina was at least four feet to the side. They all froze.

Hasina whispered, "What is it?"

Walid could hardly breathe. He said in a soft, low voice, trying to sound calm, "It's a bad poisonous snake, one that will strike if you move, if anyone moves. Stay still. Everyone stay perfectly still." Without moving his head, he looked around quickly for anything resembling a weapon or tool he could use to kill the deadly saw-scaled viper. And he realized there wasn't one. If Kissa stayed where she was, there was a good chance that anything could set off the snake and it would strike her. If she tried to move at all, there was an even greater chance of an attack, almost a certainty, and she would not be able to move fast enough from a sitting position to get out of its reach. It seemed like an impossible situation. Then, the prince did what no one could have expected.

"Nazeem! Nazeem! Help us! There's a viper over here ready to strike! A deadly snake! He's beside the bench!" Walid called out as loudly as he thought he could without any overall body moment that would agitate the serpent. Are snakes bothered by noises? Can they hear? He had no idea, but he had to take the terrible chance that this one tactic involved. There was no other option available to save Kissa from an attack that could be sparked by any movement at all around them. He didn't know whether he had shouted too loudly and perhaps in that way further agitated the creature. He also didn't know whether he had called out loudly enough, in his hesitation.

Hasina whispered again, "What should we do?"

"Just stay still. Nothing yet—no one should do anything yet. Hold still and don't move, no matter what. Help may come."

At that moment, Nazeem slowly stepped around a high shrub near Kissa, but to her side and slightly behind her, as well as behind the snake. Everyone but Kissa could see him. "Stay still, Kissa," Walid repeated. "Be a statue. Help is here."

Nazeem raised his shovel, and with what he knew to be the one and only opportunity available to him, since a miss would likely cause the attack they were all dreading, he forcefully brought down the blade of the shovel in a lightning fast movement right behind the snake's head, chopping him in two. Two more severe blows made sure there was no mistake, and then just as quickly, he instinctively shoved the blade down again and shoveled the snake body and head sideways to his left, farther away from Kissa, being as careful as he possibly could be. He was unaware that, in doing this, he had thrown the dead body onto a second viper barely three feet away and under a bush.

As he shoveled it, he yelled, "Move! Now! Away! Quickly!" And Kissa and the others scrambled to get at least twenty feet from the bench, or more.

"Oh, my!" Kissa exclaimed. "You saved me!"

But at that same instant, the second viper coiled to strike and Nazeem both heard and saw it and froze, the shovel in his hand, afraid to move and use it, in the knowledge that he could be struck in the leg before the arc of any swing would get close to the snake. The angled position of the viper and its proximity made any act of effective self-defense seem impossible.

Noticing Nazeem's sudden and complete lack of movement, Walid looked around more closely and caught sight of the other viper and said, "Second snake—everyone stay calm and where you are. I'll get this. Just stay still. No motions. Nazeem, don't move at all."

The prince was far enough away from the live snake at that point, and a bit out of the viper's presumed range of vision that he felt like he could safely inch backward, to the side, and farther away. When he got far enough from the group, he turned and ran toward where the gardener had been working and saw exactly what he remembered, a long handle hoe that was now lying there on the ground. Picking it up, he ran back, but a slightly different way, so that he could come up on the snake from behind. When he got slowly and silently into the best position available, he realized that most of the viper's body was blocked from this angle by the shrub it had been under. The low bush now stood between Walid and the snake. But its head was visible above the bush and it was still poised in a full strike position. Without hesitation, Walid forcefully swung the hoe from behind it almost like a golf club and decapitated the threat instantly, knocking its head a good distance away from everyone and into nearby sand. A shiver ran through his entire body. "Move!" He shouted to Nazeem.

"Oh, man!" Mafulla exclaimed.

"Careful, everyone, in case there's a third," Walid cautioned. "Let's move away from the bench and leave our things for now. We'll get some palace guards to come and pick them up later."

They all walked a few feet farther away and then stopped to look back. Nazeem spoke first. "I can't believe it! I just can't believe it!"

"My goodness, that was scary!" Kissa said and shuddered.

"You bet it was!" Mafulla agreed. "Nobody expected this!"

Walid said, "Nazeem, you saved Kissa."

"Prince, you saved me!"

"I've never been so shocked," Hasina said.

"It was pretty frightening, mostly because there was really nothing physical I could do," Kissa explained to them all.

Walid said, "Nazeem, would you go ask your supervisor to get two or three guards down here? Tell them what happened, and have them check the area for more vipers. But make sure they know to be very careful."

"Right away, Prince Walid."

"Have you ever seen snakes like these, in the garden, in pairs?"

"No, Your Highness. I've never seen a single viper here in all the years I've been working the gardens. They're desert snakes. I have no idea how two of them got into the palace gardens, and both in this one place. This is not a viper habitat, thank goodness. They're very dangerous."

"Yeah, and of all possible locations, they were in this place where you and I come most days," Mafulla said to Walid. "It can begin to look like someone had a surprise in mind for the two of us."

"It does sort of look like that," Walid agreed, with great concern in his heart. "I'm so glad nobody was hurt."

"Yeah," Mafulla said.

Nazeem explained, "These snakes I know about, despite never seeing one around here. I grew up hearing stories about them. They rarely deal out mere harm. They bring death. They're legendary.

But enough talk. I'll go tell the boss and get some guards out here as quickly as I can."

"Thanks, Nazeem."

As the gardener walked away at a rapid stride, Walid said to Kissa, "You mentioned that you were scared because there was nothing physical you could do. Did you do something that was not physical?"

"Yes. I did."

"What?"

"I used my mind and focused on the snake not striking. I willed it not to strike—first me, and then Nazeem. I have no idea if it did any good, but it was all I could think to try."

"It may have done a lot of good. Neither one struck."

"I hope I helped."

"I sort of tried that, too," Hasina admitted. But I was too shocked to do it at first. Then it suddenly came to me that maybe I had that option. It's just different when it's not a person—you know, a human."

"Hasina's right," Kissa said. "When it's a person, you feel like you can touch their body through their soul, or through some collective unconscious spirit connection or something, person-to-person. But when it's a creature like a snake, you don't even have that really going for you—I mean, as far as I know. You have to totally stretch your sense of possible connections. And that can be a problem for your confidence, and I've really come to realize that some level of confidence is necessary when you're trying to do that sort of thing."

"Or, almost anything," Walid added.

"Yeah, almost anything," Kissa agreed.

"I guess there's got to be a clear flow of energy, without any doubt or hesitation, or anything else to block it."

"I agree with that, completely," Mafulla said, "but I haven't been saying anything for a bit here because I've been keeping my eye on the surrounding bushes, sand, and grass, looking for snakey signs. And so far, it looks like snakey parts are all that are anywhere near us. No signs of anything else."

Walid said, "Well, thanks, mighty hunter. I've been glancing around too, but it's good to know that at least one of us has been using a degree of truly focused concentration on the job."

Kissa then said, "You know, it's sad that two living creatures had to die so that none of us would."

Walid responded, "I agree. It's odd, but I was just feeling the same thing."

"I think it was Mafulla's mention of the snakey parts."

"Yeah. It's so strange. It's like any death that's not natural is somehow to be regretted and maybe even mourned."

Hasina then said, "I hope there's a snakey heaven."

Mafulla quickly added, "Far, far away from people heaven."

"Good point. It would have to be."

"Yep."

Within a few minutes, as they continued to talk, three palace guards came running up, one with a shovel and two with guns drawn. The first one called out, "Prince, are there any signs of other poisonous snakes?"

"Not since Nazeem and I killed the two we saw."

"Ok, good. Thanks, Your Highness. You can all leave now and we'll take over. We'll make sure to get your belongings to you after we've searched the entire area. I'm so sorry that this happened to you at a picnic on such an otherwise nice day."

"It was interesting."

"I'm sure."

"Please let Naqid know that Nazeem has never seen a poisonous viper on the palace grounds before, in all his years of working here. The fact that there were two, and located at the spot where Mafulla and I often come to relax, is more than a little suspicious. You may want to do a background search on all recently hired employees and on any packages that might have arrived anywhere in the palace today, or even yesterday."

"Yes, Prince, you're absolutely right. We'll get on it immediately."

The guard speaking turned to his colleagues and said, "You two do the search. I'm going to go see Naqid about this right away." They nodded, and got to work, while he bowed to the prince and turned and walked briskly toward the nearest palace doorway.

Walid and Mafulla escorted Kissa and Hasina over to the side of the palace where Khalid and Hoda's office was located, and then accompanied them upstairs to the hallway outside the office. They talked for a couple of minutes more about what an eventful week it was turning out to be, and then said their goodbyes quickly and the boys walked back toward the private residence area.

By the time they got as far as the king's quarters, Kular came into the hallway, spotted them, and called them to come in. Already, there were eight men, directors of various departments of palace life, sitting around and waiting as the king stood by the window, conferring with Naqid. When he saw the boys, he said, "Walid, Mafulla, please take seats. You're just in time for the meeting."

"What's going on?"

"We've heard all about your scare and are about to take action."

"This quickly?"

"We need to move fast. But now, sit."

The boys walked across the room as the king gestured to a couple of chairs up front near where he stood. "I've gathered the heads of all our major departments in the palace for an emergency meeting to let them know of this afternoon's developments."

Now the king faced his executive staff. "Thank you all again for coming. I'm sorry to have to tell you that there has just been an apparent assassination attempt on the lives of Walid and Mafulla. Two deadly vipers were brought onto palace grounds recently, perhaps today or yesterday, and were placed at a location where they are known to relax most days after school. They were at the precise location today when the boys visited with two of their other friends for a picnic. And, without the fast action of the prince and one of the oldest groundskeepers, Nazeem Alfid, there could have been tragic consequences."

There were shocked, mumbled reactions around the room. Someone was heard to say, "What a terrible thing!"

Ali continued. "Someone brought these snakes onto the grounds, and it's your job right now to discover who did it. I want you to conduct rapid and extensive background checks on all current employees, and especially recent hires. I want Naqid presented with a complete list of all packages or parcels that have been delivered to your offices or anywhere on the grounds in the past forty-eight hours. I want to know where they came from and who took delivery. We need to apprehend the would-be assassin before anything else can be attempted." He paused for a moment, and then concluded, "This is all that can be said at present. Please work as quickly as you can. I thank you for your time, and look forward to your reports, which should be given to Naqid as soon as you know or suspect anything. Use whatever resources you have. And do move efficiently. Fast action is key. You may go and get to it, now. Thank you all."

The men stood and there were bows around the room as the various directors uttered, "Your Majesty," or just, "Majesty," and made their way out the door with solemn expressions. One man passing Walid said "So sorry for the scare, Prince. We're on it."

Walid nodded and said, "Thanks."

"My honor, Your Highness."

When the last man other than Bancom and Naqid had left the room, the prince turned to the king and said, "Assassination?"

"Yes."

"Wow. I hadn't thought of that term in connection with all this, but I guess that's exactly what this attempt was."

"It was. And we're dealing with it accordingly, with all due seriousness," the king said. "I know Naqid has a few quick questions for you." He motioned for his head of security to come over and sit.

Naqid moved over and sat near the boys and said, "Did you see anyone else near your picnic location today, other than Nazeem?

"No, not that I recall," Walid answered.

"I didn't either," Mafulla responded.

"So, only Nazeem Alfid was around."

"Yes, so far as we know. But I hope you don't suspect him. He came and saved Kissa, taking a big risk himself, and then I had to return the favor and kill the second snake to save him," Walid explained.

"No, we don't suspect Nazeem of having any connection with this. But we do have to note his presence. We'll be asking him whether he saw anyone else in the area, or anything odd, either beforehand or afterward."

"Did the men find any more vipers?" Mafulla asked.

"No, there were just the two. But they spotted and eliminated another serious menace."

"What was that?" Mafulla couldn't help but ask with a puzzled and concerned look.

"There were dozens of dangerous black widow spiders within about a thirty foot radius of where you had been sitting."

"What?" Mafulla exclaimed and shuddered.

"The men found a great many of them. They were the especially deadly venomous kind known as camel killers, the ones with thirteen spots on their backs."

Walid said, "Oh, my! That's horrible. And so strange."

"Yes, the white widow is better known here in Egypt, but this variety of black widow is much more dangerous. We rarely see one in the palace, or on the grounds, but the men spotted and killed perhaps as many as three or four dozen."

"That many?"

"Yes. And possibly more."

"They have thirteen spots? Thirteen?" Mafulla asked.

"Yes, and the spots are brightly colored. Unfortunately, whoever left the snakes there also most likely dumped out these dangerous creatures, as well. Their bites can kill or sicken badly. It's a miracle that none of them became a problem for you."

"We were sitting on the grass." Walid was vividly recalling the time in his mind.

"The men found many of them—most, actually—in the grass."

"We were all on a large white cloth the size of a bed sheet."

"Do you normally sit on a cloth when you visit that spot?"

"No, this was a special occasion because of the friends with us. Most of the time, we just sit on the bench, or plop down directly on the grass."

"That large cloth likely saved you. It acted as a barrier. And you would have been at least more likely to see any spiders that got near you."

"Oh, man, this gives me the goose flesh arm shivers. Vipers are bad enough, but I'm so freaked out by spiders," Mafulla revealed.

"Yeah, they're pretty creepy for sure," Walid said, looking over at his friend.

"We need to check your clothing carefully right now," Naqid instructed them. "I should have done so when you first got here, but I was distracted, focused on the meeting. I'm sorry, but we need to look you over immediately. Please stand, both of you."

"Oh, man." Mafulla said and stood up, almost afraid to move. Walid did, too.

Naqid carefully examined them, head to toe, and said, "You've not felt anything crawling anywhere on your body, or an itch or anything?"

"No, but just the idea of it makes me sort of itch all over," Mafulla said.

"Me, too," Walid agreed. "But, what about the girls?"

"We've had Hoda do a complete search of their garments as well."

"Good. That's good. But let me ask: How long do you think the snakes and spiders were there?" Walid looked at Naqid.

"Not long, actually," he replied. "Otherwise, they could have moved away from the drop spot, and that would have been ineffective for those who put them in place. We actually suspect that they were there no more than an hour, at most, before you arrived at the fountain, and perhaps for much less time than that."

"That's incredible timing," Mafulla said.

"Yes, it is."

"So, this all happened today, and likely right before we got there?" Walid was getting all the clarity he could about the event.

"Indeed. It occurred during the afternoon, likely a very short time before your visit. So we'll be tracking the whereabouts of all palace employees in the hour or so before you arrived there near the fountain. It helps to have a contained period of time for the search. We'll check not only all movements during that time but also clothing. Who was wearing thick pants and high boots? Who was seen carrying a box outside? I have two-dozen palace guards already asking these questions and tracking down the answers. We should begin to acquire some useful information soon."

"Wow." Mafulla was still trying to get his head around all this.

The king said, "Naqid also ordered an immediate shutdown of all the palace gates as soon as he got word of the problem. No one has been allowed to leave since then, and all visitors have been interviewed. Only a few individuals, with our explicit permission, have entered the grounds. We're being very careful."

"We're also getting clearance through the city police and a judge to be able to search the bank records of anyone under suspicion, to see if there have been any recent deposits that are out of the ordinary. We're going to pursue every avenue we can to unravel all this."

"I'm sure glad you're so on top of it, Your Majesty," Walid said.

"Me, too," Mafulla added.

"And Walid, if you and Mafulla wouldn't mind, I'll invite you to stay around here in my quarters for the next few minutes, while your rooms are checked thoroughly for any hidden dangers that might have been introduced during the day."

"Oh, gee, I didn't even think of that," Mafulla said.

"Neither did I." Walid took a deep breath and let it out. "Are Kissa and Hasina completely safe now?"

"We've sent guards to be with them and stay with them until we get some answers. It's most likely that you two were the direct targets, or perhaps just Walid, but we're not taking any chances."

"Why do you think I'm being targeted?"

"To answer your question, let me ask you one: How did Nazeem kill the first snake?"

"He cut off the head."

"How did you kill the second one?"

"The same way."

"Exactly. And that's what one of our adversaries is attempting to do to our government."

"But you're the head of the kingdom, not me."

"For now. And I'm sure the targeting won't stop with you. If an adversary eliminates any or all of the royal family, then that person has paved the way to step in and take over."

"Do we have a succession plan beyond just me?"

"Your father has agreed to be next in line after you, despite his alternative sense of personal mission, just to keep some sort of continuity going until something else can be devised."

"So Dad might be in danger now, too?"

"Yes, at least in principle. Even though no one else is aware of our plan and his agreement, many know he's my brother, and so that alone puts him and your mother in some degree of danger."

"Oh. Is she safe?"

"Yes. I've made sure of it. And you shouldn't worry. This has been true since the night of our revolution. Anyone plotting his own takeover would have to deal with all of us at some point. We've always known that and have prepared for it. Plus, both your parents have additional security now, since we first received word of the snake and spider scare."

"I guess we know who we can trust and count on."

"Yes, the people who have just now been in this room, the members of our families, and all the active Phi whose identities, as such, you know. Masoon, Hamid, Omari, Paki, and Amon, as well as Hoda and Layla and their daughters, and Khalid, and your school friends here in the palace, can of course be trusted fully, just like our families."

Just then, Kular came in the door and said, "Your Majesty, the boys' rooms have been cleared. It's safe for them to go back there now."

"You're sure?" Mafulla said.

"Yes. The search was thorough."

Under the chair where Mafulla had been sitting, in the shadows of its upholstered leg, a small black spider moved just a bit to the side, about three inches from the back of his open sandal.

8

Important Revelations

The man would never stand out in a crowd, unless it was a crowd consisting entirely of small children. But in the capital city of Egypt, in normal street conditions, he was always able to blend in—which was one of his many professional credentials. You could look straight at him and not come away with a good description.

He was walking quickly down the darkened street toward a working class tearoom in an old building not far away. The neighborhood here was dingy and paint peeled off most of the storefronts he was passing. As he arrived at his destination and entered the narrow door, he saw his confederate across the dim room at a small table.

He crossed the room, glancing left and right, and came to a stop a few feet away from the other man. With a nod of his head, he greeted his associate with the words, "It's certainly a fine day to be out and about."

The older fellow who had been awaiting his arrival just made a dismissive noise and gestured at a cup of now cold tea that was in front of the empty chair on the other side of the table. The younger man sat down. He was still the only one speaking at this point. "Were you able to accomplish your mission?"

"As much as it was in my power," the other man said.

"Oh?"

"I did exactly what I was instructed to do, and it should have been successful. I'll be surprised if it wasn't. But I couldn't stay around to find out. I guess we'll know soon enough. If our goal was attained, word should be out on the street in no time. And tomorrow, for sure, I'll find out. How about you? Were you able to get your own job done in the right way?"

"Well, my first visit was a great success."

"Yes?"

"Indeed. Mission accomplished. But at the second stop, no one was home. I waited for two hours. At that point, I was a little worried about being seen and questioned. Then, knowing you were going to be here and remembering how you hate tardiness, I had to give up on the primary plan, go with the secondary possibility, and get here as quickly as I could. Things should be fine."

The older man sighed. "I suppose you did the right thing. When will you double check on your effectiveness?"

"Probably tomorrow morning."

"Then, right after that, you need to leave town."

"I know."

"But you can't leave before having one hundred percent success. The one who pays us demands it."

"I know that, too. I don't want to end up expecting a visitor like you to surprise me some day. I'll make sure."

"You'll do whatever it takes?"

"Yes. Right before leaving—it's no problem. You know I will."

"Nothing's ever been more important."

"I understand. You don't give me enough credit. I'm not that new in this line of work." The younger man smiled, despite the tone of his words. He thought he had proved himself many times over by now.

The older man looked skeptical, but still nodded and decided not to challenge his associate any further. He just said, "The big difference between success and failure in our work is always the same as that between life and death. Effectiveness is fatal for one, ineffectiveness for the other."

"Well said," his colleague replied. "This is why I like working with you. Your sayings will remain with me long after you're gone."

"I'm going nowhere any time soon. I get the job done. I always have. You should know that. I'm a good role model for a man like you. Let me inspire you."

"Yes, you do and you are. You're legendary for your success."

"Thank you."

Across town, at about the time that this conversation in the dingy tearoom was taking place, two very young men were experiencing a wave of exhaustion after their overly exciting afternoon. They had just arrived in the king's private sitting room where they were for the moment alone.

"What a day!" Mafulla said, as he slumped down into the sofa.

"Yeah, really," Walid replied and sat.

"I was just replaying the whole thing in my mind and I want to say, one more time, nice shot at the second snake, my friend."

"Thanks."

"I couldn't believe it when I saw that head flying through the air. What a relief! You looked like that famous old Scottish golfer of the past."

"Old Tom Morris?"

"Yeah, or maybe his son, Young Tom Morris, both winners of the British Open, time after time, if I recall. I don't really know the difference. But I've seen some of the photos. They're both legends, like you now, of course."

Walid chuckled and thought for a second and said, "I've always liked that name, Tom Morris."

"Yeah, me too," Mafulla nodded.

"It's a solid name," Walid commented.

"It is," Mafulla agreed. "It sounds strong, even rugged, like it's the name for a man of action and legend, someone larger than life, a true champion for the ages, which is what you were today, my friend."

"Well, I had to act fast and the snake was at a strange angle, partly covered by the bush. I just did the one thing available to do."

"That's what the king's always saying. Be opportunistic in the best way. Don't get tied up in frustration about what isn't available, but find what is and use it."

"Yeah. That's a good philosophy for life, including of course, Scottish golf and Egyptian snake management."

At that moment, the king entered with a much older man. Walid and Mafulla rose to their feet. "Boys, I'd like to introduce you to our guest for the evening, Mr. Mohammed Bendar, who once worked here as the Director of Palace Storage. Mr. Bendar, this is my nephew, Prince Walid Shabeezar, and his best friend, Mafulla Adi."

"Mr. Bendar," both boys said at about the same time. The old man did a short bow in their direction, and then spoke.

"It's so nice to meet you both, but please just call me Mo. 'Mr. Bendar' is so formal. That was my father's name, and right for his time. It's an honor to be named for the Prophet, may he greatly be blessed, but I'm not worthy of being called by his name. I've always preferred Mo."

"Ok, Mo. That sounds good. It's an honor to make your acquaintance," Walid said.

"Yes, nice to meet you," Mafulla responded.

The king said, "I thought we could have just an informal early dinner this evening and talk about old times in the palace." Mo nodded and smiled. Then the king suggested, "We can go into my private dining room now and I'll have Kular bring in some food."

They all agreed and walked through the doorway into the dining room where they stood by whatever seats the king indicated they should take. He gave Bendar one end of the table, and took the other for himself, arranging the boys in between. "Please everyone have a seat," he said. Over the shuffle of chairs he continued, "Kular will be coming in soon with some good things for us, but we can go ahead and begin our conversation."

"Very nice," Mo said.

Ali looked across at their guest and smiled. "Mo, now, would you please tell us: When did you begin working in the palace?"

"Yes, with pleasure. And actually, Your Majesty, it was when I was not much older than the prince and his friend here. It was during the reign of your great father, before you were born."

"I didn't realize that your service went back so far. What was it like in the palace in those days?"

"Just marvelous! Wonderful! We all immensely enjoyed working here! And, of course, we felt quite honored at the chance to serve your father, the king, and his beautiful and kind Queen Noori. I took great pride in my job. My neighbors who did more normal work in town always admired me. They called me "The King's Man." It was quite an experience for a person of my age at the time."

"I can imagine," Ali said.

"Your mother, the queen, was so good to all of us, and so was your father. I was young, as I said, and I was first hired as a dishwasher in the kitchen. I worked hard and always came in with a good attitude. So, in a little while, I was promoted to the loading dock, where the pay was higher and my job was to help receive the supplies that came in each day for the kitchen. In that capacity, I worked with some of the other men who served the palace's supply needs more generally. And it was through them that I eventually began working in the many palace storage rooms—keeping things well organized, available, and clean."

"Was it a time of peace for the kingdom?" Walid asked.

"Yes, for most of my first few years. Then a war erupted with a neighboring kingdom. They tried to take a strip of our land by force and subjugate some of our citizens. The king would not allow that to happen, so war resulted, and we prevailed."

"Were things tense in the palace during that time?"

"For the most part, our days carried on as usual. But, now and then, the war intruded on our daily efforts. There was some treachery within the palace staff, and that was the worst thing to deal with. It seems that a few men can always be bought at the right price, but when we discovered their identities, we stopped their treason. And it was a great relief."

"I know what you mean," Walid said. The king looked over at him and smiled with a tilt of his head, and he understood that he should likely not say any more along those lines. In difficult times, discretion is always important.

Ali then asked, "Over the years, especially when you came into an administrative position as the Director of Palace Storage, did you work with any interesting or unusual characters?"

"Yes! Oh, yes, indeed I did, Your Majesty. There was one man who had been in the circus. He could balance anything. He was always entertaining us. Another man was an excellent musician who often brought an instrument to work that he played during our breaks. One man who served here for many years could have been a professional comedian and storyteller. We'd listen to his funny tales all day long. He often had us laughing on even the hardest days. The time would pass so quickly when he was telling one of his stories, whether it was about his wife or his family, or some famous historical figure. I'm sure he made up half the accounts he told us, if not more. But he had such a great talent that merriment followed him around wherever he went."

"Were there any other co-workers in those days who might have been, in some way, just … odd?"

"Let me think."

At that moment Kular brought in their main course and, with

three other palace waiters, quietly set down all the plates at the same time. Mo continued, "Oh, I remember one man—it was right after that terrible revolution when your father was so tragically killed and your mother took you into exile. We were all horrified by the events, but those awful men had enough confederates whose cooperation they had bought, and especially in the military, that we couldn't do anything about it. Our attitude changed, though, on that very day. Most of us serving within the palace ceased to think of ourselves as working for the king himself—now that we were stuck with that unjust impostor of a monarch. We hated that man for what he had done to your father and mother, and to you, of course. We began to think of ourselves as serving the kingdom and the palace, whose rightful residents we believed would one day return, as you have! We were keeping this place safe, well ordered, and functional for your future use."

The king smiled. "I deeply appreciate that. And you did your job well. But, let me ask about the odd fellow you were going to describe."

"Oh, yes. Well, he came to work some time after the revolution, years later. He was a highly intelligent young man and a hard worker—very ambitious, as I recall, and a natural leader, though a bit aggressive. But often, it just seemed that his head was in the clouds, thinking about things that made no sense to the rest of us."

"Like what?" Mafulla asked.

"Like numbers, and what he called ratios, and almost magical sounding things."

Mafulla was quite surprised at hearing this and said, "Did this individual ever talk about … the Fibonacci series of numbers, or the golden ratio that's also known as Phi?"

"Why, yes, yes I think he did. You've certainly sparked my memory! It was a long time ago, and I would have forgotten all that if you hadn't mentioned it. It's remarkable that you would guess such a thing! But then again, perhaps it's just something that numbers-minded people talk about. I wouldn't be the one to know. I learned enough basic math in school that I could have been a good businessman, and I often used it in service to the king and later to the kingdom, but I didn't know anything about the matters he was often going on about."

"Do you remember anything else about him?"

"I believe his father was a professor at the university. And, I heard that his mother was very intelligent. He also had a younger brother. Oh, I remember the younger one well. That was a difficult fellow. He, too, came to work here for a time, but he was always getting into fights. He was a hot head and didn't last long. The older brother did his own work with discipline and stayed here quite a few years before he eventually took a job in the business world. And I heard now and then, a while after that in the following years, that he had gone on to do quite well for himself, becoming rich and even powerful."

The king said, "That odd older brother, the one who went on to do so well in business: Do you remember his name?"

"Well, let's see. We had a little rhyme that I think I'll recall—if I can recite it properly." Mo laughed and said, "This is from long ago. What's his name? Ok. It rhymes with moon. Oh, yes. Here we go."

> "Farouk al-Khoum
> will own the moon,
> one day, I know it's true.
> With brains and brawn,
> he'll carry on, and then
> claim the sun itself, too."

Mo smiled, remembering the time. "Yes. That was it. Farouk al-Khoum. The rest of us liked to make fun of his ambitious talk, his very high self-confidence and such, but he was indeed smart and a hard worker, very strong and keenly committed to whatever he was doing, and yet always with an eye to promotion—more money, more power, more status, and really much more of everything. He was never satisfied."

The boys looked at each other. The king took a deep breath and nodded his head and said, "Farouk al-Khoum: that's a name that certainly rings a bell these days. He's indeed become a famous industrialist and business owner. I believe the moon and the sun are still safe, but he does already own a great many things."

Mo replied, "I'm not surprised in the least to hear that. I've not kept up with general news in the past few years. Well, since you arrived and put things right, I've been much more interested in current events. But before you came back, it was just one long parade of corruption and mismanagement and greed gone wild, so I basically left it all behind and tried to enjoy my small retirement as much as I could. I stopped reading the newspaper and did everything I could to avoid all the terrible people running the kingdom at that time."

The king took a sip of juice and said, "That was an understandable policy. I hope you're enjoying your dinner this evening, so far."

"Oh, yes, it's marvelous."

Ali then said, "The one thing that I've heard people worry about, concerning this man al-Khoum, is his excessive ambition and how that might propel him beyond the realm of ethical action."

Mo replied, "That doesn't surprise me at all. He was always an odd duck and extremely driven. Every now and then, he would look up from his work, gesture to things around him in a dramatic way and say, 'One day, this will be my house—you'll see.' Very strange behavior!"

"Really?" Mafulla said. "He meant the palace?"

"Yes! And we would just laugh and respond: 'What on earth are you saying? Do you think the king is going to adopt you as his son?' And he would answer back in the oddest way. He'd say something like: 'Wait and see! The tunnels and I have plans. The tunnels and I have plans.' What a strange young man he was, indeed."

"Did you say, 'tunnels'—in the plural, like more than one?" Walid asked.

"Yes, indeed."

"What tunnels did he mean?"

"I don't know. That's just what he said many times: 'The tunnels and I have plans.' We never had a clue what he was talking about. We had no idea. I mean: there was only one palace tunnel that we knew of, the one that comes into the maintenance room where the main plumbing is. And he never explained what in the world he meant by alluding to more, or what it could mean for such tunnels to join him in having plans. It was all just so odd."

"That room in the basement a tunnel enters is now the hub of electrical service for the palace as well as for mechanical things." Walid was thinking hard about what all this could mean.

"Oh, in my day, of course, there was no electricity. We just called that place the Maintenance Room."

"Yes, it's still so called to this day."

"We were never sure why it was there, the tunnel."

"Really?" This time Walid spoke up.

Mo went on. "No one used it. Some said it was built long ago for secret escape purposes. We mostly just kept it locked."

The king asked, "Do you think that this young man, Farouk al-Khoum, believed there to be more than one tunnel coming into the palace?"

"He could have meant that, certainly. There weren't any other tunnels that the rest of us were aware of—just the one that entered the Maintenance Room. So none of us knew of, or had ever seen, a second tunnel or more. Yet, when Farouk spoke mysteriously of his plans for the palace, he would always speak of tunnels. Always: 'The tunnels and I.' It was such a strange way to talk."

"But he never gave any clear indication of what he was referring to?" Walid asked.

"No, I'm afraid not," Mo responded. "He always liked to be mysterious. He seemed to enjoy feeling that he knew secrets the rest of us couldn't share."

"Did he ever work in the storage rooms by himself, organizing things?" Mafulla chipped in.

"Oh, yes. We turned over to him many of the more complicated organizational tasks down there and, as far as I know, the elaborate scheme he developed for storing supplies may still endure to this day. I don't think anyone ever wanted to mess with it at all. It was about those numbers you mentioned and such—too strange for most of us, but he kept reassuring us that in the numbers there was power. He was always talking about power. I think that's likely been his main life long interest and even pursuit."

"I suspect you're right," the king said. Then he added, "Unfortunately, I'm nearly sure that you're right."

"Did he ever set up combinations on door locks in the basement?" Mafulla wanted to nail down all he could about all this.

"Oh! That's a very specific question."

"Yes. I'm just curious."

"Well let me see. Remember, we're talking about a long time ago. Door locks. Most of the doors down there had keys. They were the old kind. But there were a few newer ones. And yes, yes, he did set up some of those new combinations, I think."

"Really?"

"Yes. Whenever numbers were in play, he would step up and tell us all what to do. He was so smart and headstrong that we found it easiest if we just did what he said about such things. Who were we to disagree? And really, what difference did it make to the rest of us? A lock is a lock and a combination is a combination."

"That's true," Mafulla said, "And it helps clear up a lot."

"Good. I'm glad I can be of help." Mo looked thoughtful for a moment, and then added, "The young man had positive qualities. But there were troubling things about him, as well. I guess we all have good and bad in us."

"Yes, I think you're right," the king said, and then looked around the table. "Who'd like some dessert?"

To that question, he got a unanimous positive response and so he rang a small bell to signal Kular.

"Yes, Majesty?"

"I think we'd all like to sample a few of your marvelous desserts this evening, and we're ready when you are."

"Certainly, sire! We've had a wonderful array of items just sent up from the kitchen. We'll bring them in right away."

The four diners talked more about palace history and the times that Mo had lived through. They learned that he had been married, but had lost his wife years ago to an illness, and that he had three children, all of whom still live in the capital. Walid and Mafulla were enjoying everything they were learning about the town and the entire kingdom, from all these decades past. Then, Mafulla, not one to give up a topic before he thought he had exhausted all angles, said, "Mo, do you remember anything else about that odd character you've told us about, that Farouk fellow? Since he was about our age or a little older when you knew him, I'm just keen to hear more."

"Well, now that you ask, there were certain rumors about him."

"What sort of rumors?"

"I almost forgot about this. There were rumors that he could do unusual things."

"Do you recall any examples?"

"He had a habit of always getting his way."

"Really?"

"People could just not say no to him. It was sometimes almost as if he had others hypnotized. I know it sounds silly, but that's how I remember it. And he was very intense. I once overheard him threaten another young worker, and it wasn't the normal, 'I'll break your face,' or 'If you want to live,' or anything like that. It was sinister sounding—something like, 'The new day will rise with bright sunshine on your dead and rotting corpse,' or other words to such an effect."

"Oh, my. That's indeed pretty extreme language."

"Yes. He tried to hide that side of himself most of the time, but it came out now and then. It made us worry."

"Did anyone know him especially well?"

"No. I don't think so. But wait, I take that back. I remember now my old friend Kaza used to sit down with him a lot to talk. Kaza was about my age at the time—well, I mean, he's about my age still, of course. He's as alive and well as I am."

"Wait." Mafulla said. "Is this Sayid Kaza?"

"Why, yes—the son of Fayed Kaza. Do you know him?"

"He works for my dad at the Adi Shop in the marketplace."

"Your dad is Adi?"

"Yes!"

"He's a very good man!"

"Thank you. I agree wholeheartedly!"

"You're Adi's oldest son?"

"Yes, I am."

"Oh, my! What a small world! I know your father. I know Shapur. I knew your grandfather. And I used to pal around all the time with old Kaza when we were young. We still see each other at least once a week. I had no idea!"

"Wow, it is a small world!" Mafulla was thrilled. He could talk to Mr. Kaza to get more details about Farouk al-Khoum. Who would have known? We must have potential resources all around us for all sorts of things. And these are likely resources that we may never have access to unless we make it a point to talk about what we're interested in and what we need. And then, as if by magic, we can discover all these unknown connections with people and things we wouldn't have imagined. The king was right. The simple appearances of this world often hide deep riches and profound, practical things that are available behind the scenes and around us all the time.

If we don't customarily speak up about our concerns, our needs, our goals, and our curiosities, we can miss out on many gifts that would otherwise be ours for the taking, and some that are perhaps the most ready for our use at only one fleeting moment of time. But then again, the best connections with other people often come from first asking them about their own concerns and lives. As we learn more about others, we may discover things that relate to our own goals.

All this was flying through Mafulla's head as he sat listening to Mo talk some more. Walid knew what Mafulla was thinking, and so did the king. This could be a major turning point in their access to information about a dangerous adversary. But the boys didn't know what the king knew—not yet, at least. And they had no idea about all that he had done to make this dinner possible, taking many actions without which it never could have happened. Least of all did they even suspect the terrible events that were even now on their way, in connection with this time of discussion and vital discovery. Much was yet to be revealed.

9

A Dead End Lead

When the king rose from dinner with words of gratitude to all and the boys stood instantly in response, old Mo got slowly to his feet and with a big smile thanked the king profusely for his gracious hospitality. Ali, in turn, thanked him again for his time and company, as well as for all he had done in service to the kingdom. Then Kular, at that same moment as if summoned, came into the room and walked over to Mo and took his arm and began to escort him to the door.

"I'd love to do this again some time," Mo turned and said as he reached the doorway.

"Yes, I would, too," the king replied, while knowing it would be impossible, but not exactly why or how. "It's been a great pleasure to make your acquaintance. One of the palace guards will see you home and make sure you arrive there safe."

"It was my honor," Mo said, and he added, "Goodbye, for now," as he accompanied the head butler out the door.

As soon as the door had been closed once more, the king said, "Boys, if you would, please take your seats again while I duck out for a second. I have a quick story to tell you in just a moment."

"Certainly, Your Majesty," Walid said.

"Sure thing, Your Majesty," Mafulla replied, as he pulled his chair back out to reseat himself. The king walked briskly out of the room. And before Mafulla had fully sat down on the chair, he had a strange question suddenly come to mind that made him straighten back up and look at his friend.

"Walid, is this table expandable?"

"What?"

"Does it have what they call leaves in it, sections that can be put in or taken out to make it longer or shorter?"

"I have no idea. Why do you ask?"

Mafulla laughed. "I have no idea either, to be honest. Idle curiosity, I guess. It's strange. I'm not a furniture guy. But I seem to remember the table is sometimes longer than it is right now. Let me check." At that, he bent over and got down on his hands and knees and looked under the tablecloth for the cracks or seams and any other apparatus that would be found on the underside of an expandable table. There were some clear seams that could not be detected above the table, since it was covered with a pad and a starched white cloth that overlapped the edges. And there were some wooden pieces that appeared to be exactly the apparatus that would allow the table to be slid apart in such a way as to accommodate an extra leaf, or section of wood to make it longer. Then, Mafulla saw something unexpected that would lead to a bigger surprise.

"Wow. It looks like something's written on the underside of the table top near the end where Mo was sitting." Mafulla crawled a few feet to see it better. "I think it's a maker's name and signature, and the date 1759. That's interesting."

"It is," Walid said. "That makes it a modern table in terms of the sweep of Egyptian history."

"Yeah, but still, I think, really old compared to you and me—and especially me."

"Yeah. Also true. What else do you see?"

"I see … Oh no! My Goodness! Yow!"

"What?"

Mafulla had a strong shiver run through him. He said, "Come down here and look. Right where Mo was sitting. Something black on the carpet that I think is a dead spider. Yep. It's the sort of spider that Naqid was describing, the super poisonous black widow. Jeepers."

"No way!" Walid got out of his chair and bent down to look.

"Yeah, right here! I think that's what it is, but it looks dead."

Walid got closer. "Does it have those spots?"

"Yeah. It does. Oh, man, oh, man, oh man." Mafulla backed away and made a noise through his teeth. A spasm of repulsion again ran through his body.

"Did spiders get put in the palace after all?"

"I don't know, but there's only this one, as far as I can see."

"Do you think it came in on our clothes? Yours or mine?"

"I bet that's what happened. Oh, that just weirds me out totally."

"But Naqid checked us out pretty well."

"I know, but maybe it fell off one of us or jumped off, or whatever spiders do, before we got inspected, and it's just been in here."

Walid said, "That makes sense."

"Yeah. Oh, man."

"This is creepy to the max. But at least we didn't get bit. That's a really close call. And you're sure it's dead?"

"Yeah. From where it is, it looks like Mo might have just accidentally stepped on it with his sandal and killed it."

"He didn't look like he got bitten by it, either. He didn't say ouch or grimace or anything during dinner."

"It probably just ran across the floor and got under his sandal and he put down his foot and … goodbye, spidey."

"Oh, gee. I'm still creeped out by the idea that one of those things was on one of us."

"Me too—I was sure we had avoided those guys."

"Yeah."

"The thought that this one may have gotten a ride on one of us from the garden all the way here is just too creepy and scary."

"I completely agree."

Just then, the king came back into the room and said, "What in the world are you gentlemen doing under my table? Surely, there was more than enough food available tonight and you're not scrounging for crumbs down there."

Walid was quick to answer. "No, Your Majesty, Mafulla just got under the table to see if it was the sort that could be lengthened or shortened with those expansion pieces called leaves, and then he saw a maker's name and a date, and then over at Mo's chair, a dead black widow spider."

"Oh? Let me see," the king said and walked over to the chair in question. He bent down and stuck his head under the tabletop and, without touching the intruder, said, "Yes, this is indeed the dangerous black widow, one of the poisonous spiders of the sort found outside today in the garden."

"How do you think it got in here?"

"Well, there's been no one out of the ordinary in here today, and there have been no other spiders sighted, so I'm strongly inclined to think that this one rode in on the clothing one of you was wearing this afternoon. It just fell off before Naqid checked you over."

"That's what we thought, too," Walid said.

"We're lucky neither of us got bitten," Mafulla said.

"It was apparently not to be," the king replied. "Their bites are not always fatal, but can be for young people and older people."

"And here we were, a table full of nothing but young people and older people," Mafulla said. He thought for a second more and said, "You know, it's been a pretty remarkable year. Never before in my life have I had so many opportunities to feel glad to be alive, either because of the great things I've experienced, or the bad things I've narrowly missed."

"Yeah, it's been a wild year," Walid agreed.

"Well, if there are no more deadly arachnids around, I would love to have the two of you sit for a second. But, now that I think about it, it would be nice to go into the other room where we can be more comfortable. I'll alert Kular later to our dead creature under the table."

"Good idea," Walid said. "Let's get away from that thing." The three of them then walked into the king's main sitting room and he invited the boys to have a seat and relax. As soon as they were all well ensconced in their favorite cushioned chairs, Walid spoke up again. "Your Majesty, do you think we should begin to search right away for another tunnel in the basement?"

"Yes, I do. I'll have a crew of palace guards start tomorrow. I'll instruct them to examine every square inch of the basement—floors, walls, and ceilings. If there's a second tunnel, one long ago known about by Farouk al-Khoum, we must know of it also, and as soon as possible."

"Good."

"Now," the king said, "I'd like to share with you both something that I've recently experienced. Do you recall how, a couple of days ago, I first told you about Mo—that Bancom had met him and that I had invited him to come and share a meal with us?"

"Yes, I do," Walid said as Mafulla nodded.

"Well, when Bancom was originally telling me about him, I knew I had to invite him over and I knew when it should be. I had a very strong feeling that it was today that he should come by, and that it should be for dinner. I didn't know why I was having these feelings, but they were strong, and I trusted them. We do well to respect such inklings. Mafulla, tell me again why you went under the table in the dining room."

"To check to see if it was expandable."

"And why did you want to know that?"

"Actually, Your Majesty, I have no idea. The question just popped into my head and it had a sense of something almost like urgency attached to it."

"And would it make sense to you that you felt such an urgency about the question then?"

"Not really. Not at all."

"Did you spend any time analyzing the issue, or questioning why you wanted to know, or trying to talk yourself out of caring, or thinking that the whole matter was just strange, or did you instead simply go with your question and begin to investigate the answer?"

"I went with it. I took action."

"Why?"

"It just felt like I should. I had a really strong feeling—despite the fact that having the feeling didn't make any sense."

"And you discovered something important as a consequence, something that was there that we needed to know was there."

"I guess so," Mafulla said.

"And it had nothing to do with table expansion."

"Yeah. That's right."

"This is important for us to reflect on for a moment."

"Why, Your Majesty?" Mafulla looked a little perplexed.

"It's one more example of something speaking to your unconscious mind and pulling you in a certain direction, and then you immediately rationalized the desire to go under the table by asking a question that made at least some sort of sense, on its own terms."

"Yeah, I suppose so."

"And as a result of your instinctive action, you ended up being at the right place to gain new knowledge."

"You're right."

"That's why, as I'm always saying, we should typically trust our hunches and those otherwise sometimes strange promptings that may come to us in ways we don't fully understand."

"I think we're getting better at responding to these feelings," Walid said.

Mafulla quickly added, "But I still don't fully understand why we'd need to know about the spider or, I mean, what that knowledge would do for us except to spook us out."

"Are you aware that most spider bites don't hurt at all?"

"No sir, I didn't know that," Mafulla answered.

"If any of us had been bitten, there would most likely not be a pain sensation accompanying the bite to let us know."

"But then, how would we know that it happened?" Walid asked. "Do you just die?"

"No. A bite mark would appear, caused by the poison and bacteria. It would then itch or later begin to hurt, and you would start having internal symptoms of various kinds like a cramp or pain in your stomach, or muscle problems, or trouble breathing."

"Now, you're making me dizzy just describing all that," Mafulla commented and put his hand over his heart.

"You're a very suggestible young man."

"Yes, I think I am, now that you suggest it." He grinned a bit, and looked over at Walid with a quick eyebrow jump.

Ali smiled. "It's fine. There's nothing wrong with that at all. In fact, it can be a sign of high intellect, wedded to a heightened imagination, accompanied by a lively emotional life. Many medical students, highly intelligent individuals, begin to think they have every disease they study, and sometimes even show one or two of the symptoms. Your suggestibility is a keen testimony to many of your virtues."

"Thank you, Your Majesty." Mafulla turned to his friend. "See? I've been trying to help you understand how highly intelligent, imaginative, and sensitive a soul I am—not to mention, virtuous."

Walid just smiled and shook his head. The king added, "But it can also be a weakness. So be watchful of it."

"Oh, Ok, like everything else, I guess. It's a matter of the two powers."

"Yes. And now we should exercise our own power and send a guard out to check on old Mo, to make sure that he's all right and not having any of these symptoms himself."

"So, he could have been bitten and wouldn't have felt it at the time?" Mafulla was clearly concerned.

"That's correct."

"And … wait … so could I?"

"Yes."

"Any of us?"

"Yes, any of us. So pay attention especially to your feet, ankles, and legs over the next few hours, but even your arms and neck. If you have any new redness or cramps or physical difficulties of any kind, let me know. I'll have Rumi to be ready in case there's any need for his services."

"Oh, man. I could be a ticking time bomb." Mafulla said.

"Me, too," Walid added and started looking at his feet and ankles, and then his hands and arms.

"Hopefully, not," The king reassured them.

"Yeah, hopefully not." Mafulla took a deep breath. "Ok, Ok, I'm not going to get all worked up about this. I'll be fine. We'll all be fine. I hope old Mo will be fine."

"I do, too, and that's what I wanted to talk about with both of you for just a few moments."

"Oh, right, that's what we were talking about," Walid said.

"Yes. As I said, I had a strong feeling that Mo Bendar should be invited to dinner tonight. And shortly after that, I had thoughts of his being in danger, and that it was important for me to bring him here for a couple of hours, at least, and talk to him now. I'm not sure why, but I had a strange feeling that we had a limited time, a small window of opportunity, to hear what Mo had to say."

"Do you mean that, maybe, you had a feeling he'd have a fatal spider bite?"

"No, not in particular, or I wouldn't have gone through with the dinner and brought him onto palace grounds where we experienced our spider problem earlier. But I had a sense of immediacy and need and that our time with our new friend would be, or might likely be, brief. In the arc of our lives, the time had fully come for us to meet, and we did. I suspect a benevolent power brought him to us. And he may soon be unavailable, for whatever reason."

"Oh. Ok. And, actually, that's what I think I want on my tombstone. I've always wondered what it should say." Mafulla looked like he had just had a great insight, a light bulb moment, in popular parlance.

"What?" Walid asked. "What do you think you want on your tombstone?"

"Unavailable, for whatever reason. Or maybe it would be better for it to just say: Currently Unavailable."

Walid laughed and said, "Altogether unbelievable. How can you joke at a time like this? No, never mind, I know how. But I'm still amazed. If there's ever a modern plague, you may turn into the world's greatest comedian—or at least our most prolific humorist."

Mafulla said, "Especially if that plague eliminates most of my comedic competition, but I thank you for the vote of confidence that you've so graciously expressed while I'm still ... available." That last word was accompanied by the famous double eyebrow jump.

The king shook his head, smiled and said, "There's more... while you're both still available."

"Sorry," Mafulla said quickly and grinned. The two boys looked at the king expectantly.

"I activated some senior Phi yesterday," the king said.

"How? What do you mean?" Walid asked. The king just pointed to his head, and then to his heart.

"Oh."

"I felt it was important."

"Really?"

"I was strongly affected by a sense that lives are in danger, or would soon be in danger. I didn't know which lives, but I suspected our new friend Mo. I had no idea who else. So I mentally sent out a need, to the minds of those few senior Phi members whose abilities would allow them to receive the thoughts I was projecting, even if they had no idea of the sender. I wanted to surround any of our potentially endangered friends with some protection, at least up to the end of the dinner that we just now enjoyed, so that we could talk with Mo and perhaps learn something we might need."

"You can do that?" Mafulla seemed surprised.

"Yes, I can. I didn't know whether I could cover with safety all who might be needing it, and even felt that, perhaps, I could not—I sensed that some of the matter might be beyond my intervention, but I had to try to do all I could. And I did. Plus, I know that the other Phi responded right away. You boys then, very shortly after that, avoided being bitten by the snakes and the spiders today, at least so far as we know. And Mo made it here to talk with us, despite whatever threats there might have been against him. Somehow I'm sure that, otherwise, he would not have been ... available, if dinner had been set for tomorrow, or if I had not responded to the need I felt, when I felt it."

"You mean, it was like a prayer that you made?"

"Yes."

"With other Phi?"

"Precisely. I'm telling you boys all this for several reasons. First, I want to help you deeply appreciate an important truth, even more than you already do. We as individuals are part of a community of souls, connected in ways we can't see. When we sense a need in the community, we respond, whether we understand fully what we're doing and how it works or not. We allow ourselves to be led by and to the good that summons us. And we respond in the best ways that are available to us. That's our obligation and our privilege."

"That makes sense," Walid commented.

"Good. Second, I want you to understand that there is an ongoing danger for us and those we love. Today's garden incident was not an isolated event. Someone has begun a campaign of preparation for something that's yet to come. If Farouk al-Khoum plans to make a move on the palace, he may already be preparing the way through hired agents and assassins. We must all be on guard constantly."

"But what would that have to do with our new friend Mo?" Walid looked confused.

"Farouk may suspect that we'll try to find out as much about him as we can at this point."

"Oh. That makes sense."

"And he would, of course, want to eliminate any potential source of information for us."

"Oh, no! Mr. Kaza!" Mafulla said.

"Do you know where Kaza lives?" The king asked.

"Less than a mile from the shop," Mafulla replied.

"Do you have the address?"

"I don't know the exact address, but it's not far from the shop. I've been there and I can draw you a map."

"If you can do that now, we'll have someone immediately call the Sakat brothers, since they're probably closest to Kaza's home, and ask them to go check on him as soon as they can."

"Good. I hope he's all right. But I have to admit that, as soon as he occurred to me just now, I got a very bad feeling, a quick one, but a bad one."

"You can find a pen and some paper in the top center drawer of my desk. Please go over and get from that drawer anything you need, and do your map right away."

'Yes, sir, Your Majesty," Mafulla said. He quickly walked over to the desk, got out paper and pen, and took only a few seconds sketching out the map with street names. While he was doing that, the king called Kular into the room, told him about the spider, and asked him to go fetch Bancom right away, or whoever might be in charge of the communications center for the evening. He also instructed him to send for Naqid and Masoon, and to do it as soon as possible.

Kular was still feeling the effects of The Stone of Giza, which he had kept in his possession, thanks to the king's kindness, for a full month a while back, and as a result he was still enjoying the energy of a man decades younger than his current age. Because of that, he was able to make haste to summon these men, and Bancom appeared within less than five minutes. Meanwhile, Mafulla had given the king his carefully drawn map and they had talked for a few more minutes.

As the head of communications entered the room quickly, he said, "Your Majesty."

"Yes, Bancom: Please get the Sakat brothers on the radio, tell them that a friend of the Adi family and a man I need to speak with may be in danger."

"Certainly. Who's the man?"

"His name is Sayid Kaza and this is a map to his home from the Sakat shop. Give them directions. Warn them that there might be an assassin out for Kaza, so caution them to approach the home with all due alertness. Tell them to be on the lookout for men who are trained killers, or for poisonous snakes, or even for black widow spiders."

"Right away, Majesty."

"And let us know what you learn, as soon as information is available."

"It will be done." Bancom took the map from the king and left in a hurry to convey the message to the two soldiers who watched the Adi business and acted as security for Mafulla's family whenever they were at work.

"Your Majesty, do you think they would use the snake and spider approach again?" Mafulla asked.

"It's possible. I wanted Badar and Mumar to be alert to the potential for this, which is something they wouldn't normally have even thought of, I'm sure, so that they wouldn't be taken by surprise, in case our adversaries do use the same unlikely tactic."

At that moment, Kular opened the door and announced, "Naqid's here, Your Majesty."

"Please send him in."

The head of palace guards came into the room, greeted the king and the boys, and took a seat, as requested by the king. But before he was even settled on the cushion, Kular was bringing Masoon into the room as well. Ali made sure they were both up to date on all the events of the afternoon and the discussions at dinner with Mo Bendar. He told them of the danger to Kaza and the fact that he had asked a palace guard to accompany Mo home. Naqid suggested that he could send two extra guards to intercept them and provide an additional measure of security, in light of the possible danger, and the king immediately agreed. A word to Kular in the outer room was all it took for this to be set in motion, and then Naqid rejoined the king, Masoon, and the boys.

Ali began to strategize their responses to these events and possibilities. Masoon had some good ideas, and so did Naqid. They had been sitting and talking for no more than thirty minutes when Kular opened the door for Bancom again. "Your Majesty, we have some very bad news."

"What is it?"

"Mr. Kaza was found dead in his home."

"Oh, no," Mafulla said. "Oh, no." He felt his eyes welling up with tears for this old friend of the family whom he had known since he could remember. "Poor Kaza. My parents will be completely shocked. They'll be distraught. What happened?"

"How did he die?" The king asked Bancom.

"It seems he was stabbed some time before the Sakats arrived, likely a few hours ago. But Badar says that there was something else discovered at the scene, something very odd indeed, in his words."

"What was it?" The king asked.

"He didn't say. But he did tell me that he would be here in a few minutes to give us a full report and that he'll bring the surprising discovery with him."

10

The Discovery

Mafulla spontaneously stood up and walked over to the window where no one could see the single tear running down his cheek. Mr. Kaza had always been so nice to him and kind. He was like an uncle, or an elderly great-uncle. The whole family loved him. Mafulla's younger siblings, little Sammi and tiny Sasha, thought of him like a dearly cherished grandfather. They always hugged him when they first saw him. And he could be relied on to greet them with a big smile and a word of hearty welcome. Often, a small treat for each of them would appear as if by magic from his pocket. He wasn't just an employee or an old friend—he was a real member of the extended Adi family, adopted by all, as he had adopted them in his heart.

Mafulla instantly had a feeling of great concern about the kids. But at the same time, he had some sort of a strange sense of peace that he now noticed and yet didn't really understand. It surprised him. He had no idea that the king had already been at work in the realm of the spirit to help prepare him for dealing with this news. And he also had been helping the rest of the Adi family in this same way, despite their current lack of any knowledge about the tragic event. Inner places of peace and comfort were being prepared for them. A path of calm and acceptance was being provided for them to walk along.

Walid didn't know whether to get up and go stand with Mafulla, or leave him alone for a few minutes with his feelings, which he assumed must be intense right now. Situations like this could be painfully awkward. You never really know how to act or what to say. With the unexpected diagnosis of an illness, or even with a sudden injury, you can always speak words of encouragement and hope. But with an unanticipated death, it's often hard to know what to say to anyone who has been intimately affected. You want to be there for them and show sympathy in the deepest possible way—but how? You yearn to be helpful, but by doing or saying what? The thing you fear most is saying something stupid or worthless, or even worse, unintentionally hurtful. How can you come up with just the right thing?

Ultimately, comforting a friend is about being there, simply being present for support. It's about trusting your instincts. You don't need to have answers. You just need to take action. So, without any answers to all these questions, Walid summoned the dose of courage needed to get up and walk over to Mafulla, a courage that was made possible, as it most often is, by love. "Hey, man. I'm really, really sorry about this. Mr. Kaza was a good man, and we all respected and loved him. He always made me feel so welcome in the shop."

Mafulla sighed audibly. "Thanks. I know he was old and probably didn't have that many more years ahead of him anyway, but why now? And why did he have to go so violently?"

"I was just asking the same things in my own heart. The one thin compensation is that he must have gone quickly, which is a rare mercy that was, of course, totally unintended by whoever did this to him."

"Yeah. I suppose so."

"Most ways of leaving the world are not so quick, and many

involve lots of terrible pain over days, weeks, months, or even years. Mr. Kaza was pushed onto a road that we all have to travel at some point, I guess. And, at least, his steps on it were few."

Mafulla tried to wipe his face with his hands in a way that wouldn't be too conspicuous. "I just hope it wasn't absolutely terrifying for him to go through—I mean, someone you don't know suddenly attacking you with a knife and stabbing you, and you realize you're dying, or at least that's what you think and fear for those last few seconds."

"Well, but remember the bomb explosion, and the things we've learned about time slowing down, and the transcendent above-it-all perspective that can come to you. And remember the strange peace you can feel in the middle of it all when it's you undergoing the trauma, and you have this calm awareness that's completely unconnected with the apparent horror of the situation from any onlooker's point of view."

"Yeah. That's true. Thanks for reminding me."

"I bet Kaza had all that calm and weird confidence and peace. In fact, I'm sure he did. It's the oasis within us. It's in us all for whenever we need it."

"Yeah. I hope you're right. Actually, I feel, as soon as I hear you say it, that you are right, and I need to let that sink in. It was surely just like what we experienced when the bomb went off, and that was Ok. It was what came afterwards, when we didn't die, that hurt so much."

"Yeah, and Kaza didn't have to feel any of the awful hurt. He was gone before it could happen."

"You're right."

While the boys were talking, the king had been conferring with Bancom and Masoon and Naqid. Just then, Badar Sakat came into the room and the king's men all turned and rose to greet him.

"Your Majesty." Badar bowed as soon as he saw the king.

"Welcome, friend. Tell us what you found," the king requested.

"Yes, sir. Mumar and I got there very quickly after Bancom's radio message. We approached the house cautiously, thanks to your warnings. We knocked and there was no answer. My brother was first through the door, which was unlocked. Kaza was just inside, as if he had been attacked while answering the door, or by someone waiting inside as soon as he had entered the house and closed the door. We couldn't tell which was the sequence of events. He was face down on the floor with a knife wound to the heart and to the throat."

"I see."

"When we got some light turned on, what we found on a table close to the body surprised us. It was extremely strange."

"Bancom told us of an odd discovery," the king said.

"Yes, it was a sealed white envelope of high quality stock addressed with the words, 'To King Ali Shabeezar.' Mumar picked it up and handed it to me. I took the liberty of opening it. Inside was the big surprise—the envelope contained nothing but a single small black widow spider, very much alive and active. I just managed to avoid any unfortunate contact."

"How interesting and sinister. There was nothing else inside?"

"No, sire, nothing. Of course, I killed the spider instantly, dropping the envelope and stomping it sufficiently to know that I had accomplished my goal. And then I double-checked." Badar looked a bit perplexed and said, "If I may ask, why would Your Majesty imagine that such a thing had been left there like that?"

"Well, two compatible possibilities occur to me right away. First, that this killer wanted us to connect the tragedy in Kaza's house to some events this afternoon on palace grounds, where two poisonous snakes and dozens of these spiders had been placed at a spot that the prince and Mafulla visit almost daily at about the same time."

"Oh, my. I'm so sorry to hear that—and surprised."

"Yes. The boys, as you can see, escaped any immediate harm.

The spider is, at least for now, the calling card of this man or group of people who have been sent on a mission of creative assassination."

"That's very odd and unsettling."

"The second possibility, wholly compatible with the first, is that the assassin was hoping that, by some means, the envelope would be put unopened into my hands, and he might have an indirect shot at me tonight, as well."

"That makes sense in the larger context, unfortunately," Badar said. "May I ask who's doing this?"

'We don't yet know the identity of the person or group of people most directly involved in these events today, but we have reason to believe that they're operating on orders from Farouk al-Khoum, a wealthy industrialist who may have our kingdom in his sights. Kaza was a man who knew him well many years ago, and al-Khoum may have thought it important to eliminate such a source of potential information for us at this juncture in his unfolding plans. We discovered just tonight that Mr. Kaza might have indeed been able to supply us with important background knowledge about this dangerous foe, with whom he once worked here in the palace decades ago."

"I hate to interrupt, Your Majesty," Mafulla said, "But it just occurred to me: How would Farouk have known that we talked to Mo tonight and just learned of Kaza's connection to him? Could we have another traitor in the palace?"

"I don't think so, Mafulla. I suspect the explanation is simpler, and deeper, and even more disturbing than that."

"What do you mean?"

"Even with an insider's eyes and ears around here, Farouk couldn't have known that Kaza was discussed tonight. It was more likely a more subtle warning from his innate rare sensibilities, as keenly as his concentration has likely been trained on us lately."

"Oh."

Kular suddenly appeared and said, "Excuse me, Your Majesty, but one of the palace guards has come in with urgent news."

"Send him in," the king said.

The man came into the room, bowed and said, "Your Majesty, I was sent with my partner to join the guard escorting Mr. Bendar to his home and provide extra security. But I'm afraid we arrived too late."

"What do you mean?"

"We found them both just outside Bendar's apartment building. They had been ambushed and were already dead."

"Oh, my. Both of them?"

"Yes, Your Majesty. There was nobody anywhere nearby on the street, and so apparently the attack wasn't witnessed by anyone."

"I see."

"Oddly, beside the guard's body, there was an envelope addressed to you." He pulled it out of his pocket and held it toward the king.

"Please drop it to the floor and step on it with all your weight," the king said. The guard looked puzzled but did as he was told. "Now, do it again, step on every part of it, two or three more times." Once more, the guard complied.

"Thank you. Now, Naqid, would you do us the honors?"

"Yes, certainly, Your Majesty."

Naqid bent down, picked up the envelope, now soiled by the sole of the soldier's boot, took it over to the king's desk, and with the use of a letter opener shaped like a small dagger, he slit it open and poured out, onto a white piece of paper, another dead black widow spider.

"May I ask what that is, Naqid?" The guard was peering over toward the desk.

"It's a dead and otherwise deadly spider, a black widow of the most venomous sort, killed by you just now before it could become a killer. You can tell your children that you just saved the life of the king."

The guard looked at Ali and said, "But … how did you know?"

The king replied, "We received another note exactly like this one just minutes ago, and so we expected its content."

"Oh."

Naqid spoke up and said, "It's a message to the king from an unsavory source, as you can imagine, in addition to being a rather unlikely and highly creative attempt on his life."

"I'm so sorry I carried such a thing back here to the palace, Your Majesty."

"Don't worry about it at all, my good man. You did exactly what you should have done."

"I sure had no idea what I was carrying. I figured you would want to see whatever was in the envelope, since it was addressed to you."

"You did the right thing. We now have further confirmation for our picture of the adversary."

"You'll likely also want to know that the bodies have been brought back here to the palace for a medical examination."

"Thank you very much, my friend. Please alert Hamid and Rumi," the king replied.

"Yes, sir."

"We value all of your service this evening. And I'm sorry for what you had to see. You may go now, with our thanks." The man silently bowed and left the room.

"These people are serious indeed," Naqid said. "We'll do all that we can to find them and stop them before they bring any more harm."

Walid and Mafulla had been listening from over by the window. The younger boy turned and asked his friend, "Do you think we're still in danger, I mean, the two of us?"

"It sure sounds like it," Walid replied. "Check your room and your bed again for creepy crawlies tonight."

"Ugh. I hope I don't find anything. Or, let me rephrase that: I hope there's nothing to find, but that if there is, I can find it and deal with it in the safest way possible."

"Yeah, nice precision of statement. I hope for the same thing."

The king then spoke to Mafulla with great love and concern for his loss. Their talk was relatively brief, but it was miraculously healing. Ali knew just the right things to say for support and condolence, and even encouragement in such a time. Then, it wasn't long before he suggested that the boys go on down to their rooms, get ready for school tomorrow, and turn in early. As they were leaving, he said a few more words about what was going to happen to initiate a search for a second basement tunnel and what new protective and security measures would be put in place for the palace, the boys, and their friends. And then, he bid them a good night.

Over the next three days, three memorial services were held in the palace, one for Mr. Kaza, one for Mr. Bendar, and one for the guard who unexpectedly gave his life on that short mission for the king. Friends and family members were admitted for each of the occasions, and the king briefly spoke at all of them. Mafulla's parents were, of course, shocked and saddened to hear of Mr. Kaza's death at the hands of a criminal assailant, but they were also strangely comforted in contemplating his passing. The younger children were instantly sad, as children are, but the sadness was, as it turned out, neither deep nor long lasting. Most people would say that this was due to their innocence and incomplete understanding. But in a more profound sense, it may have been due to a lack of the unfortunate misunderstanding that adults generally come to develop about death.

This is an interesting and ironic feature of the human adventure. When, as very young children, we seem to know and understand so little, we tend not to grieve over death in a way that's both deep and long. Then, if we ever eventually attain the higher reaches of spiritual understanding as adults, we can sometimes arrive at a place where, once more, we'll tend not to grieve over a death in a way that's both deep and long. But in that vast, extended desert trek between first innocence and a more complete enlightenment, we can suffer greatly from knowing what can seem from a philosophical perspective to be both too much, and yet too little, at the same time. Both children and sages allow mystery to be mystery, and move on in this world to whatever is next, as is properly their way.

In adulthood, it's only the supremely spiritual person, which is to say, the humbly enlightened soul, who knows enough to let go, sometimes of our fondest wishes and desires, in hope and trust—the proper twins of faith and love. In this way, he or she can overcome the otherwise intense sadness that reflects the greatness of a loss, and be at peace with both the ways of the earth and also the greater dimensions of reality, as they play out here below. The higher understanding that affects this consists not in having explicit answers to every question, but rather in having a broader and higher and yet also deeper perspective, with the ability it provides to live with and transcend the lack of answers we so often experience during the journey—in via, as the ancients would put it, "along the way."

The enlightened soul has a big picture that puts into perspective the smaller snapshots of life and provides an overarching context for understanding, with a measure of acceptance, even in the midst of what seems to be inexplicable tragedy. The king, as a person who had attained this state of inner peace long ago, did all that he could to share bits and pieces of that equanimity and deep assurance with the others around him who might not, on their own, have a direct access to it in the circumstances.

After the memorial services had all been held and the three wonderful lives had been celebrated, the next day was the last school session of the week. The boys had all shuffled into the classroom at various times, the way boys do after they've developed a sense of comfort with their surroundings. Most of them were timing their arrival a bit tight, but all were in their seats at the appointed hour.

Khalid sat on the edge of his desk and said, "Well, it's been quite a week for many of us around the palace. I'm sure that by now, most of you have heard about the poisonous snakes and spiders that were brought onto palace grounds and placed in a certain spot where two of our classmates often go to relax and read and think. The three deaths we've mourned this week and the lives we've celebrated were of men cut down by enemies of our kingdom—the same adversaries, apparently, who tried to take away from us our good friends Walid and Mafulla." Khalid looked at the two of them, who were sitting in their regular seats, and said, "We're all very glad they failed."

Both boys secretly hoped that Khalid wouldn't mention the fact that Kissa and Hasina were with them on the day in question, and he didn't, to their great relief. It's not as if the guys in the class would have been surprised. In fact, some of them may already have known. And their special friendships were certainly recognized by all. But it was still kind, Walid thought, for Khalid to narrow the scope of his remarks here, and not refer to the presence of the two girls at the site of the danger, especially when one of those young ladies was his own daughter, and naturally the focus of his greatest concern.

"There's a reason I'm mentioning this today. Well, actually, there are two reasons. First, I want you all to be aware that there are some bad characters plotting things against the palace and the monarchy, and I want you to be on the lookout for anything unusual on or around palace grounds and here in the building. But the second reason is less serious. The king has decided that we all need something that will help us shed some of the stress of recent days. So he's proposed making up for the cruise on the Nile that we missed because of the heinous kidnapping some time back."

"Really?" Jabari was instantly excited.

"Yes. So find your little monkey some proper boating attire. The king has suggested that we get on a royal barge at the nearby docks and cruise down river to Alexandria, the ancient capital of our land during the time of Cleopatra, and the location during one stretch of our kingdom's life for what was possibly the most important library in the history of the world, a massive collection of ancient documents that no longer exists."

"What happened to the library?" Mafulla was the first to ask the question that had come to nearly every mind in the room.

"It reportedly burned to the ground," Khalid said. "And with that one fire, many of the manuscripts of the ancient world were totally lost to us, incinerated from ideas to ashes, and much of the world's great cultural art and wisdom went up in smoke."

"You're not kidding?" Set said.

"No, not at all. The Royal Library of Alexandria was the greatest repository in the world for ancient texts, in the form of papyrus scrolls, and when it burned, the only copies we know of for so many great ancient works perished, and in many cases the so-called copies were actually the originals—plays, poems, essays, and books of science, mathematics, and philosophy. It was probably the single greatest intellectual loss of all time, except for when Mafulla misplaced his short essay last week on stoic ideals."

Jabari and Set both laughed out loud and then both together said, "Sorry." Everyone else smiled.

"Don't worry. I promise to make it up to you, the class, and all of humanity," Mafulla said quickly. "I'll likely find it, yet. Meanwhile, I'm maintaining a suitably ideal stoic attitude."

There were more smiles all around, and then Bafur asked, "How did the famous library fire start?"

Khalid answered, "Historians don't agree on this. Many say that Julius Caesar or his soldiers set fire to some ships in the harbor, for one reason or another, and the fire jumped onto the docks, then to some nearby buildings, and finally found the library, taking it down to the ground. Others believe that the Royal Library was located too far from the docks for that to have happened, and that its big fire must have started in some other way."

"Why's there a disagreement?" Bafur asked.

"Well, there were at least three libraries in Alexandria at about that time, and some later accounts of the great fire may have misidentified whether the conflagration of the ships spread to the big library or just to a dockside repository of books that were mainly commercial and shipping records. But, regardless of who set the famous fire or how it started, we do know that the massive library burned, and we think that its total contents were lost."

There was silence for a few seconds. Then Malik said, "It's pretty tragic that so much was lost. I mean, there are probably things about the ancient world that we'll never know, and just because of that fire."

"Yeah," Haji added, "Think of all the wisdom that might have been wiped out forever."

Khalid looked out the window for a few seconds, and then said, "As we all know, the fire that's the source of life, the flame that warms us in the cold and cooks our food, the element that illumines the world and lets us see, and thus brings us access to most of our knowledge, that same source of heat and light can take away knowledge forever."

The class just sat and looked at Khalid. This was one of those philosophical moments that often punctuated their time together. You never knew what sort of insight might be on the horizon.

He went on. "When a great conflagration happens, like the one in Alexandria, it's not just that books are lost, and in its case, many sole existing copies—tragic enough in itself, as you suggest, Malik—but also various other forms of art, valuable unique artifacts that would have connected us with the past in special ways, with all the memories and triumphs and tragedies that those things encoded. Almost inevitably, too, there was likely some loss of life."

Set spoke up, "So, the element that gives knowledge can take it away, and the same element that gives life can take that away."

"That's right," their teacher affirmed. The class sat in silence for a moment.

"Opposite things," Bafur said. And then he added, "I've learned from my father that a big meal can give you enough good fuel to power you forward, or enough mind-numbing bloat to shut you down."

At that, everyone laughed. Walid smiled and then said, "Yeah, the king calls it the two powers, or sometimes the Double Power Principle." He looked over at Bafur and grinned more. "Maybe your dad calls it the Double-Up Principle. Whatever we call it, it explains a lot. Many things in life, maybe even all things that have power for good have corresponding power for ill—it's most often up to us how we use that power, and what happens as a result."

"Very good," Khalid said. "And true. If people could just understand that principle, they might not condemn half the things they disparage, or so enthusiastically praise other things without caution. The world could be a different place. Power, for example, generally, is one of the many things that are misunderstood in our world." Khalid stopped and stared into the distance for a second. Then he said, "But now, of course, without any further musing, I must use my power to get us back on track, first with a few more details about the trip, then with a review of our history lesson that was planned for today—the history of something other than Alexandria and its famous library."

Walid always enjoyed witnessing their teacher's talent for launching into a philosophical conversation about almost anything, and then cleverly pulling the class back to the practical matters of the day. Khalid was a gifted instructor and they were very lucky to have him to guide their educational adventure in the context of the palace school.

With everyone's attention back on track, they all talked about the upcoming trip for a few more minutes, and several other questions were answered. Khalid gave them all the particulars he knew, and then they focused on their lessons for the morning.

In the girls' class, Hoda did as her husband had, and started the day with an announcement about the upcoming trip. The girls were at first just as excited as the boys, but then a few of their comments also made it clear that there was some residual ambivalence about traveling together in public again, a concern that stemmed from the traumatic events of the last class trip and the recent threats to life directed at people connected to the palace.

"Aren't we sort of a target when we all go out in public together—a really big target, as the last trip proved?" Ara seemed the most worried and was the first to voice the feeling that several of the girls were having.

"Well, that was a unique situation we all went through together and, remember, we came out of it successfully," Hoda said. "The men responsible for those troubles aren't around to bother us again."

"But there are always others, aren't there, like the people behind the current threats?" Ara replied.

"There's certainly that possibility. But the king has assured me that we'll have much more security this time, and no one outside the small circle of our families and his most trusted men will even know we're going. Plus, the trip will be short. One day of barge travel, one night in Alexandria, a time to explore, and a few hours back by train."

"And no fake reporters?" Ara asked.

"No reporters of any kind."

"Why Alexandria?" Cabar asked.

"Well, the Nile flows in that direction, and Alexandria was the original, and very important capital of our kingdom, the place where Cleopatra lived and Julius Caesar visited her. It's also the place where some smart people realized that the world isn't flat. It's where we think geometry was discovered and a steam engine was first built. It's where the entire earth was mapped more accurately than ever before. It was also the main repository for ancient knowledge."

"That's a lot," Khata said.

"Yes, it is. The Royal Library there housed the greatest collection of poems, plays, histories, philosophies, and treatises of all kinds on the face of the earth. A great fire destroyed all those books, many of which had no copies, and some say the ghosts of the books still haunt the city."

"Books don't have ghosts!" Bakat said and laughed.

Hoda smiled and laughed as well. "I'm just reporting to you what people say. Some will tell you that they've felt the spirits of Aeschylus and Euripides and Epicurus, and even Aristotle, among many others, still articulating and energizing the words and ideas, the concepts and claims, the sayings and sagacity that were ripped from the world on the day the fire spread throughout that massive structure and consumed so much of human art and achievement."

"Yeah, but really," Bakat said.

"Well, wait a second. What is a book? Is it the papyrus scroll on which it originally might have been? Or is it one, or all, of the perhaps three or thirty or three hundred complete copies that might have been made later by scribes?"

"It's the original."

"Well, suppose the original was destroyed after several complete and perfect word-for-word copies were made. Did the book itself cease to exist, as a book, or was it just the original manuscript that ceased to exist, while the book continues on, embodied in the copies, and is thus a book we can still read and benefit from?"

"Hmm. Ok. I guess the book continues to exist in the copies. I get that."

"Would one copy be enough for the book to continue to exist, or would there have to be many copies?"

"I think one would be enough."

"Now consider this. What is it that the original has in common with the copy? The material it was written on could be very different. So, is it the ink? But the ink could be very different as well."

You could tell Bakat was really concentrating at this point. But

Ara spoke up before she could, saying, "It's the words, or concepts, and they have to be in the right order, saying all the exact same things that the original said."

"What if the words were different?"

"It would be a different book."

"But what if the words were different only because it was a translation of the original into another language?"

"Oh. Ok. That would be fine."

"The book could continue to exist, just in translation. We could read the book, but in the translated language."

"I see what you're saying."

"So it's the complete intellectual and basic stylistic content of the book, really, that is the book, right?"

"Yeah." Bakat and Ara answered at the same time.

"But that content can be embodied in different forms, couldn't it? It could be embodied in a papyrus scroll at one point in history, and in a printed and bound book in our day. You can even imagine someone speaking all the words of the book into a microphone and, through the wonders of the modern recording studio, its being etched into the surface of a record, or a set of records, that we could play and listen to. It would still be the same book, but in the very different form of an audio recording."

Kit spoke up and said, "So if that happened, you could listen to a book someone else had read on paper, and then you could both talk about it, and you'd be discussing the same book."

Hasina jumped in at this point and said, "That sounds really strange but it also seems right."

Ara was puzzled and asked, "But how can it be right? A book is one kind of object, and a record is a different sort of thing."

"But think more about it," Hoda said. "Suppose that a book was read onto a recording, every word of it, and then every paper copy was lost in a fire. Would you say that the book no longer exists at all, or that we still have it, only just in audio form?"

"Hmm. I guess you're right. We could listen to the recording and take dictation and create another paper copy from that and I guess we wouldn't be bringing the book back into existence, just back into its original form, or a more standard form.

"Well, if that's true, the book itself is starting to sound more like a soul than a body, since it can inhabit, or be embodied in, more than one physical body through time, almost like a version of reincarnation."

"That's really weird, but I guess it's true," Bakat said.

Hoda loved this kind of thing. The girls could tell. It's part of what attracted her to Khalid. So she went on, looking at Ara and then Bakat, and said, "Now, consider another angle. Is Aristotle's Ethics the physical object on your desk, or is it perhaps the distinct physical object on the desk of Walid, or Mafulla, and in another room?"

"I guess it's all of them."

"But remember our math. If A=B and A=C, then B=C as well. If Aristotle's Ethics is the object on your desk, and it's the object on Walid's desk, and it's the thing on Mafulla's desk, then the thing on Walid's desk is the very same object as the thing on Mafulla's desk, and I know that's not true. The thing on Mafulla's desk is worn and has lots of drawings in it, silly cartoons that I've seen, pictures doodled by, not Mr. Aristotle, but Mr. Adi, and the thing on Walid's desk does not contain such drawings; therefore, they are different objects and neither can be the exact same object as Aristotle's Ethics. As the soul isn't the body, the book isn't the particular embodiment, but something else—more like … a ghost, perhaps."

"Ha! There's got to be something wrong with that reasoning, but I can't say what!" Bakat was smiling now, like a small child who had just witnessed a magic trick. There had to be an explanation. But she had no idea what it could be.

Hoda was beaming at this point. She concluded, "Some say the book is just the thoughts in the mind of the author, but couldn't an author forget completely in his old age most of what he wrote in a book composed during his youth?"

"Sure," Hasina said.

"So the thoughts are no longer in his mind. When he wrote the book, he created something physical, but also something non-physical as well—the content. Some astute medieval thinkers concluded that every such object must be a thought in the mind of God, however extended and complex. And God's mind is eternal. God cannot forget. Otherwise, what exactly would be the form and nature of the content's existence, distinct from its temporary embodiments?"

"Wow, this is deep stuff," Bakat said.

Kissa looked puzzled. She said, "But, Mom, doesn't that mean that no actual books burned in the fire of the Royal Library after all? I mean: If books are non-physical objects, they can't burn. So, the things that burned were just temporary embodiments of books."

Hoda smiled and said, "Excellent reasoning. And this just shows us how people might think you're crazy if you've done a lot of philosophy and bring them your unexpected conclusions."

"That's funny," Kissa said. "And it totally explains dad."

That made the other girls laugh, and Hoda, smiling, picked up the thread by saying, "What it really shows us, of course, is that our ordinary language is not really clear about such things. We speak of the physical objects on your desks and mine that are made of paper, ink, glue and thread, and call them books. And if that's what we say they are, and it's a normal use of language, then, for all practical purposes, they are. But you and I have just discovered some deeper metaphysical complexities behind the simplicity of ordinary language. For convenience, we don't talk about book bodies being on our desks, or embodiments of books. We talk about books. But now, you and I know the deeper subtlety that lies behind our normal talk."

"It's so strange," Bakat said.

"We speak with the multitude when we say that many books burned in the Royal Library in Alexandria. And, understood as we mean it, it's true to speak this way. But, unlike the multitude, you now know what else is going on in our talk about books. And, of course, that same reasoning in slightly different terms applies to other forms of art, like poems, songs, and symphonies but not, interestingly, to paintings and tapestries and sculptures. Different works of art, across different media, are metaphysically different types of things. But that's a topic for another time."

"Wow. This is really deep," Bakat said.

"Yes. There are many mysteries around us. There are mysteries behind some of the most ordinary things in life, as well as some of the most remarkable."

Hoda's words applied more widely to events around the palace and throughout town these days than even she realized. There were various mysteries that the king needed to clear up, and soon. No one, though, would be able to guess how soon some of the mists of mystery would begin to vanish, and what a role unexpected violence would play in all of it.

II

A Nice Walk Interrupted

"We need to go for a walk." Mafulla said this from a sitting position on the floor of Walid's big room. The window was open and a light breeze drifted across the space.

The prince nodded his head in agreement. "Ok. I'm up for it. You want to lap around the palace grounds a couple of times?"

"No, I think I'm more in the mood to go to my parent's shop. I want to get in the extra exercise and check on whoever's there—you know, to make sure they're doing all right."

"Oh. Ok. Good idea. We should tell the king."

The boys got up and walked down the hall to Kular's office. Walid knocked on the frame of the open door. "Hi Kular, is the king in?"

"Oh, hello, Your Highness. Hello, Mafulla. I didn't realize you were back from school already. This day has gotten away from me! Too busy, too busy!"

"Our day has flown by, too," Walid said.

"That's a good thing. It means your minds have been engaged."

"For sure," Mafulla said.

"As to the king's whereabouts, he's actually downstairs right now in a big meeting. Given the nature of the gathering, and what it says here on his calendar, I would estimate that he'll be tied up there for the next couple of hours, and be back in time for dinner. Is there any message I should leave him for you?"

"Yeah, would you just let him know that we're walking down to the Adi Shop for a little bit? Mafulla wants to check on everyone and make sure they're doing Ok—with the recent loss of Mr. Kaza and everything."

"That sounds like a good idea. I'll convey the message. But I do know that he always wants you to have a security escort when you leave the palace now, in light of the unfortunate recent events."

"Yes, you're right. I hope this doesn't go on forever, but I totally understand. Could we choose the escort?"

"Why, of course. You're the prince."

"I keep telling him that," Mafulla said. "But I don't think it's completely sunk in yet."

"Ha," Walid replied, and then said to Kular, "Ok, then, we'll go down to the main guard room and see who's on duty this afternoon, and I'll exercise some princely discretion."

"Good idea, Your Highness."

"What's that smell?" Mafulla was sniffing loudly enough that Kular and Walid could both hear him.

"Oh, fresh nut rolls, hot from the oven, baked with cinnamon and glazed with sugar. They got here about sixty seconds before you did. Would you like one?"

"Yes! In fact, two might prepare me royally for our walk."

"Two it is!"

"And some coffee, black."

"Ah, I remember. You like the stuff full strength, like the top warriors, Masoon and Hamid."

"You remember well."

"I'd say you're in very good company."

"Thank you. The three of us have what I think of as a similar proclivity for the robust."

Walid raised his eyebrows. "A proclivity for the robust?"

"Certainly, my friend," Mafulla said as he took the wide plate that Kular had just offered him, adorned with two wonderfully large sticky buns, themselves festooned with glistening candied nuts. "An inclination, or tendency, or habituation, towards things of strength."

"Oh. I see," Walid said with a big smile. He turned to Kular and said, "My own proclivity would also be for two of these rolls and some equally robust dark beverage."

Kular laughed and said, "As you wish, Your Highness. You both have a proclivity that's easily satisfied today."

Walid got his rolls and coffee and the three of them chatted about the day as the boys nibbled away and sipped their cups of the rich brew. After about five more minutes, it was time for them to take off, so they said goodbye to Kular and made their exit, heading down the hall and quickly descending the nearest long staircase to the first floor.

Walid turned to Mafulla and said in a low voice, "Do you have your sand mask?"

"Yep."

"And your wristband, just in case? You never know."

"Check."

"All right, then."

"But, we're going to be accompanied."

"Still. You never know."

"True. We have to be ever ready, just in case we have to flip the case and chase an ace of common crime."

Walid smiled. They turned and walked down a hallway leading to the main palace guard station. As the prince crossed the threshold, there was a shuffling sound of chairs being moved and everyone in the room stood up quickly. "Your Highness," was muttered by several voices, as all present bowed slightly.

"Good morning," Walid said, as Mafulla hung back a few feet.

"Good morning," all of the men variously responded.

"Please, as you were, men," Walid said with a small gesture of his right hand. The guards who were scattered around the room on break or awaiting assignments all took their seats, or got back to whatever they had been doing before the prince appeared.

Just then, Naqid walked into the room and said, "Your Highness, and Mafulla: How can I help you two gentlemen today?"

"Hi Naqid. We're going to walk down to the Adi Shop to see Mafulla's dad or mom, whoever's there. I know the king wants us to have an escort for now, whenever we leave the palace grounds, and I was wondering if I could choose someone to accompany us."

"Absolutely," Naqid said.

"Is it possible that Omari or Paki or Amon might be available?"

"Paki's around the corner in the guard kitchen having a snack. He just came in for the next shift of duty. I could free him up for your walk if you'd like."

"That would be great."

"Would you need a second escort? Omari and Amon are outside training a couple of new guards and won't be finished until later today, but you could pick anyone else."

"I think Paki can do the job of two or three other men, and especially if he's fresh and rested," Walid said.

"I agree," Naqid replied with a smile. "I'll also let the Sakats know that you'll be at the shop. They'll function, like always, as extra backup while you're there."

"Great. Thanks, Naqid."

"I'll get Paki." The head of the guards did a slight little bow and then turned and left the room at a brisk walk.

Mafulla said, "I forgot how many palace guards are on duty each day. It's pretty impressive."

"Yeah, there are a lot of them."

"They seem to be wearing different colored patches on their uniforms. I've never really paid attention to that before. I wonder what they mean."

"I'm not sure," Walid said.

Just then, Paki walked up, did a quick bow and with a smile said, "Your Highness. I hear we're off to the market. Hi Mafulla."

'Hi Paki," Mafulla replied.

Walid said, "That's right. We're going to see Mafulla's dad, and maybe his mom, too. Can you come with us?

"Absolutely and with pleasure."

"Are you ready now?"

"Lead the way." As Paki said that, he motioned toward the door and let Walid and Mafulla go first. When they got to the outer entrance of the palace, Paki said, "Doesn't the king want us all to wear sand masks on trips like this, especially when there's a breeze, to make it a more natural thing to do?"

"Yep, you got it right," Walid said. "Let's go ahead and put them on. It's a bit windy today, so they'll be useful for more than one reason."

Mafulla added, "And, since there are three of us, not just two, we won't likely get any annoying Viper and Storm comments."

"Those guys haven't been in the paper recently," Paki said.

"No—except in cartoon form," Mafulla replied.

"Oh, yeah, that's right. I do enjoy the cartoons. But there haven't been any recent actual reports of any exploits around the city."

Walid remarked, "The mystery men have become even more of a mystery."

"Indeed."

As they walked out the door and down the stairs, now suitably masked, Mafulla said, "Paki, I was asking Walid a minute ago about the different colors of patches I noticed on the guards' uniforms just now, and I realized I'd never really paid attention to that before."

"Oh, yes. You're right. There are three main colors."

"What do they mean?"

"The color green is the lowest level of security clearance. It's for guards who are given full access just to the grounds and gates and outer buildings. They can come into the palace only to the main guard room—unless, of course, they're otherwise ordered or invited by someone more senior."

"Ok."

"A blue patch is for all that access plus the entirety of the first floor of the palace, and the basement, where, as you know, the main guard storage room is located."

"Yeah."

Walid then asked, "What's the color red represent?"

"That color on a guard patch is for the all the lower access, plus the common areas of the second floor. And a fourth, actually, gold," he explained, "is for the highest level of security and access to the entirety of the palace, its grounds, and any other government owned building, in its full extent, as well. There aren't many of those."

"That's what you wear," Mafulla said. "I've noticed but never thought about it."

"Yes. I have the gold patch on all my uniforms. Of course, I came in today in street clothes that also have the patch, a small version, in case it's needed for identification, and that's the best thing anyway for our walk to the marketplace, rather than wearing an official uniform."

"I didn't realize there were all these different levels of security clearance for the palace."

"Yeah, it's all about how well a guard is known to his supervisors and to Naqid, how well he's performed, and how much he's trusted. It's a little bit like seniority. But only the king can confer the gold patch."

"Who all has it?"

"Omari, Amon, Masoon, Hamid, Naqid, and me—we all have it. And, that's it."

"But why do you need it? Everybody knows who you are."

"It's mostly symbolic, and something for the other guards to aspire to. Plus, there are staff members in the palace who aren't guards, like Kular and the other royal butlers. If a new butler came on duty and I came in to see the king, he'd know right away that I have access. It's part of the training for any staff."

"Oh, Ok," Walid said. "But wait. My dad doesn't have a gold patch. And we don't, either."

"Oh, that's different."

"What do you mean?"

"You and your father have total access to everything, but not because of anything symbolized by a security patch. You're the royal family, not military, and the patch is just for military men who can serve on the palace grounds as guards or in any other function. You and Mafulla both have that level of access, of course, but Mafulla doesn't need to be given a patch, either."

"And we both get access because of the king," Walid said.

"Yes, well, you, because you're the prince, a crucial member of the king's royal family, and Mafulla, thanks to the king, is … something almost like … extended royal family. No patches needed."

"I got it," Walid said.

"I like the concept of extended royal family," Mafulla added, and he turned to Walid. "So, one day in the future, when I begin having little Mafullas running around, with the assistance of the beautiful Hasina, of course, but you can keep that to yourself at this point—as if she doesn't already know that she's the luckiest girl in the world, but still—then, you'll be Uncle Walid. At least, you'll actually, technically, be Extended Uncle Walid, quite regardless of your height or weight at that point, but we'll just call you Uncle Walid, for short."

"Very funny."

"And, then, of course, when you want to pass down keepsakes and heirlooms to my children, all you'll have to do is stretch them a bit." Walid looked puzzled. "So that," Mafulla explained, "they'll be suitably EXTENDED family heirlooms."

"Clever."

"And then, when you tell my kids tall tales about when we first met, and all our many adventures, you'll only have to stretch the truth a little bit for them to be perfectly good extended family stories."

"I get it. I promise," Walid said.

"Ok, just making sure. Otherwise, I can run with this as long as you need me to."

"I'm good. Believe me."

Paki had been smiling all the time this was going on. He said, "Are you guys always like this?"

Walid answered, "Only when Mafulla's a little nervous. Then, he gets in a really jokey mood. Sometimes, the jokes are actually funny, but don't hold your breath."

"Hey," Mafulla said.

Walid ignored him and said, "But then, I get nervous, since he gets truly funny only when he knows we're really in a super bad situation. So here's the simple rule: good situation—no jokes; decent situation—bad jokes; but really bad situation—good jokes, at least sometimes."

Paki said, "Well, that's good because I guess the worse the situation is, the more you actually need a laugh."

"True. And this is the guy who will always try to provide it—most often, over and over and over again."

At that, Mafulla spoke up and said to Walid, but also for Paki's ongoing amusement, "Well, humor of course is in the eye of the beholder, and it does take a certain higher level of mental function to recognize it when you see it, my friend, if it's of the more subtle form. And you know, at such times, whenever a piece of potential humor presents itself, we both do like to extend it—because … that's the kind of family we are." This final tweak on the theme of the hour got the double eyebrow jump version of visual punctuation, and seemed to satisfy Mafulla's current need to riff on Paki's apt phrase.

"And there you have it," Walid said, to bring this line of conversation to its proper conclusion.

But Mafulla still felt an urge to reflect a bit more, aloud, on his own tendencies, in order to make sure that Paki understood what he was being exposed to here, so he added: "I will have to say that my innate risibility often expresses itself in something like the equivalent of American jazz, with its lively juxtaposition of given themes and highly creative improvisations." And Paki just laughed again.

"Ah, your risibility," Walid said in a very serious voice. "Your deep propensity to be risible, which is often quite visible—I hope you know how much of a glow it gives the rest of us, or at least the best of us—jokey jazz fans that we may be, by happy happenstance and more."

"Oh, very nice rhyming word play, my friend. And, yes, consider the birth of all this mirth to be my gift to you. Or perhaps a gift conferred on all those around me by vast and generously benevolent forces far beyond my control, or ken—meaning, quite simply, my wide scope of knowledge, or range of awareness."

"Good. I'm keen to hear more about your ken, especially now that you are—in an extended sense, of course—my very own kin," Walid said.

Paki chuckled once again. "I should volunteer for more duty with you guys, or at least just basically follow you around. It would improve my vocabulary a lot and it could even be good for a few laughs."

"Any time, my friend," Mafulla said. "Any time. We consider you … almost family—in the most extended sense, of course."

At this point, they were already half way to the marketplace. As they approached a large café with both indoor and outdoor seating, Paki said, "This may sound strange, but I have a sudden feeling we should duck in here for just a few minutes."

They all stopped walking. Walid said, "I'd trust that feeling."

Mafulla said, "Me, too. We do strange things all the time."

"Ok, then," Paki said in a happy voice, "Why don't we go in and sit down and have a cup of tea and see if something existentially significant awaits us here?"

"Very good," Mafulla said with a look that indicated he was quite impressed.

Walid smiled and replied, "Let's do it." The three of them walked through the main door of the café and asked for a table. They were then shown through a side door and back outside where all the open-air seating was located, and were told to select any spot that might appeal to them. Paki walked by several open tables and right to an empty one that was next to a couple of large men who were clearly deep in conversation.

The first words that Paki heard as he sat down were hard for him to believe. One man said in a low voice, "The thing on the grounds failed completely, but the two old guys were taken care of properly."

That was all it took for Paki to rise back up from his chair and turn around to face the two men, who were having black coffee and sweet rolls. "I'm really sorry," he said, "but it's against the law to eat and drink at a commercial establishment like this and leave without paying your bill, which is what you're about to do. And I have a feeling that you're also going to be breaking several other laws within the next couple of minutes. So, you're under arrest. You'll both have to come with me."

The heavier of the two men looked at Paki with a completely puzzled expression and said. "What are you, crazy? Are you out of your mind? We're not going anywhere." He was an individual with fat arms and a thick beard, to match the rest of his body. Walid and Mafulla, who were at this point just completely confused, also quietly stood back up, despite the fact that they had just taken their seats. They hadn't heard what Paki heard, and so had no idea what was really going on, but they knew enough to back up their friend, and just be confident that he had a good reason for whatever he was doing.

The other man said, "Are you a cop who's lost your uniform and your mind, or are you just trying to show off or something for your kids? Is this something like a very bad joke?"

"No, I'm not a cop, and these aren't my kids, and this isn't a joke, but I am going to have to make something like an arrest right now. As I said, you're about to break a number of laws and so you'll have to go to jail. So, if you wouldn't mind, I'll have to ask you to stand up."

The first man, the bigger one, replied, "You're completely insane. Get out of my face and far away from me if you don't want to get hurt."

"No, I'm sorry. I'm very sane and totally serious. You're both coming with me, right now, like it or not. So, one more time: Would you please stand up and show me your hands?"

Paki then noticed the bigger man's right hand go down below the table. He said, "I wouldn't do that if I were you."

"But you're not me, are you?" The man replied with a sneer, and he slowly pulled out a large knife and laid it on the table. His companion then did the same thing. "Look," the heavy man said, "why don't you just get lost, you and your little friends? We'll pretend like this strange conversation never happened, and you'll have a nicer day. Stay healthy, walk away, forget about us, and keep your mouth shut. You'll be much better off as a result."

"I have a different idea," Paki said. "Why don't you both leave your nice cutlery there on the table where it belongs, stand up slowly, turn around, and clasp your hands together behind your back? You'll be much better off, as a result."

"You're a dead man. You just don't know it yet," the heavily bearded antagonist said with a scowl. What he didn't know was that Walid and Mafulla had each instinctively reversed their watchcases and covered their watches with their stretchy cloth wristbands while all this was going on, and had picked up a couple of items off their table, a dinner knife and a heavy glass ashtray, and were now holding them behind their backs. They had remembered their lessons well. Whenever you're confronted with a sudden problem or unexpected danger, you stay calm, use what you have, and prepare to move quickly.

The boys both stepped around behind the smaller of the two big men while his eyes were on Paki, knowing that their guard could handle the larger antagonist just fine. And as they did so, however, both men slowly got up from their chairs, knives in hand. The big man looked at his friend and smirked and then said to Paki, "You can't say I didn't warn you."

What happened next played out so quickly that others sitting around the café heard only a frighteningly loud commotion for a moment and saw a blur of movement that, in less than four seconds, resulted in an overturned table, many chairs scattered about, and the two big coffee drinkers on the floor, unconscious and separated from their weapons. Paki had known that they needed to make sure these men were captured and not killed in the fierce and sudden fight that he was forced to launch. And the boys somehow also understood. The resulting thunderous noise and shouts from other tables had drawn the attention of two city policemen who had been almost a block away when they first heard it, and they had now dashed down to the café in response. They quickly entered the outdoor area of tables and chairs with their guns drawn and yelled out, "Freeze! Hands up! Stay still! City Police!"

"Palace Guard, Paki Alexander," Paki quickly stated.

"What?"

"Palace guard. Look at the patch I have." He turned slowly so they could see.

They both saw the small gold patch and one of them said, "Oh! Sorry, sir! Very sorry! What's the problem here? How can we help?"

"These two men just attacked me and my young companions. I'm afraid I have to arrest them on the king's authority and ask you, as my deputies, to take them to the palace jail right away. Hand them over at the main gate for high security custody, to be put in separate cells, and apart from each other."

"They're to be separated?"

"Yes. And they're not to speak to each other."

"Got it."

"They should regain consciousness soon. So please cuff them now. They're bad characters. They're also very strong and must not escape, under any circumstances."

While the men got to work doing as he had asked, Paki continued, "You'll be well served to put them in full walking restraints, as well. I'm sure the café has something you can use for that purpose. And this is important. No word of their capture should include any description of them at all. This is highly sensitive kingdom business." He then drew closer and said, "These thugs are guilty of crimes against royalty and the state, plus a likely involvement in two recent murders. And in case you didn't recognize the taller of the young men with me, he's Prince Walid, and was just assaulted by them."

"Oh! My goodness!" Both policemen turned toward Walid, and one said, "Your Highness! We had no idea! I'm so sorry!" The other one bowed and mumbled a word of apology.

Walid smiled and nodded. He said, "Thanks. We appreciate your quick action to get here and help out."

Paki spoke again. "Can you do all that I've asked, and take care of it immediately?"

Yes sir!" Both policemen replied instantly and got straight back to work, and with the help of a waiter, they bound the legs of the two criminals so that they could walk slowly, but not run.

Paki had asked the policemen their names, made sure they knew his, and emphasized again the importance of these men not escaping. He also repeated that they had committed crimes far beyond the present situation and, receiving ample reassurances from both uniformed officers, he turned to Walid and Mafulla and motioned toward the door. On their way out, he said to the stunned owner, "Don't worry, my friend. You'll be compensated for their food and drink and any damage—for which we're very sorry. Someone from the palace will be in touch later on." The older man just nodded his understanding.

An unseen individual had walked up and around the corner a second or two after all the action in the café, and had caught sight of the policemen rushing up on the scene where his meeting was to have taken place. He stopped for a moment, taking it all in. He saw the two men who had been expecting him. But they were on the ground and not moving. And there was another man standing over them, and two boys. The man with the boys had a sand mask around his neck, as did they. And the policemen spoke with them for a minute or more. He couldn't tell what was going on.

As he watched, he remained inconspicuously out of sight, but quietly managed to get close enough to the outside café tables to be able to hear some of what was being said. He knew at that moment that he had to follow either his prospective colleagues or the other three. He reasoned that he couldn't likely overpower two armed policemen, especially on busy streets in the middle of the day, and get his friends out of both the cuffs and the leg restraints he now saw being put on them. So that was a nonstarter. But he could follow the man and two boys. The taller boy, from what little he could see, seemed to match some descriptions he had heard of the prince. And he had been told that the prince was often to be seen with a friend about his age, but a little younger, a boy whose father owned a shop nearby in the market. That could be the shorter one. Who then was the man? He had no idea. But if he followed them from a distance, an opportunity of some sort might present itself.

Paki, Walid, and Mafulla shortly after that walked out the door and down the street in the direction of the Adi shop. They all put on their sand masks again. Once they were about half a block away from the café, Walid said, "Ok, what in the world was that all about?"

Paki replied, "I thought you might be curious."

"I am indeed."

"Me, too." Mafulla said.

In a low voice, Paki explained. "When I got to the table a bit ahead of you two and turned to sit down, I heard a voice behind me say these words: 'The thing on the grounds failed completely, but the two old guys were taken care of properly.' Those were the exact words the man said."

"No way," Walid said.

"Amazing," Mafulla said and glanced back.

"Of course, I knew what they were talking about, and I had to decide instantly: Do I follow them to find out who they are, or do I detain them? Following seemed too risky. What if they somehow lost me? And I'm with you. It would have been much harder for the three of us to follow them inconspicuously.

"That makes sense," Walid commented.

Paki continued, "So I had to arrest them on the spot, but on what grounds? If I gave away that it was because of what I heard, then we'd be compromised, right off the bat. They'd know that we knew what they were involved in, however big or small their part. People like this—you can't let them know too much, too soon. It undermines what you might be able to accomplish."

"I see," Walid said.

Mafulla had to ask, "So, how did you come up with arresting them for leaving without paying, when they were still sitting there?"

Paki laughed. "That was a little creative, I admit. But I went with it because I knew they'd leave in restraints of some sort, and wouldn't have the chance to pay. I also knew they'd at some point assault us, including you, Walid, and so commit multiple lawless acts, that would include a crime against royalty. Plus, by saying such a crazy thing, I could catch them off guard a little, and to some extent confuse them, which worked in more than one way to my advantage."

"Very clever. I think you really messed with their heads," Walid said with his own laugh. "They thought you were insane."

"Yeah, they didn't have a clue what you were up to," Mafulla said. "I can't really claim I did, either."

"That's exactly the way I wanted it," Paki replied. "It was also important for my little ruse that I didn't touch them first, before they made movements intended to inflict bodily harm or death. They had to initiate an assault. I couldn't physically provoke it. But they seemed like the kind of guys I could depend on for that. And my hunch proved to be right."

"Yeah," Mafulla laughed. "You got that one right."

Walid looked genuinely impressed. He said, "Man, oh man, I figured you knew what you were doing, but I had no idea all of that was going on."

"We learn to be innovative when necessary."

"Yeah, well, it was pretty amazing. So," Mafulla said, "it sure sounds like those guys were both somehow on the inside of the attack on us in the garden, and the deaths of Kaza and Mo. They both had prior knowledge and some form of involvement, it seems, however direct or indirect."

"Yes," Paki replied. "So it's important for us to find out who they are and who they work with, where they're from, what they're doing in town, where they're staying—basically, all sorts of things. And, in the palace jail, we'll have a chance to learn what we need to know. But now, we still have our intended visit yet ahead of us."

"Every time we leave the palace, something crazy happens," Mafulla said. "I hope these guys can lead us to whoever killed Kaza and Mo."

"And who tried to kill us," Walid added.

"Yeah, not to mention us," Mafulla agreed.

As they continued to walk briskly toward the market, Paki said, "This is what investigators call a break in the case. Now, of course, as Phi, you'll both realize that my desire to stop into that café at the exact moment we did so wasn't random, or a coincidence. A thread of some sort presented itself and we followed it to where it led."

"Yeah, it's wild how that works," Walid commented.

"It is," Paki said. "We don't always know what our feelings mean, but we do well to respect them and take appropriate action when we feel led to go somewhere, or to speak with someone."

"It happens to us all the time," Mafulla replied.

"Good. I would expect that."

It was a warm, clear day, but not too hot. Strong breezes came in gusts with intermittent but extended lulls. There was moderate traffic on the street they were walking down, but it was mostly pedestrians and donkey carts. Within just a few more minutes, they were on another street and in sight of the Adi shop. Paki split off for a minute to tell the Sakat brothers they had arrived. Walid and Mafulla came up to the entrance of the shop, and right away saw Mafulla's dad arranging some vases on a table.

"How's my favorite shopkeeper of all time?" Mafulla said in a masked lower voice.

Shapur turned around, and the look of surprise on his face was just what Mafulla wanted to see. "Oh! What are you marvelous boys doing here?" he exclaimed with a big smile. "Good to see you! Good to see you! Come and hug your old man!"

"Old? I see no one old, but I'll hug you anyway." Mafulla walked up to give his father a big embrace and Walid followed closely behind.

"A royal hug also for an extremely loyal citizen?" Mr. Adi asked, as he continued to grin.

"Of course," Walid answered, and gave him a big hug, too.

"What brings you famous and powerful people into our small and humble shop today?"

"We had a free afternoon and just wanted to check up on you and see how you're doing," Mafulla replied.

Shapur's countenance changed in that moment. "Well, you know, it's still so tragic what happened to our good friend Kaza. It's sad not having him in the shop or in his house or anywhere in this world, after all those years of knowing him and working with him and feeling I could count on him for anything. I enjoyed his company a lot. He was really like one of the family."

"Well, we have some good news about the ongoing effort to solve the crime," Mafulla said.

"What is it? I could use a piece of good news."

"A few minutes ago, on the way here, we captured two men who apparently have knowledge of the murders and might have been involved."

"Oh, my! You captured some men?"

"Yes."

"But, what do you mean?"

"We got two bad guys arrested and carried away, with the help of Paki Alexander, a top palace guard who's with us today. But this minute, he's across the street saying hello to the Sakat brothers in their shop and letting them know we're here."

"How did such a thing as this arrest happen?"

"While we were walking here from the palace, with Paki along as our security, he had a strong feeling that we should stop into a big café that we were about to pass, the one with the moon and some stars over the door. You know the one I mean?"

"The Big Sky Café."

"That's it."

"The one with so many tables outside."

"Yeah, that's the one. Well, Paki initially thought we should stop in for tea or something. He had no idea that the something was a capture of likely accomplices to the murder of Kaza and Mo Bendar, and also a palace guard."

"Really?"

"Yeah. So there sat two big men, next to where we were going to take a table, and Paki actually overheard them talking about the murders in hushed voices, and in very indirect language that proved they both had knowledge of the events before they happened, and since. That tipped him off and he took action, and we just backed him up and assisted in their capture. City police are taking the men to the palace jail right now. They're likely there already."

"Oh. My goodness. You were never in danger, I hope."

"No, not at all."

"Good. I'm so relieved. I'm glad. Your days are too exciting."

"That's very true. But somehow, we're getting accustomed to it. Is Mom around today?"

"Yes, she's helping out in the back. Now that we don't have … our old friend here with us, her help is more needed than ever."

"I'll go say hello."

"Me, too," Walid said.

"Ask her about the strange invitation that we just received in the mail," Shapur said.

"What invitation?"

"Ask your mother. She probably has it with her. It's very odd—very odd, indeed."

12

A Strange Invitation

"I'm sorry to interrupt while you're working, Farouk, but this just came for you and your brother."

"What do you have, Tau? Is it about operations in Egypt?"

"No, I'm afraid not. There's no word yet. This looks like it might be a formal invitation of some sort."

"That's strange. Where did you get it?"

"It had been left in the box at the gate."

"Did you see anyone leaving it?"

"No, no one. I just went out to check the box and it was there."

"Ok, give it to me."

Farouk al-Khoum was sitting outside alone by a large swimming pool where he had been reading some reports compiled by his brother Faraj, when Tau, his head of security, had approached him with this word of a delivery.

The man handed an expensive looking square envelope to his boss, and Farouk looked it over carefully before opening it. He said, "No return address on the outside."

"It must have been brought by messenger, and not as a part of the usual mail delivery."

"Ok. Let's see. What do we have here? 'His Royal Majesty

Rasul Appolonium'—well, this is unexpected—'requests the presence of Farouk al-Khoum and Faraj al-Khoum for tea at Sea Watch House, Tripoli, Libya' … and then it gives the address, as well as the day, date, and time."

"The former king of Egypt, their recently deposed ruler, is now suddenly inviting you and your brother to tea? And it's to be held somewhere in Libya?"

"Apparently so. You know, I had heard that some Italians were hosting him there in the capital city, but I didn't have any details. I haven't really cared to keep up with him, to be quite honest. He was useful to us for a time, but I never liked him."

"An invitation like this, out of the blue, to tea at his current hideaway is pretty strange."

"Very odd. I wonder what the old has-been, or former-but-no-longer wants?"

"Access to some of your money, perhaps—or maybe your men? Or possibly some other form of support?"

"Support for what, though?"

"I have no idea. Now that his political kingdom's been taken away from him, he could be in search of a financial realm to rule, and he wants your advice, or a very large loan."

"You might be right."

"Do you think he knows of your plans?"

"No, not at all. How could he?"

"Word travels on the desert breeze."

"Yes, it does. Ok, maybe he knows I'm collecting some favors and gathering some materiel, but he would have no idea what I'm doing with the men, arms, and money being brought together. He could never be in a position to know about most of what's going on."

"He could have a guess."

"I seriously doubt that he thinks of me in political terms at all."

"I see. You're likely right."

"He knows me only as a businessman, a very focused and, one might say, highly successful industrialist."

"That's true."

"He could have no clue what my true ambitions are. They're known only to a few fundamentally trustworthy people, and of course also to my brother."

Tau laughed. "Maybe he just thinks that you and your brother will be enlightening and entertaining company for a little light afternoon tea talk."

"You're a funny man, Tau. I'm sure he wants something. Otherwise, why go to the trouble of having someone come all this way just to deliver an invitation?"

"Are you at all inclined to accept and travel there?"

"I'll actually think about it. He may have something I need, or at least that I can use—even if it's just information. After all, he lived in the palace for many years and still has friends and allies in the city. Maybe I do him a favor and he does me one. Who knows? It might be worth looking into."

"That's probably right."

In Cairo, within the vast sweep of the big marketplace, and inside the old familiar shop where the boys had just arrived for their visit, Mafulla walked quickly to the back room. As he came through the door, he said, "Mom! How are you?"

"Oh! My son! Mafulla! Sweetie-pie! What a nice surprise! What are you doing here?"

Mafulla grinned and rushed forward to hug his mother. "Walid and I just decided to take a walk and come visit."

"I'm so glad!"

Mafulla ended the quick hug and looked at his mother and said, "You're Ok? I mean: you're doing Ok since, you know, Mr. Kaza's unfortunate passing?"

Shamilar sighed and said, "Yes, yes, as Ok as can be expected. It was quite a blow to lose dear old Kaza so suddenly and so violently. Our hearts were broken for him. But none of us is here permanently, you know. And we're trying to keep that in mind. We grieve his departure, but are also endeavoring to be strong in his honor, like he would do for us, and keep working hard, as he always did."

"I guess there's got to be a lot more work to do without him around, helping out."

"Yes, despite his rather advanced age, he was quite a diligent helper, totally dedicated to your father and me and the shop. His passing has left a big void here. We miss him a lot and in many ways, every day."

"I do too, already," Mafulla replied. "How are the kids taking it? Are they Ok?"

"It was hard for them at first, very tragic, but you know kids. Their grasp of such things is only partial, even your brother at his age, and so they rebound after a day or two. Sasha started drawing right away to express her sadness and confusion. But she bounced back. That's the way the youngsters are made, so that they'll be resilient and return to the flow of life, almost regardless of what they have to face."

"Where are they now?"

"Reela's taking care of them. He's home again, just back from another trip. The poor man returned, seeming very tired, but he was more rested this morning after a good night's sleep and he offered to look after the children. Well, of course, Sammi spent the morning and early afternoon in school, but Reela stayed with Sasha and then took her to pick up Sammi from the schoolhouse. He'll watch them both now until we get home. I'm sure they'll play games and have lots of fun together until we return."

"Good. I know they both love to be with Reela."

"It really perks up their spirits. And they seem to energize him, as well. He laughs a lot when he's with them."

"Very nice. Now, Dad told me a minute ago that you just got some sort of a strange invitation."

"Oh, yes, indeed. It's the oddest thing."

"What is it?"

"We've been invited to tea at the home of the new ambassador from Tunisia."

"Really?"

"Yes, can you imagine that? We've never been invited to an ambassador's residence before, ever. What do you make of it? Here, let me show you." Mrs. Adi walked over to a desk and opened a folder, picking out a large beautiful card and handing it to Mafulla.

"Well, you're right. This is a very formal invitation to tea. I have to admit, I'm more than a little suspicious about this."

"We were just puzzled. Why do you say that you're suspicious?"

"Walid and I met the ambassador's son at a palace reception for his father the other night, and there was something not quite right about the kid."

"What do you mean?"

"He was tall and handsome and witty and charmed many of the girls, of course, but he didn't seem to have a sense of social propriety, of appropriateness regarding his actions and words. He appeared to be overly selfish in every way, and almost oblivious to the context."

"Oh, dear."

"Yes. He was quite forward with the young ladies there and, while some were clearly flattered, in at least some ways, the more sensitive among them were visibly uncomfortable with his stark boldness. It was all a bit awkward."

"I can imagine."

"It was almost as if he had a sense that the evening revolved around him—well, actually, more than the evening; he seemed to have a feeling that the entire world revolves around him."

"Oh, dear."

"And, when you see that in a kid who's fifteen, it often says something about how he was raised, about his parents and maybe even their character."

"It does."

"Walid and I were reminded of the old American saying, 'The apple doesn't fall far from the tree.' Of course, we have our own version about figs and fig trees and, applied to him, I'm afraid it implies some unfortunate things about his father."

"I see."

"But there may be more."

"What do you mean?"

"Walid and I are both a little concerned about why we even have a new ambassador from Tunisia. We were told that the former top diplomat just retired. But—why now?" Mafulla lowered his voice and bent down closer to his mother. "This is completely confidential, Mom, but we have reason to believe that some enemies of our kingdom have recently moved to that very same country of Tunisia and have been seen with high Tunisian officials. Then, shortly after that, we suddenly get a new ambassador from there. So, is this diplomatic change a mere coincidence, or is it something we should be concerned about? That's the problem."

"Oh, my goodness."

"I've just had a strange feeling about it."

"Tell your mother."

"Maybe I'm paranoid, but we know that our government, and in particular King Ali, has enemies, and some of them are in the capital of Tunisia, at last report."

"But how could such a wonderful man as our king ever have actual enemies?"

"There are devious people, criminals really, who prospered under the previous regime, and because of the corruption of those officials. They want them back. And then there's another powerful and evil man who doesn't want the old king back, but rather has different plans. He apparently wants to be the king, and replace King Ali."

"That's terrible."

"Yes. And a man like that can use others to seek to attain what he wants. Walid and I have just learned to be careful about new people whose agenda we don't know. And so, I feel very cautious about the new ambassador, and even suspicious. The old rulers of our kingdom were exiled to the north. And, they could have gone west. As far as we know, they might be in Tunisia, too. I'm just concerned."

"My goodness. But why would we—your father and I—be invited to a formal tea by this new ambassador?"

"I really don't know. It could be completely harmless and sensible. Maybe the new representative to our country wants to meet a group of prominent business people, a range of citizens in the city, to better understand your impressions of world and regional affairs, or to sense how you view his own country."

"That could be true, but why us? Our store is small."

"But it's well-known. And, small as it might be, it's busy and prosperous, and many of the top families of the city and throughout the kingdom shop here. You even have customers from afar."

"That's true."

"The shop is certainly well established. And it's known for the high quality of all the merchandise."

"Yes, it is."

"Maybe that's enough to qualify you for an invitation."

"I suppose so."

"The ambassador could simply want to talk to people like you and dad about commerce, the economy, and your impressions on various issues."

"Ok. I could see that."

"Or, on the other hand, it could be just a sneaky ploy to gain leverage over me, or Walid."

"Oh! Really?"

"The ambassador may be using this invitation to get to you, in order to get to one or both of us—most likely and ultimately, of course, Walid. Because of my friendship with him, you have a connection to the prince and, through him, to the king, which is a level of access that very few people have."

"I guess that's true, although I've never thought about it like that before—I mean, in terms of access."

"Well, remember, that's why you have special military protection here across the street and at the house."

"Yes. I have to admit that I sometimes forget the unusual nature of your friendship with Walid and what it might mean to us, for good or for ill. It's hard to imagine that, in a matter of mere months, I've gotten so accustomed to the prince being around and his being your best friend that it typically just seems normal to me, and of no real consequence. And that's despite the alternately wonderful and traumatic events that already have come to us all as a family due to our new connection with royalty. I'm just so silly!"

"No, no, not at all. I'm glad it ordinarily seems normal. It is normal, in many ways. Most of the time it doesn't really matter to me that Walid's a member of the royal family—I mean, in my mind. I hardly even think about it. But, at some level, it's always important, and we should remember that. We don't want to do anything to endanger him, or the king, or ourselves."

"Of course, you're right, we'd never want that."

"Look, Mom, I don't mean to worry you at all about the invitation, but maybe I should mention it to the king and get his impression."

"That's a good idea, if you could."

"I'll do it right away and let you know what he says."

Walid came into the back room at that point and smiled and said, "Hi, Mrs. Adi! Good to see you."

"Hello, Walid! How's my favorite royal prince?"

"I'm good. Thanks for asking. We just thought we'd drop by today and check up on you."

"We're certainly glad you're here! We love visitors."

"And, now, suddenly, you have even more than just us," Walid said, and turned to Mafulla with a grin.

"Who's here?" Mafulla asked.

"Well, our friend Paki, the palace guard, has come in and is talking with Mr. Adi. And then, there is a Mrs. El-Bay with her daughter and her daughter's best friend."

"No way!" Mafulla exclaimed.

"They said they wanted to stop in and say hello."

"Oh, my goodness," Shamilar said. "I've never had so many personal callers here at one time!"

"Well, you just don't know how popular you are, Mom. Come on, let's all go say hello."

The three of them walked into the main part of the shop where Hoda was talking to Shapur and Paki, while Kissa and Hasina were admiring a nearby bright blue vase ornamented with cream speckles under the glaze.

"Shamilar!"

"Hoda! It's so nice to see you. You look wonderful!"

"Thank you. You're so kind. We were in the market today and just had to stop by to say hello and check on you and Shapur. We wanted you to know how sorry we are about the loss of Mr. Kaza."

"Oh, thank you so much. It's indeed been a big loss for us all. We loved Kaza like family."

"I'm sure you did. He was a sweet man, and was here with you for many years."

"Yes, it's hard to imagine the future without him. So far, I'm just trying to pretend he's on vacation. It's helping me make the transition."

"I understand completely. That's a sensible approach. It's a very imaginative way to adjust to his absence."

"Thank you. I knew I had to do something to help me cope. Otherwise, it's just too hard."

"I know."

"It's so kind of you to come by and visit. Mafulla speaks highly of you all the time and of your husband, who is his favorite teacher ever, he keeps telling us."

"That's great to hear. I'll have to pass it on to Khalid. He's really enjoying this particular class of boys. They have lots of lively discussions, and there's not a single sour grape in the basket, he always says."

Shamilar laughed and replied, "That's good, and it's far too rare these days, from what I hear."

Walid and Mafulla had been glancing at Kissa and Hasina while the moms were talking, and then Walid spoke up and said, "Hoda and Mrs. Adi, I'd love it if Mafulla and I could show the girls a new shop that we like down the street, if you might want to talk for a bit longer."

"Yes. Oh, yes, that would be fine, Walid," Hoda said. "Shamilar, if you have a few more minutes, could I take you to tea nearby?

Shapur spoke up and said, "Business is slow right now, and I've got it covered. Why don't the two of you go have some refreshment? The teashop down the lane has some new lemon poppy seed bread that's delicious. I'll be fine here. In fact, I may ask my friend Paki if he can help me move some boxes in the back while you go about your visit."

"That would be fine," Paki said. "I'd love to be of help. It'll be nice exercise. Walid, how close will you be?"

"Just down the block on this street, only about four shops away—very close."

"Ok. I think it's good with the four of you together. I'll be here if you need me. Don't be too long."

"Thanks." Walid knew that Paki understood how much more comfortable it would be for them to be able to go down the street without any older person along. Security often got in the way of spontaneity. And they were all Phi, after all, and could take care of themselves pretty well. Paki surely had this in mind. He was happy to give them a little space. They could just speak more freely and be more relaxed on their own. It was pretty quiet at this time in the marketplace because of the heat, unlike the mornings, which were crazy crowded. So Walid led the group out the door as Hoda and Shamilar followed them, and then the moms turned in the opposite direction to stroll down to the little tea and muffin shop within sight.

Mumar Sakat was outside and nodded to everyone as they appeared on the street. But just then, a customer came up and the two of them went inside to talk sandals and tired feet. It looked like a sale might even be imminent.

Walid said to Kissa, "This is a really nice surprise, for sure."

"For us too. We had no idea that you and Mafulla would be here today. Mom needed to do some errands and we offered to tag along with her."

"My man wanted to come check on his parents and I was in the mood for a nice walk myself, so here we are."

"Has it been a calm, peaceful day for my two favorite crime stoppers so far? I know how it is whenever you guys leave the palace grounds together."

"Well, now that you mention it, we did have one small incident on the way here."

"With Paki? Does he know about the secret identities and the stealthy mission?"

"No, I don't think so—not yet, at least. We all had on our masks because of the wind, and because the king normally prefers it for us when we're off palace grounds, and especially if there's someone with us, so it's three of us, not just a potential Viper and Storm show. But Maffie and I always have our wristbands handy, just in case."

"Just in case."

"Yeah. It's realistic to be prepared. But, anyhow, we were on the way here and Paki had a sudden urge to stop into a café that we were going to pass. He told us he just had a feeling we should go in for a few minutes and asked us if we'd like some tea. Then, as we walked over to a table, he got there first and while he was sitting down he overheard two guys at the next table talking. He told us later that the first remark he heard included the words, 'The thing on the grounds failed completely, but the two old guys were taken care of properly.'"

"What?"

"Can you believe it?"

"No, that's just amazing."

"When he heard those words, he knew they were somehow involved in the snake and spider attack on us and the murders of Kaza and Mo, however directly or indirectly. So he stood up, turned around, and told the guys they were under arrest for soon leaving without paying for their food, and for other crimes they were about to commit."

At this point, Hasina said, "What in the world did the men say to something as crazy sounding as that?"

Walid answered, "Well, they weren't amused and, within a minute or so, things got pretty ugly. Big knives appeared and it took a little Phi action to take care of the guys."

"Are you both Ok?" Kiss asked.

"Oh, yeah, just fine, thanks to a constant diet of intense training with our good friend Masoon."

"And lots of protein," Mafulla added. "Mainly, goat cheese." He showed the muscle in his arm and did a double eyebrow jump. Hasina laughed.

"And Paki did the really heavy work," Walid had to say.

Kissa smiled and shook her head and said, "What happened to the suspicious men?"

"First, they took a nap. Then, two policemen heard the racket and came up thinking we were the bad guys, but Paki explained it all and they took the men, handcuffed and restrained, to the palace jail for us. We're going to find out who these guys are and what they know."

"Wow, that's pretty wild," Kissa said, looking impressed.

"Yeah, in the old days, I would have thought it was an incredible coincidence that we were walking right by where those guys were, and that Paki had his feeling, and that we stopped in exactly when we did, and that Paki walked way across the outside seating area and picked the particular table he chose where he could be in the right position at the right time to hear that one specific sentence. I would have once thought, 'Wow, coincidence piled up on coincidence, layer after layer of it. What totally wild, random luck!' But now, I know better. I've sort of come to understand that this is how things can work when we're deeply tuned in and paying attention."

"Yeah, you're right. Paki is a pretty advanced Phi. He must be really tuned in. But you guys have often had the same sorts of things happen, like at The Luxury Shop when we were riding down the street in the new palace car."

"Yeah, it was just like that in a lot of ways," Walid said. "And we've had other situations like it. But with Paki being the one tuned in to the strange leading feelings, it was interesting. I had no clue. I didn't think anything big was going on when we walked into the café. It never crossed my mind. I was—and this is one of Maffie's favorite words these days—oblivious."

Mafulla chirped in and said, "Actually, me, too. I didn't realize anything was going to happen, either. So, to our great surprise today, we got to do some Viper and Storm style action, taking down bad guys, and we had help. At least, that's the way I like to look at it. Although, of course, I guess it was really more a case of Paki taking down some bad guys and the Viper and the Storm being along for anonymous backup. But, either way, we'll take it. We were still in action, doing our thing."

"Yeah and it was nice to have a more advanced Phi present. We got to concentrate on one guy—the smaller of the two."

"But they were both really big," Mafulla said. "Gargantuan fierce giants."

"Maybe not quite giants," Walid laughed. "But basically, it's true. They were both really big, and Paki took on the larger one, so we were able to surprise the smaller guy and focus on him."

"Well, he was the less huge of the two enormous guys, and still bigger than you can imagine," Mafulla said and made Hasina laugh. "Then it was time for the old divide and conquer."

"Yeah, the good old divide and conquer," Walid agreed.

"Works every time," Mafulla added.

"Yep." Walid then pointed and said, "Here's the shop." He gestured for the ladies to enter first, and Mafulla followed them in.

"Wow, this place has all kinds of stuff, and everywhere," Kissa said, looking around.

"It's pretty incredible," Mafulla replied. "It started out as a small book store. I first noticed it a long time ago when we came to the nearby office and school supply place. I looked in once after that and was amazed at the collection of books. And then they added other things. First records, then framed photos of famous people, then postcards from around the world, then toy stuffed animals, then all kinds of trinkets and even some nice looking but fairly inexpensive jewelry."

"Look at all the records," Hasina said. "American records!"

"There's a brand new record player in the palace," Walid said.

"Really? We should get some records and play them."

Just then, a man stuck his head in the door, a fairly nice looking and well-dressed man, and he said aloud to the store in general, "I'm sorry, is there someone here named Walid? If so, you're needed outside for just a minute. Some gentleman has a message for you but says he can't come in." The man looked puzzled at his own message, and shrugged with a hand motion that conveyed as much.

The prince said, "Right here, I'm the one."

The man smiled, nodded his head, and said, "Good, I'll … tell the fellow you're coming," and disappeared from the door.

Walid looked at Mafulla with a momentary and almost comical expression of perplexity, and then said, “Just a second. It may be important. I’ll just dash outside to see what this is all about, and be right back.” As he was speaking, he turned toward the door and walked out.

Mafulla said, “But who?” Then Hasina called out to him from across the store, and he twisted around and stepped toward her to answer.

Kissa, who was over beside the shop owner’s cluttered desk next to where there were some beautiful postcards on display, had a thought run through her mind—simply, “No. This is strange.” And, after a few seconds of hesitation, she spontaneously picked up something off the desk without anyone’s noticing, and she moved closer to the door, still looking at merchandise that was arranged on tables nearby. But her mind was following Walid and wondering what was going on.

As soon as the prince had stepped outside, he saw the man at the corner of the building, saying into the alleyway, “Yes, sir. He’s there. I told him. He’ll be right out.” The man then looked back toward the door and said, “Oh, there you are. The man’s right over here.” He then waved the prince forward and moved into the alley and Walid warily followed in that direction. It was just a few feet away. When he reached the corner and turned into the alley himself, he saw the same man not fifteen feet away, facing him now with a gun in one hand and a pair of handcuffs in the other. That second, he tossed the open handcuffs to Walid with the words, “Put these on instantly or I’ll shoot you dead right here where you stand and then go kill your friends. You’re all more useful to me dead than alive, except for one thing. Do it now! You’re coming with me. Do it! Put them on!”

The completely surprised young man had caught the handcuffs in the air, and now slowly clicked one around his left wrist, while he tried to think of what to do. “The other hand, this instant, or you’re dead and they’re all dead!” The man nearly hissed out his words.

Walid then took a deep breath and, with no other clear options that he could think of, clicked the second cuff into place. "Ow!" The man yelled out loudly and looked at his right arm just as his gun clattered to the ground. A heavy, dagger-shaped letter opener was buried nearly halfway into his flesh. Kissa had just rounded the corner and thrown it as precisely as a balanced knife and as hard as she could without any sacrifice of aim. The man grabbed at his wounded arm. Walid moved toward him, and before he could recover, in the second that he was looking from the projectile in his arm to his gun, now on the ground, Walid kicked the weapon far away from him, down the alley.

"Why, you!" He grabbed the letter opener and jerked it free and the blood really started flowing. As he was moving to attack the still-bound Walid with this makeshift weapon, the prince spun around and kicked it from his hand, bouncing it off the wall nearest to them. Kissa then stunned her friend even more by catching it mid air and, in one seamless motion, and lunging toward the man, as she noticed that Walid had momentarily lost his balance and fallen to the ground. That instant, while the prince was quickly getting back up, she drove the sharp, knife-shaped object into the man's back with a shout of great power, and he staggered forward with a loud gasp and fell to one knee. Mafulla and Hasina appeared around the corner just in time to see Walid explode into one more kick, straight to the man's face, that made him suddenly collapse on the ground, unconscious.

"Is he dead?" Mafulla asked, moving quickly toward the crumpled figure. "Did you kill him?" He looked over at Walid.

Kissa replied, "I don't think we did. I tried to hurt him and stop him without killing him."

"You did? Mafulla said," mouth open. "What did you do? I didn't see!"

Walid interrupted and asked her, "How did you ever catch that thing in the air?"

"What thing?" Mafulla said.

"Phi reflexes, my friend, and lots of training," Kissa responded.

"And you didn't hesitate."

"I saw what was going on as soon as I came around the corner, and I had already prepared myself for pretty much anything. I grabbed the opener off the shop owner's desk."

'What opener?" Mafulla asked.

Walid said, "The guy had a gun on me and was too far back for me to do anything. And he threw me these handcuffs and said if I didn't put them on instantly, he'd shoot me and kill all of you."

"What?"

"Then, suddenly, I heard a noise behind me and there was this knife looking thing sticking out of the guy's arm and he yelled and dropped his gun. I kicked the gun away and he pulled out the knife, or as it turns out, the very dangerous letter opener, and lunged at me. But I kicked the blade away and Super Woman here grabbed it in the air and gave it back to him, pretty forcefully—in the back. And then I kicked him in the head, right in the face, and you showed up. And so, here we are."

"Oh, man, really?" Mafulla said. "All that just happened?"

"Good girl!" Hasina said with a big smile. "That's awesome. I'm really sorry we missed it."

"Me, too!" Mafulla added. "Me, too."

Walid looked at Kissa, right into her eyes, and said, "You're even more amazing than I realized."

"Thanks. You're not bad, yourself."

"You threw that thing so well and hard that it went into the guy's arm like a really strong man had thrown an actual razor sharp army knife at him!"

"Well, yeah. We've done a lot of training with sharp objects. It had a nice point and was heavy enough, and it had decent balance, and I have to admit that I'm not bad at such things. I practice when I can. You should see the holes in things around my house."

"Oh, man," Mafulla said, bending down. "You really got him

good in the back with it."

"Who is he?" Hasina asked.

"I have no idea," Walid replied. "But could you guys go through his pockets and see if you can find a key to these cuffs?"

Mafulla and Hasina searched the man and Hasina found a key, which she then used to open the metal cuffs that had bound Walid. He rubbed his wrists and said, "Good, that's better."

"Glad to help in some way," Hasina said. "It's just too bad we missed the real action."

"I wish we had all come out," Mafulla said.

"Me, too," Hasina agreed.

Mafulla added, "But it was so sudden and puzzling and harmless seeming, at the time. The guy looked completely legitimate, and not at all sketchy. I was a little surprised at what he said, but I never thought there was a threat."

"It's Ok," Walid said. "Everything worked out, thanks to Miss Kissa's instincts and skills. But now, Kissa, could you and Hasina go get Paki? Maffie and I can guard the guy. We've got to do something with him and figure out why he attacked me. I'll get the gun up off the alley and be ready when he wakes up."

While Walid was talking, two things happened. One was that the guy did in fact wake up, and he was plenty mad. It was a very good thing that something else had also just happened.

13

Some Suspicions Confirmed

Literally seconds before Walid's attacker regained consciousness, Mafulla had clicked the handcuffs around both his wrists, which he had pulled around behind the guy's back with the simple thought about dealing with danger that he had often heard from Walid, who got it first from the king: "We use what we have and move quickly."

The man woke up cursing and squirming and groaning. By the time he had looked around from his limited vantage point, face down on the alley and with his hands in restraints, Kissa and Hasina had already disappeared around the corner on their way to Paki, who was less than a block away.

"What happened to me?" He croaked out the words.

"You got opened up like an envelope," Mafulla said. "Now, we just have to find out what the letter inside has to say."

"Nothing. I say nothing," the man replied.

"Oh, I think you'll say something when I begin to twist this knife around that's already in your back, and fish for some of your internal organs. You're lucky that the person who stabbed you was careful not to kill you. But I'm not as skilled. So I hope you'll forgive me if you accidentally happen to pass away during our little conversation."

At that point, Walid walked around to where he could see the man's face and said, "Why did you try to take me away? Why did you threaten my friends? Who are you and what do you want?"

The man was silent. "Ok," Mafulla said. "I hate to do this."

"Who's speaking? Show yourself."

"Sorry, I can't. I'm busy."

"What do you mean?"

"As I was saying, I hate to do this, but if you insist on being stubborn, you can have your silence—it's yours to enjoy for as long as you can maintain it, if that's what you want, but you'll also get some other things right now that I promise you're not going to want or enjoy."

He moved closer in toward the man and crouched down and put his hand gently on the letter opener's handle. Even the slightest touch of the object made the man groan loudly with a truly terrible sound. "I'd hold very still if I were you," Mafulla said. Then he turned and said, "Walid, could you stuff something into this guy's mouth? If he isn't talking anyway, we won't miss anything, and I need to be able to work freely here without his screams attracting any unwanted attention."

"Ok, Ok, Stop. I'll tell you. It's not worth this."

"What is it, then? What can you tell us?" Walid asked.

"I saw you at the café a little while ago when those men were being led away by the cops. I didn't see what happened to get them arrested. So it was a big surprise. I had spoken with one of them previously. I was supposed to have a meeting with them both today and I was on my way there when I saw them being tied up."

"Who are they?"

"It doesn't matter."

"Yes, it does. I should really tell my friend to pull this knife, or, actually, dangerous letter opener, out of your back, but the problem is that, without proper medical attention, you might bleed to death right here in the alley, if I do. I can help see to it that no such thing happens, but only if you'll answer all my questions. You see, we really need to know. Who are those guys? You have to tell us now."

"Ow. They work at the embassy."

"Which one?"

"Tunisian." The man groaned again and loudly said, "Oh, Oh, Oh," and "Ow" again when he tried to move.

"How long have they worked there?"

"They came in with the new man."

"What new man?"

"The new ambassador—the guy who just got to town, Omar somebody. They're both embassy guards that he brought with him. They're from Tunis."

"Did they identify themselves to you as guards at the embassy?"

"Well, no, but I'd seen them there, and I asked around and learned who they are. I think they were actually trying to keep me in the dark a little bit about who they are."

"Why did they want to meet with you?"

"I have no idea."

"Sure you do. Think for a minute. What are your special skills? What's your knowledge that they might need? What was your motivation to meet with them? Why did such a meeting make any sense to you?"

"They promised me a lot of money."

"For what?"

"To help them out."

"Ok, this is becoming tiresome. You'll have to tell me the whole story. I don't have time for bits and pieces and uninformative answers. And, judging by your condition, you don't have time for that, either. You need medical attention right away. I promise you this. If you don't get that attention soon, we'll have to find a way to carry your body to the morgue. And I don't have time for that."

"Ohhhhhhhhh." The man moved and paid a high price in pain for his trouble. "Please take this out."

"What do you know about two recently deceased gentlemen, Sayid Kaza and Mohammed Bendar?"

"Who? Nothing. I don't know those names. Ow. I'm a chemist, an expert in drugs and poisons. I have no idea exactly what the embassy men wanted me to do for them. That's what the meeting was supposed to be about. But, now and then, I do some work … outside the strictest understanding of the law."

"Oh? Tell me more."

"It happens that, recently, I've been through a tough time and I'm in need of money. They wanted me to do something for them. They didn't say exactly what, except that it would be easy and I would be paid handsomely for it. The only specific thing the one guy had said to me was 'You're going to help us bag Prince Walid.' That's what he said. I didn't know whether he meant capture or kill. But I didn't want to know. I've got nothing against you, assuming you're the Walid they want, and I think you are. I mean: it's not personal."

"Everything's personal."

"This was just business. I was simply going to apprehend you and hide you away until I could find somebody in the embassy to take you. Maybe then I'd still get my money, even if those two were in jail, for whatever reason. So, I was earlier on my way to meet with them at that café to find out in detail what they wanted me to do. I had the cuffs and gun just in case I had to go do the job without any time for preparation, and in case things got messy."

"You're a chemist who carries around a gun and handcuffs."

"I thought maybe the Tunisians were going to send me out to get you right away, and I have things I carry with me for rough situations."

"But you don't have chemicals or poisons on you."

"No, no. The client has to tell me what they want me to do, and I decide what to use, and then I get it and they pay for it. I don't carry around a lab of chemicals with me. And I don't accept every job. Maybe I wouldn't have agreed with everything they wanted, once they explained it. I try to have standards."

Paki had quietly walked up in time to hear these questions and their answers. Kissa and Hasina were right behind him. At this point, he spoke up. "Do you have any names for these men?"

"No, they wouldn't tell me their names. And, who is this new voice behind me?"

"Paki Alexander. I'll gladly tell you my name. I'm a senior palace guard and you're under arrest for attacking a member of the royal family with a deadly weapon and with the intent to kill."

"I wasn't going to kill him."

"You can tell that to a judge. Aiming a gun implies your intent to use it. You've also made death threats to others and have attempted a kidnapping through force. That should be enough to worry about for quite some time. It tends to be a problem with no solution, from your point of view."

"Can you get the knife out from my back now without me bleeding to death here on the street?"

"Actually, it's a dagger shaped letter opener, an impressively large one. And I can try. I'm pretty good with basic emergency medicine."

Just then Badar Sakat walked up, took in the scene, and handed Paki some items. Paki said, "My friend here from the Egyptian military has just walked over and brought me a small battlefield medical kit. I'll be able to clean your wound and stitch it well enough to get you to jail without too big a mess on the alleyway here, where people have to walk. It's not going to feel good, but I think you'll live—for now, at least."

"Just get the thing out, please. It's too … Ow! … painful."

"First, one more question: Are there, to your knowledge, any other individuals such as yourself in pursuit of the prince at the present time?"

"No, no, just me. They told me they attempted to get the prince with some snakes and spiders, and I said, 'Are you kidding?'

And they explained they were trying to do the job without leaving any evidence or a trail to follow. They also like creative methods. They'd heard good things about me and wanted me to take the job now and do it right. It would be left up to me, they said. But again, I had no details."

"Why do people in the Tunisian Embassy want our prince killed or captured?"

"Nobody told me anything about that. Just, please—Ow! You have to fix my back. The pain, it's getting worse. I may pass out."

"Ok. But did the man you spoke with say anything else to you at all?"

"Only that if I got the job done quickly, then his boss and a couple of other guys were going to be very happy, and they'd make sure that he and his partner were happy, too—that's all."

"Who were the men he was speaking of?"

"I don't know."

"His boss—that's the ambassador, I'd guess—and a couple of other guys. All right. I'm going to put a clean rag in your mouth. Bite down on it. The really painful part will take less than half a minute, maybe only a few terrible seconds. Prepare yourself for some very long and fully unpleasant moments. The clock will seem to slow down now and time will be of no help to you in the upcoming extended seconds of your distress."

And in that period of time, Walid, Mafulla, Kissa, and Hasina all suddenly felt a bit sorry for the man and what he was now going through, despite what he had just done and threatened to do. But they were not surprised. The agony of another should always be distressing for a good person to witness.

Down the street, Hoda and Shamilar had been having a very nice time at tea, talking about their children and discovering that they had several mutual friends in town, and also laughing about Mafulla's various forms of, well, Mafoolery. At the moment that Walid had turned the corner a block away and had seen the barrel of a gun pointed at him, Hoda had experienced a sense of something's being wrong, of something's happening nearby, but she didn't know what it was. Within seconds, she had a feeling of reassurance that Kissa somehow was dealing with the situation, whatever it might be, and that everything was fine.

She didn't say anything to Shamilar about any of this, and managed to keep a pleasant expression and tone of voice throughout it all. But Hoda was keenly attuned to her circumstances in the broadest possible sense, and especially to her daughter's well-being, however near or far away. She often seemed to have a way of knowing beyond words and far beyond any physical means of information conveyance. And she had learned to keep such things in her heart unless she knew that it was appropriate to say something or take action. On this occasion, she simply continued with the conversation.

Shamilar took a bite of a small biscuit and said, "It was the strangest thing to get that invitation to tea at the Tunisian ambassador's house. We're not usually a part of such circles."

Hoda replied, "I've always wondered what an ambassador's home is like. Is it full of rare artifacts and pictures from his homeland? Does he have an obligation or is there an expectation that his décor will represent his nation? Or is he free to decorate as he chooses?"

"I'd never thought about that. Those are interesting questions."

"I'm sure there are budgets—there must be—and that he just inherits most of what's in the house, for the duration of his service, but it would be interesting to find out how free he can be to do his own personalization in the new environment."

Shamilar smiled and said, "Why don't you come with me?"

"What do you mean?"

"You could accompany me there to see it all."

"Really?"

"Shapur doesn't like formal occasions. He's more comfortable in the shop, or at home, or with friends. And if we both go, someone has to watch the kids."

"I thought Reela usually does that for you."

"When he's in town. But I believe that on the date of the tea, he's off again on business, this time to Morocco."

"Well, the invitation was for the two of you, husband and wife."

"I'm sure I could simply explain that Shapur couldn't make it, but that you as a friend agreed to accompany me. If they want a business person's opinion on something, I know as much about the business as Shapur."

"Do you really think that would be Ok?"

"I do. I mean—what do I know? But, why not?"

"I would like to see inside the home of an ambassador." Hoda smiled conspiratorially, and Shamilar laughed.

"Let's do it," Shamilar said. "We'll go together—Girls on the Prowl for Diplomatic Decorating Details. Oh! I sound like Shapur, or Mafulla!"

"I like it," Hoda replied with a laugh. She had an inner sense that it was somehow right, or meant to be, that she should go to this formal tea, for reasons beyond what they were discussing. But again, she kept that sense to herself as they clinked their teacups in agreement.

"But poor Shapur," Hoda said, "He won't get to hobnob with the muckety-mucks."

"Lucky Shapur, you mean," Shamilar replied. "He won't have to get all dressed up. The wonderful man never saw an old worn piece of clothing or a wrinkle in his clothes that he didn't like. I'm sure you can tell by looking at him that he dresses for comfort, not elegance."

"Well, in his work, that likely helps."

Shamilar smiled and sighed and said, "Sometimes, I think the elegance would help more, given the clientele that we often have, and would like to have even more of. But I understand. I didn't marry a movie star. Yet, he was a little bit of a dandy in his early days. Still, he'll be relieved that he doesn't have to get all fixed-up now for the formal tea—which just means more crumpets for you and me!"

"Well, I'm all for doing a favor for poor, wrinkled Shapur," Hoda said.

Shamilar laughed, and then quickly became serious again. "There is one thing, though."

"What is it?"

She leaned forward and said, in a much lower voice, "I don't know how to say this, but Mafulla has expressed to me some worries about the new ambassador. He just confided to me that some very bad men, enemies of our king, had been seen recently in Tunisia and in conversation with government officials there, at a time right before the old ambassador was called back and this new man was sent here in his place."

"Really?"

"Yes. So, I'm not sure what this man is, or might be, up to. He could be trying to use our family as a conduit to the prince, through Mafulla, of course. So Mafulla said we should be careful."

"That's a shame. But careful we shall be," Hoda replied in a lower voice. "The man is messing with the wrong people, if messing is what he intends. The two of us will certainly not let him get away with anything."

At about that moment, across town in the palace, Kular came into the king's office and said, "Your Majesty, Bancom is here to see you."

The king looked up from some papers and said, "Oh? Thank you Kular. Please send him in."

As Bancom walked through the door, he did a small bow and said, "Your Majesty, there's some interesting news. I've taken the liberty to ask Naqid, Masoon, and Hamid to meet me here, and they should arrive any moment."

The king rose from his chair and said, "If it's not too urgent, I'd like to go down to the sitting room where we can all be more comfortable."

"That would be nice," Bancom replied. "The news is important, but its nature will allow us to enjoy the greater comfort. It can wait." The king led the way and, passing Kular, asked him to bring in some tea for them and the three gentlemen who would be joining them shortly. Less than a minute after the two of them were in their seats, Naqid came in, followed by Masoon and Hamid. They all bowed.

"Your Majesty."

"Majesty."

"Sit, sit, please, everyone," the king said in welcome. "Bancom tells me that he has some news to share with us."

When they were all seated, Bancom began by explaining, "I just got a call from Badar and Mumar Sakat. It seems that Prince Walid, Mafulla, and Paki, on their way to the marketplace this afternoon, stopped into a café for a moment, and Paki overheard two men speaking about the recent murders and the attempt on the prince with what sounded like insider knowledge of a conspiratorial sort."

"Oh?" The king looked surprised.

"Yes, Your Majesty. And soon things got crazy." Bancom then went on to relay to them all the entire story of what had happened at the café, and later with the man who had attempted to abduct Walid, and he recounted everything that had been learned.

The king suggested that these events may point to the involvement of Farouk and Faraj al-Khoum, and then said, "We need to question all these men thoroughly."

At that moment, Kular ducked his head in, waited for a second, and said, "Excuse me, Your Majesty, but the boys are back here with Paki. They wanted to clean up for a minute, but will be right in after that. Mafulla says that he has an important piece of information for you, and a question."

"As soon as they're ready, please send them in."

"Certainly, Majesty."

Mafulla had already washed up quickly and changed clothes. He was sitting on the edge of Walid's bed, waiting for him to finish up doing the same so that they could go down to the king's sitting room, where everyone by now would be expecting them. Kular had told them of the meeting that was underway.

"Come on, man. They're likely all looking at their watches by now."

"I'm almost done. Thirty seconds." In ten, Walid came walking out of his large bathroom, still drying his hair with a towel. "Just a quick comb and we can go."

"Well, make sure it's perfect. You know how demanding Masoon is about the parts in our hair. And if it's sticking up again in the back, I'm sure Naqid will just freak out."

"Very funny."

A quick comb in front of the mirror, accompanied by Mafulla's sardonic exclamation of, "Very nice, indeed," and Walid led the way out the door, with his friend close behind. A distance down the hall and right beyond the door to the king's sitting area, they saw a palace guard with papers in his hand, a man Walid didn't recognize, and he appeared to be writing or drawing on the paper, looking up at the hallway and then the king's door, and down again. His uniform didn't really seem to fit him very well. And that was a bit unusual. Walid looked more closely and, as the man turned his body slightly in their direction, he saw a small gold patch on the front of his shirt.

When the guard was looking down at his papers, Walid turned to Mafulla with a look of great concern and pointed to the spot on his own upper left chest where Mafulla should look at the man. Then Walid stuck out two fingers, the index and middle finger, in a V shape, and made sure Mafulla saw them. He did, and walked by the man, as Walid stopped on the near side of him and said, "Oh, are you here about the new carpet?"

"What? Oh, yes. I'm … I'm getting down all the hallway sizes and door openings for the carpet layers who'll be coming in some time tomorrow."

"Well, I'm sure glad to see you. We have a bad problem right inside this door, if you could look at it with me for just a second."

"But I'm not the specialist, myself."

"It's Ok, you can tell him when you see him."

"Oh. All right."

Walid smiled and opened the door and, taking the man by the arm, said, "Kular, this man needs to see that problem we've talked about," and then practically pushed him through the inner door, into the king's sitting room, where he was now facing several men who were obviously in a meeting, and who looked up at him at the same time.

"Oh! I'm so sorry." The man looked appropriately surprised.

"You soon will be," Masoon answered, seeing his ill-fitting uniform and the gold patch.

14

Time for Tea

The palace gardener Nazeem Alfid had gotten off early from work because of a sore back. He was sitting in the front parlor of his small apartment reading the paper when his wife Aswan came into the room wearing one of her best outfits and carrying a tray.

"It's time for tea, for you and me," She said this in almost a singing voice as she swirled around the room and placed the tray down on a table.

"What's this?" Nazeem said and laughed. He added, "You look so good! What are you doing?" as he looked up from the paper.

"You're almost never home in the afternoon at teatime. Today you are, so I dressed up for you and I have some special tea freshly brewed and, to go with it, the most marvelous little crisp cookies that I've baked for us."

"Well this is different," Nazeem remarked, "and very nice, I have to say. I should come home early every afternoon! I didn't know I'd be getting special treatment here today."

"I can't do much to help with your sore back, but I can help refresh your worn out spirit with a little pick-me-up here in the late afternoon."

"This is very kind of you." He put down his paper.

"You do kind things for me all the time. I just wanted you to have a pleasant little surprise while you're home."

"I've heard that good tea is always best when sweetened by a kiss," Nazeem remarked with a sly look on his face.

"Ha! You've heard correctly, I think," Aswan answered. "But here's the problem. If I kiss your tea, I might burn my lips. It's still far too hot."

"You're so funny. There's only one solution to that problem I can think of," Nazeem suggested. "You must administer the sweetener much more indirectly."

She laughed, bent down, and gave him a big kiss on the lips. "That's what I'm talking about! Everything will taste better now."

Aswan made a face and said, "You don't think that my tea and cookies will be tasty enough on their own?"

"Oh, how we husbands get in trouble with our jokes!" he said, and they both laughed.

"I'm just kidding, too. I know you love my brewing, along with my cooking and baking."

"To the extent that I do indeed have a strong feeling my back is going to be acting up more often from now on."

"Good! Then I can nurse you back to health each time with baked goods, along with the best and sweetest tea in town!"

"That sounds great. Now sit, sit, and let's drink, nibble, and talk."

Aswan poured the tea for them both, and placed two cookies on a small plate for each of them. There were folded cloth napkins and old silver spoons for stirring the hot delight.

I've been meaning to ask: "How has work been since you helped save the prince and his friends?"

"It's been marvelous. I told you how our supervisor praised me at that gathering in front of all the other gardeners and grounds crew. What I found out just this morning is that, at the end of the month, I'll have a little something extra in my pay envelope, courtesy of the king."

"Oh! That is good news! It's very kind of the king. They've been so good to us, in many ways."

"Yes, they have. I'm blessed to work for such people."

"You are. But I'm still getting over the snake and spider story. How scary that must have been! And how strange! Have there been any other unusual things happening around the grounds since then?"

"No, nothing really. Not like that, at least. But, actually, there has been one thing that was a bit odd. If you hadn't asked, I may have simply forgotten about it."

"What was it?"

"I had just killed the snake that threatened the young woman, the friend of the prince, and he in turn had killed the other snake that was prepared to strike me. Then, when it was all over, I was walking back to the main tool shed and I approached a storage building where some of the oldest horseback riding equipment is kept, along with other old outdoor sporting things. It's a building that's hardly ever used these days, since they moved most of the stables to the edge of town. And to my surprise, for the first time I can recall, I saw the door hanging just ever so slightly open."

"You did?"

"Yes, it was cracked open just a bit."

"Isn't it normally locked? I mean, if it isn't regularly used."

"Well, actually, no. Since access to the palace grounds is so limited, I suppose they feel no need for locks on small outer buildings like that one. But they do need to keep the door closed, so there's a latch, and a thick nail usually holds it in place, just stuck through the hole at the end of the latch, and also through a connector on the frame around the door. But when I noticed the door hanging a bit open, I walked up to it and saw the nail on the ground."

"What did you do?"

"I picked it up and put it back into place after I had shut the door tightly."

"Well, someone may have gotten something from the building and they just forgot to close it up securely."

"It's possible, but then this afternoon, I saw the exact same thing. The nail was out and the door was just a bit open, only a crack."

"Was there anyone around?"

"Not that I could tell. And in all the years I've worked on the palace grounds, I've only seen someone go into that building maybe three times, and they've never left the door open like that, unattended. Then, suddenly, this happens, not once, but twice."

"That is perhaps odd. Did you mention it to anyone?"

"No, I just fixed the door again and went about my business. I really didn't know the person to tell. Darwishi, the head driver for the king, used to be in charge of the horses also and all their equipment, but someone else may be doing that now, mainly at the building out at the edge of town. But again, there was little to tell. Someone's just being sloppy, I suppose. But it made me feel strange when I first saw it on the afternoon of the snake and spider attack."

"Maybe you should tell Darwishi when you go back tomorrow," Aswan said as she poured more tea. "He'll know who else needs to be informed. It might be relevant to their investigation of the incident."

"You're right. But, for the moment, I believe I have fresh tea in my cup that needs to be sweetened."

Walid, Mafulla, Kissa, and Hasina were not the only students from the palace school who had been having an eventful afternoon. Malik and Haji had left class with no idea what the rest of the day would hold, and no clue that they were shortly going to make a stunning and vitally important discovery. Right after Khalid had dismissed class for the day, the two of them had gone on a walk to look at the palace cars, especially the new ones from Rolls Royce. Haji on the previous day had just gotten a magazine that was a special edition entitled, "Great Cars of the World," and two of the cars featured there were described as being owned by the king of Egypt. He wanted to go see for himself, and he brought along Malik, who was also a big fan of modern automotive design.

They found Darwishi and told him about the magazine and, right away, he knew the sedan and the convertible they were talking about, and let the boys get into the cars to explore every nook and cranny. They loved it. These particular vehicles were used so seldom that they still had that new car smell. The leather was luxurious, and as the boys sat in the back seat, they pretended they were being driven around town to important formal events.

After about an hour of admiring these "exemplars, nay, paradigms of beauty and power," as Haji put it, quoting from the article, and then taking their time to look at a few other cars in the garage, they thanked Darwishi and began to walk back toward the palace. But as they passed the old out building that was used to store some equestrian equipment and other gear, Malik noticed that the door was slightly ajar and that no one was around.

"I wonder what they keep in here?" he said.

"I have no idea," Haji replied, and he walked over to the door and said, "It's open."

"Yeah, I just saw."

Haji took hold of a small handle, and pulled it toward him a little more to look inside. Glancing around quickly, he said, "I didn't see anyone nearby who might have been in here. I wonder if it's Ok to take a peek and maybe look around."

"Why shouldn't it be?" Malik responded.

"I guess you're right. If it was the sort of place that was off limits, it would be locked or something."

"Let's have a little adventure and check it out."

"Ok."

"I'll go first."

"Sure. After you—what's the old saying I've heard? Oh yes. Age before beauty."

"You're very funny." Malik slowly opened the door a bit more, and the angle of the sun allowed a good measure of light into the small building. He stepped in and said, "Wow, there's a lot of stuff in here."

"Yeah." Haji was now right behind him, looking in as well.

"What is all this?

Haji followed him in and said, "It looks like a lot of really old equipment for the king's horses."

"But the horses are kept in another place now, miles away. This must be the stuff they don't use much anymore."

"Well, there are a few horses still on palace grounds. Remember the small stable next to the garages."

"True. But this stuff looks really ancient."

"It does."

"Let's poke around some and see what else is in here."

The boys stepped farther into the space and began to pick up things, looking under and behind the saddles, saddle blankets, straps, and many other items that had been in storage there for apparently years.

"It smells pretty bad in here, like everything's moldy old," Haji commented, and then added a grunt.

"Yeah. Wow. Check this out," Malik said.

"What?"

"Some old guns."

"Really?"

"Yeah. Look at this one." Malik picked up an ancient looking rifle. "This could have been used for hunting."

"I guess—or shooting snakes."

"I bet you could bag something big with this one."

"What are they doing in here?"

"Who knows?"

"It's like this stuff has been forgotten or something."

"Unbelievable."

"What?"

"Some exercise equipment. What's this doing here? Wait. Here's an old medicine ball."

"A medicine ball?"

"Yeah, a heavy leather ball that people throw back and forth for arm and back exercise. Think fast!" Malik threw the ball to Haji without warning, and Haji twisted and stumbled trying to either catch it or get out of its way. He somehow managed to snag it and hold on, but the unexpected weight of it shoved him backwards into some large boxes, which he hit hard. The boxes then all fell down, and Haji started laughing, which was good, because Malik had been worried that he might have hurt him with the unexpected toss of such a bulky, heavy thing. As the boy lay on the floor surrounded by boxes, with the medicine ball now on his chest, they were now both laughing.

"Good catch," Malik said. "Really nice. Graceful, too, with the expert use of all the boxes."

"No, no, perfect throw," Haji replied. "I can't take all the credit. But I'm glad you like the way I used the boxes to back me up."

"Very athletic," Malik said. "And improvisational."

Haji was still laughing and said, "Well, now that we've reduced this place to a chaotic shambles, maybe we should quietly slip away while we can."

Malik wouldn't let up. He said, "First, I want to make sure you know how very much I do love your technique with handling that ball. It was extremely creative, I'd say."

"Stop it," Haji said with a pretend frown. "I caught it, didn't I? Help me get all these boxes stacked back up."

"Ok, Ok," Malik responded and walked over to where his friend still lay on the floor, offering him a hand up and then bending over to look at one of the boxes. "This one's labeled 'Nets, Rackets, and Balls.' Tennis stuff?"

"Sounds like it."

"Maybe there's more sports stuff here."

"You're right. Wait. Here's one labeled, 'Croquet.' Very cool."

"I wonder who we could speak with to get permission to use some of this stuff?"

"I don't know. We should ask Walid. He can find out."

"Good idea."

"But then we'd have to admit that we've been in here."

"So what? Walid won't care. And it wasn't locked or anything."

"True. Hey, what's this?"

"What?"

"Step to your right so you aren't in the way."

"In the way of what?"

"I think … wait. There's a door in this wall behind where the boxes were."

"Really?" Malik walked over to where Haji was standing and looked at the back wall carefully.

"Yeah, look." Haji pointed to a smooth vertical crack in the wall. And it was obvious that this door was also standing a bit ajar, as they had found the outside door of the building—but this one, not nearly as much.

"There's no handle or nob or anything."

"I guess you just have to put your fingers in the crack between the door and the frame to pull it open from this side. From the other side, you just push."

"Well, let's see what's behind it," Malik said, and began to pull it farther open. "It looks like another little room, but it's really dark. Was there an old lantern back near the horse stuff?"

"I don't know. I didn't see one."

"Well, let's go back for a second and look."

The boys turned around and walked back to the front of the

building where all the equestrian stuff was stored. There was indeed a lantern off to the side and nearby, not far away, an old box of matches.

"It probably doesn't have oil in it," Haji said.

"Wait," Malik replied, and rummaged around a bit more. Within twenty seconds, Haji heard him say, "Aha! Lamp Oil!"

"No way."

"Here it is." Malik got to work, opening the oil bottle and then testing the lantern's wick with his fingers. "Hey, this is already wet, like it's recently been used."

"Really?"

"That's strange." He unscrewed the small cap on the lamp, saw that it was half full, and filled it the rest of the way with the oil he had found, remoistening the wick a little more. He then got out a match, struck it on the side of the box, and touched it to the now ready wick.

Haji said, "Let there be light."

Malik held the match to the wick for one second, two seconds, three seconds and then said, "Voila!" The light blazed and illuminated the entire room. Haji closed the nearby outer door most of the way, as it had been when they first saw it, since they didn't need any daylight now that they had the lamp. Plus, he was a little nervous about being in the building without an invitation or permission or anything, and didn't want anyone to see the light they had just created inside.

Malik picked up the lantern by its handle and carried it quickly back to the door they had just discovered. Pulling the door open more and then stepping into it, he was instantly glad he had thought to get light first, and had remembered seeing the lantern when they first entered the building. He stopped short and said in a loud whisper, "Whoa!"

"What is it?"

"There's an open trap door right where we would have stepped."

"What?"

"Yeah, right here. One of us would have been in major trouble. I think we just avoided a broken leg, or even worse."

"Let me see." Haji moved around to get a better look. Not four or five feet beyond the door they had discovered and opened, there was indeed a wooden trap door whose top had been pushed open and to the side. If they had entered the room without light, chances are that one of them indeed would have stepped into the open hole.

"Boy, did we get lucky! Hold the lamp down here so I can see a little better," Haji said, as he now bent down next to the opening. Malik swung their light over the hole and got down on his knees as well, so he could lower it down a bit.

"Oh, man," Malik exclaimed in a hushed voice. "There's a ladder, an old wooden ladder, and it goes down maybe, what, ten or fifteen feet?

"Yeah, and there's a big, horizontal hole at the bottom, at the back side. Can you see it? It looks like … the start of a tunnel. We need to tell somebody about this."

"We will. We will. But, first, let's go see what's down there."

"Are you sure?"

"Well, we've got a lantern and there's nobody around, and we're two strong guys who can take care of ourselves."

"Ok. Age before beauty."

"Again?"

"Sure, it never gets … old."

"I'm just two months older than you."

"Yeah, that's right. Experience leads the way. So, after you."

"All right, but you can hold the lantern until I get down. Then you can come down with it and, if you lose your balance and fall or anything, I'll be there to catch you and the light."

"Ok, that sounds like a plan."

Malik handed the lantern to his friend and turned around

to put his foot down on the top slat of the ladder. He tested it and it seemed strong enough to hold his weight. He then slowly and carefully found his footing on the next slat down, and began descending with a touch more confidence, but still carefully. Only five or ten seconds passed.

"Made it. I'm on the floor now. Put the lamp on the edge, get your footing, and when you're, like, two steps down, you can get the lamp in your right hand and still have a good grip on the ladder with your left. I'll get up a couple of steps on the ladder, or so, and sort of meet you before you get down, and you can hand me the lamp, Ok?"

"Ok, that sounds good. If you're sure about this."

"Yeah, it's fine."

Haji did what Malik suggested and made it safely to the bottom. "Hey, did you notice that a few of the slats on the ladder look really new?"

"No, I didn't have the lantern like you did just now."

"Yeah, most are old but a few are new, like someone's recently fixed the ladder."

"Hmm. I wonder why—and who."

"I have no idea. So … let's see what's in the tunnel."

Malik turned to the big opening behind them that was maybe six feet high and held the lantern out into it. "Wow, look at this. This thing is long. I can't see any end to it. It goes down for a while, like a gradual descent, but that's as far as I can see. Let's take a few minutes more and check it out."

"I don't know," Haji replied. "This is kind of spooky. And we're all by ourselves here. Maybe it would be safer to have some palace guards along for exploring this thing."

"I totally agree. But we can get them later. Maybe if we just go into it for a short distance, we'll have more of an idea of what it's like and we can give them a more detailed description."

"Ok, I guess that makes sense, but just a little bit into it should do the trick."

"Sure, we won't have to go that far to get a better sense of what this is and maybe why it's here." Malik held the lantern in front of him and began to walk forward very, very slowly, looking up, side to side, and down to make sure there weren't any holes or unseen dangers like snakes or spiders, which he had recently heard plenty of talk about in the palace. Haji followed him closely. They walked ten feet into the tunnel, then twenty, then forty. They were going gradually down a subtle incline, as Malik had detected. And after about thirty yards, it seemed to level off.

Haji loudly whispered out a panicked sounding, "No!"

Malik whipped around fast and whispered back, "What? What is it?"

"Nothing. I was just messing with you, Captain Courageous."

"Well, don't do that again. You made my insides jump about a foot."

"Ok, Ok. So lead on, Fearless Leader."

They continued walking. In all that distance, there had been nothing new to see. The tunnel was lined with stone. It was maybe six feet wide and seven feet high. The rock on the walls was cool to the touch, and here and there, even a little cold. The whole thing smelled damp—not terrible, but a little stagnant and maybe moldy. At one point, as they silently and slowly moved forward, Malik saw the light of the lantern reflected in a pair of glowing little eyes up ahead, close together and very low to the ground. "Uh-oh."

"What?"

"Up ahead, it looks like there's a rat or something else."

"Well, Ok then. That's enough for me. Exploration ended. We need to go tell somebody about this, right away."

"About the rat?"

"About the tunnel."

"Oh, yeah. Ok. But where do you guess this goes?"

"I don't know. We could be outside the palace grounds already."

"You think?"

"Yeah. We've maybe passed under the street out back and who knows where we are. I also think we've been brave enough for the moment and have something really important to report here. And I think we should get back and do it now. Naqid and the king will want to know about this right away, I bet, and also our dads."

"Ok, you're right. We need to report in. I haven't heard anyone talk about a tunnel here and I'm sure everybody would want to know. Let's go back. We can come down here again with backup. That'll be better. If we're going to face critters like rats, and maybe worse, I'd rather have a long stick with me, anyhow."

The boys turned around and made their way carefully but a lot more quickly back to where the ladder was. The time it took them to retrace their steps revealed how truly far they had gone. The excitement of danger and adventure they had experienced while initially walking through the tunnel had affected their sense of time and distance. Now, they realized what an impressive tunnel it actually was.

They climbed back up the ladder and then closed the trap door over the opening behind them. And as they passed through the inner door behind where the boxes had been stacked, they also closed it and pushed some of the boxes back up against the door, without even thinking why they were doing that, except maybe just to leave it as they had found it. And then they shuffled toward the outer door. But just as Haji was getting close to the door, Malik said, "We won't need the lamp any more," and he turned down the wick, putting it out the second before Haji pushed on the door to open it back up.

"Oh, no."

"What is it?"

"Somebody locked the door. It won't open."

"What?"

"We're locked in here."

"Are you sure?"

"Yeah."

"Oh, man! I just put out the lamp. How are we going to find the matches again in this dark?"

Haji replied, "Give it a minute. Our eyes will adjust. Meanwhile, I'll bang on the door in case whoever shut it is still close by and can hear us." He did just that, and banged loudly, many times. Then, with his hands cupped around his mouth and up against the crack in the door, he yelled out, "Hello? Is anyone there? We're locked in this building. This is Haji and Malik. Hello?" He banged on the door a few more times and then listened. All they heard in response was silence.

"It's pretty late in the afternoon. Maybe nobody's around."

"I think I can see a little better now. I'll look for the matches."

"Ok."

"Ouch!"

"Watch where you're going. There's a lot of stuff around."

"Oh, yikes! I think I just touched some sort of live thing. Gross."

"Hope it's not a spider!"

"Yeah, me too! But it seemed bigger. Ok. There. Got 'em. I've got the matches. Give me just a second. Where's the lamp?"

"Over here."

"Ok, I got it." There were some scratching sounds in the dark, several, actually, then the match suddenly burst into flame, illuminating the room and the exact location of the lamp and wick. Haji bent over, lit the wick, and the room came back into full illumination.

"Good job, man," Malik said. "You've got awesome eyesight in the dark."

"Yeah, it's pretty decent."

"What do you think we should do now?"

"Well, banging on the door and yelling didn't work. I think we need to see if there's something we could use as a tool, something really skinny that will fit through the small crack around the doorframe, because, if I remember correctly, there's no real lock or locking mechanism on the door, just a nail that's supposed to stick through a loop. I bet we can fish it out and get out of here."

"That sounds like a good way out," Malik replied, and got to work, silently looking around the room they were in. Haji was doing the same thing.

"Wait. Did you hear that?"

"What?"

"Shh."

15

An Uninvited Guest

In the king's sitting room, Masoon, Hamid, and Naqid slowly rose from their seats. The uniformed man who had just entered with Walid said, "I'm so sorry, so sorry to interrupt you. I'm just here to prepare for some … carpet installation. This young man wanted me to look at a problem in this room."

"Oh, there's a big problem in this room," Masoon said.

"Can you show it to me?" The uninvited guest continued to try his bluff, although he was increasingly uneasy about it and even a bit panicked, and that showed in his voice.

"Well, the most obvious part of the problem starts with your uniform not fitting as it should," Naqid said.

"I'm quite embarrassed. My regular uniform is being cleaned. I had to borrow another one today from a friend."

"What's the name of your friend?"

"Oh, I'm sure you wouldn't know him."

"I'm sure we would. You see, only six people in the entire kingdom have the gold patch on their official uniforms that you have on this one, and three of us are in this room. We know the other three as well as we know each other. Which of them is being helpful to you today?"

"I wish I could say. I'm so nervous being in front of you exalted gentlemen that I've lost all memory of his name. It's completely slipped my mind. I'm expecting him any second," the man said, glancing around with evident nervousness. "Let me look into the hallway and see if he's here yet." With these words, he turned to leave, but both Walid and Mafulla simultaneously took his arms to restrain him, with what to him were shockingly strong grips.

Naqid replied, "I'm afraid you're meeting no one, and that you're not leaving this room under your own power unless we know who you are, where you came from, how you got into the palace, and what your real business is here today."

The man reached for a hidden weapon, a knife, but shouldn't have wasted his time. Mafulla had him disarmed in a split second, and Walid put him on the floor, face to the carpet, as Naqid stepped around him to handcuff first his left wrist, then his right one. The head of palace guards then began to address the king, but decided, as the first word was leaving his mouth, that he'd better not say anything to identify the monarch to this man, in case he didn't already realize whose presence he was in.

Naqid's words were: "Your … indulgence is appreciated, all of you. I'm very sorry about this intruder. I'll find out the answers to our questions and get back to you quickly. Masoon, if you'll help me get the man into the hallway, I'll have guards take him into custody, and relocate him to a more appropriate part of the palace for questioning."

Naqid bent down again and looked the man in the face. "Palace guards don't install carpeting, or help in its installation. Those are fine jobs, important jobs, but we don't do them. We have other jobs, and you'll find out very soon what they can involve. Now, get up on your feet." Masoon jerked the man upright and, taking one arm, with Naqid holding the other in a tight grip, they walked him out the door, through Kular's greeting room, and into the hallway.

The king said, "Well, that was interesting."

"Sorry, Your Majesty. We saw that guy in the hallway outside the door, noticed the patch, and knew we had to deal with the situation fast," Walid said, adding, "I shouldn't have surprised you like that."

"No, no. There's no need to apologize. Remember what I've always said. Life is full of surprises. Something unexpected is always happening around here these days. Think nothing of your dramatic interruption. In fact, I quite like what you decided to do and how you chose to do it. It was quick and creative. You surrounded yourself with strong backup instantly, and now the scoundrel's in custody. Maybe he can help us to plug some leaks around here."

Naqid and Masoon quickly came back into the room, reporting that Paki and another guard had taken the man down the hall, and that Paki would be returning as soon as a second man could be found for the job. The king invited them all to have a seat and for Walid and Mafulla to join in their conversation. He brought the boys up on what had been discussed, and they confirmed Bancom's report about the marketplace incident, while adding a few details about what was learned from questioning the man who had attacked the prince.

Mafulla then took the opportunity to tell the king about the invitation to a formal tea that his parents had received from the new Tunisian ambassador. He said that, right before coming back to the palace, he and Walid had stopped by the shop briefly and had learned that Hoda, rather than his dad, was planning to accompany his mother to the late afternoon social occasion at the ambassador's residence.

"Your Majesty, I didn't say too much to discourage her attendance, but just mentioned my personal doubts about the Tunisians and the fact that I'd be telling you about the invitation and asking for your opinion. Mom said she'll do whatever you think is best."

"You did the right thing, Mafulla. In fact, before this new twist, I might have discouraged her attendance, but with Hoda going, we can turn this in a new direction. I'll have a word with her later on, possibly tomorrow, and we'll see how we can use the occasion for a little more information gathering. When and where is the Tunisian tea?"

"It's going to be held tomorrow afternoon, at five o'clock at the ambassador's home."

"Good. There's plenty of time to speak with Hoda about it and coach her on the role she can assume."

"Do you think there's any danger for Mom?"

"No, none at all. The way we can play this out, she'll be one of the most welcomed and appreciated visitors the ambassador has ever had respond to an invitation of any official nature."

Mafulla looked puzzled.

The king continued, "Let me put it this way. Hoda will be the most delightful uninvited guest the ambassador has ever had, and he'll be so over the moon to speak with her that your mother, who will have brought her, will be held by him in the highest possible regard."

"Ok, that's good—but what if something goes wrong?"

"Hoda will know how to handle it."

"You're absolutely sure, Your Majesty?"

The king smiled. "Yes, Mafulla. Rest easy. I'd never endanger a member of your family in order to gather information, or for any other reason."

"I know. I'm sorry I'm so nervous about it."

"No, that's quite all right," the king said. "I understand completely. But, trust me, Hoda is fully capable of meeting any unexpected challenge with aplomb and complete mastery. Your mother will be as safe as she would be in the company of Hamid or Masoon, or perhaps the both of them." The two men referenced smiled and nodded.

Mafulla was a little puzzled to hear such a comparison of Kissa's mom to the legendary warriors, but just said, "Ok, thanks. I'm sorry for my concern."

"It's absolutely natural," the king said.

Talk turned back to the men arrested during the course of the day, all of them, and the king suggested various ways that the pieces of the puzzle might fit together. Then, he did a bit of a summary for everyone to hear, and either approve or correct.

"So, it is clear that the two men Paki arrested at the café had prior knowledge, and most likely, complicity in the snake attack on palace grounds, as well as in the murders of Kaza and Mo. These men work in the Tunisian embassy, came to town with the new ambassador, and call someone who wants the prince captured or killed their 'boss.' They also speak of two other people who want this to happen. We know that the two al-Khoum brothers are in Tunis, or have been, and that they've been seen with government officials. So this would be the most obvious connection. But we shouldn't bet everything on that conclusion. The former king, Rasul Appolonium, is still out there, as far as we know, and so is Ari Falma, two other people who might have this same aim. Evidence so far points to the brothers, but we won't rush to judgment."

The other men were listening and nodding as the king spoke. He continued. "The first thing we need to know is how these men or their associates got the snakes and spiders onto palace grounds and out to where Walid and Mafulla relax after classes. We also have to find out how they knew the spot to take their unconventional, venomous weapons. Then we have to learn how this man just now, our hapless carpet installer, got into the palace and stole a uniform for use. We clearly need a more secure building and grounds area. We can't have such enemies moving among us."

"You're absolutely right, Majesty," Masoon said.

"Furthermore, we need to discover whether the ambassador himself is involved in all this. And whoever is the point man in the embassy, we need to know who he's working for and reporting to in Tunisia. Finally, we need to gain a sense of what's coming next. What are their plans? What should we prepare for? How can we stop them?" He paused and said, "Does this seem to sum it all up?"

"That covers everything I can think of, Your Majesty," Hamid offered.

"I feel the same," Masoon said. Naqid nodded.

"It sounds good," Walid commented.

In the old storage building out back on the palace grounds, there was a state of high alert. "Quick, over here!" Malik whispered. "Take this and get on one knee and put out the lamp again."

"But ..."

"Just do it!"

Their lamp's small flame was extinguished again. The room went dark again. They could both see a slight ray of light from behind the inner door they had just minutes before closed most of the way behind them. There was a faint shuffling sound and then a thud. After a second of silence, that door began to creak open, pushing some small boxes aside, and light once again flooded the room. Malik and Haji were off to the side now and blocked from immediate view by some other boxes stacked up between them and the door. But they could see through a small crack that was between the stacks. A man who was maybe in his late thirties and carrying another lighted lamp slowly entered through the door. He was dressed in the uniform of a palace gardener. He had a large bag with a strap slung over his shoulder. The boys were silent, and the small building they were in was just big enough that he didn't notice them in the shadows, off to the side of the cluttered room.

The man quietly made his way straight to the outer door, put down his lantern, and pushed on the edge of the door. When it didn't yield, he took something from a pocket, slipped it through the crack between the door and its frame and, with a jerking upward motion, released the nail on the other side that had been keeping the door closed. He then slowly pushed the door open, quickly looked around outside it, returned the tool to his pocket, and ducked back in the door to bend down and put out the lamp. But before he could touch the lantern, a low voice surprised him.

"Stop right where you are. Don't move your hands. Go down onto both knees immediately, or we'll shoot you where you stand."

The man's head jerked up toward the boys and he saw them for the first time, each of them on one knee, and each pointing a hunting rifle straight at him. "Who are you?" He hissed out the words.

"Wrong question. Who are you?" Haji demanded.

"I'm a gardener for the palace grounds and, anyway, it's none of your business," the man answered.

"You're no gardener. I've never seen you before," Malik said. "What's in your bag?"

"Nothing of interest to you—just equipment I need, supplies."

"Why did you come through the tunnel?"

"Who are you to be asking me all these questions? I'm a gardener here at the palace and I use the tunnel to bring in supplies from an underground storage room."

"Where's the storage room?"

"Just a few yards from the opening of the tunnel. And let me ask you: How do I know you have any bullets in your guns?"

"We were out hunting today and target shooting, and we have a few bullets left for you."

"I doubt it. You're just boys playing at being tough."

"Do you want to be the next target?"

"I think your guns are empty. I think you have no bullets.'

"Well then, maybe one of us should prove that we do. Malik, would you like to shoot him in the foot or leg, or should I?"

"Let me," Malik said. "I can't think of any other way I'll get the chance to do such a thing any time soon."

"Ok. Go ahead."

Malik cocked the gun and aimed it down at the man's right foot.

"No, no, stop. There can be no shooting near my bag. I can't take the chance of it."

"Why not?"

"There are fertilizers in it that could ignite and explode and kill us all."

"Because of the bullets we don't have?" You could tell Malik was now almost enjoying this, despite his pounding heart. The man just glowered at them both, unwilling to take the risk that they were not bluffing and the guns were actually loaded.

"Ok, then, lie face down on the floor and you won't get shot. But if you try anything, we'll shoot you very carefully, in a part of your body that's not near the bag. It'll be our choice as to exactly which part."

"I swear to you: You boys are going to be in a lot of trouble."

"No, you're the one in a lot of trouble," Malik answered. "Face down!"

When the man had assumed the desired position, Haji grabbed some rope, put down his gun, and walked over to tie his hands behind him. As he straddled the stranger, the man grasped his left ankle. But Haji reacted with a move he had seen his father Masoon do many times in workouts with lesser force, and instantly stomped into the man's lower back with his right foot. The man howled in pain, and Malik was over him now as well, swinging the butt of the rifle at his head. As it made contact with a loud crack, the jolt caused the rifle to fire and shoot a bullet through the roof of the building with a thunderous report. The man was now unconscious and couldn't hear the shot, but it scared both boys half to death.

"Holy Moly! I didn't know the stupid gun had any bullets at all!" Malik said.

"Geez, I didn't either," Haji said. "The guy didn't know what he was dealing with here!"

"I guess we didn't either."

"Good point. Tie him up and let's get him out of here and get somebody's help."

"I hope I didn't kill him."

"I think you just knocked him out."

Malik got to work with the rope Haji had dropped and within a minute or two they had the man tied up, hands and feet. The job then was to drag him out into the open where maybe someone would see them and give them help. They got the man out the door and into the area in front of the building, still unconscious. And now in the distance, they could see Omari jogging in their direction. Malik waved his arms and yelled out, "We need help over here!" Darwishi and two mechanics had also come out from the palace garage nearby and were also running in their direction.

"Who fired a gun?" Darwishi shouted.

"I did, by total accident," Malik said. "But there's an intruder! Come help us!"

As Omari and the other men came closer, Haji yelled out, "This man entered palace grounds through an underground tunnel that we just discovered, and then pretended to be a gardener. We tried to subdue him, and he fought us and I kicked him and Malik hit him with the butt of an old gun, but that made the gun go off, and we didn't even know it had bullets in it!"

The men were all there now and Darwishi said, "This man claimed to be a palace gardener?"

"Yes," Haji answered.

"I've never seen him before here at the palace, have you?" Dar asked the other men.

"No, no, not at all," one man said.

"Never before," the other confirmed.

Omari said, "Interesting. I've seen him once before, I think, recently, just in passing. He was carrying a box across the grounds." He then looked at Haji and asked, "What did you say about a tunnel?"

Haji pointed and said, "There's an underground tunnel hidden in that building. We just saw the door hanging open and were curious what was in there, and we went inside. I know we probably shouldn't have, but we did, and we found a hidden doorway and behind it a trap door and an underground tunnel."

"Really?"

"Yeah. We actually went down in it a few minutes ago and

walked what must have been at least a city block before seeing a rat or something and we turned back to go report what we had found. But when we got back into the building, we realized that someone had closed the outer door and locked it, and we were stuck. Then we heard a noise and it was this guy coming up from the tunnel. He didn't see us, and we found these guns, and when we asked him what he was doing, he lied and said there was a storage room a few yards down the tunnel and that he had gone there to get fertilizer. And he had a bag on his back that he said was the fertilizer."

"How'd you get out?"

"Oh, he opened the door with some sort of tool before we revealed our presence."

"Where's the bag you mentioned?" Omari asked.

"Right inside the door," Malik answered.

Omari walked briskly to the door and through it. He was in the storage building for no more than fifteen seconds, and when he emerged he said, "The man lied more than once. There's no fertilizer in that bag."

"What's in it?" Malik asked.

"Sticks of dynamite."

"No way!" Haji said.

"Oh, my goodness," Darwishi added. "Dynamite on palace grounds. I wonder what he was going to do with such dangerous stuff hidden in a bag."

"Nothing good, I would imagine," Omari said. "The king needs to know of this right away, and Naqid, and perhaps Masoon and Hamid. Boys, can you go to the king's office, or ask Kular where he might be found? He'll want to hear your whole story."

"Will we get in trouble for going into the building?"

"No, not at all. You'll be heroes for what you've discovered. Now, go! I'll deal with this guy and move him to the palace jail with the help of our friends here."

Malik and Haji did as Omari had asked. They ran to the back entrance of the palace, up the outer stairs, then through the door and down two long interior hallways and up a big flight of stairs toward the king's quarters. One guard initially stopped them, but then recognized both boys, and when they reported the urgency of their mission and Omari's instructions, he let them go on to Kular's office.

They arrived completely out of breath and explained to Kular that Omari had told them to come and see the king. Kular said, "Your fathers are in with His Majesty now. Let me tell them all that you're here." He disappeared for a moment and then returned to say "They'll see you right now. Please follow me," and he led them through the door into the king's sitting room.

The king, Hamid, Masoon, Naqid, and Walid and Mafulla were all still there, at this point having a snack and some juice. Kular formally introduced the boys into the room and, on the king's urging, they launched right into a fast and complete version of their story.

The king listened and then exclaimed, "It's truly remarkable that you've found the mystery tunnel we've been seeking! We had reason to think there was such a thing, but we had no idea that it would come up in an out building like that old equestrian and sports storage shed. This is good news, very good news, indeed. You two are officially heroes for the rest of the day, and, for at least part of tomorrow."

The boys both smiled really big and Malik said, "Thanks, Your Majesty."

"Yeah, you guys did great," Walid said.

"You sure did," Mafulla added. "Dynamite work." Walid just shook his head.

Haji laughed and said, "Thanks, guys."

"Yeah, thanks," Malik added. Hamid looked over at Masoon and smiled, while nodding his pride.

The king then addressed the boys again. "Omari said he had seen this man before on the grounds?"

"Yes, Your Majesty, at least once and carrying a box."

"I wonder if that box might have contained snakes and spiders?" The king mused aloud.

Masoon spoke up and said, "There's a good chance, Majesty."

Walid looked at his friends and said, "So this man had a bag of dynamite, and the individual we apprehended in the palace just a short time ago, the self-identified carpet installation man, seemed to be drawing up a map of this floor of the palace. I wonder if it was a map to guide the placement of … explosives?"

"That's a very disturbing thought, and it's likely accurate," the king replied. "We have to get to the bottom of all this as soon as we possibly can."

The king then thanked Malik and Haji again, as well as all the others, and told them they were all free to go, and that he would be in touch whenever developments warranted. As they left the room, Walid said, "Malik! Haji! Wait up."

The two of them stopped in the hallway. The prince walked up to them with Mafulla right behind him and said, "I just want to say that what you guys did was really brave and totally awesome!"

Malik said, "Thanks, man. We were curious about that old building. We'd never seen anyone going in or out and wondered what was in there. We had no idea it would end up being such an exciting adventure."

"So what was down the tunnel?"

"There was absolutely nothing at all, as far as we went. It was just an old, musty passage."

"And you went maybe the length of a city block?"

"Yeah, I think so—and it could have been more. It seemed like that, but it was hard to judge."

Haji jumped in and said, "I agree. I think a block or more. We just felt it was time to turn around at that point and tell somebody what we had found. I remembered how that other tunnel in the basement of the palace had been used by some bad characters before, and I was afraid that history was going to repeat itself if we didn't report this fast. I had no idea that we'd actually come across an intruder before we could leave the building."

"Yeah, well you guys dealt with him pretty decisively," Mafulla said. "Top notch performance."

Malik replied, "Thanks, man. I'm just sorry we didn't get curious long ago and find the tunnel before some evil guys could use it to bring in poisonous snakes and spiders and such."

"Well, you stopped the dynamite."

"True. And you guys escaped the slithery and creepy crawlies just fine."

"Yeah, fortunately."

Haji said, "I wonder what exactly these guys were planning."

Walid answered, "I don't know. But I hope we find out soon. That way, we can stop their Plan B as well, whatever it is."

Mafulla nodded and said, "Yeah, whatever it is."

16

Ambassadorial Delight

The next day, the morning was bright and almost cool, with unexpected breezes coming off the Nile. The school sessions in the palace were a bit hectic, especially in the early afternoon, with more talk of the upcoming trip to Alexandria and new assignments to read before then for everyone. The king had decided that the overall security situation would still allow for their planned excursion. He firmly believed that, even in dangerous times, life has to go on.

When the school day finally ended, Hoda went straight home for a short rest and a change of clothes. The afternoon had arrived for the formal tea at the Tunisian ambassador's home. The king had already spoken with Hoda and had offered her one of the older palace cars that could be taken without its identity being too easily recognized. She then sent a message to Shamilar that she would come by in the car and pick her up at a quarter to five. They could arrive at their destination in comfort, safety, and style.

The driver was Rahib Nasula, a trusted member of the palace staff who reported directly to Darwishi, the head driver for the king. Rahib had been instructed to let the ladies out near the ambassador's home but not directly in front of it, so as to be less conspicuous and to reduce the possibility that he might be recognized by anyone on the diplomatic staff. He was then to wait there for them.

When the car pulled up in front of the Adi home, everyone poured out of the house to see it. Sammi came running out, followed by little Sasha and with their father, Shapur, close behind. Several neighbors came to their windows or stood in their doorways to admire the fine long automobile, the likes of which was not normally to be seen in their neighborhood. Rahib opened Hoda's door, and she happily invited the children to get in and look around.

While all this was going on, Shamilar was making final preparations and looking into the mirror once more. Then she came out the front door, which was opened for her by Rahib, who introduced himself on the spot. He then accompanied her to the car and, as they both approached Shapur, the proud husband looked at his wife and smiled and clapped his hands and said, "My, my, my! You look absolutely wonderful! Simply marvelous!"

"Thank you, sweet husband," Shamilar said with her own big smile as Rahib opened the back door of the car for her. Looking inside, she saw Sasha squirming and squealing with delight, and Sammi with a huge grin across his face, bouncing on the dark maroon leather seat next to a laughing Hoda.

Their mother then laughed as well, but said, "Calm down children! You'll wrinkle our Hoda!" And then she bent down and looked more closely at her friend and exclaimed, "My dear, you are stunning!"

"Thank you, Shamilar! And I should say that you look quite beautiful yourself—like you go to these events all the time."

Shamilar laughed again. "So you can't tell that this is my first tea with an ambassador?"

"Not at all!"

"Or that I'm extremely nervous about it?"

"Not a bit! You look cool, collected, and elegant."

"Good! Now, children, it's time to get out of the car. Mommy has to go to her party. I'll be home soon." She guided the two of them out from the car door and turned them over to Shapur, giving him a little kiss on the cheek.

Sammi said, "Vrrroooom!"

Shamilar did a little wave and said, "Back soon!"

"Have fun," Shapur replied.

"I'm sure I will!"

"I guarantee it," Hoda said from inside the car.

Shamilar got into the back seat and said to Hoda, "Oh! You should have seen me this morning! I was so nervous earlier, much more than now, and then I just thought: Why am I worrying about this? It's tea and cakes at someone else's expense. I get to dress up, go out, see you, and enjoy a delightful experience. So, I'm a lot less nervous now. I'm just pretending like it's normal—or at least, almost normal."

"I'm glad to hear that. You shouldn't be nervous at all. The king sent one of his best drivers for us today. Rahib's a man with extensive military training. He'll get us there safely and he'll be just outside the residence at all times, waiting for us while we enjoy the event. If we're not out by six-thirty, he'll come for us and introduce himself as your driver, saying that he's been instructed to keep you on schedule."

"Good. I've met Darwishi, the king's main driver, but never Rahib, until just now, I mean."

"Dar's too widely known to people in diplomatic circles. Rahib isn't. The king wanted us to be protected and well cared for without any obvious sign that the palace was in any way involved."

"Well, I'm very happy to be so pampered and protected."

The driver who was being discussed had just finished exchanging a few friendly words with Shapur, and had taken his seat up front at this point. He said, "If you ladies are ready, shall we depart?"

"Yes, by all means," Hoda replied, and the car pulled away smoothly, with the family waving from the front of the house.

Shamilar waved back and said, "I wish they could all go today, but there will be other times for special rides, I'm sure."

"Yes, I'm sure," Hoda said. "There will be many more parties and events—at least, now that you're clearly on The List."

"What list?" Shamilar laughed.

"Oh, the list of the socially important—party version," Hoda smiled and joked. "I'm just so glad you invited me to come along today!"

"And that was before I knew you'd come with your own car and driver. I should invite you more often." Both ladies laughed. On the way to the ambassador's home, they talked about their children, recent events, and kingdom matters generally. Shamilar was always impressed with Hoda's keen intelligence and understanding of current events, and she recognized a strong intuitive sense that Hoda seemed to have about people, a sensibility she also admired.

Rahib soon looked into his rear view mirror and said, "Excuse me, ladies. We're about three blocks away now and should be arriving momentarily."

"Oh, good. How's my hair?" Shamilar asked Hoda.

"Very nice. Perfect, in fact," she answered. Rahib pulled up to park a short distance from the main entrance to the ambassador's home, got out of the car, and opened the door for the ladies, helping them out and escorting them most of the way to their destination.

"I'll be with the car in case you need me," he said with a smile.

"Won't you get bored just waiting?" Shamilar asked.

"No, no, I always have a book to read," he said. "And today, a very good one I've started already. It's about the country of India and all its deep philosophy. I'll have a marvelous time with it while you enjoy the party. I like the quiet time alone."

"Very nice," Shamilar said. And she added, "We'll see you in just a bit." The ladies walked the rest of the way by themselves and, as they approached a very official looking doorman who was dressed in a beautiful uniform, Shamilar said, "I'm Mrs. Shamilar Adi, here for the ambassador's tea, and this is my guest, Mrs. Hoda El-Bay."

The man said, "Oh, yes! You're most welcome to the ambassador's home. Please allow me to check your names off the list." He opened a little book and made a mark and said, "I'll announce your arrival." Ushering them through the grand front door, he said in a rather loud voice, "Mrs. Shamilar Adi and her guest, Mrs. El-Bay."

As the ladies walked in, they could see two or three-dozen people already there. Beautiful flowers were everywhere, brought in especially for the event. A string quartet, tucked away at the top of a large curved stairway, was playing a light and festive melody. Shamilar recognized several important merchants in town and their wives, along with some other prominent individuals. In the middle of the room was the ambassador, talking to four or five guests who had recently arrived and were standing around in a cluster, laughing at something he had just said.

The king had been absolutely right. The moment Hoda walked through the door, the ambassador caught sight of her and was completely mesmerized. He continued talking with his other guests for another half minute or so, but kept glancing back her way. He had seen her at the palace party given in his honor, where she had looked like a goddess, but his time with the king and other officials had not allowed him to break away and speak to her. At the earliest possible moment, he excused himself from his current conversation partners and walked quickly in the direction of Hoda and Shamilar.

"My goodness! Two such exceedingly lovely ladies! Your presence is a great gift to me, and an extravagant adornment to my humble house! Welcome to my new home!" He gushed and beamed.

"Thank you so much," Shamilar said.

"Please allow me to introduce myself. I'm Omar Sassi, the recently appointed ambassador from Tunisia, at your service."

He looked right at Hoda with a big smile and Shamilar spoke up again, saying, "It's so nice to meet you. I'm Shamilar Adi and this is my friend Hoda El-Bay. My husband Shapur couldn't be with us today, but that just gave me the opportunity to bring my friend along."

Omar turned to Shamilar and said, "I'm so glad to make your acquaintance, and I'm very happy that you brought along such a charming companion. I'm sorry I'm not able to greet and speak with your husband, but please do thank him for making it possible for you to bring this delightfully lovely lady. Now, come, both of you, and let me get you some tea and cakes to enjoy on this fine afternoon."

"Oh, that would be so nice of you," Hoda replied, with charm nearly oozing from her voice. "For a man of your exalted position to be taking care of us personally is so gracious and kind."

"It's my great pleasure," Omar said. And taking Hoda's arm lightly, he felt a thrill of excitement at the touch that he'd never before quite experienced. The word 'extraordinary' came into his head. He led the two of them toward a nearby buffet table where an array of teas and baked delights were sitting at the ready. Then, composing his emotions a bit and looking at Shamilar again, he said, "I've heard great things about the Adi family, even before my arrival."

"You have? My goodness. In Tunisia?"

"Oh, yes. Your shop is well known. You and your husband are quite famous in certain circles for the quality of merchandise you carry, and for the way in which you can find whatever rare items your customers desire."

"Thank you. I'm honored. I'm sure you know that's very flattering to hear," Shamilar said, blushing.

The ambassador continued, "Your brother-in-law is also well

known among diplomats, and I've even heard superlative things about one of your children, a young man who, I'm told, is living in the palace and being educated alongside the prince."

"Why, yes! You're absolutely right. We're so proud of Mafulla. The king seems to have taken quite a liking to him. We think he's a fine boy, but as parents, what could be expected of us? Still, even without the natural parental prejudice, we know he's an exceptional young man."

"And it's certainly no surprise. I'm sure that he's every bit as accomplished as we all might expect from your outstanding family, and even more so, I would imagine."

"That's so kind of you to say."

The ambassador smiled. He clearly knew the way into a mother's good graces, and at this stage Shamilar had completely forgotten Mafulla's worries about the man. "And Mrs. El-Bay, may I ask your role in kingdom matters?"

"I'm a teacher of the girls in the palace school."

"Marvelous!"

"It's indeed a wonderful job that keeps me involved in the life of the palace and at the center of the monarchy."

"A better role model for young girls could not be imagined, from everything I can tell about you already."

"You're most kind, Ambassador Sassi."

"Oh, please, you would do me a great honor if you would both call me Omar."

"I'd be delighted, Omar." Hoda said his name with special emphasis and almost a tone of intimacy, and then added. "And, just now, hearing you praise Shamilar's son so appropriately, I will have to say we've heard reports that your own son is sharp as a razor, very athletic, and about as handsome as a young man can be."

"You're too kind," the ambassador replied.

"Well, his attractiveness and charm are certainly no mystery, now that I've met you." Hoda was every bit as clever as Sassi, and as he attempted to lure Shamilar and her into a trusting and quite favorable disposition towards him, she was doing the very same thing to him. And she was much more effective in her methods, determined as she was to make the most of this rare opportunity.

"You flatter me. I've never been so deeply complimented by such a beautiful woman." He turned and said, "Shamilar, you've done me a great service by honoring me with your presence this evening, and by bringing your lovely and gracious friend into my home … and a dedicated teacher, of all things—certainly the noblest profession."

He moved in closer to Shamilar and lowered his voice so that just the two of them could hear him and said, "I wonder if you would mind my borrowing your friend for just a few moments. I would love to get a teacher's perspective on a collection of books that were in the house when we moved in. I'm trying to decide what to do with them. And if I could show them to Hoda, perhaps she could advise me—if it's not an inconvenience, of course."

"Oh, no! That would be fine," Shamilar said. "I'm sure she can provide you with great insight."

Omar nodded with a big smile and took Shamilar lightly by the arm and said, "I happen to have heard somewhere that you appreciate nice jewels. Is that right?"

"Oh! I do. I don't really own anything extravagant, I can assure you, but I do enjoy seeing nice things."

"As do we all."

"I love both ancient and modern jewelry of an artistic design."

"Excellent! Then I'd love to introduce you to one of the top jewelers in our part of the world, in case you don't already know him. He'd be so keen to meet you, I'm sure, and I'll have your friend back to you before you know it." He looked at Hoda and said, "Please pardon us for just the most fleeting moment."

"Certainly," she nearly cooed.

He steered Shamilar about four feet away and to a group of

people clustered around, talking, and said to an older man in the group, "Mr. Ahmed, I'm sorry to interrupt your conversation, but do you know Mrs. Shamilar Adi? She's a lover of fine jewels."

"No, I don't believe we've ever met. Are you involved with the famous Adi shop in town?"

"Yes, that's my husband's enterprise, and I help to run it."

"Oh, it's a fine place—fine, indeed, and it has always had a sterling reputation."

"Thank you so much for your gracious words! I've heard many wonderful things about you over the years, as well."

"That's very kind of you to say."

"I'll leave you two alone for a minute," Omar said. "But I'll be right back, I promise. Ahmed, do tell Shamilar about those new gorgeous rings you just got in."

"I'll be happy to." The jeweler smiled and nodded.

Quickly returning to Hoda, who was at this point sipping her tea as she watched things proceed, Sassi had to force himself not to stare inappropriately, but instead, he made direct eye contact with his lovely guest and smiled again and said, "I'm sorry for leaving you unaccompanied for that brief second."

"I'm glad as a result to have you completely to myself."

"Oh! Not as glad as I am."

"Omar, you make me blush."

"I'm delighted to hear it. And I hope you don't mind my whisking you away for a moment or two."

"Oh, no," Hoda said, "Not at all. I was quite hoping we could have some quiet time to chat."

"Oh?"

"Yes. I'd love to see more of your home. And I'd be delighted to look through your … books." By this point, Sassi's heart rate was nearly through the roof. He was so excited at the prospect of time alone with this gorgeous woman that he could hardly think straight. He had never seen her equal, in all his travels throughout the world.

The king had heard that Sassi enjoyed quite a reputation as a lady's man, and it was confirmed during their conversations on the night of the palace party in his honor. Because of what he heard and saw that evening, the king knew that, at the first sight of Hoda walking into his house, Omar would do all that he could to get her alone, so that he could focus on her. His full energy would be devoted to winning her over. His ego needed to know that he could awaken in such a remarkable lady a desire to talk to him, one-on-one, and bask in the aura of his charm. Already, what he was hearing from her was stroking his need for conquest, and immensely satisfying his ego.

"The volumes of which I speak are in my private library, if you would not mind accompanying me there for just a few minutes."

"Please, show me the way," Hoda said. "I'll follow you anywhere."

Sassi heard these words and could hardly believe his good fortune. He motioned her forward and followed close behind her, just to take in the sight of her graceful movement across the light parquet floor. He guided her around the lively, chatting crowd, and down a side hallway toward a back room that turned out to be quite an ornate library with a high ceiling and intricate woodcarvings throughout.

"Here we are, my dear. But before I show you the books, I feel that I have to be somewhat bold and share a thought."

"Please do."

"I hope you won't mind my saying this, but the moment I first saw you, I said to myself: This must be what Cleopatra was like. This has to be the sort of sight the great Julius Caesar was presented with when he first laid eyes on the famous Queen of the Nile, before Mark Antony experienced the same wondrous vision. In your presence, dear lady, I feel the glory, mystery, and beauty of Egypt. I would never want to embarrass you by revealing my inner thoughts in this way, but I just had to convey them to you. I hope you don't mind."

"Oh, no, Omar, quite the contrary. I'm very flattered that my illustrious ancestor would come to mind when I first entered your home. You're kind to say so."

"Your ancestor?"

"Yes, indeed. I try not to speak of it much, but I'm blessed to be her direct descendent."

"Oh! What a thing to learn!" He laughed and said, "As if your personal beauty and poise weren't enough alone to set you apart from all the other women in Egypt! Then, to have this background! It's quite extraordinary. My goodness. That explains a lot, then. Yes, it certainly explains a lot."

"Oh, it does?"

"You're quite extraordinary, Hoda, beyond the reach of words—if I may say so. There are many beautiful women in your kingdom, and in my country as well, but they don't even begin to compare."

"What a sweet thing for you to say."

"I'm sure you hear this all the time. Your husband may just be the luckiest man on earth."

"Thank you for such a sentiment. He was the first deeply intellectual soul, and the first Oxford man, I ever knew—handsome, brilliant, strong, and dashing. I was smitten right away. But then, you surely know what I mean, since you're both cut from the same cloth." Hoda was playing her part well, in fact, perfectly. She knew how far to go and where to stop. She went on to say how amazing the university connection was, and that she had a suspicion there were other cords that might tie them together. Omar gestured for her to sit, and he sat down very near her, utterly entranced by what she was saying.

The minutes passed as if they were seconds to him, and somehow Hoda made a natural transition into the territory where she wanted to go with the conversation. "I've always been entranced by powerful men. I don't know if you ever met our previous king, our Rasul Appolonium, but he was certainly a man's man, and a woman's—the type of man who stirs a lady's blood and quickens her pulse, the rare sort of individual who knows exactly what he wants and goes out to get it with no hesitation or apology."

Omar was stunned at what he was hearing and he was at this point totally unable to control himself. He said, "I know Rasul very well. He's one of my oldest and closest friends. He and I have had many dealings together, and do even to this day. We have mutual friends who say that we're so much alike, we could be twins!"

"I'm not at all surprised to hear this," Hoda replied in a near whisper, and almost a purr. "You project the same strength and confidence. I can feel it. It's wonderful." Sassi was watching her mouth form these words and thinking what extraordinarily voluptuous lips she has—their shapes so perfect and distinctive. Then she said in a low and conspiratorial tone, "I've often wondered if there's any chance Rasul will come back to the kingdom."

"Yes, yes, it can be so." Omar moved even closer to Hoda and said, "He's been asking me to help him make it happen."

"Really? Oh, my. That's very exciting. What can you do to help?" Hoda asked this with a look of pleased astonishment on her face.

"Oh, I've been doing many things since I arrived, many things."

"You have?"

Hoda now gazed into Omar's eyes with an expression of great eagerness. He hesitated for a moment and then, overcome, said, "Yes. Yes. I have. In fact, I've been playing quite a game with another man and his brother, two ambitious individuals who also want to rule your kingdom. They've recruited my help, and they've paid me royally for it. But everything I do that they believe is for them is really for my old friend Rasul."

"Really? How fascinating!"

"They don't know that Rasul is after the same thing they seek. They're fools, thinking that an old friend of the powerful Rasul Appolonium would ever go into league with the likes of them, new money tycoons who have no clue what a kingship involves or requires. Our friend Rasul knows. As do I. And he's promised me great power in the second reign that's to come—I tell you, such power as you can't imagine, unless you think back to your own incredible ancestor, and the impact she's had for so long."

"Oh, my goodness, Omar, this is far beyond exciting, and wonderful," Hoda whispered.

"Yes, it is."

"You must tell me more! You must! I want to know everything!"

"I have a feeling that I'll be telling you absolutely everything in due time," Omar replied. He took a deep breath and continued, "But now I must somehow tear myself away from this wonderful moment and unique connection we're having and get you back to your friend. I can't have anyone suspecting that I've found in you a deeply kindred spirit, and perhaps even a muse for my bold endeavors. I'll ask you back again soon, and to come alone, if that's not too much to hope, and then I'll share with you in every way, and freely."

"Please, make it soon," Hoda said.

"Yes, I will," Omar assured her with a rush of excitement that he could barely contain. "In fact, it just occurred to me that, since you're friends with Shamilar, I think you may be able to help me get through to her son, and by that connection, we should be able to make some truly great things happen soon, things that will hasten the outcomes we both want to see."

"That would be so wonderful!"

"We can do it together. And I feel that there will be other things for the two of us, matters of which we must not yet speak."

"I hope so, Omar. I do. I want to hear all your thoughts, even your most secret ones. But for now, you must indeed take me back to the party."

"Yes. You're right."

"And there's just one more thing."

"Whatever you ask, my dear."

"For the moment, for my sake please, you must not touch me in an overly familiar way. It would inflame me too much, and all would be lost. I hope you can understand. I need to keep my head so that I can be of help in the things that need to be accomplished. Then there will be a time when my heart can rule and my head will nod to its greater wisdom and authority."

"Yes. Yes, dear one." Omar's own heart was racing like never before. He suddenly came to himself and said, "Oh! I almost forgot. I must ask you, in case anyone inquires about it. Please look at this section of books quickly and give me your opinion." He gestured toward a nearby bookcase.

"You're a man who desires the truth, or mere opinion?"

"Yes, I love the truth, when it's both available and convenient—and especially from such a one as you. It makes things more intimate."

Hoda stood up and gazed at the shelves that the ambassador had indicated. She stretched to reach a book on a higher shelf. He watched her movement and was overcome and touched her arm. She said, "No. Please, Omar. Don't push me over the edge. Not yet. This is not the place or time. We have great work to do."

And he came to himself again and said, "You're right. You're wise, and you're right. I can sacrifice this moment for those to come; for those incredible times that await and call out to us."

"Yes, sacrifice is often needed for the greatest things to happen." Hoda spoke quickly and then looked over the book she had pulled down. She flipped a few pages and glanced back up at the other shelves for a few seconds, and then returned the book to its proper place. Omar stared at her profile again as she did so. And she spoke again. "These books are all important classics and will be useful in the education of your son. You should keep them and use them. You should also encourage him to take them and read them." She paused and ran a finger down the spine of one volume and said, "I see a few that a man such as you would relish."

He noticed the title on which her hand now rested. She slowly tugged it out from its lower shelf and held it silently for a moment, and then she gently stroked its edges with a single finger that traced its shape. He took her meaning with an additional burst of inner excitement and, after a moment of speechless near paralysis, said, "Thank you, my stunning new friend and my advisor. I thank you from the depths of my heart."

"Yes." She spoke just the one word.

And then he continued. "Now, against the full magnetism of desire that pulls me in another direction with the greatest force I've ever felt, I must do what's right for the long term, for the future, our future, and escort you in a gentlemanly way back to your friend." He reached out to take the book from her that she was holding, and carefully placed it on a table next to them, where he could consult it later.

Hoda then said, "Thank you, Omar. You're a man who knows how to get what you need and what you deserve. You will receive everything you deserve very soon. And I will exult in it."

17

A Night and a Day

"You were certainly right about the ambassador, Your Majesty." Hoda had stopped by the palace after the formal tea with Shamilar Adi and Omar Sassi, and had just entered the king's office. Rahib her driver was waiting with the car to take her home after she had a quick meeting to report on what she had learned.

The king sighed and said, "That's too bad. Please, take a seat and tell me what happened. I hope it wasn't too unpleasant for you."

"No. It was much easier than I thought. He's a man with very little self-control in these matters," Hoda said. "He actually had a bit more discipline over himself than I had suspected, but not enough to prevent our plan from getting its start." She then went on to recount the sequence of events at the ambassador's home, including the entirety of their conversation.

"Oh, my. Well done, indeed," the king commented. "This is extremely important information, with quite a surprising twist that I didn't expect. By any chance, did the ambassador intimate any imminent threats to the palace or to any of us personally? Did he give away what might be coming next?"

"No. It didn't get to that point. But I'm sure things are ongoing and that we should continue to be on our guard. If I may ask, Your Majesty, what can be done about this awful man?"

"I hesitate to do anything immediately, except to watch him. We're in a position of strength right now, since we know some of the most crucial aspects of his involvement, and none of the men who are the ultimate threats to our kingdom are aware that we know. We may be able to use this position of knowledge to thwart their plans."

"Good. I just want to reassure you that I'll be available for more information gathering, if more is needed, however unpleasant."

"Thank you, Hoda. You're in a unique position to uncover things for us, and I appreciate your willingness to be put in such uncomfortable situations for the greater good. If I didn't know your abilities to take care of yourself, of course, I'd never ask such things of you."

"I'm fully aware of that, Ali, and appreciate your concern. You and I understand each other well, and we both want what's vital for the good we seek. I'm keen to do my part to help defeat these enemies of the nation. And I know how to keep a man like Sassi in line."

"You're sure it's not too compromising a situation to be in?"

"His eyes can't take from me anything I'm not willing to give for our purposes and, as you know, he's otherwise unable to take anything from me at all, including my inner peace and comfort."

"Yes. That's why I knew you could help us in a distinctive way."

After a few more words between the two of them, Hoda departed and returned home to a dinner that had been prepared by Khalid. They talked of her ride in the king's car, her time with Shamilar, the ambassador's home, the décor, the books in his library, and the many guests who were at this quite festive occasion.

"Oh, on another topic," Hoda said, "I've been meaning to ask. Are you, my good man, making all your final preparations for the big trip the day after tomorrow?"

"Yes, yes indeed," Khalid replied with a smile. I've set everything up with the hotel in Alexandria and I've confirmed that they'll be ready for us. The tour guide is all lined up. The king's transportation people have the barge ready for us, and food's going to be prepared and put on board for our cruise right before departure. The train for the return trip has also been reserved. And I've done all the reading I had planned to do in advance, so that I can be a fully prepared expert on all things Alexandrian."

"Have you learned anything surprising?"

"Yes, as a matter of fact. I have to admit that I was surprised to learn how many philosophers were in Alexandria in former times and how ecumenical and urbane the atmosphere could be."

"Well, apart from the truly unfortunate fate of that great lady philosopher, Hypatia whom you can claim as a distant relative."

"Yes, and I'm proud to make the claim. But her fate was a really unprecedented and awful anomaly in the fair city, and mostly due to an ignorant and inflamed mob of people from out of town who had come into Alexandria precisely for the sake of making trouble."

"True. I do think it would have been at most times a great place to visit, just to sit in on all the amazing conversations," Hoda said.

"I was thinking the same thing. I wish we could recreate that in the present day, and here in Cairo."

"Well, there are a few great minds, and quite a number of impressive scholars at the university."

"True, but I don't think they get together to talk as scholars did in the old days. They teach their classes and write, and just stick to their individual routines without as much fertile give and take among themselves, as was once the norm."

"Surely there are exceptions."

"Perhaps a few. But I've even heard that the only time most of them sit and talk to each other at all is at departmental meetings when they decide issues like hiring and promoting and adding new classes to their offerings. They don't really share ideas to the extent that they once did. They don't have a place, or even much of an inclination, it seems, to gather and discuss the deeper issues in life like the ancients."

"That's too bad. But I hope it's something that can change," Hoda said. "You know, when the boys in your class and the girls in mine get a little older, it could be that they'll offer our fair city the spark it needs to create a new culture of books and ideas. They're so energetically engaged in the grand enterprise of learning together. I'm often surprised at how deep they'll go."

"You're right. We do have some pretty thoughtful and sharp kids in our classes right now. The boys spark a lot of great conversations and keep me on my toes constantly," Khalid said with a smile.

"I think this trip will play an important role in getting them to talk and think together even more," Hoda said.

"I agree." Khalid began clearing the table of dishes and said, "So, how did you like dinner? Be thoroughly honest, completely candid."

"It was excellent! Much more than could ever reasonably be expected from a trained philosopher in the kitchen."

"I cook, therefore I am."

"You eat, therefore you are … a little more than a year ago," Hoda replied with a laugh, patting her own flat and muscular tummy but referring, of course, to his.

Khalid laughed. "Hey, my being takes up the perfect amount of space. You're looking at a man who's fit as a fiddle, whatever that means, or at least a cello—and no, don't say anything about a double bass." Hoda laughed, and then Khalid yawned really big, and said, "But, fit or fat as I might be, I'm certainly tired, and therefore I yawn."

"Me too," Hoda replied. "It's been a long day. Let's get to bed early so we can begin the new day with energy and effectiveness."

"Good idea. Is Layla planning to take Kissa to school tomorrow with Hasina?"

"Yes, it's one of their normal sleepovers, with all the extras."

"Ok, good. So, there will be no young person around to make fun of us tonight for going to sleep so early."

"I think even Kissa would agree that you definitely need your beauty rest tonight, and all of it that you can get," Hoda said playfully.

"Ha, ha," Khalid replied. "I'll have you know that when I lie down, the pillow whispers to me completely unsolicited compliments about my handsome and nearly ageless countenance."

"So, now you're hearing things, too, and believing as a result that even the furniture's smitten with you. Old age is playing its share of tricks on your mind, my friend."

"Middle age, I insist," Khalid responded with a grin. "And even the very earliest middle age, at most."

"Well, then, you still have a lot to look forward to," Hoda said, "and so does your pillow." Then she added, "I'll be back in here to help you clean up in a few minutes. I need just a moment of meditation."

"Ok, great. But don't linger too long in your timeless state of mindfulness. Remember, I'm getting older by the second, unlike you, and will need even more help cleaning up as I increasingly succumb to the manifold vicissitudes of age while the flow of time here in the kitchen continues to run down life's drain."

"Don't worry, my poetic and very early middle aged friend. I'll be back in here with you within fifteen minutes. And even those marks of the clock I can persuade not to lay a hand you. I'll find you as young as you are at this moment. You can rest easy, and even take a rest until I'm finished, if you'd like."

"Actually, I have something I wrote today that I'd like to look over for a few minutes and reconsider while you tune in to the Great Beyond. Then, come get me, once you're renewed. I'd love to wash and dry together, which the warmth of your presence will only assist." Hoda laughed and gave him a kiss on the cheek, and walked out of the room.

In the ambassador's private office at the Tunisian embassy, Omar Sassi's chief of staff had just informed his boss that two of their most trusted associates were missing. They had gone out to a late lunch on their scheduled day off and now, a good deal more than twenty-four hours later, they had not returned to the embassy or to their rooms. The last thing on their schedule had been a meeting with a gentleman who was well known in certain circles. But, so far as it could be determined, he was also missing. Or, at least, his current whereabouts were not known by any of the people who would ordinarily keep up with him. The chief of staff was concerned, but the ambassador tried to rationalize it all and dismiss it from his thoughts.

Admittedly, this bit of unexpected news puzzled Sassi, but it didn't yet alarm him. "Perhaps they're personally pursuing the matter I assigned them, in league with their new partner, and it requires a temporary disappearance," he said. And he added, "We don't know otherwise, and we shouldn't worry about it." But he did note to himself that it was unusual not to have heard from them at all. Yet, the assignment they were on was extra sensitive and might not allow for communication back to the embassy or the official residence. He would sit tight a bit longer before allowing himself the distraction of real concern.

His chief of staff, by contrast, was clearly agitated. "What do I say if I receive a call … from out of town?"

"You say that everything is proceeding as planned."

"But how should I respond if I'm asked for details?"

"You tell them that we're taking care of all the details."

"But."

"You tell them that everything's underway, and we'll report back at opportune times to let them know what's been accomplished."

"The last time we talked, they seemed to be in a big hurry and pressured me considerably."

"If that happens again, then all you do is reassure them that good things take time, and that proper results are worth waiting for. I've learned that in many areas of my life. We care about this as much as they do. Remind them of that. They've succeeded in making their plans our top priority and concern, and that's not going to change. Tell them that, as well."

"And if they still press for more?"

"End the call. Hang up mid sentence."

"Really?"

"Yes. The telephone lines between us are not at all reliable. And remember this: These men are not the power we serve. But we need to keep the illusion intact as well as we can for the meantime. Soon, though, no such pretense will be necessary."

It had been an eventful day in and around the palace. Walid and Mafulla had gone down to Walid's room after all the excitement with the intruder, and had just hung out for a while and talked about recent developments, speculated about the future, and joked a lot about the upcoming boat trip. Then, the best friend of the prince said good night, went down to his room, and just collapsed into the bed. Both boys fell asleep quickly and slept well.

The evening was a blank void for Walid. But Mafulla dreamed of a small red book. He saw it on a shelf in a huge room of bookshelves that seemed to go on and on and on. Then he looked back at the place the book had been, and it was gone. A slender volume that had been beside it now leaned over its empty space and touched another book that had been to its left. It just wasn't there.

Then the scene changed. The red book reappeared on a much shorter shelf in a vastly smaller space. This was a home library inside a grand house in Alexandria. How Mafulla knew that within the borders of the dream, he had no idea—but that's where it was. Then he saw through the window some flames at a distance, giant flames and smoke. He could see the book, and through the window, the fire, and somehow he knew that the original shelf and those two small companion books would soon be gone. The red book alone would survive from that shelf and that room. But: why? Was it random happenstance? An accident? Meaningless probability? No. There was a feeling within the dream. There was … something more, something significant and important, even vitally necessary about this book and its survival. It had to last. It was meant to be. But the dream itself would not give up the mystery as to why.

The sight of the book and the feeling of its value stayed with Mafulla after he awoke, and it would haunt him now and then for two days. But he didn't say anything about it. He thought he had nothing solid or specific to tell. It didn't strike him as anything that should be told to Walid or reported to the king. There were no threats or dangers associated with what he had seen. It was just an odd little dream. A couple of times though, when it came to mind, he started to mention it to his best friend, but on both occasions something happened to interrupt his train of thought, and he never said anything.

The new morning had dawned full of expectations for the class trip, now just a little more than twenty-four hours away. Walid and Mafulla were determined to enjoy this entire day, devoid of incident, bereft of criminals, and utterly without any enemies of the kingdom to tangle with and subdue. A quick, early breakfast gave them plenty of time for a little football outside with Malik and Haji before classes started for the morning. It was a time of fun, physical exercise, and good companionship that they all had needed.

Walid reinforced to these friends how important their discovery of the new tunnel had been. He told them briefly the whole story about how the king had recently received some information that there might be a second tunnel onto the palace grounds, but that all searches had been without success until their discovery. He emphasized, again, that they were genuine heroes for having found the tunnel, as well as for capturing the guy who had been using it, and he repeated that he knew the king was indeed proud of them and immensely grateful.

This was really nice for the two boys to hear. Like some of their friends, they had often admired from a distance the things that Walid and Mafulla were able to do for the kingdom. And they each had sometimes felt a little sidelined, a bit like they were on the edge of exciting things but never in the middle of it all. It would go too far to say they were jealous of Walid and Mafulla, because they had good hearts and would never allow anything like the corrosive poison of envy to take root in their feelings. But they often had wistful thoughts about the greater role in kingdom events that the prince and his best friend played. And yet, at the same time, they had seen clearly what happened when their classmates Jabari and Set had changed places with Walid and Mafulla for just a day, and it obviously wasn't all wonderful, by any means. So, there was some small bit of complexity in their attitudes toward their classmates. But, deep down, they knew Walid and Mafulla were good guys, and they liked both of them a lot. They had nothing but positive feelings for the two of them as people. Plus, both Malik and Haji had been raised to be loyal to the true monarchy and the kingdom, and they knew they'd always be loyal to Walid, as he took on even more official duties in the coming years.

Their time outside before class was great, and it was needed. It was probably the longest stretch of football or anything they had ever experienced together, just the four of them. They laughed a lot, and all showed impressive levels of skill in ball movement and game tactics. Walid was impressed with how strong Haji and Malik were, as well. But then he remembered that growing up with fathers like Masoon and Hamid would likely have encouraged exercise and various forms of strength training.

Class was fun that day, as well. Khalid was in good spirits, and their lessons seemed to roll by at an extra fast pace. Everybody was excited about the upcoming trip, and the jokes were flying around about Jabari and his personal flying monkey. The cool thing was that Khalid had given Jabari official permission to bring Manni along, the view being that you never knew when a wild monkey might come in handy. Jabari just had to agree to several sensible rules, along with a promise that he would be careful with his pet, and all would be well. His good friend Set would back him up as monkey handler, and no one else would have to worry about Manni wandering away or taking a swim off the side of the boat, or just generally getting into trouble.

Lunch went quickly and their afternoon lessons focused on philosophy, which was a topic that all the boys typically enjoyed, especially the way Khalid taught it. And the topic, by chance, was luck, or chance. The boys debated whether there is any such thing as random luck, or whether everything happens for a reason, either seen or unseen, known or unknown. The class was pretty evenly divided on this one, and the discussion was lively.

They had learned how to argue a point in the philosophical way, so that no one took a criticism or objection personally, since they all realized that they were in a mutual search for truth. To argue for your point of view was just to state how things struck you at present, and to marshal reasons in support of that view. But as Khalid had taught the boys, there was absolutely no embarrassment whatsoever in listening to contrary views and taking in new information, and perhaps revising or giving up a claim in light of what others were saying. That could signal a very positive development of intellectual progress and be an important part of the learning curve toward new insight. The point of debate is to marshal the resources of many minds together and attain a perspective that might otherwise be elusive.

Most people don't understand this at all, and assume that any argument is like a fight where there has to be a winner and a loser. But there would be no such thing as modern science, successful business, or effective government if sincere, intelligent people hadn't learned how to argue properly and reason together from something like an open and even relatively objective mindset. It's fine to advocate a point of view or perspective, or hypothesis, and in fact it can be important to do so when you believe it might get you closer to the truth, but it's always equally important to test that point of view and elicit the help of others in evaluating it. That way, you can see whether it can withstand scrutiny, or will rather wither or change in the face of opposing argument. The winner then, ideally, is the truth revealed in the end, not one of the people in the debate.

The classroom discussion got into issues of human free will and determinism, fate, destiny, and many other things that fascinated all the boys. Is luck an objective category, or merely a matter of perception? If it was an objective thing, Set argued, there couldn't be total determinism in the world. There would have to be undetermined, pure chance, or randomness. Jabari agreed and suggested that there couldn't be universal determinism anyway, since they all had free will, and true freedom is impossible in a world where everything is caused by impersonal forces to happen just as it does. And once you deny determinism, then chance has a chance to rush in along with freedom and provide, on some occasions, what we call luck, good or bad, for the people it affects. But it's also possible, Khalid explained, to deny both determinism and chance. In principle, it could be that all non-determined events in the world are not random, or chance events, but are rather the actions of free will.

Khalid also pointed out that some advocates of determinism, impressed with a picture of the world as in many ways like a huge machine, argued that our strong intuitive feeling of freedom must be illusory. Their perspective is that, ultimately, all our thoughts are determined by the functions of our brains, and that brain events are nothing more than physical things that are all caused or determined by the natural forces impinging on us at each moment. Thus, any apparent choice, as a thought, must be determined by forces outside us, and not free.

The boys asked how believers in free will might answer such reasoning. Khalid explained that most philosophical advocates of freedom would simply draw attention to the fact that our own sense of free will is something we experience with a strong degree of directness, vividness, and even certainty that greatly exceeds the directness, vividness, or certainty of any premises that lead to a conclusion that there is no real freedom. And they would then draw attention to a basic rule of reason that it can never be rational to abandon a belief that's certain, or compelling for a contrary one that's less certain and less compelling, all things considered. To overturn such a widespread and forceful affirmation as the belief in free will, a critic needs an argument built on more forceful premises and ending with an even more certain conclusion.

Mafulla then asked whether many people hadn't for a long time far in the past felt very sure that the world is basically flat—and been very wrong in that certainty. So couldn't the determinist suggest that we can also be wrong about our basic freedom?

Khalid had an interesting answer. He said that you shouldn't just compare your initial feelings about a developed view with your feelings about its opposite. But instead, you should construct the best argument you can for each view, and then compare the premises or steps of the arguments for how compelling they might be individually, as well as in total, along with a consideration of all the available evidence. The earth still looks relatively flat to us, he suggested, but a thorough consideration of all the relevant evidence and steps of argumentation for deciding the issue eventually led, step-by-step to our current understanding of the earth's shape. What immediately seems true is not always a good guide to what is true, but is always a sensible starting point for asking questions and gathering evidence.

Walid then suggested that there might be deep connections between things and a sort of purposiveness behind apparently coincidental events, without this at all indicating that everything is connected in a fully deterministic way. Deep patterns that go beyond the surfaces of things can still allow for genuine freedom in our responses to them. Mafulla then advanced the idea that true free will might not be either as illusory as some think, or as extensive as others believe. On that view, we're truly free, but not as often or as continuously as we might normally tend to think.

In the middle of all this, Khalid looked down at his watch and said, "Oh! Bad Luck! I just, by chance, looked at my watch and realized that it's time for us to go. And I can't let this wonderful discussion deterministically make any of us late because of how much we all may yet have to do in order to be ready first thing in the morning for our freely chosen excursion. So, therefore, class, it's hereby decreed, whether by fate or me, I'll leave you to decide: Class is dismissed."

And, for the first time ever, Khalid heard a lot of the boys say things like, "Oh, man!" or, "No, not now! Or, "Geez, just when it was getting good!" And he was glad to hear such forms of friendly complaint.

He reassured them all that there would be plenty of time to continue their conversations on the barge in the morning, and shooed them out of the classroom and into the rest of their day. In the hall, Mafulla and Walid went in the direction opposite from that taken by the rest of the boys. There were various goodbyes and Malik yelled "See you later!" to them both.

Mafulla turned to Walid and said, "I was just thinking. You know, it was impressive what Malik and Haji did to get that fake gardener guy subdued and in ropes. Plus, they were pretty brave to explore the tunnel by themselves in the first place. They're more like us than I realized."

"Well, remember who their dads are," Walid said.

"True."

"I'm sure Masoon has taught Haji a lot, and Hamid has shared a bunch of skill and life attitudes with Malik as well."

"Good point. I keep forgetting that. I wonder why they're not our brothers in Phi."

"We don't know that they aren't."

"Why don't we just ask?"

"I don't think we're supposed to."

"Why not?"

"Well, I've got the feeling that the king tells us what he thinks we need to know and when he thinks we need to know it, and he's surely in a better position than we are to decide."

"Yeah. I keep forgetting that the king hasn't shared everything about Phi with us, generally—just what we now need to know."

"Yeah. And even if Malik and Haji aren't literally Phi, that still leaves a lot of room for them to be great allies for us to have. I mean, when you think about what we saw Set and Jabari do to fight the bad guys, and what we now know that Kissa and Hasina can do ... well, we're sort of surrounded by some pretty impressive friends."

"Yeah, we are," Mafulla agreed. "And we may need all of them on our side sooner rather than later."

"You got that right."

"Ok, this has nothing to do with anything," Mafulla said, "but I had a strange dream last night."

"Did anything bad happen to anybody we know?" Walid asked this right away because of their history with Mafulla's dreams.

"No, it was nothing like that," he answered. "I just dreamed about a little book."

"A book?"

"Yeah, a small red book. There was this book in a big room, like that huge Royal Library in Alexandria we've been talking about in class. Then it was gone."

"The book?"

"Yeah. And there was a new scene in the dream. The book was in what looked like a private library, on a smaller shelf, and I could see it. And I noticed a window nearby and through it I caught sight of a big fire at a distance—really gigantic, with huge flames and smoke.

"You think that was the famous fire?"

"I do. It was so clear. The great library was burning, and the dream showed me that this little book had survived, and that it's somehow important."

"Did it look like a modern book—you know, with hard covers and paper pages inside?"

"Yes."

"But the books in the great library weren't like books now. They were on papyrus rolls, right?"

"Yeah, sure, but a dream can be symbolic."

"Ok."

"I saw a modern book that, I don't know, maybe represented an original papyrus scroll that might have eventually been recopied at some time and made into the form of what's now a modern book."

"I see. So is it a book that we need to find while we're visiting Alexandria tomorrow?"

"I don't know."

"What's it about? Did you see a title?"

"Yeah. I think it was, 'The Superior Intellect of Mafulla Adi,' but I could be wrong. However, according to the title itself, that would be unlikely."

"Quit kidding."

"Ok. Then the answer is: No. I have no idea what the title was or what it's about. It's sort of red, or orange or reddish orange, or maybe a little more like orangey red. Mostly red."

"I get the idea," Walid said. "I think we should take this seriously. We should take all your dreams seriously."

"I take the ones very seriously that feature the lovely Hasina."

"Yeah, I'm sure you do. But this one, too, should be given a good measure of attention and consideration. Let's tell the king."

"Tell him what?"

"Just what you've been telling me."

"But we don't know what it means."

"That's why we'll tell him. He might know."

"Oh, Ok. That makes sense," Mafulla said. "And once again we have a clear indication of why you're the prince, and despite the possible magnitude of my overall intellect, I'm just the sidekick."

"Hey, there's no 'just' about it. You're the one who has the weird dreams that are so important for all the rest of us to hear."

"True. I am an unbelievable source of oddly strange and often even useful information."

"Oddly strange. Yes. You are. And as such, as well as for many other reasons, you're both exalted and indispensible …and sometimes indecipherable, especially when you verge on the oracular."

"Oh! Oracular. Ok, see? I told you."

"See you told me what?"

"This is, again, why you're the prince, and I'm the very important, exalted, crucial, occasionally indecipherable, almost oracular, and absolutely indispensible sidekick."

"Yeah, so be careful never to get dispensed," Walid said.

"Or, even fully deciphered. I promise," Mafulla replied with his double eyebrow jump.

By that time, they had bounded up the staircase to the wing with the private quarters of the royal family, and there stood Walid's mother, Bhati, and Hasina's mother, Layla.

"Oh, hello, Walid's mother and Hasina's Mother—or should I say, 'Mrs. Mothers,' to be appropriately appropriate?" Mafulla did a deep bow and the ladies both smiled.

"Hi, Mom," Walid said, "It's been three days since I've seen you or Dad at all!"

"Yes, it has! I've been really busy on a project with Layla."

"The big charity?"

"Yes. That's the one. And your father has been taking care of all the annual physicals for the palace staff and the top executives of the monarchy. We've hardly had a chance to catch our breath! How are you doing, best and dearest son of mine?"

"Very well, best and dearest mother of mine," Walid said.

"And you, Mafulla?"

"Very well, as well, or as well as I can tell," Mafulla answered, and grinned at them both.

"We have the big trip tomorrow," Walid said to his mother.

"Yes! The barge trip to Alexandria! I hope you have such fun! It seems like forever since your father and I were up that way. Alexandria is a fascinating place. I think you'll enjoy your short adventure to our former capital city."

"Good. We're actually hoping it won't be quite as adventurous as our last and only joint class trip—the overly exciting train-ride to Memphis."

"We all hope for that," Bhati said.

Layla then added, "Hasina told me all about the excitement of your recent walk in the marketplace. It seems like, whenever the four of you are out anywhere, some very crazy things tend to happen. So, be ever aware."

"We always are," Walid said. "And it's because you're right. A few crazy things and people seem to follow us around, any time we leave the palace gates, and even on occasion inside the gates."

"I know," Layla said. "It's a good reason for each of you to be cautious at all times."

"Careful is always good," Bhati said. "Now, give me a hug. We're off to a meeting. Let me know as soon as you get back from Alexandria!"

"I will," Walid said and put both arms tightly around his mother.

"Ok, I get to hug you, Mafulla," Layla said.

"Really?"

"Yes! You need a hug, too—a Bon Voyage hug. Come and be hugged! And take good care of Hasina on the trip!"

"I will!" Mafulla said, as he hugged Layla, or rather, in a flash of shyness, let her hug him. "We'll see you soon and bring back lots of good stories."

"Please do," Layla said. "We love good stories."

The ladies went down the staircase and Mafulla turned to his friend and said, "Like mother, like daughter."

"What do you mean?" Walid asked.

"Beautiful ladies clearly can't keep their hands off me."

"Ha!"

18

From the Palace to the Docks

"Darwishi! Hi." Walid had just walked into the palace garage and he saw the head driver polishing the hood of a gleaming sedan.

"Good morning, Prince Walid. How are you today?"

"Fine! I hope you are."

"Yes, indeed, fine and dandy. Are you and your friends excited about today's trip?"

"Very much so," Walid replied.

"I'm glad. It's a beautiful day for a river cruise. By the way, where's Mafulla? I never see the two of you apart."

"Oh, he's with the girls, right over there."' Walid pointed to his friend at the opposite end of the large garage, surrounded by four or five members of the girls' class, all laughing at something he had just said. Dar and Walid then caught sight of him making a big gesture in the air and they heard laughter burst out again.

"I see he has quite a way with the ladies," Darwishi said.

Walid took a deep breath and let it out. "Yes, yes he does. He keeps saying that if I'm around him enough, it'll one day rub off on me, but I'm not so sure."

The king's driver laughed and said, "You can't fool me, Your Highness. I've often seen you in the company of the most lovely and gracious Miss El-Bay. No more popularity than that is ever required, or even possible, throughout the entirety of a gentleman's lifetime."

"Yeah, you're right," Walid said with a smile. "I'm very lucky, or fortunate, or just blessed." More laughter was coming from the direction of Mafulla, and Walid said, "I'd better go and break this up. Otherwise, we'll never be ready to go on time, and that would be bad, despite how fully entertained the ladies might be."

"Yes. You're a wise man to think ahead."

"Thanks. But of course, I'm not worried about Mafulla. With the reception he's getting now, even if he missed the boat altogether, he could probably walk on the water all the way to Alexandria."

At that, Darwishi laughed loudly and said, "I think you're probably correct again, Prince. You'd better go rescue him from his own success. Otherwise, it will indeed go to his head and, as you say, perhaps even to his feet."

Walid walked down toward where Mafulla was holding court, and patted Malik on the back as he passed him. "Hey, man."

"Hey, Prince."

Then, coming up behind his best friend and waving a small and silent greeting to the girls, Walid spoke over a new wave of laughter and said, "With all the commotion down here, I thought the real Caesar had joined us for our trip down the Nile."

"There's no one here who is named after a salad," Mafulla turned and replied in a serious tone.

"Very funny, my friend. But the salad was created just ten years ago by another Caesar, an Italian guy with restaurants in America and Mexico, Caesar Cardini."

"Ok, how do you know that?" Mafulla asked, and Walid just smiled. Then he added, "No, really. That's a factoid worthy of me. Where in the world did you pick it up?"

Kissa said, "My brother taught Walid all he knows about salads." She had just walked up to the group and overheard the strange topic of the moment.

"Yeah, Kissa's right. I was talking to Baqid one day about food and he regaled me with the history of salads. I would love to tell you all about it. Lettuce discuss it further." Walid, of course, emphasized the word 'lettuce' as he said this. And that led to a big grin on Mafulla's face.

"Oh, cheese, that's good. I'm ready. Let me egg you on. Pepper us with the facts. Come on endive into it! I mean olive for this sort of thing! No, really. Oil eat up every bit of it, every crumb of information you can dish out. Serve it up! Bowl us over. And don't be so slaw about it." There were groans all around, mixed with a few laughs. Mafulla then paused and made a funny face and said, "I can tell that being around me is paying off for you, my comic friend, and of course, for the rest of us as well, especially those who truly relish good food humor. I have to admit, I'm a—may-onaissed."

"Ok, that was a bit of a stretch."

"Hey! Don't criticize my salad humor, these fresh jokes I've just tossed off. Peas! I beg of you. Otherwise, I'll have to withhold, until later today or tomato, all the other jokes that romaine in my head."

"This gag is making me gag."

"No! It would be awful if you artichoke on my puns."

The girls and Walid smiled at that, and shook their heads, or made faces.

Just then, Jabari walked up with an overnight bag and a back-pack. "Hi, everybody!"

"Jabari!" Mafulla said, "Is our very favorite simian all ready for the trip and suitably excited?"

"Yes! I sure am!"

Mafulla laughed and then said, "I mean the other one, the slightly smaller and more intellectually astute one."

"Oh! Of course! All ready for the cruise, comfortably ensconced in his favorite backpack, and astute as always!"

"He's so cute!" One of the girls bent down to look at him.

Mafulla then also bent over to peek into the pack and said, in a formal and louder than necessary voice, "Manni—on behalf of both classes, I would like to officially welcome you to our second class trip. Please keep your hands inside the boat at all times, and refrain from biting or scratching anyone who is not clearly a bad guy, or a personal irritant to me."

A little screech came from the bag, and everyone laughed.

"You two communicate pretty well," Jabari said.

"They came from the same tree," Walid replied, and added: "I believe they were last seen in the wild, fighting over a banana."

"Very funny," Mafulla said. I just cut it in half for him. We both like a good banana … split."

Everyone reacted to that with appropriate grimaces and other funny faces.

"Usually, I scream for one just like he does – get it? I scream … ice cream—as in … a main ingredient for … Man, this is one tough crowd today! Come on!"

There were several chuckles and groans among the gathered students and a few humorous comments, as they watched Mafulla go through this, one of his classic impromptu routines. Walid laughed, too, but inwardly he knew that Mafulla was nervous about some aspect of the trip, and that was going to be worth talking about.

Khalid and Hoda walked up, and Khalid said in a loud voice, "Ok, everyone, it's time to load up. Pick a car and put your stuff either in the trunk or on the floorboard in front of where you'll sit. It's only about a ten minute drive down to the dock."

Mafulla turned to Kissa and said, "Where's Hasina?"

Kissa answered, "She said she might be a few minutes late this morning, but not too late."

"I hope she gets here soon!"

"She should be here any minute."

Mafulla then turned and looked toward where Khalid was

standing and said, "Professor! We need to wait for the honorable and studious Hasina!"

"Don't worry, Mafulla, she's on the way. She'll be here momentarily. We won't leave without her. But we do need to load up."

"Ok, loading up," Mafulla said and touched Walid's arm. "Let's get a car and save the lovely lady a place."

"Will do," Walid replied. "And I think our car's already been assigned."

Kissa turned to the prince and said, "Could you help me with one of these bags? I'm balancing more than I realized."

"Sure. No problem." He picked up Kissa's main overnight bag and led the way to the car in which he was supposed to ride. A palace guard had waved him in its direction. Once they had put their bags in the trunk and had chosen their seats inside, a smiling Hasina pulled open a door and jumped in.

"Hello, friends and family! You weren't going to leave without me, I hope!"

"Not at all," Walid said.

"No way!" Mafulla chirped in. "I had already talked to Khalid about holding the cars, the boat, and the tides if need be. Alexandria will wait, I told him—it's been waiting for centuries already—a few extra minutes won't mean a thing."

"Well, I thank you, kind sir," Hasina said.

As the cars loaded with students, teachers, and security escorts began to pull out of the garage, Kissa let out a deep breath and said, "I hope this trip isn't nearly as eventful or as filled with adventure as the last one."

"We've sure kept it secret," Walid said. "And this time, there aren't any bad guys hanging around the garage to find out about it."

"It also looks like the king has provided even more security today than last time," Hasina observed.

"Yeah, and you won't believe what's waiting for us at the docks," Walid replied. "Uncle Ali told me. Nobody's taking any chances now."

"Ok," Mafulla said, looking at Hasina. "We're officially on the road. So we can begin."

"Begin what?"

"I have a secret. I'm thinking of a number between one and ten. What is it?"

Both girls started laughing. Hasina said, "Last time, it was cards. This time we're just guessing numbers?"

"I forgot the cards."

"Well, why should we do any game?"

"You're kidding, right? Tell me you're kidding. Travel and games go together like falafel and hummus, or camels and sand, or me and deep wisdom. Whenever my family travels, we play games."

"Why?"

"Why? Games engage the mind. They bring people together. They often allow me to win. And they make the time pass quickly."

Walid jumped in and pointed out, "It's only a short ride to the docks, you know."

"How many minutes?" Mafulla asked.

Walid answered, "Ten."

Then Mafulla sighed and said, "Well, that's it. You got it."

"What?"

"The number. My secret number was ten." Walid just shook his head with a smile.

"Now I have another one. Guess it."

"Three," Hasina said.

"That's right!" Mafulla said with a look and a tone that revealed how impressed he was.

Hasina said, "That was easy."

"The next?"

"Seven," Hasina answered.

"Whoa. That's correct, once more." He paused and said, "Ok. I have another one."

"One."

"Yeah. Jeepers. I shouldn't have said it."

"What?"

"I said I have another one."

"Oh. Ok, Silly."

"Next?"

"Nine."

"Next?"

"Seven again."

"Ok, something just occurred to me."

"What?"

"You're a dangerous young lady to know. I can't keep any secrets from you at all."

"Why would you want to?"

"Ah—a snappy rejoinder and a very good point all rolled into one. Plus, I suppose it stands to reason at this juncture that, if I had a reason, you would not have asked that, but already would have known."

"True enough," Hasina said. "Or at least, I'll let you go on and believe that."

Mafulla pointed at her and said, "What do you mean?"

"I don't know what everybody's thinking all the time. I don't even know what most people are thinking most of the time. It's a matter of focus. And even that won't guarantee anything."

"Yeah, it's the same for me. This thought access stuff is pretty elusive. It's real, and it's often helpful, but it's still unpredictable."

"I agree with Kissa completely on this," Walid said.

"But Kissa hasn't said anything," Mafulla replied.

"No, but she just thought something, and I agree with it."

"What?"

"Focus on her thoughts and find out for yourself."

"Oh! I know now, and I agree, too!" Hasina suddenly said with excitement in her voice.

"Ok, Ok. And so, suddenly it seems that I'm the odd man out," Mafulla said.

"You're always the odd man," Walid said with a grin.

"I see."

"But I'd never count you out."

Mafulla waved away this last comment, and he said in a fake spooky voice, "Let me concentrate. Shh." He looked at Kissa and didn't move. Then he began to move his hands around in front of him, sort of framing Kissa's face with them, and bobbing them up and down and sideways in a sort of circular motion that made Walid laugh. Hasina's eyebrows were in what commercial airline flight attendants now call "The upright and locked position," as she observed these antics, or shenanigans—she wasn't sure which.

"What?" Walid said.

"Shhh." Looking at Kissa still, Mafulla now put down his hands, smiled big, and said, "You agree that this thought access stuff is indeed a bit elusive and unpredictable, but you also think that we're all getting better at it."

"That's right," Kissa said. "You're exactly right. And so am I. See?"

"Good point. But the real question is: Why was I the last to get it? To pick up on what you were thinking."

"Well, you were most likely not focused properly, and so I helped you a bit."

"You helped me?"

"After having the thought, and when you started trying to read my mind, and were not getting a result—when it was clear that the very creative hand movement thing wasn't working at all—I concentrated on the thought again, and on sending it out to you, my brain to yours, and then, as I think you might say: Voila! You got it."

"So, I needed help."

"Apparently."

"Remedial Phi 101."

On hearing that, their driver turned around and said, "Please excuse me, Prince, and Mafulla and young ladies, and I hesitate to say this, but are you absolutely sure that you want to discuss such a topic in front of, or actually in the case at hand, in back of, but in the full hearing of, a palace driver?"

"Oops," Mafulla said and grimaced. "Good point. Thanks, Dar. My mistake."

"We wouldn't do it if it were any other driver than you. I promise," Walid said.

"Good, that's what I was hoping to hear," Darwishi said, and smiled into the rear view mirror. "You know how the king is about discretion and being careful."

"Yes, definitely," Walid replied. "Thanks for reminding us. We'll have to be more cautious."

"Yes, we'll try not to Phi-get," Mafulla said. And Walid shot a mock serious look at him in response.

"Ha! We haven't had such entertainment around here in a very long time," Darwishi said. Then he smiled again and announced, "Well, we're almost there. You can see the docks up ahead."

Within four or five minutes more, all the cars had arrived at their destination. The drivers opened the doors and pointed the students and staff to the right place on the main dock area for the royal barge that was nearby. Then they began taking out their bags and setting them down beside the cars. "Wow, that's big!" Jabari said, as soon as he saw their next ride. "That is indeed the greatest quintessential large barge of my dreams."

Mafulla walked up and, hearing this, said to Jabari, "You get a charge from a very large barge?"

"Yes, and I go positively daft for a big royal craft!" Jabari responded.

Set said, "You guys should be a comedy team and go on the road together."

"Or at least the water," Mafulla, of course, replied.

"Jabari, you're right." Khalid, who was standing nearby, commented. "This is the ultimate river cruise boat. And I think they're ready for us, so why don't we get on board?"

Walid saw Paki, Omari, Amon, and Hamid among the crowd.

He also caught a glimpse of some other palace guards he knew well, who were also in civilian clothes. But the biggest surprise of all was that Layla, Hasina's mother, was there already and waiting for them.

Walid pointed her out to his best friend and Mafulla said, "Hasina! You didn't tell me your mom was coming along!"

Hasina laughed and said, "I couldn't tell anyone, not even Kissa. She wanted it to be a surprise for Hoda. Khalid suggested just last night that she come. He had left a note at the house. That's why we were late this morning. She had to get herself ready, while helping me."

"Oh! I thought you just slept late, or something!" Mafulla said.

Walid looked around and said, "From a security point of view, you know, this is pretty impressive. I see lots of palace guards, and lots of people … with advanced defensive skills."

Darwishi turned around and said, "If you look around in the water, Prince, both in front of the barge, behind it, and to the side, you'll see more small boats that look like they have on them ordinary working men, but they're all top military in civilian clothing. I've never seen so much security. The king is very serious about protection on this trip."

"I wish he could have come along with us," Walid said.

"Me, too," Mafulla agreed.

Darwishi smiled and said, "He's always been a big fan of water travel. In fact, he wanted me to tell you that as soon as you get on the boat, go into the boathouse and ask for the royal barge director, and he'll personally make sure that you're well taken care of on the trip."

"Thanks, Dar, I'll do it," Walid said, and then added, "I'll get our bags out of the car and take them aboard."

Mafulla was back at the car, already grabbing a few of the bags to take onto the boat. All the boys were doing the same thing at their respective rides, and the girls were helping out. The barge was indeed impressive. It was painted white, with dark blue accents. It wasn't the main ceremonial royal boat, but rather one without the markings of the monarchy, one that could be used more discreetly whenever officials of the kingdom needed to travel for diplomatic purposes and not call undue attention to their presence on the water, or at their destinations. There was plenty of room for people inside, or outside on the deck. It had only a few sleeping compartments for the captain and crew, but lots of enclosed space in case the weather might become inclement.

Walid and Mafulla hauled all their own stuff and the heaviest bags from Kissa and Hasina onto the boat, and followed Khalid's directions about where to store them. Kit and Cabar talked Set and Bafur into helping with their bags, and Malik and Haji were assisting Ara, Bakat, and Khata. "I thought the teachers said to pack light," Malik said as he hefted a big bag brought by Ara.

"I did! This is light—for me, at least! I'm totally roughing it on this trip," she said and smiled.

"So far, the only person it's in any way rough for is me!" Malik replied.

"You're so sweet," Ara said.

"Hey, you should feel this one," Haji said as he hefted up Bakat's duffle bag and slung it over his shoulder. "Good thing we get lots of exercise!" He turned to the owner of the bag and said, "Are you sure this isn't going to sink the ship?"

"Ha, ha. You're very funny. How do you know it's not full of flotation devices that you'll need if the ship does sink?"

"It feels more like a bag packed with anchors."

"Very funny."

In the midst of all this merriment and complaining, Walid got his little group on board and, putting down his bag, walked over to a member of the crew who was standing next to the boat's enclosed quarters. He said, "Hi. I'm Walid. I'm supposed to introduce myself to the royal barge director as soon as I've gotten on board."

"Oh, that old guy?" The crewman said with a laugh. "I have to tell you, Your Highness, he's sort of honorary around here, but we defer to his age and experience. He knows everyone. I'm sure he'll be able to see to it that you're well cared for while you're on board." The man turned his head into the enclosed area and yelled out, "Shabby! Shabby! There's somebody here to see you." Turning back to Walid, the man said, "I hope you can overlook his rumpled and stained appearance, one of the reasons for his name. That's just the way he is. He likes to be comfortable while he's working."

Walid said, "No problem. That's fine. We're all casual today."

"Shabby! It's the prince!"

"Oh! Just a second!" Walid heard a gruff voice as a bent-over man backed out of an inner crew cabin, dragging something behind him. "I have to get this stuff out of here."

"Shabby, please, Prince Walid is here to see you."

"Ok, Ok," he said as he jerked one more time on whatever it was he had been removing from the inner cabin. He turned around, and Walid could not have possibly been more surprised.

19

A Trip Down the Nile

"Welcome aboard, young man!"

"What? I can't believe it! What are you doing here, Uncle Ali? I mean, Your Majesty!"

The king laughed loudly and then he said, "I thought this might surprise you."

Walid also laughed as well. "I couldn't be more surprised. Are you coming with us?"

"Yes, indeed, I am."

"You're amazingly good at keeping secrets, for a man who's also generally pretty down on secrets."

"But this is a good one, you have to admit."

"Yeah, you're right. It's a very good one. But, hold on for a second. Turn around again, if you don't mind, just for a moment—and of course, not for much longer. I have to share the surprise."

The king smiled knowingly and did as he was told, turning and bending down to work on something near his feet.

Walid yelled, "Hey Mafulla, Kissa, Hasina, come here a minute! Right now! Hurry!" He gestured to them in a way that made them move quickly in his direction.

"What is it?" Mafulla asked as he walked up, followed by both the girls.

"You remember that Dar wanted us to meet the director of the royal barge?"

"Yeah. Sure."

"Well, he's in here, the old guy himself, and he's worth meeting right away. They call him Shabby."

"What?"

"It's a reference to how he looks."

"Oh."

"Hey, Shabby," Walid said as he gestured toward the man's bent over back. "Say hello to my friends."

And, at that moment, Shabby straightened up and turned around to face them and said, "A warm hello to you, my friends also."

Walid burst out laughing at the look on Mafulla's face, as well as the shock and surprise shown by Kissa and Hasina as they saw that it was the king, shabby stained clothes and all.

"Your Majesty!" Mafulla said. "What are you doing here and … like this?" He darted a glance back and forth between Walid and the king and sort of generally gestured toward Ali's worn, rough clothing and context.

"Oh, I'm doing a little work on the boat for the duration of the trip. Someone has to clean up around here. Sorry, I would shake hands with you, but they're a little dirty from the morning's toil already." The king said this with a big smile as he wiped his hands against each other. "However, please, let me greet you warmly, even without the customary handshake in these circumstances." He finished with a nod of his head.

Kissa and Hasina did quick bows and, when he saw them do this, Mafulla looked back at the king, then at them, then the king, and then he did the fastest, most awkward bow anyone had ever seen. That made Walid laugh out loud again.

"What?" Mafulla objected. He then turned back to the king and said, "But wait a second, Your Majesty. You're the director of the royal barge? You? The king?"

"Shhhh." The older man said with a smile. "We should keep our voices down for now. When we cast off and get going, I'll reveal my presence to everyone. But currently, only you and the crew and, of course, all the security people know that I'm on board."

"Your secret's safe with us," Mafulla whispered a bit loudly.

"Good. Thank you. And now, I should get back to work. So, why don't you make yourselves comfortable again out on the deck, and we'll be underway soon."

"This is great—really, really great," Walid said. "Thanks for coming along … Shabby."

"Yeah, for certain," Mafulla agreed. "Shabby Shabeezar, director of the royal barge—I just can't get over it."

"Honorary director, actually," Shabby said. "They defer to my age and general life experience. But it's the captain who really knows what he's doing, fortunately for us all. Now, please, scoot, before your friends come in and discover me! And close the door behind you."

"Amazing," Mafulla said, and he shut the door once they were out. "Your uncle is full of surprises."

"I wonder if any of the Alexandrians know he's coming," Walid whispered.

"No, I bet they have no idea that … he's going to barge right in," Mafulla said, giving his little joke the patented double eyebrow jump.

"Oh, that was bad," Walid said.

"But clever, very clever as always," Hasina pointed out.

"Yes, and in fact, it's so bad, that it's actually pretty good. I admit it," Walid acknowledged.

"So, why do you think the king came along, and in a disguise?" Kissa asked.

"Well, I know he loves the water," Walid said.

"He was likely just in the mood for a rip-roaring riparian adventure," Mafulla suggested with a completely straight face.

"Once again, we have here the walking dictionary of rarely used terms," Walid commented. "Riparian—you mean, of course, having to do with rips, as in his clearly disheveled workingman garments?"

"No, no, no, my friend. I'm pleased to provide the information that riparian means having to do with rivers—and especially the banks of rivers."

"Ok, my second guess was going to be 'having to do with repairs' as in repairing rips. So, I guess, I'm aquatically challenged in my limited vocabulary."

"Yes, you're challenged aquatically, and emphatically. I'm assuming you also don't know the meaning of 'estuary' and that you wouldn't even be able to … guess-tuary."

"Ha!"

"Boys, boys," Kissa said. "I'm sure Walid has a perfectly adequate vocabulary for dry land and, in fact, much more than adequate. He probably knows twelve different words for sand."

"Well, actually …"

"Never mind. The prince is a deep thinker, nonetheless, and that's a fact," Mafulla said, while patting his friend on the back, "but perhaps more of an intellectual spelunker than a diver or sailor over more speculative seas."

"Spelunker?" Hasina said.

"I know that one," Kissa replied. "It means an underground cave explorer."

Mafulla said, "Yes!"

Kissa said, "I'm relieved."

Mafulla smiled, and then he turned to Walid and added, "However, before I completely dismiss your nautical knowledge … everyone deserves one more chance: Quick—tributary."

Walid laughed and said, "Ah! This is a no-brainer: One who gives tribute."

Mafulla exhaled loudly and said, "Yes! A no-brainer indeed! Ok, then, this is pretty hopeless. But, water you going to do? … water … Get it? Anybody? Anyone?"

"I think I'll go talk to normal people for a while," Kissa said, adding, "If you need me, just wave. Get it?"

"Ah, you're eminently able to go with the flow and channel my own particular brand of humor in its maritime branch. Very impressive," Mafulla replied. "In fact, I'm flooded with admiration—hook, line, and sinker."

"Oh, gee," Walid said with a smile and walked off with Kissa.

Mafulla looked over at Hasina and made a face. She said, "Don't worry about them. They may think you're all wet, but I think you're very impressive. They'll sea. S-e-a. Get it?"

Oh! That's good!"

"You know how to give a girl a good time, in fact, a marvelous, merry, maritime!" she added with a grin.

"Hoo! Hoo! Very good, indeed! And I think you're a perceptive genius, a very beautiful and totally perspicacious sage of the highest order," Mafulla concluded, "with a full appreciation of anything having to do with the pelagic and thalassic side of life."

"The what?" Hasina laughed.

"Oh, yikes! I'm not even that sure, myself, other than … having to do with waterways, swimming, boating, and such. But, now, on to other topics." Mafulla gave her his most winning grin, and said, "Let's find Jabari, and see if the monkey likes being around the water, so far. There's a gentle rocking to the barge, even in dock. I don't know if monkeys ever experience something like this."

Just then, Khalid called out above all the various conversations. "Is everyone on board and settled in, and ready to go?"

"Yes!" A shout from many voices answered him.

He looked at a crewmember standing on the dock and said, "Then, let's be off!" The man lifted a thick rope, looped on the end, off a vertical piling, a large beam of wood tethering the ship to the land. And then he wrestled loose another one and ran up the short bridge to the barge, picking it up behind him with the help of a second man, as the boat slowly moved away from the dock. A cheer and scattered applause erupted from the passengers, and they were underway.

As the barge maneuvered toward the middle of the river, Walid could see six other smaller boats around them, an entire flotilla blanketing them with protection. He took a deep breath and let it out slowly with a sense of relief that, maybe, this trip would not be quite as wild and tumultuously adventurous as the last. But at the same time, a thought whispered to him in the very back of his mind that he needed to talk to Mafulla about anything he might be feeling. The prince didn't notice that, as he was looking out over the water, the man who had unhitched the barge was now turned around, looking intently at him.

Across town from the dock in Cairo, the new ambassador from Tunisia was finishing up a note to the deposed former king of Egypt. He held the pen in his hand and thought for a second and then wrote: "Two of my men have gone missing, right before the planned top operation was to begin. I have no idea what's happened to them, and no one seems to know. The proprietor of the café where they were to have their meeting says that there was some sort of scuffle, and he saw the men led off by two individuals in police uniforms, but there's no record of their presence at any of the police stations or public jails in town. The man they were to meet has also vanished, as if into thin air. I suspect some sort of foul play, of course, but have no idea who would do such a thing."

As a matter of fact, he did have some worries that the al-Khoum brothers may have guessed he was something like a double agent also serving interests other than theirs. They could now be buying off or taking out anyone implementing his plans just to confuse him or intimidate him, or somehow force his hand to slip up and perhaps reveal where his true loyalty might be. But of course, he couldn't tell the former king this in his note. And he certainly could do nothing to let the king's new associate Ari Falma come to suspect that he was also taking money from the al-Khoums, and in that way seeking to benefit from two opposed parties who probably still did not know of their mutually incompatible goals. It was a messy, delicate situation and not one to be handled bluntly or carelessly.

By writing that he suspected foul play, Omar was hoping that if Rasul had any suspicions at all about Farouk and Faraj and their possible intentions, he would take the initiative to act against them on his own. And this could happen without any possible hint that the brothers had been paying Sassi all this time to do for them most of what the former king was asking for, as well. Omar couldn't let anyone realize that he had been double dipping from rivals and thus playing both sides for maximum gain. In reality, he simply detested the al-Khoum brothers, and nearly revered the former king. But then, that was mostly because of his love for the trappings of royalty, and especially the decadent court life for which Rasul had been known.

Appolonium had always surrounded himself with the finest luxuries and beautiful companions intent on pleasing him and his friends in every way. His court life had been one long party. Sassi would be firmly in his element in such a setting, if only the former king could be restored. The al-Khoums were just, by contrast, in his mind, simple thugs—violent mobsters posing as businessmen, with endless ambitions for their own gain but no desire to share the wealth in terms of lavish living for anyone who helped them attain their goals. Life under their regime would be no party at all. But, in a newly restored Appolonium monarchy, supporters could expect one long indulgent celebration, and Sassi was sure that he would be well ensconced at the center of the festivities, every day and night. And he was accordingly determined to help that become a reality.

The ambassador finished his note by writing: "I hope that we can clear up this mystery in some way soon and get back on track. If there might be anything you can do on your end, it would be greatly appreciated. Meanwhile, I may need to find one, or possibly two, new security men here until this issue is resolved." He then signed off: "I remain, in all things, your servant and fervent supporter, looking forward to your imminent reinstatement. Faithfully, Omar."

He contemplated his words as the ink dried on the paper, then folded the sheet of thick letterhead, placed it in an envelope, and slipped it into a diplomatic pouch labeled and bound for Sea Watch House, Tripoli, Libya. He coughed and then called out to his chief of staff and said, "Hello? Hello out there! Chief! There's some business!"

The man came through the door and into the room. "Yes, sir?"

"I have something here that needs to be done."

"Not a problem." As Sassi held up the diplomatic pouch, the younger man moved forward to take it.

"Would you get this out as soon as possible? It's of the highest importance, and even urgency."

He replied, "Yes, immediately. And I also have a message for you, one that's marked 'Urgent and Personal.' It seems to have arrived only a few minutes ago." He handed Sassi the envelope.

"Thank you. Please get this letter of mine in the pouch out quickly. We can talk more later."

"Yes, indeed, right away," the man answered.

As his colleague left the room and headed for the outer door, Omar sat back down in his comfortable desk chair and took up a letter opener, noticing both the ink color choice and the handwriting script of the address, along with the markings of "Urgent and Personal" on the front of the envelope. He slit open the length of the envelope along the top and pulled out the luxuriously heavy and high quality piece of stationary it contained. His curiosity was piqued. Sassi then unfolded the sheet of paper and smoothed it on the desk pad in front of him, taking note of the elegant cursive script that spilled across the page. He focused his eyes and read the words: "My Dear Omar: I know that you're worried about your men and are looking for them. I'm doing what I can to find out anything on my end. Be careful and take steps to protect yourself. I'm on a trip now and will return soon." The letter was signed, simply: "With Anticipation, H."

Kissa walked across the deck of the ship to where Hoda and Layla were standing by themselves at the railing, apparently deep in conversation. Hoda saw her approach and smiled. Kissa said, "Hey, Mom! Hi, Layla! I had no idea we'd have the Dynamic Duo, the Terrific Twosome, the Profound Power Pair with us on this trip! I'm really glad you could come along, Layla!"

"Khalid invited me right after we saw each other yesterday, and even though it was as last minute as last minute can be, I knew I just couldn't miss the chance to do this with you," Layla said. "It's been a long time since I was on a river cruise or a boat of any kind, and I'm loving it again already."

At that moment, there was a sound of laughter from a group of students on the other side of the deck, where Jabari had just taken his monkey out of the knapsack. Manni jumped onto Jabari's shoulder, then onto the top of his head, doing a happy screech, and just as quickly, he leaped onto the nearby railing of the barge and began running along it, away from the boy. The important ten-foot leash that was attached to Manni's collar and that gave Jabari such a sense of confidence in letting him out of the bag was now the only thing keeping the little monkey controlled and safe. But it did seem secure, at least until it suddenly slipped out of Jabari's fingers, the moment Manni got far enough down the railing to pull it tight.

"Oh, no!" Jabari shouted. "Manni! Stop!" The monkey kept running, whether out of excitement or fear at these new and unexpected surroundings, no one could know. Then he suddenly jumped from the rail to a bit of deck no wider than four or five inches that stuck out under and beyond the edge of the protective railing for the full length of the barge. "No, no, no, no! Bad Monkey! Come back here right now! Manni!" Jabari was already moving toward the little guy as he shouted these words, but the alarm in his voice may have just served to frighten Manni more.

Bad situations often get worse before they get any better and so, in the spirit of this cosmic truth, everyone could see the small monkey scramble down a bit farther from the deck and onto the top of a large white life preserver that hung from the side of the boat. Now, nothing but a slippery surface and the morning air stood between Manni and the waters of the Nile. Jabari quickly climbed over the railing and, holding onto it, inched his way along the edge of the deck toward where the monkey now sat and jabbered, as if telling his owner to get him off this barge this very minute. At that point, some of the other students had run up close to where Jabari was and saw him squat down and reach out to where Manni was sitting, in order to grab him and bring him back. But, of course, in strict accordance with what we can call The Law of Bad Situations, when Jabari leaned down, he momentarily lost his balance and fell overboard into the water with a shout of "No!" but hardly a splash to mark his contact with the river.

Set yelled out, "Oh, No! Jabari can't swim! Man overboard!" He leapt over the rail to grab the top of the life preserver where Manni was now crouching and screeching loudly. "Manni, get on me!" The little monkey jumped toward Set and landed on his shoulder, clinging fast, just as he lifted the heavy life preserver off the hook that held it to the boat and with one huge swing threw it toward where the boy had hit the surface and disappeared. In a blur, two figures simultaneously dove from the side of the barge into the water.

"Jabari fell off the boat! Jabari's in the water!" Bafur yelled to anyone who would listen. "He can't swim! Stop the boat!"

Walid and Mafulla ran toward the railing near the front of the barge where some of the others had gathered. But just then, someone yelled, "To the back of the barge! We're passing him! Stop the boat! We have to stop!"

The boys turned quickly and dashed down along the railing toward the back where they saw two military escorts already dropping a dark raft into the water and rappelling fast down two ropes into it. As they passed by, Walid yelled at a member of the crew, "Somebody fell into the water and can't swim! Stop the boat!" The man ran off and, within seconds, the order was obeyed, but then of course, to some extent, the boat's forward momentum continued.

Omari and Paki were the two who had dived over the side within seconds of Jabari's fall. They were searching for him now and he had not resurfaced. Walid, looking over the side, could see the two of them come up a few seconds apart, gasp in a deep breath of air, and dive down again under the cool skin of the murky Nile. It was almost impossible for them to see anything under there. But they were doing their best to use their eyes, their arms, and their other keenly developed senses to detect the boy's location. And yet, he was nowhere to be felt or seen. Then suddenly, Mafulla and Walid saw Jabari's face appear above the water for a fraction of a second, some short distance away and just long enough for him to yell "Help!" and gasp for at least a mouthful of air.

"Over there! He's over there!" The boys pointed at the spot in the water as Jabari disappeared again beneath the surface and shouted at the two soldiers close by, "He was there! Over there! Right back there!" One paddled the raft quickly in the right direction as the other jumped into the water to join in the rescue of the young man, who was obviously in terrible distress and danger at this point.

Omari had a feeling to turn to his left and swim underwater as rapidly as possible. At that same moment, the king, who had been inside, heard the commotion and realized that someone was overboard, and now appeared on deck to find out what was being done. Most of the people on board were too focused to notice his unexpected presence among them. A few did see him and were very surprised. He quickly made his way to Walid and asked, "Who is it?"

"Jabari, and he can't swim," Walid said. "There are two or three men in the water already looking for him. He was somewhere over there, just seconds ago." The prince pointed as exactly as he could.

As soon as the king had appeared on deck from the wheelhouse of the boat, four palace guards converged on his location. He now looked up at them and said, "Who can swim well?" Two of them raised a hand. "Into the water, the two of you!" Both men dove over the side, and then the king himself followed close behind them, pushing off from the side, and he entered the water without making more than a tiny ripple. By contrast, the two guards had hit the surface of the river with a great slapping noise and created a considerable splash.

"Uncle!" Walid shouted as he saw the king leap over the railing.

"Oh, no!" Mafulla said. He looked at Walid and added, "This is too dangerous! I can't believe the king jumped in!"

Walid replied, "I can't either! Can you swim?"

"No, not really. Can you?"

"No. The king was going to teach me not long ago, but something happened and he couldn't."

Hoda, Kissa, and Hasina had seen what was going on as soon as it happened, and were all using the power of their minds to both request and provide assistance to poor Jabari himself and the men who were now risking their own lives to rescue him. Layla had started the same quiet mental and spiritual process, but then suddenly climbed over the rail before anyone could notice her, and she leapt overboard at about the same moment that the king had dived into the cloudy waters, or maybe a fraction of a second later. "Mom!" Hasina called out in shock.

Now five guards, the king, and Hasina's mother were all in the Nile, seven searchers looking intensely for young Jabari. His monkey continued to screech as Set held onto him tightly, both wrapping an arm around Manni and grasping his leash as firmly as he could. There were then more shouts from the deck as several members of the crew threw more life preservers overboard toward where the rescuers had entered the water. Another raft was being lowered as well, and three more guards were getting into it.

"They don't have long," Mafulla said.

"What do you mean?"

"They don't have long to find Jabari. I've read about this. It's hard for a non-swimmer to last very long in these conditions."

"How long?"

"Two or three minutes, maybe … a little more, possibly, if they're really lucky, but that's rare and super hard for even a well trained swimmer. The survival time gets cut down real fast if he sucks water into his lungs in a panic."

"But … he came up once for air."

"Yeah, that was good. And that sort of restarted the clock, so we're looking at maybe two to three minutes from then, but no more."

"Oh, wow," Walid said.

Just then Hamid ran up. "Where's the king?"

"He went in to try to help find Jabari." Walid answered instantly.

"Into the river?"

"Yes."

"How long ago?"

"I don't know. A minute, maybe two."

"He hasn't been back up to the surface yet?"

"No. No he hasn't."

Hamid frowned.

"Ok," he said, "I'll need your help. If anyone is brought back onto the boat in the next few minutes unconscious, I'll need you to help get that person up on to the deck and positioned as I tell you. I'll have to clear water from their lungs and restart their breathing. If their heart's stopped beating, I'll attempt to get it going again as well. And every second will count. So stay close to me in case I need your help in any way at all."

"Sure," Walid said. "We didn't know what we should do to be of help."

"If someone is brought up in distress, just do what I say, and as quickly as you possibly can."

"You think Jabari will need that?"

"Yes. And maybe more than just Jabari."

"Oh," Walid said and looked very concerned as he stared over the railing.

20

The King

"Are you absolutely sure this is a good idea, after all that's just been said?" Faraj al-Khoum looked over at his brother with skepticism. They were in the back seat of a roomy black four-door sedan, bouncing along the road between Tunis and Tripoli. Four other large cars followed them, and two trucks trailed the cars at a distance.

"Yes, as I've been telling you, it's a very good idea," Farouk replied. "I've been thinking about the old king now and then, and wondering what he's up to. When we received his invitation, my first thought was that a visit would give us a chance to assess his situation and determine if he poses any danger to our plans, or would rather like to ride our coat tails into some new situation of power or profit."

"But, as I've been saying, this whole thing could just be a trap."

"Of course. And that's why I've had you bring some of your men along with us today."

"But if it's a good enough trap, we could still be overcome, with only our small security detail."

"Why haven't you said this earlier?" Farouk was now playing a momentary little game with his brother.

Faraj said, "I just got the map of Sea Watch yesterday, quite late, and this morning I was able to determine all the ways that the king could sneak troops in to surround us—if that's what he has in mind."

"So, it has you worried?"

"Yes. It has me worried."

"That's too bad, and completely unnecessary. There's no reason for you to be worried, and I don't like to see it."

"What do you mean?"

"You have so little faith in me, brother. I was going to keep this a nice little surprise for later, but I'll tell you now to settle your worried mind." Farouk smiled in a way that could be read as friendly, or that could be seen as just condescending. Then he said, "I've received some news since the invitation came, and it's important information for which I've paid a lot of money."

"What information?"

"The former king may indeed have invited us into a trap."

"What? How do you know?"

"A well placed informant has revealed to me that Rasul is well underway with his own efforts to retake control of Egypt."

"Really? I've heard none of this."

"Yes. He will never accept what you and I want, and if he even suspects it, he will certainly try to eliminate us. Moreover, there's some reason to think that he's been informed of our goal. And if so, there will indeed be a trap. We can count on it."

"Then, why in the world are we going?"

"Because," Farouk said with a look of ultimate triumph, "I've prepared for him a better trap."

"What sort of trap?" Faraj seemed both puzzled and immensely agitated at this surprise.

"I have a small army arriving in Tripoli by boat today, under the guise of being oil workers for one of our new ventures in the area."

"You do?"

"Yes."

"How many men?"

"Roughly a hundred, and they're all well-trained, top mercenaries, provided by our friends in Tunis and Morocco. They'll look like a labor force, but their equipment will be military. They'll be positioned in such a way as to prevent any adversarial force from gaining access to Sea Watch while we're there. Plus, they will be the men who attack, and they'll take out our enemies."

"Good, that's good." Faraj said, but inwardly he felt a mix of relief, assurance, shame, resentment, and irritation toward his older brother. "Who's leading the operation? You?"

"No, no. Senior officers with vast experience are in charge, under my directives, of course. But the tactical details are of their devising. I'm sure you'd approve. It's all quite impressive."

Faraj was both puzzled and deeply offended. Why hadn't he been told earlier about this? He could have helped in the planning, or could have done it all. He really didn't have enough men under his own command, or enough authority at this stage. But he could have led this mercenary force. His brother found ways to stay in control of their most important resources, and that galled him badly. Farouk was no military man. But he thought of himself as such a great leader and never sufficiently appreciated the extensive training and military intellect of his brother. Faraj was thinking all this to himself as they continued down the dusty highway.

Then Farouk decided it was time to bring his sibling in on the full plan. He ran through some scenarios and established some signals to be used when the time was right. Faraj, at this point, could only go along, in order to secure his own physical safety and wellbeing. And so he put all his negative thoughts and feelings behind him for the moment and concentrated his efforts on making a few suggestions to fine-tune various elements of the plan, at least regarding the two of them. And they were ideas that, to his surprise, Farouk accepted.

At Sea Watch, the large mansion now being occupied by the former Egyptian king, Rasul Appolonium, Ari Falma had just entered the dining room where the king was having lunch. He walked over to the table and said, "Your Majesty, I have word of something troubling."

"Oh? What is it, my friend?"

"It's about the al-Khoum brothers."

"Are they not coming, after all?"

"No, no, they're still coming in response to your invitation. And because of that, I'll be leaving soon. I've told you that there's a history between Farouk and me, and I don't trust him at all."

"Yes, you've said that many times."

"I've warned you often that he may have his own political ascendancy as an aim."

"Yes, I know you worry about that. But as I always remind you, just as repeatedly, I've known him for years, and I can assure you that he's a businessman, not a politician."

"So far," Falma said. "But that's why this news is so troubling."

"Well then, tell me the news."

"I have reliable intelligence from a well placed informant—a man who has been richly compensated for this information—that Farouk has been paying Omar Sassi to do for him what we've been paying him to do for us."

"What?"

"Omar is working for al-Khoum as well as for us. He's a double dealing traitor."

"This can't be true."

"I've been assured that it is, and by someone who is in a good position to know."

"This is not just more of your ongoing attempt to paint our old friend al-Khoum as dangerous?"

"No. He's been hiring Omar to do work for him and to help him in the pursuit of his own goals, aims that are likely at complete odds with ours."

"This is a total shock. We're so close! What could Omar be doing for al-Khoum? What's Farouk asked of him?"

"I'm not sure, but I've heard a rumor that he's paying for the elimination of the royal family and the preparation for an attack on the palace."

"What? Why would al-Khoum want this?"

"I can assure you that it's not to reinstate your rule."

"Then what's he doing?"

"Precisely what we're doing—that's my best guess. He wants to remove the Shabeezars as much as we do. But he craves the throne for himself."

"That's impossible."

"No, I'm afraid it's very possible. He's ultimately power hungry, not money hungry. And he'll kill anyone he thinks to be in his way. The business ventures are all to provide him resources for his actual game, the grab for real power that he intends to make very soon."

"I can't believe it! I've invited him into my house for the purpose of planning alliances with him as a businessman. And he's coming here while preparing to take over my kingdom? He must be stopped."

"Yes, these are my sentiments exactly, Your Majesty. There's one rightful king of Egypt, and it's you, Majesty. I'm the one and only businessman you need at your right hand. We can take al-Khoum's resources by force, and I can provide you better guidance than he ever could. I know Egypt, and I know Cairo. That's why he once hired me—to know what he doesn't know, and do what he can't do. I have friends and associates, as you're aware, at every level there."

"But what can we do now? Farouk's on the way and will be here within mere hours."

"I say we prepare a trap for him and his brother, a surprise he'll never expect. I've even been asking around in preparation for this, in case we had to do it. And I have men available."

"You do?"

"Yes. And we're in a good position for a surprise. Farouk knows you think of him as a potential ally, and not as an enemy. He'll suspect nothing. He'll be easy prey for a simple plan. I'll alert the men I've contacted and have them in position to storm the grounds and eliminate him after he arrives, along with his brother and any top aid or security team he brings."

"Good. Your wise preparations will protect us. Thank you."

"Anything for the cause, Your Majesty."

"Make your final plans quickly, and make sure they're effective."

"I will, sire. I'm loyal to the one true sovereign of Egypt." Ari Falma walked to the door, turned, and said, "Long live the king."

On the Nile, things had gotten a bit frantic. Now, everyone left on the barge was leaning over the rail and staring down into the water. Several soldiers from the other small boats were also in the water, searching either for Jabari or the king.

"Where's the king? Has anyone seen the king?" Hamid was looking back and forth at the crowd who had been observing the water for too long now.

"The king?" Malik looked at Haji with surprise. "The king's here on the boat with us?"

"I didn't know," Haji replied. "I haven't seen him today at all, or heard anything."

"Dad! Is the king with us?" Malik shouted toward his father.

"He's in the water, looking for Jabari!"

One palace guard emerged from the deep, gasping for breath, then two other military men surfaced. They were all looking around, and, seeing nothing but each other, dove back under. Then two other men repeated their actions.

"It's been too long," Mafulla fretted. "There are limits."

"Yeah." Walid didn't know what to think.

Hamid felt a pull inside his soul. He took his hands off the railing and turned around, looking intently at the other side of the barge, where there were no spectators or members of the crew. He then slowly began to walk in that direction, almost automatically, without conscious intent. No one noticed his movements except Amon, who followed right behind him, leaving all the others peering over the side.

They quickened their pace and, arriving at the opposite rail, glanced over a part of the river on that side of the boat with no apparent activity either on it or in it. Hamid noticed a ladder on the side of the barge and, turning around, got onto it and began to descend toward the water—again, with no real thought as to why. Just two rungs down, he heard a sound. It was someone breaking the surface of the water right behind him. He twisted around to see what it was and was shocked to see the king now holding Layla, who was herself cradling a limp and unconscious Jabari. Hamid was at that moment perfectly positioned to step down one more rung and reach out to take the boy. Amon could also bend over the side to assist in bringing the small boy onto the deck. Layla, gasping for air, passed him into the king's grasp, and Ali lifted him up toward Hamid.

As Hamid was bending and reaching out to receive the boy's body, he saw past the king, behind him, and also behind and to the side of Layla a shocking sight that nearly made him lose his grip on the ladder. A large, menacing, fifteen-foot long Nile Crocodile, the royal predator of the river, was just now visible a mere three or four feet beyond the bobbing head and shoulders of Hasina's mother. As the reptile's eyes appeared above the water and the rest of his large head quickly came into sight, his huge jaws began to open wide for the unexpected meal he now planned to have.

"Layla! Behind you!" Hamid yelled as loudly as he could. She turned in time to see into the gaping mouth moving toward her, its sixty-eight teeth poised to take what this prehistoric monster had noticed in its path. There was no time for Layla to escape, and she was utterly exhausted from the underwater dive and search for Jabari—plus, she had nothing she could use for a fight.

She had first found the boy, following her intuitions to go under the barge. The king had then been quick behind her. And he had now successfully handed Jabari over to Hamid who, with the assistance being offered by Amon, was pulling him up onto the deck. The king had hardly a split second to turn around and see the attack coming. He was also without a weapon and was too far away from her now to get between the terrifying beast and his friend.

It was at that moment when time decided to slow and nearly stop for all involved. There was a fullness, a plenitude, an expanse between that second and the next one that would inevitably come, a stretched out reality that allowed for all to see a fluid snapshot of their dire and seemingly impossible situation. The sequence of events that had been transpiring was paused just enough, floating in its own cosmic bubble, for a second shape to emerge suddenly and without warning from the water.

Omari came up beside the croc and, using all his arm strength, clamped down on the jaws of the creature, forcing them shut. He didn't know the scientific truth that the musculature opening this frightful trap could be resisted from just the right angle and forced down, and yet without any conscious awareness of this fact, he spontaneously did precisely the right thing and managed to close the awful trap before it could slam down on Layla. He held it shut, shoving it to the side, and the angry predator struggled, powerfully slashing with its tail. It was all that Omari could do to hold on. The king grabbed Layla and pulled her to the ladder on the side of the barge, pushing her up onto the first visible steps. And just as he turned to go back and help Omari, Paki came up under the crocodile and his knife found the exact spot of the reptile's heart, penetrating two of its three chambers and ending its violent reaction to Omari's long, fierce embrace.

On the deck, Hamid had a limp and apparently lifeless Jabari in position and was clearing his lungs right before starting an effort at resuscitation. Layla crawled over the railing near them and the king was right behind her. They were thoroughly drenched, of course, and their clothing, which was not made for swimming, weighed them down with what felt like many pounds of water. Layla immediately saw what was going on and stretched out her hands, not to physically touch Jabari or interfere with Hamid's work, but to direct her focus and healing thoughts to him. The king walked by her and joined Hamid over the body. He took Jabari's motionless head into his hands for three or four seconds, then ran the fingers of his right hand down the boy's left arm, and ended this motion by holding his hand for a moment and then closing it into the form of a clenched fist.

Doctor Hamid was bent over Jabari with his palms on the boy's chest. He pushed downward then released, pushed again, then released, and again and then up. And he continued in this rapid rhythm as he spoke low some words that were heard by no one else around.

The moment he had pulled Jabari over the railing and put him on the deck of the barge, someone on the other side saw it and yelled, "Jabari!" It sounded like Bafur. In any case, it was the large boy who immediately ran across the deck, followed a second later by most of his friends, both boys and girls, and nearly everyone else. But seeing the body without its familiar movement, and witnessing Hamid place it carefully onto the deck, Bafur stopped in his tracks in shock. And then so did everyone else, held back as if by a force of collective surprise and fear, along with a near inability to process what they were seeing.

Omari then climbed up the ladder and jumped over the railing onto the deck and, close behind him, Paki did the same. Both of them walked toward the clustered group of students and others with their hands spread wide in front of them.

"Please stay where you are," Omari said.

"Let Hamid and the king do their work," Paki added.

"Say a prayer for our friend," Omari then suggested.

Walid was the first to go down on one knee. Mafulla followed him in this gesture. Then the others began to do so as well. First, Kissa and Hasina and Malik and Haji knelt down. Then Bafur and Set, and Ara and Khata and Cabar, and everyone on deck joined in. Without any flicker of self-consciousness, Walid then put his other knee to the deck and bowed forward and stretched his hands in front of him and down to the wood beneath them all.

No one had ever seen a prince or king in this position of humility and supplication. It was almost too much to imagine. But it instantly seemed both right and powerful, and they all then saw Walid in a new light, and yet one that was deeply continuous with how they already viewed him. And still, this physical posture of his and what it connoted took them all to a new place in their estimation of who this young man is, what he values, and what he might ultimately be able to do.

After a second in which they all took this in and quickly pondered their instinctive reaction to it, every single person on that deck followed along Walid's path and humbled themselves and asked and opened their hearts and directed their love and concern and faith toward the need of their friend. And a soft breeze blew across the deck.

Hoda created a small opening within her spirit and enlarged it and then let it grow until it became bigger than anything she had ever experienced. And then she felt a powerful connection with the small unconscious boy in his time of need. And, joining with Layla and Hamid and the king and Paki and Omari and now Amon and the others, she offered herself as a conduit to whatever was needed. Then she meekly got out of the way of the power that she alone could never have mustered or applied. The silence on the deck was thicker than the water beneath them and the mud under that as the boat bobbed slightly in the midst of the channel. The longest ten seconds they had ever experienced were then suddenly split asunder by the roar of a throaty cough and air was sucked into and heaved out of Jabari's lungs. His heart leapt awake from its slumber and his eyes opened with a loud gasp from his mouth. An invisible energy seemed suddenly to indwell the boy and emanate from him to those close around.

Those first sounds pulled everyone from their prayer positions and drew their eyes straight to their newly animated friend. A cheer erupted from the group and instant applause. "Yes!" Someone shouted.

"Oh, man!" one of the guys exclaimed.

"Oh! What? What? What happened?" Jabari lifted up and coughed repeatedly and turned on his side. "What's happened to me?" He was speaking to Hamid or anyone nearby who might answer.

"It's Ok," Hamid said calmly. "You fell overboard trying to get Manni and you hit the water and went under, and many of your friends who can swim followed you into the Nile to look for you. And Layla found you, and brought you out again."

"I don't remember all that! I just reached out for Manni and lost my balance, I think," he said.

"You had a bit of trouble, but you should … be fine now," Hamid reassured him.

"Where's Manni? Did he fall, too?" Jabari started wiping his eyes and blowing air through his nose to clear out some of the river water that was still in his head.

"No, no, he's good and dry. Set has him."

"Set?"

"Yes. Set grabbed him right away, when you fell in."

"Wait. I was underwater?"

"Yes, for several minutes."

"Under the Nile?"

"Well, in the Nile's murky water and, for part of the time, under the boat."

"But it was so bright!"

"Bright?" Layla spoke up at this point, as she moved closer. "We could hardly see anything an inch in front of our eyes, it was so thick and dark from river silt."

"No, no, it was bright and amazing." Jabari stopped to cough a few more times and breathe deeply, and then he continued. "I mean, I remember it now! For a second I was scared when I was falling, and it was strange. And I must have passed out or something, and then it was dark at first and a little cold. And I was moving fast, and then it was bright up ahead of me and I came out of the dark and into this strange light, and it was just amazing. It was the best thing I've ever felt, and the light was inside me, not just outside me, and it was all through me and I was just so, so happy. And then, wherever I was, I knew I couldn't stay but had to come back here, but that one day, I can go there and take it all in and be and do new things. But first, I have stuff here to get done here, and the light will wait, and all this was just sort of pouring into me and now …" he coughed loudly twice more, "Here I am again!"

The king smiled knowingly. Walid had just walked up and heard all this and said, "Wow."

"So, what was all that? What happened?" Jabari looked around at everyone.

"You visited the source, my friend." The king looked into Jabari's eyes, and Jabari knew that the king understood what he had just experienced.

Layla said to him, "Back here in the manifest reality of our kingdom, Manni had jumped onto the railing and then the deck outside the railing and then onto a life preserver on the side of the barge. And you tried to reach him and fell into the water. Then many friends and helpers who are expertly trained swimmers followed you in to rescue you. I sensed powerfully that others helped in different ways."

"How did you find me?"

"We followed our inner promptings," Layla explained. "I guess we followed the light that we couldn't see but only feel in our hearts."

"Wow," Jabari said. "Thank you so much. Thank you all. Manni wouldn't know what to do without me." He coughed three more times and spit out some more river water. "Sorry, I'm still water logged."

"That's quite all right," Hamid said. "You get rid of it any way you need to. We're just glad to have you back. The light, indeed, will wait."

Layla softly added, "Yes. It will wait. It always does, with great patience and support and hope for us while we're here."

As all this conversation was going on around the soaking wet Jabari, who now had a thick blanket around him, thanks to Amon, the other students looking on had their arms around friends, or hands on backs, or intertwined fingers as they waited in anticipation for what might be next. And that "next" was Hamid helping Jabari stand up, a jerky, off-balance movement that elicited another cheer from the group and lots of happy screeching from Manni, still held tightly by Set, as he brought the monkey across the deck and up to his friend.

Jabari said, "Hey, Set. Thanks man, for taking care of Manni while I was … otherwise occupied."

"You're welcome," Set said. "I figured no one should have to fish two of you out of the water, so I made sure this guy stayed on the boat."

Far away from this scene on the river, along a major road in the nearby nation of Libya, but in the midst of vast spaces where no other traffic could be seen, Farouk and Faraj a-Khoum had now ridden in silence for about thirty minutes. Farouk was reading. Faraj was looking out the window. And then, suddenly, Faraj spoke.

"Remember what our father used to say about power?"

Farouk looked up from his book and studied the face of his

brother for a second before answering. “Yes, I do. He would say it often. ‘Power is the only thing that matters.’ It was his philosophy of life.”

“Yes, it was. When I was young, I always wondered why he then often added the words, ‘So, this means that something matters.’ And he never explained that to me.”

“He explained it once to me.”

“He did?”

“Yes.”

“What did he say?”

“You never knew how his father died, did you?”

“No. All I was ever told was that he died young.”

“Not so young, but before his time.”

“How?”

“He apparently went mad one day.”

“What do you mean?”

“He had always been a quiet man, brooding and extremely negative about things. He had a steely temper and was prone to outbursts of anger now and then. One day, his young daughter died of a terrible fever, a disease no one understood.”

“His daughter?”

“Yes, our father had a younger sister.”

“I never knew that.”

“He didn’t talk about her. I believe her death was so painful for him that he was unable even to speak of her life, except for a couple of times, ever. I suspect that most of what he did as an adult was meant to block thoughts of her, to distance himself from the pain. He loved her and he lost her, and then he was lost.”

Faraj just stared at his brother. “What more do you know?”

Farouk continued. “Our grandfather brooded for days over the death of his young one. Then, one morning not long afterwards, he emerged from his room ranting like a mad man, saying and then eventually screaming, ‘Nothing matters! Nothing matters at all!' He grabbed a scimitar off the wall of his home, an old one, an antique, and ran through the village randomly attacking people with the sword, yelling the same thing, 'Nothing matters! Nothing matters, don't you see?' Several people were severely injured. Two were killed. Then a group of strong men intercepted him and took away the scimitar and used it against him, ending his rampage and his life right there in the street."

"I've never heard any of this."

"You were young when I learned about it and had to promise not to speak of it. It was a solemn and frightening promise."

"I see."

"And do you know what our father said to me in reflecting on all this?"

"No. What?"

"He said that it cannot be that nothing matters, because if that's what his father thought he had discovered, and the discovery set off such unexpected and violent action, then this just proves that the so-called discovery mattered to him so much that it turned him into a different man. So, our father concluded, it cannot be that nothing matters. Something must matter."

"That seems right."

"And then, in further reflection, as the years passed, he concluded for himself that what matters in this world is power. Power, and power alone, matters. Power over disease would have prevented the young girl's death. Power over his emotions would have prevented our grandfather's violent actions and early demise. If our father had possessed the power to stop his father from leaving the house with that sword, the life and history of the village would have been very different. Our family's life and history would have been very different."

"I see."

"It's all about power. We're here to get it and grow it and use it. And that's what he taught us as we grew up."

"I can't believe I've never heard this story, not a word of it. But, yes, that's what he always taught us. And now I see why."

"I think our father believed in his heart that if grandfather had somehow had more power, he could have found medical help for his poor daughter and saved her life from the sickness that ultimately had power over her. He then came to think that power is everything."

Faraj said, "It's then no accident that we're so focused on this one thing, you and I, so careful to gain it and guard it. We trust no one else with it." He then thought to himself, "Not even each other—or, especially, not each other."

Farouk continued, "And that's why it's so important for us to see to it that no one has power over us. That's why we're visiting Rasul today. We'll make sure he doesn't twist and manipulate us, or succeed at any plan to eliminate us. We'll make sure that we have the power."

But as they drew closer to their appointment with destiny, Rasul Appolonium and Ari Falma were making careful preparations to secure their own power and protect it from these brothers. As the former king now listened to Falma's final report on what had been done and what was being prepared for their visitors, he nodded his head and slightly smiled as he gazed at an old, antique scimitar, displayed on a table in front of him, set into a wooden base.

21

Destinations and Destinies

After Jabari's unexpected adventure and amazingly fast recovery, everything eventually got back to normal on the royal barge. The other students were at first, of course, patting him on the back, saying nice things to him, and even making pretty good jokes about Manni's gymnastic abilities. Jabari was glowing in the warmth of everyone's affection, but more than that, he seemed to give off a new sort of deeper glow to all who spoke to him. Only a few people had heard his entire story about the time under water, and he didn't think it was necessary to repeat the tale for everyone else. He was already the center of attention and didn't want to do anything to enhance that even more. He was good with just being Jabari, and didn't want to be thought of mainly as a visitor to, or an emissary from, some wild metaphysical reality beyond our familiar cosmic neighborhood.

The students were all surprised and delighted that the king had decided to join them, and they loved his little disguise as one of the barge mechanics. But they soon found out that it was no simple pretense or joke. He really liked working on the boat, and had natural mechanical abilities that no one would have imagined. His quick participation in the rescue of Jabari had also impressed everyone as well. He wasn't a leader who expected others to do all the difficult and dangerous work. He dived over the side without hesitation, as soon as he learned what was going on. And he had worked tirelessly to find and save the smallest of the boys.

Soon afterwards, lunch was served and everyone had a great time eating together as they watched the banks of the Nile go by. Khalid gave a lecture on the history of the great river and its significance in Egyptian political life, religion, and commerce. Fortunately, he kept the talk relatively short, because now everyone was in more of a vacation and adventure mode than in a classroom state of mind. He was wise enough to realize this, and he also knew that it would change once they were in Alexandria at their destination. The ancient city would fascinate and intrigue the students and open them up to the new learning that he always looked forward to providing.

Khalid's parents gave him a love for knowledge that had lifted his entire life to a higher level. From even his earliest years, he heard from both his father and his mother that education matters. No one can live a good life without a carefully cultivated knowledge of the world. At every age, we should look, listen, and learn from those who are a little farther down life's road. We need to ask questions about things we don't understand and explore more deeply those things that we think we already know. Knowledge is liberation. Ignorance is servitude. The more we grow in understanding, the broader our personal freedom becomes. And Khalid knew that for such freedom to be used well requires both wisdom and virtue, qualities he also sought to impart to his students as he could.

This love of learning had set Khalid apart from many of the other children his age when he was growing up, and it had impressed his teachers at every educational level. During his magical time at Oxford, and later Yale, he had come alive in even new ways to the realm of the mind and the world of ideas. Now he drew from the resulting treasure trove to give to his students freely and even lavishly, both in class and in social settings. He saw these young people as his sacred responsibility. He felt he had been entrusted with one of the most important things in their lives, and he would always do his utmost to honor that trust. Plus, Khalid simply loved his job. He truly enjoyed his work, day-to-day. And that showed in his ongoing enthusiasm for it all.

Hoda noted with pride how well he did this little lunchtime chat about the Nile, and how wisely he timed his remarks to be both informative and brief. When he finished with a bit of a rhetorical flourish, she clapped, and then so did a few others. He smiled, bowed to her, and said to the students, "When I speak, my lovely wife always pays rapt attention. But when I stop, she applauds. I think she likes the stopping most of all." That got a good laugh from all the students, who then of course applauded much more, and with enthusiasm.

"I get the hint," he said. "The rest of the cruise today will be utterly free of any organized education. But make sure to explore and pay attention on your own. The only true education is what you acquire for yourself. And to acquire more information on the Nile, in depth, below the surface, please consult our friend … Jabari." Hearing his owner's name, Manni then let out a happy screech that made everyone laugh again.

In his office in Cairo, Omar Sassi, the Tunisian Ambassador, sat at his desk with a very serious expression on his face. He said to his chief of staff, who was at the moment standing in front of him, after delivering a message. "You're telling me that our men are just gone?"

"Yes, sir, so it seems. They've vanished without a trace. No one has seen them. There's no report of them or from them, whatsoever. We've checked in every possible way. The initial mystery is now even more puzzling. There is no sign of them." The man looked worried.

"Ok, then, at this point, I suppose we should assume that

they've been killed or abducted, but most likely killed—both our men and the other contact." The ambassador tapped his fingers on the desk.

His top associate gestured questioningly with his hands and said, "But who would do that and why?"

"You know I've suspected al-Khoum from the beginning. But what we have very good reason to believe now is that one of the interested parties has discovered that we've been playing both sides in this matter over the future of the monarchy here. And someone's out to stop it, or just to get revenge and punish us."

"It can't be King Rasul! He knows you're loyal."

Sassi sighed aloud. "I've never, of course, confided to him that I'm taking money from the al-Khoum brothers, and I worry about that a great deal."

"Yes, but if he somehow found out, then surely he knows you're just seeking to make a profit from men you would never help all the way into the Golden Palace. He's certainly convinced of your loyalty."

"We can only hope such a thing, but I'm afraid that it would be assuming far too much."

"Really? You think he might doubt you?"

"Look. I believe in being optimistic but not in willfully deceiving ourselves."

"Still, on balance, I think it's much more likely that Farouk has killed our men. It surely couldn't be a lesson from Rasul. Such extremes are more the style of Farouk."

"Yes, I agree. That would be more like the way he operates—sudden death and intimidating silence. And he has people everywhere, unlike the former king, men who are in his various business enterprises."

"But then, that means with a certainty that he's discovered our treachery toward him and we ourselves aren't safe."

"That's the terrible implication I've been trying not to think about. But I've already written the king a very indirect letter asking for help. If we can get through to him quickly and explain what's now happened, then we can throw ourselves on his mercy and ask him to deal with the al-Khoum brothers."

Sassi's assistant felt his heartbeat increase. Now was the opportunity. He said, "Yes, I agree. We need the king's help immediately. And, if I may say so with all due respect, this is no time for you to sit here in the office and depend on a letter. You're too vulnerable if you remain here at this stage. The only thing that makes any sense for you to do is to go see the king in person right away."

"In Tripoli?"

"Yes. And I think you should leave immediately. We need to bring Rasul in on this now, but with a careful spin on it all. You can explain that we were misleading the al-Khoums whenever they contacted us to help them, and that we were doing so to learn of their movements, and actually set them up for failure, in case they were indeed, as we suspected, competing with the true king for the ultimate prize here."

"Yes. Yes. Good."

"Then you can say that they somehow discovered our loyalty to Rasul and began killing our men. Surely, he will then gladly give us good protection. Our ongoing fidelity will be confirmed."

"Yes, with that explanation, it should work. I'll go immediately. But first there's someone I need to get word to."

"Who?"

"It's a personal matter."

"Well, you need to leave soon—today, and no later, and even within a couple of hours, if possible. Otherwise, who knows what might happen next?"

"I agree. Get my son. Tell him we need to make a sudden short trip. We'll take our destinies into our own hands."

"Why your son?"

"I don't want him here while I'm gone, if people are indeed killing those who are close to me. So, you should be careful, too."

On the long road from Tunis to Tripoli, as Farouk and Faraj

drew closer to their destination, Tau looked into the rear view mirror, and his gaze lingered for just a moment on his boss. "Farouk, we're close now."

"How much longer?"

"If we take the direct route, it's a bit less than half an hour, I would estimate."

"And if we approach more cautiously?"

"Add twenty or thirty minutes."

"That's not bad. Go cautiously, then."

"As you wish."

"And then the plan can begin."

"Indeed. We'll first meet up with some of the other men before we drive over to Sea Watch."

"Yes. The leaders know where to wait for us, as you're aware."

Almost an hour later, the small caravan of cars and trucks pulled up to the edge of a large, busy marketplace. They kept far apart from each other, but within sight. Tau turned off the engine of the main car and got out, opening the door for Farouk and Faraj, who emerged from the backseat, stretched a bit, and casually looked around. The vehicles were all covered in the dust of the road and, also because they were far apart, didn't attract unwanted attention. The dress of Tau and the al-Khoum brothers was nice, but also not too expensive or eye-catching. Seeing a familiar and expected face at a booth on the edge of the vast market, Farouk and Tau slowly walked over in that direction. Faraj strolled back to the next car in their procession and conferred with the driver.

Within about five minutes, they were back in their car and headed for the mansion by the water where the next stage of their destinies was about to play out. Their hosts were now in position to greet them, in hopes that their invited guests were about to arrive and have their last cups of tea.

Three cars pulled up to the entrance of the long drive. The other vehicles stayed back. A guard car was now first in line, then the one with the al-Khoums, and a third large automobile brought up the rear. Two guards jumped out of the back seat of the first car and, seeing no security at the elaborate gate, opened it wide. They quickly returned to their seats and the first car pulled onto the drive and slowly rolled through the gate and toward the large home up ahead, about fifty yards away. The impressive house itself was perched on the water, with an expansive view along its back. In the front, there was a gravel parking area nearly as wide as the structure itself, and with a working fountain in the middle. The day was quiet and the air was still, as if in expectation of what was soon to come.

As they pulled up in front of the house, the three cars parked in the formation of a spread apart and upside down U, the main car parallel to the home, the guard cars at angles. And at that moment, two butlers appeared with big smiles to greet the guests, emerging from the tall, dark wood double front doors of the mansion. Tau got out of the main car, walked around the rear, and opened the back door on his side for Faraj and Farouk, who emerged from where they had sat.

One of the two butlers approached and said, "Good day to you, gentlemen! Welcome to Sea Watch!" He bowed toward the al-Khoum brothers and continued by saying, "My associate and I will be happy to provide you with any assistance you may require."

"Thank you," Farouk said. "I'm Farouk al-Khoum and this is my brother, Faraj. I believe we're expected."

"Yes, indeed!"

"These other men are our security and communications teams who always travel with us."

"They're certainly welcome as well! We have a place in the entry where they can store any weapons or other personal items they may have with them. We like an atmosphere conducive to an uncluttered and peaceful enjoyment of one another at Sea Watch."

Farouk said, "That's good. We'll bring just one of our closest associates into the house with us. The rest are fine to wait outside. That's part of their job."

"Oh! Yes. Whatever you wish. We'll even deliver a snack out to the cars." The butler looked at both the other vehicles and said, "How many men will we be serving?"

"Six men from the other two cars. And I know they'll appreciate anything you can bring them."

In contrast with all this apparent pleasantness, the two large teams that had independently traveled to Tripoli under the guise of oil workers now quietly converged toward the house from the east and west sides of its large, walled property. Their advance scouts had spied small groups of armed men on two nearby roads, and had managed to avoid being spotted by them, in turn. Their disciplined diligence allowed them to guide their larger companies of men behind them toward approach avenues where they would not likely be seen.

The plan was that a small group would first approach by water and plant diversionary explosives on that side of the property. When gunshots were heard from the mansion, the bombs there would be detonated to attract attention seaward, and the main force would breach the walls from two other directions. At that moment, a major assault on the house would begin from three sides. The men knew in advance where their allies and superiors in the house would most likely be found. Farouk, who was never one to leave anything to chance that he could secure in advance, had managed to locate a man who once worked in Sea Watch, and had questioned him about all the rooms and potentially safe places in the mansion.

By contrast, the thirty or forty security guards in the employment of the former king had plans to stream in through the main gate. They would disable any vehicles in the drive, rendering motorized escape impossible. And, along with about half a dozen military men who were dressed as servants already inside the house, they would then quickly engage and overpower the visitors and whatever small security team they might have brought with them.

As Farouk and Faraj walked behind Tau and the two butlers toward the front door, stealthy movement was already commencing all around. Heavily armed men were getting into position for their various assignments. And, despite surface appearances, it was at this stage unclear who had the advantage in the situation. The al-Khoum team had more men and information as to the existence and initial placement of potential opponents. But the Appolonium team had the distinct advantage of proximity. They had forces inside the house that could in principle strike their victims before anyone else knew what was happening. Farouk's plan might be able to nearly guarantee the obliteration of the former king and his men, but perhaps only at the cost of his own demise, as well as that of his brother, early on in the process. Whether he knew the full range of dangers he faced was at the moment uncertain.

The butlers apologized for a quick but thorough personal search they were required to do at the door, to check for any concealed weapons that might have been forgotten, but Farouk said that he understood completely. And nothing was discovered. So, within moments, they were inside.

The house was quite elegant throughout its interior, with a huge, high ceiling entry greeting them, a glistening black and white tile floor, ornately carved marble columns, and lots of dark wood everywhere. Monumental tapestries in subtle geometric patterns hung on the walls. And there were flowers in large ornate vases here and there throughout the entry. It was a nice touch, Farouk thought. The head butler turned toward them and smiled broadly again, saying, "Gentlemen, please follow me to the sunroom where tea will be served shortly. I'll let His Majesty know you're here."

Farouk looked into the man's eyes and said, "Thank you. But while my brother and our associate make themselves comfortable, I would like very much to visit the nearest bathroom, if that's possible. It's been a long drive, and I'd love to freshen up before seeing the king."

The butler instantly felt that this was a marvelous idea and found himself saying, quite spontaneously, "Oh, certainly. Please help yourself. It's just down that hallway and to your right."

Farouk nodded and glanced at his brother for only a split second before turning down the hall to which the butler had gestured. The plan the deposed king had formulated involved having his visitors sit for a few minutes alone in this very attractive and comfortable room to just enjoy the view, hoping that it would relax them, take them off guard, and keep them from suspecting that anything dangerous was afoot. But that made Farouk's own plan even easier to implement.

The house was a big one and the hallways were long. When Farouk came to the open door of the bathroom and entered it, closing and latching the door behind him, he quickly looked around and got his bearings. It was all dark wood and beautiful light marble, with highly polished, glistening hardware. He quietly began opening drawers, and in the second one found a long pair of scissors, and then a straight razor and soap. Clearly, insufficient caution had been taken in preparation for their visit. The former Phi smiled and took both sharp implements and hid them in his clothing before returning quietly to the hall. But, rather than walk immediately back to the sunroom, he first stepped a few feet in the other direction and, at a crossing hall, almost ran into a fellow who was approaching rapidly from his right.

There was something about the man that evoked a sense of warning. "Oh, I'm sorry!" Farouk said. "I was in the bathroom and it seems not to be working properly. Could you come and look at it for a second?"

The man was clearly caught off guard and shoved something into his right pocket that Farouk did not quite see but that looked as if it might be a small handgun. "Certainly. I'm so sorry for the inconvenience. Please, after you." The man gestured for Farouk to lead the way.

Turning back into the room, Farouk said, "It's the toilet mechanism," and as the man bent over to look, he pulled out the razor and slit his throat from behind, holding the man close, a hand over his mouth, and dropping him gently down to the floor. Then he closed the outer door of the room with his foot and quickly went into the man's pocket to pull out what was indeed a small loaded handgun. He slipped it into his own pocket, and tucked the man's legs fully into the water closet, the little room around the toilet, and then closed its door and, turning to the sink, he carefully rinsed some blood off one of his hands. He dried himself, put the towel into the closet with the dead man and, closing the bathroom door behind him, walked back down the hall into the room where Tau and Faraj were waiting, still alone.

"That was greatly needed, and nice. Faraj, would you like to freshen up a bit as well?"

"Yes, thank you. Now that you mention it, I think I would, indeed." Faraj reached out his hand, took something quickly from Farouk, and then retraced his brother's steps, but instead of going into the bathroom, he began searching farther down the hall for anyone he might be able to come across. Two men were right inside an arched doorway not more than twenty feet from the bathroom, an opening that seemed to lead to a large kitchen and pantry area. They were speaking in low voices and one of them was gesturing as he talked.

Faraj came up with a quizzical expression and said, "Oh! Hello, there. I'm so sorry to interrupt you gentlemen. But I just arrived and was attempting to use the bathroom down the hall and I'm afraid the sink isn't working properly. Could one of you please help me and take a look? I'm so glad you're here. I have only a few minutes before I meet the king."

Faraj repeated the actions of his brother, a plan they had

hatched well in advance of their arrival, in anticipation that there would be men in the house whose assignment might be to eliminate the guests during tea. The brothers initially would at least seek to reduce quietly the number of adversaries they could face, and well in advance of any signal to strike that the king might have arranged.

Faraj dispatched this second man over the sink. There was just barely enough room for his body in the closet, but Farouk's younger brother managed to get the door closed and then returned quickly to the kitchen entry where he found the other man waiting.

"I'm sorry to bother you again. But your colleague asked me to come get you. He's struggling a bit to fix the plumbing in there and wants you to hold something, he said, and he might need you to get some part. I'm not sure. I know little of such things. He just sent me to fetch you. He didn't want me to do anything to soil my clothing."

"Oh, Ok." The second man followed Faraj, who opened the bathroom door and struck instantly, leaving his body in the middle of the floor, but near the door. He searched him and took another revolver from his pocket and then, as he left, he closed the door behind him in hopes that no one would seek to enter the room before the rest of their scripted actions were able to play out, as intended. Faraj knew there could be many more men in the house, but at least they had eliminated three of the closest adversaries they could find. And any change of the odds in their favor was a good one, in their estimation.

The younger al-Khoum walked rapidly but quietly back to the large, bright sunroom and, with Tau and his brother still sitting there alone still awaiting the king, he looked at Farouk and nodded, while flashing two fingers on his right hand, as inconspicuously as possible, and Farouk nodded back twice.

Faraj sat down and Farouk stood as they heard approaching footsteps. First into the room was the butler again, who now said,

"It pleases me greatly to announce His Majesty, Rasul Appolonium, the Rightful King of Egypt."

Appolonium then entered the doorway and moved toward his guests. His thin beard was no longer salt and pepper but now pure white, and he had put on some weight since Farouk last saw him, over a year ago. A third man followed close behind him and, as he entered, stepped to the side in front of a large bookcase and stood still, hands folded at his back. Farouk smiled and Faraj and Tau both stood up, now also smiling.

"Welcome to my current home! Welcome to the famous Sea Watch!" Appolonium smiled broadly and stretched his hands forward in a gesture of greeting. "It's so good to see you again, old friends."

Elsewhere in Sea Watch at that very moment a guard of the former king was growing concerned and began looking for the colleague who was supposed to have brought him some extra ammunition. He had left their post to get it and now, over five minutes later, was still not back. The remaining guard knew that things were to happen in the next few minutes, at the very latest. He abandoned his post near the entryway and walked rapidly down a corridor in search of the man.

As the king spoke his initial words of welcome, two other gentlemen in formal serving attire entered the room with large silver trays. There was a teapot on each tray, with one cup and a small plate of round sugar cookies on one of them, and three cups with a larger plate of cookies on the other.

The former king said, "We've prepared some special tea for you, brought in from India for the occasion, and we have some distinctive baked delights to accompany it. Let's sit and enjoy these delicacies and catch up a bit before we begin our more serious conversations."

It was the simple intent of the host to poison his visitors, with a severe and quick acting dose of a rare, powerful toxin that would create nearly instant paralysis and death within seconds. That way, there would be no fight, no struggle, and no loud sounds that could even possibly be detected by any of the security men at the cars in the drive out front. And those men could then be set upon with total surprise, shot where they stood or sat, by both snipers from the roof and men rambling down the drive in what would seem to be an old grocer's truck. It was to be a quick and twofold operation. The new enemies of the former king would be eliminated within the next four to five minutes, along with all their associates.

But few things in this world go completely according to plan. And right now, some quite unexpected things were about to occur. The man on the floor of the bathroom behind the door who had been left there for dead had just stirred and opened his eyes and, bleeding profusely, had crawled a few inches to the door and raised up as much as he could in order to pull it open. Any shout or cry from him would change the sequence of events that was about to unfold fairly radically. But it would have been impossible, even for someone with visual access to all parts of the house, as well as to everything in and around its grounds, to know exactly what was about to happen next.

A vast collection of destinations and destinies, coming together in one complex whole, was getting ready to unfold and to launch several lines of action that would affect the lives of countless people forever.

22

The Watch

When the royal barge began drawing near to the mouth of the Nile, Walid was toward the back of the boat, sitting in a circle with some of the other students who were taking turns telling stories about their lives. Mafulla had hatched the idea that they should use an empty bottle they found on board, put it in the middle of their circle, and give it a spin. When it stopped spinning, the person the neck of the bottle pointed to had to tell a quick story about something that had happened in his or her life, a short tale that was to go on for no more than thirty seconds to a minute, at the longest, and then that student should give the bottle another spin. No one could go twice in a row.

Ara told about her first camel ride when she was little. Walid spoke about the first time he saw Cairo from on top of a dune outside of town and how amazing and overwhelming it was. Bakat told a story about her grandmother's beautiful artwork. Bafur described in detail the best meal he ever had. Jabari talked about the day he got Manni as a present from a cousin who worked with a circus. Everyone was learning interesting stuff about everybody else and really enjoying this unusual time together.

Right in the middle of it all, Khalid walked up and said to the group, "Sorry to interrupt. But King Ali wanted you to know that, any minute, the sea will come into view, and that anyone who has never seen it before may want to move up to the bow or front of the barge to watch for it and be able to catch a first glimpse."

"Oh! I've been so keen to see this!" Walid exclaimed and said, "Do you guys mind if I run up front?"

"Go ahead," Malik said. "We know how much a first view of anything impressive can mean to you." Walid shot a glance at Kissa and grinned and then blushed.

"Why don't some of you guys come, too?"

"Ok, sure," several voices said. And Kissa, Hasina, and Mafulla then also stood up, as did Ara, Cabar, and Haji.

"So, let's go!" Walid said and led the way. They all went up front and stood, holding on to the rail, as they waited for the new view to open up in front of them.

Peering into the distance, Mafulla said, "You know, the Atlantic Ocean and the Pacific Ocean, and also the Indian Ocean are all much bigger than the Mediterranean. I read about them recently."

"Yeah," Cabar said. "So I've heard."

"But some day, we might see one of them as well," Walid pointed out, hopefully.

"Yeah, that would be nice," Cabar remarked.

"You gotta start somewhere," Walid said.

"Hey, this is going to be really good," Haji told them. "You don't always have to compare stuff—a big ocean, a middle sized sea. Everything is what it is. I mean, the Nile is impressive enough, but the Mediterranean Sea? Compared to anything I've ever seen, it's bound to be huge. It's going to be great in a really different way. And how big other things are doesn't really matter."

"That's a good point, man," Walid said. "It's important for us all to keep in mind."

Haji continued, "Just remember all the famous historical stuff that happened because of the water we're about to see. And we're going to go out into it for a short time to get to the port of Alexandria. We're going to be on the water where so many big things took place through the centuries."

They were all standing and peering forward when the king walked up behind them and put his hand lightly on Walid's shoulder. "I'm excited too, and I've seen it many times," he confided, to both Walid and the other students.

"Your Majesty," three or four of them said at the same time, and, turning, did small bows in his direction.

"Thank you so much, but for now, outside the palace and any other formal circumstances, you may relax your greeting to me. No bows are necessary when we're alone together like this," the king said and smiled at all of them.

"Uncle Ali, I mean, Your Majesty, we were just talking about the fact that the sea we're about to glimpse and shortly to set sail on for at least a brief time is big and yet, at the same time, relatively small in comparison to other oceans."

"Yes, you could say that," the king replied. "But it's just as true to say that the variously named oceans and connected seas are all part of one vast ocean encompassing the globe, and that when you see one of its parts, you're seeing it—whether your vantage point is at the edge of the Mediterranean, or the Caribbean, or perhaps the Atlantic, Pacific, Indian, or Arctic Oceans, as they're called. But in reality, there is simply one great ocean spread around the world, in addition to many smaller bodies of water that are in most ways bounded by land. And yet, even they are indirectly connected with the larger expanse."

The students were all impressed with this perspective and listened intently as the king went on to add, "There is an ancient saying from the Tao Te Ching that captures this singularity and more. The text says that the ocean is the greatest of all bodies of water, because it's lower than all the rest. They empty themselves into it."

"That's pretty interesting," Mafulla commented.

"Yes. And this, of course, alludes to the deepest and most vital keys to great leadership."

"What do you mean?" Mafulla asked.

"The best leadership requires a vital combination of nobility, which is a sense of greatness and vision, with humility, a counter-balancing proper sense of self that maintains a deep respect for, and eager openness to, others. These are two qualities that must be cultivated together in all our personalities." He paused to let this idea register properly, and then went on. "The Taoist wisdom is a wonderful statement about leadership. The ideal leader combines the nobility of the ocean with its humility or open lowliness. Others are drawn by both these qualities to feed their time and talents and commitments into the projects that the leader with such balance brings to them. The leader's followers are those who help make the leader great, as he or she in turn guides them to worthy pursuits of excellence and their own forms of greatness."

"Wow," Bafur said. "That's a mouthful of wisdom."

"And you would know a mouthful, my friend," Mafulla said, grinning.

"You bet," Bafur said and smiled.

"So, we wait and watch in order to catch a glimpse of the greatness of our humble and noble sea. And I think … that may be it, right now. Look!"

Everyone strained to peer forward, many now shading their eyes to help them see as far and as clearly as possible. There was a pause of maybe five seconds. "Yes! I can see it!" Walid was the first to confirm the king's glimpse.

"Where?" Kissa asked.

"Look straight there," Walid pointed and helped shade her eyes.

"Oh, yes! I see it, too!"

Now all the students were exclaiming, one after the other, then two at a time, as the sea came more clearly into view for them all. And of course, then, every few minutes brought a wider expanse into view, by small increments at first and then by a larger sweep. The ensuing conversations grew lively all over the barge. Khalid and Hoda both smiled to see such enthusiasm on the part of the younger people. Their spirits clearly were fertile soil for new knowledge, and much of that would be forthcoming very soon in the city of Alexandria—more, even, than either Khalid or Hoda could now imagine.

It wasn't much longer before they were clearly leaving the waters of the Nile and entering the broader sea. The barge made a slow, gradual turn to the left, or to the port side, as the crew said. Now the excitement of all the younger passengers had reached a new level. They realized that, in not too long, they would be coming into view of their famous destination.

At about that same moment, some distance up the coast, at Sea Watch, Tripoli, Farouk al-Khoum looked at Rasul Appolonium with a smile and said, "Your Majesty, before we sit, I must express the full extent of my appreciation." And that last word was the predetermined code. Farouk quickly pulled the loaded handgun from his pocket and shot the king, point blank. Faraj did the same with the man in front of the bookcase, hitting him square in the chest. The two servers were next with rapid second shots from both guns. Tau ran to the guard at the bookshelf, slumped on the floor, and found a pistol hidden away on him as well. Now all three were armed with something beyond the razor and scissors that two of them still held, in case they would also be useful. Two other men then ran into the room with guns drawn and were cut down as soon as they appeared. Ari Falma peeked in from another direction and, seeing the king crumpled up on the carpet in a pool of blood, he turned and ran, from both stark terror and the fleeting thought that now he must save himself so that he could live, and perhaps, even himself come to rule. But it was a fool's thought.

A loud, staccato firefight outside the mansion could then be heard. Appolonium's men had attacked the three cars parked in the front of Sea Watch, with the few men left in them who had come that day with the al-Khoum brothers. But they were extremely well prepared to defend themselves for the short time it would take before backup would intervene in massive numbers. The first sign of the larger army arriving was an explosion on the dock, followed by a second one that distracted Rasul's men long enough for the main assault to begin. Surmounting two walls and pouring through the gate, al-Khoum's forces quickly overwhelmed the house guard contingent, killing them all. Then more soldiers outside the gates put an end to the former king's other assault teams that had been poised to attack. As Ari Falma ran out a side door, a man with a rifle and an aim that was much better than Falma's luck cut him down instantly.

When a very small baby had once come into the world and was, in his first hour, named Aristomi Alimbar Falma, there was no path of destiny already laid out through time that would take him all the way from his crib to this bullet and a sudden death in the hot dirt of Libya. Many things were possible, countlessly many things, and some of them wonderful. The deck was stacked against him because of his family background, but there had been many chances along the way for him to take his destiny into his own hands and shape it into something good or even great. Yet, corruption came into his heart, and it had become over time more and more difficult for him to see and feel anything other than treachery, and an endless quest for the money and power around him in the world. All the efforts he had expended, all the organization and strategy and careful planning to gain and become what he valued had eventually came down to this, with his body lying bloodied and lifeless in the sand of a foreign land.

No one should make mistakes that are so numerous and terribly bad that their cumulative effects come to this. No soul who enters this wondrous and challenging realm of life should act in such a way that his great potential will go unrealized and be cut off from all the true good that could have resulted from his existence among us. But it's all too common. And it's always a tragedy.

Within ten minutes, the former king, the crime lord, and all their gathered forces were dead. Farouk had lost four men, and several others were wounded. But he, Faraj, and Tau had not been touched by the violence of the day—at least, in any physical way. The wounded man in the hallway bathroom who could have ruined it all had simply not lived long enough to open the door or cry out the alarm that might have changed everything.

When it was clear that all their adversaries had been eliminated, Farouk asked Tau to gather the victorious mercenaries for a rallying talk about their next opportunity, and all the glory, honor, and riches that soon awaited them in the neighboring kingdom of Egypt. He then spoke rousingly and said that, due to their success on this day, everything was now in place for the last battle and the final achievement they all needed. He elicited cheers from the men as he described the fabulous wealth and fame that awaited their next victory. And he felt in his bones that the time for this was very soon to come. He smiled and shouted and laughed and led a final, roaring cheer.

And yet, in Farouk's heart, there was a darkness that the most enthusiastic words could not change. The ambition that had warped his entire life had just poured into his soul a new measure of poison, and it created a fever of need and a lust for power that would indeed soon take him to his destiny—one that he envisioned in the most ecstatic terms, but whose reality might be quite different from his wildest imaginings. There was nothing noble and nothing humble within his heart at all. His leadership over his many companies and men was cynical and manipulative and all about his felt needs, which was quite the opposite of everything that Ali Shabeezar had been discussing with the students of the palace school on their barge trip together down the Nile and into the nearby sea.

The captain of the barge had now just informed King Ali that they should begin to watch for Alexandria, which would soon appear up ahead. The king told Walid and Mafulla, who then passed the word on to Khalid and Hoda and Layla, and nearly everyone else. Several of the students quickly gathered again at the front of the barge to begin their new vigil for a first glimpse of the city of legend, the playground of Cleopatra and Caesar, the ancient repository of antiquities, and the great, cosmopolitan port of Egypt.

Mafulla said to Walid, "I just basically forget most of the time that there is this other great city in our kingdom."

"Me too," Walid admitted. "We tend to think that our own surroundings are the center of the universe. We need to be reminded of all the amazing things and people out in the world far beyond the horizon of our daily experience."

"I guess that's maybe a universal tendency, until real wisdom wakes you up," Mafulla commented.

"What?"

"Thinking that the bubble we live in is at the center of everything."

"Oh, yeah."

"And then assuming that anything outside the bubble is less valuable, less important, or even less real."

"I think you're right. And that's the opposite of the humility the king was talking about."

"True."

One of the girls said, "Alexandria should come into view any second now."

And just then, Jabari suddenly spread his arms wide apart and starting singing, as he swayed back and forth, gesturing dramatically and crooning as if he was in a Hollywood musical:

"Alexandria, the crown
Of the great Egyptian coast!
I'm glad I didn't drown,

Because, if I was a ghost, then
I could not enjoy the town
I want to see the most!
Oh, Jewel near the Nile,
You can see me smile
In anticipation …
Of … youuuuuuu!"

He drew out that last note, and then did a quick bow as everyone broke out into applause and cheers.

"Thank you. Thank you. Thank you very much." Manni of course screeched and twirled in a tight circle. Set was holding his leash for the duration of the little performance, and had to laugh aloud at both Jabari and the monkey, who were equally flamboyant performers and were always prepared to offer some form of welcome merriment.

Ara turned to Cabar and said, "How did he come up with that? Did he just make it up?"

Cabar laughed and replied, "I don't know—probably. Jabari's pretty sharp, like Mafulla. He's just normally quieter about it."

Mafulla then walked up to Jabari and said, "You, my friend, are a sure star of stage and screen … and the large barge, of course."

"Why, thank you, my good fellow. Coming from such an astute observer and man of the world, with your appropriately high standards, that's quite a compliment."

"Hey, I appreciate a good song and dance man. Not many can spontaneously compose and perform at the level you just attained."

"You're so kind, but I'm afraid there was nothing level about it while I was belting out my little ditty—as we were listing starboard and port, as they say, and up and down." Jabari held his hands out, palms up and wiggled his arms back and forth.

"Oh, of course! And now that we're … listing the obstacles you had to overcome, to further highlight your stunning accomplishment, the acoustics out here aren't the best, either."

"So, it had to be part of my project to project more than usual."

"Boat … you did it, magnificently.

"Ah. Thank you. I had to make sure the audience could hear."

"And yet, you do have to wonder," Mafulla added. "Were they clapping just for you and the performance, as I would surely believe, or at least in part because of the very low price of admission for the concert?"

"Yes, especially when it was so much smaller than even I am," Jabari retorted.

Kissa and Hasina were just staring at these two. Hasina said to her friend, "This sort of silly dialogue sounds strangely familiar, don't you think?"

"Yes," Kissa replied. "I think we hear a version of this form of exchange all too often."

"All too often," Hasina said, then laughed. "But they are constant entertainment."

Just then, someone yelled, "There's Alexandria, up ahead!"

Mafulla had to respond by yelling back, "Ahoy!" And then, "Ahoy! Up Ahead!" as he quickly walked forward, gesturing for the others to inch forward even more as well.

Walid turned to Kissa with a smile and said the word, "Ahoy."

"Yes, definitely: Ahoy," she responded, chuckling at them both.

Everyone who wasn't already there rushed for the very front of the barge again, and up ahead in the distance they could see the first appearances of the great and famous port city. After a brief session of group gawking at the still barely visible signs of civilization in the distance and much lively talk about what they all wanted to do there once they arrived, Khalid announced to the students that they should put their things together in about twenty minutes. There were lots of items to be packed back up, and they all got to the task within a few minutes. The time then passed quickly as they were working, and they made it into port just as the sun was first beginning to set.

The large and wide boat was slowly brought in, positioned up against the main dock, and firmly tethered to huge posts by local workers who had been waiting for them. Then a wooden walkway was placed down. Everyone grabbed their bags and, stepping through an opening in the railing, walked the short distance onto the dock, which felt sturdy, like dry land.

"Oh, it feels good to stand on something that's not moving," Mafulla said, adding, "except of course through space, as we spin on our own axis and continually orbit the sun. And along with it, as they tell us, we also travel amid the galaxies, wandering through the vastness of the cosmos at appropriately astronomical speeds, but still, even so, the feeling as if we now stand upon a relatively motionless place for my feet is, again, a good one."

"Yeah. I agree, my fellow cosmic wayfarer. It feels good, but also strange, after all the hours on moving water," Walid replied.

"Yes, strangely strange."

"I still feel almost like I'm moving back and forth, and up and down, in a sort of ghostly way." Like Mafulla, Walid was carrying his own bag and one other, as the boys helped Kissa and Hasina with their things. But at the moment, he was standing motionless to feel what he thought of as the slight movement of the dock.

Paki and Omari were already some distance away, talking to the drivers of three trucks that had earlier backed up close to where they all now were gathered. The guards checked their paperwork, interviewed them casually, and were then greeted by two military officers who had just driven up in a small truck of their own. One of the two men was an old friend of the king and had come across the desert with Walid and his uncle in the camel caravan that had brought them to Cairo. He was clearly looking around for Ali as soon as he stepped out onto the street and, seeing him, walked briskly straight over to him.

"Old friend!" he said with a big smile and the slightest bow. The greeting was intentional. The few soldiers of Alexandria who knew of Ali's presence with this group had been instructed in advance not to acknowledge the king publicly as their monarch in any overt way. The trip was to be kept as low key and private as possible. It was one of many simple security measures that had been planned.

"Hamal, my friend! It's so good to see you here in the domain of your fine ongoing work!" The king was smiling broadly. He hugged the man and slapped him on the back.

The officer replied, "It's good to have you here, YM. We have a nice place prepared for the group, in the Palace Hotel, which is, of course, appropriate enough. We have two entire floors reserved for you. And from your rooms there, you'll be able to see the best sights in all of Alexandria."

"Excellent," The king said, and then looked over his old companion, head to foot, adding, "You seem quite fit, my friend. Does the work here suit you?"

"Yes, it's a good assignment. I have a disciplined and loyal band of soldiers. And we've made great progress in recent months in our efforts to provide them with a noble conception of their jobs, as well as new skills for doing that work. I'm quite pleased with the results."

"That's very good to hear."

"It's important for them to know what you stand for, and what our nation now values. We've gotten rid of all of the old corrupt and incompetent hangers-on and now we have a group of just top notch, highly committed men."

"That's a fine thing, my friend." The king looked back at all the students and their escorts and said, "I suppose we should get everyone to the hotel so they can have dinner and rest up for tomorrow. You and I can talk more once we're there."

"Right away! As you wish." Hamal motioned for one of his assistants. "Let's load up and be off."

The man nodded and turned to the nearby trucks. He quickly

gave orders and a half dozen other soldiers who had been standing close to the vehicles began loading up all the bags of the students and their teachers. Mafulla was saying something to Walid when he suddenly noticed over his friend's shoulder and about a block away, in the shadows up against the corner of a building, a man standing still and looking in their direction. Few other people were around the dock, apart from their group and the soldiers who were there to help. Any individuals who were on the street nearby were all walking somewhere, singly or with someone else, or they were obviously men working on or near the docks. This lone man was just standing there, apparently staring at them. He was almost hidden from view by the back of a tall cart and some dark shadows cast by an overhanging bit of roof above him. It was nearly dark out anyway at this point, or at least deep twilight, and Mafulla wouldn't have been able to see the man at all were it not for his stark white clothing.

At that point, the best friend of the prince bent down his head and said in a low voice, "Walid, I want you to turn around slowly as I move around you, and look across the street to what will be your right. There's a man in white just staring at us from behind a donkey cart and up against a building." But when they both turned and Walid looked up, the man was gone.

Walid glanced all around and said, "I … don't see anyone."

Mafulla twisted back around and visually scanned the area. "He … just disappeared. That quickly, he vanished. There was something odd about him."

"What was it?"

"He was clearly watching us."

The prince replied, "It was probably just some curious guy wondering who we all are, arriving here together at nightfall on a big barge."

"Maybe. But I had a feeling."

"What sort of feeling?"

"I don't know. I'm not sure. It was just … odd."

"Well, tell me if you see him again and we'll look into it."

Between two buildings farther down the street, Mafulla then saw a flash of white and a cluster of butterflies launched into flight inside his gut. And then, something made him look at his watch. He had no idea why.

23

Alexandria: City of Mystery

The ride to the Palace Hotel was a fairly short one, despite the overall size of the city. The hotel had clearly been located for good reason at a spot conducive to the arrival of guests from the sea. And it was simply magnificent. Architecturally stunning and built on a small hill, its upper floors offered a great view of the surrounding city, and some of the rooms on those floors enjoyed amazing vistas of the water as well. No expense had been spared on the elaborate construction and decoration of the building, inside and out, as well as on the extensive landscaping all around it.

The evening air was cooling as the students and their teachers and companions climbed down out of the trucks and stood admiring their new home for the night. The imposing façade of the hotel announced its importance, but the lights around it added a warm festivity to the welcome it extended these tired and yet still excited travelers.

The soldiers who had driven them were now taking out all the bags and putting them in a line on the walkway to the main door of the hotel. Khalid got everyone's attention and explained that their first official tour would be of the hotel lobby and its fine dining room, where they would all have dinner together in a private back alcove. But before that, he explained, their job would be to follow him to the front desk, collect their individual room keys, and go up to their rooms where they could leave their bags and freshen up for a few minutes before meeting back in the lobby in exactly half an hour.

"Students: You're all sharing rooms, so look for the envelope at the front desk that will have on it your name and the name of your assigned roommate or two for the evening. Take the elevator up to your floor or walk the stairs if you'd like the exercise. But I have to warn you that, because of the high ceilings, there are a lot of stairs. And remember, by the time you get to your room, you'll have a limited amount of time to put away your things, wash up, and get back down to the lobby on the side where you'll see all the chairs and sofas."

With that last message, Khalid waved everyone toward their luggage and then the front door, which was opened on cue, left and right, by beautifully uniformed doormen. He then escorted them all through the lobby and up to the front desk where staff members were waiting with their keys. Mafulla suddenly stopped and looked around and said to Walid, "Wow, this is almost like the palace at home. Look at all the marble, gold, and cut glass chandeliers. And this entry area is huge."

"Yeah, it's pretty impressive," Walid replied, stopping with his friend. "But we can stand around to admire the place later. Let's get our key and go put our stuff up."

Khalid was helping the boys, and Hoda and Layla were both assisting the girls in finding their envelopes and room keys. Of course, Mafulla had to try the stairs, explaining that they both needed exercise after so much standing around and sitting on the barge. So he and Walid grabbed their keys and found the stairwell, at first bounding up the steps, and then by the third floor, slowing to a steady slog, with their heavy luggage in hand.

The prince, who was in front, paused for a second and said,

"This was a good idea, man. We're going to spend the entire time we have just getting to the fifth floor and the room."

"Hey, it's not that bad," Mafulla replied. "Consider this to be simply another form of endurance training. It'll help prepare us for the day we might have to outrun bad guy hordes."

"Up endless flights of stairs?" Walid replied.

"Very funny," Mafulla said. "But you never know."

"Well, I hope you've noticed that we're the only ones who took this particular option."

"We're the true warriors on the trip."

"Except, of course, for those other guys who might also count—like Hamid, Paki, Omari, Amon, and the king."

"Oh. Yeah, except for them. But they've got the leg strength and endurance already. We're the ones still working on it."

"I think I've worked on it enough for today. We'll go down by the elevator—executive decision, and I'm pulling rank on this one."

"Ok, Ok. Hey, look. The door on the stairwell up ahead has a 5 on it."

"Finally!" Walid responded. "But look, if you want to continue your important exercise climb all the way to the top, I can take the bags to the room, and you can stop by whenever you've had enough leg training for the day."

"Hardy, Har, Har," Mafulla answered. "Actually, I think I've gotten to the point where my knees are discussing with each other the real possibility of just quitting, so the elevator will be fine with all of us, and we thank you for suggesting it."

"No problem. But what you said just now reminded me of something else."

"What's that?"

"Are you sore at all from the new strange exercises that Masoon gave us this week?"

"Yeah, very much so, and I didn't realize how much my legs hurt until we were up to the third floor."

"I'm pretty sore, too."

"You know," Mafulla said, "I'm not sure I like the new exercises. They're unfamiliar, uncomfortable, and I'm always worrying about whether I'm doing them right. I'm not in a flow with them like I've been with the others we've been doing for what seems like forever now."

"Well, I guess it doesn't really matter if they're unfamiliar and uncomfortable," Walid said. "What matters is whether they work, and they must work, because both of us are sore. That's the true test of any new workout."

"Good point."

"There's a deep truth here. If you don't do anything different, you won't be anything different. And we should remember that."

"True."

They finally got to the landing, and Walid opened the stairwell door. He led Mafulla into a wide, plush hallway and glanced left and right. They could hear voices from behind some of the doors already.

"What's our room number?" Walid asked. He had put the envelope in his bag.

"515. I suspect they didn't want to overtax our memories."

"Ok, over here, this way," Walid said. He walked up to a door whose brass numbers said 515, put down his large bag, pulled out the envelope, got the key, and carefully placed it into the door's lock. "Hey this is the first time I didn't have to use the golden ratio to open a lock, in what seems like forever."

"Yeah, you're right, but at least all the numerals in our room number are Fibonacci numbers."

"Huh. That's right. Funny. But not everything has to fit the mysterious pattern."

"True. And yet, I'm always on the lookout." Mafulla had a serious expression on his face but still did his famous double eyebrow jump, for dramatic purposes only.

The room was large and beautiful with a thick carpet. It contained two double beds with ornate headboards, two dark wood night tables, a desk and desk chair, and two overstuffed armchairs nicely upholstered to play off the color and design of the wallpaper. A low table in front of them held several magazines and newspapers.

"Wow, this is pretty elegant," Mafulla commented. "I could get used to this, for sure."

"Yeah, it feels just like home," Walid replied. "But it's maybe even a little fancier."

Mafulla walked over to a door along one wall and opened it. "A nice huge bathroom, fit for … a prince and his best friend, the duke, or the earl, or satrap, or whatever it is that I am."

"You're many things, my friend," Walid said with a big smile.

"I am multitudes," Mafulla replied mysteriously.

"Walt Whitman," Walid said in recognition. "That's a quote from the American poet."

"How did you know?"

"I'm worldly, too. You should realize that by now—well read and immensely cultured. I pick up things. Stick with me and learn."

"Hey, that's what I always say."

"Well, see? I picked it up. So now it's my turn."

"I guess I finally rubbed off on you."

"Yeah and too bad, there's no time for a bath." Walid made a face and said, "We'd better get down to the lobby. I hear other doors up and down the hallway closing already. We don't want to be late."

They both headed out the door and saw Malik and Haji coming out of the room across the hall. Malik said, "Hey, where did you guys disappear to?"

"Oh, my friend here wanted some exercise so we climbed three thousand stairs to get to the room."

Malik nodded his head with an expression of approval on his face, and Haji said, "That's pretty impressive."

"Or ridiculous, depending on your perspective," Walid said with a smile.

"Now he wants me to carry him to the elevator," Mafulla said.

"Yeah, My-Mule-a," Walid replied and, at that, they all laughed.

The boys got down to the elevator, pressed the button, and waited. Within a minute or so, they heard a clanging behind the closed door, and suddenly it opened, to reveal what looked like a small room containing smiling girls and a man in very nice official clothing. The man said, "Lobby?"

"No—Adi, but really good, and close enough," Mafulla smiled and said as he stepped into the device. The elevator operator just looked perplexed.

"Yes, lobby, thanks. He's just joking about his last name," Walid quickly responded, and also got on. Kissa, Hasina, Ara and Cabar had all changed clothes and were smiling at the boys.

Looking over the new arrivals, Cabar said, "You guys didn't have to get so dressed up."

"Yeah, in the clothes they put on this morning," Ara commented, and they all laughed.

"Were we supposed to change clothes?" Mafulla looked puzzled.

"We were only in our room for about thirty seconds," Walid said. "No time to change anything, except maybe our minds … about how to get to the room next time."

"What took you so long to get up there?" Ara asked. Kissa and Hasina shared quick knowing smiles with each other, but stayed quiet.

"The mountain climber here wanted to take the stairs," Walid explained.

"Yes, today the stairs of the Palace Hotel, tomorrow, the slopes of Everest," Mafulla said.

"No, tomorrow, we rest and walk only downstairs and downhill," Walid said.

"Ok. No argument here, I promise." Mafulla conceded.

"Good."

He admitted to the group, "It was a little harder than I thought. At least now I know why somebody invented elevators."

"And it wasn't just to go down," Walid said, "You know, there's a hint given by the name itself, in case you hadn't noticed."

"Oh, elevate—I get it."

"A little late." Walid turned and gave the girls a funny look.

By then, they had reached the lobby level and the lift operator announced "Ground Floor Lobby" and opened the door for them. Half the class was already milling around on one side of the wide, open space that was lavishly ornamented by beautiful furniture and lamps. Conversational clusters of large armchairs and sofas could be seen around the various lobby areas. Bellmen moved rapidly through the space every few minutes, and gentlemen and ladies in fine dress were gathered here and there in convivial groups, some awaiting dinner, others just using the hotel's convenient amenities to visit with local friends and acquaintances.

"Huddle up," Khalid was saying and motioning the boys and girls to gather around him. "Come in close for a few instructions."

Set and Jabari walked over to join Bafur right in front of Khalid. Khata and Bakat had been looking at some intricately decorated boxes on a nearby table and they now stopped what they were doing and moved closer to Khalid. Hoda and Layla were also right behind him. As Walid, Mafulla, Malik, and Haji walked over from the elevator together, the prince snuck an appreciative glance back at Kissa, who looked very nice in her change of clothes, and who had stopped for just a second, whispering and laughing with Hasina and Ara. Then they too walked quickly over to the teachers.

"A few preliminaries," Khalid said. "First, our most illustrious companion on this trip, our surprise guest and boat mechanic, has business this evening, and so won't be with us for dinner. But when he is around and you speak to him, for the rest of the trip, please refer to him as 'YM'—an abbreviation, of course, for the customary terms of respect, and a salutation that can be nicely misheard by any bystanders outside our group as the proper name 'Wayeem.' That will help us keep his unofficial presence among us private. He's not recognized on sight yet by most in the city, especially in normal civilian clothes, and so can enjoy just being with us in a relaxed and informal way. It also makes the security situation much easier."

"That makes a lot of sense," Mafulla whispered to Walid.

"Yeah."

"As you may have noticed, around the room there are clusters of other people—hotel guests, and local leaders and businessmen who are here for their normal night out, or for late meetings. Among them, you may come across some who are wearing a small green ribbon on their clothing. This signifies that, even though you might not recognize them, they are here for us, and for our protection. If you have any emergency trouble of any kind, feeling yourself in any sort of danger, and can't find anyone in our group, you can go to one of them for assistance. But you may want to hold off with ordinary needs and not show any special recognition of them apart from a true emergency, so that they can remain undercover and available for the most serious and remote possibilities. After the trip to Memphis, I don't have to say anything more about such unfortunate vicissitudes, which always in principle hover in the realm of the potential, however highly unlikely."

"It's good to have backup," Hasina whispered to Kissa, who just nodded in response.

"Now," Khalid continued in a bit louder voice, "if there are no questions, I'd like to tell you a bit about the history of this fine hotel." He then went on to give a short account of the building of the place, and a few of the mysteries that haunted its early years. First, no one seemed to know where the money came from to build it, more than a century ago. Then there were stories about mysterious guests who may have been involved in various forms of international espionage and who apparently often met, off the record, and beyond prying eyes, here in the port city of Egypt. The hotel had a history of intrigue, as well as of formal diplomacy. Many heads of state had stayed here, and other high ranking governmental officials from the region and around the world. Legends abounded that the site of the hotel was the very location where Cleopatra had often entertained her most famous suitor, Julius Caesar. The two most powerful figures of their day in the entire world were said to relax here and plot international adventures from a luxurious building that had previously occupied this spot, many centuries ago. The stories often recounted in town were that their spirits still could be felt, now and then, in various parts of the hotel. There were even rumors about sightings of white ghostly figures here late at night.

Khalid told all this with a clear intent to entrance. It was the closest he would ever come to a spooky story, and he obviously enjoyed the telling of it. Now and then, he looked over and caught the eye of Hoda, and a couple of times, Kissa, who as descendants of the Queen of the Nile, would both find these stories to be of special interest. The philosopher really seemed to relish relaying his last point that, on rare occasions, the spirits of the two world leaders were reported to actually have been seen in the hotel's hallways, glowing in white garments and then disappearing quickly.

Oddly, at the moment Khalid mentioned this, Mafulla had a strange feeling and turned around a bit to see across the lobby and in a doorway what from a quick glimpse seemed to be the mysterious man in white garments he had noticed near the docks earlier in the evening. Again, even indoors, the elusive man had found a shadow to stand in, so that his face was not as clearly visible as it should have been, even despite the considerable distance between them. Mafulla touched his friend's arm and leaned close and whispered, "The guy from the building at the dock, the one in white who was watching us, is over to your left in a doorway off the lobby." Walid turned and looked, and again saw nothing.

"No man in white that I can see," he whispered back.

"What?" Mafulla looked again and now he saw only an empty doorway where the man had been.

"Are you sure?" Walid whispered.

"Yeah. It's strange. He just disappeared again. I need to get over there and see what's going on."

"Not yet. Stay put for a second," Walid counseled, still in a whisper and with his hand on Mafulla's arm. At that moment, Khalid directed the group to walk across the lobby, not too far from where the man had been, toward the dining room, where he said he'd give them just a bit more of the history of the place before they sat down to dinner. As they approached the doorway, Mafulla shot a glance at Walid, and the prince nodded and said only the words, "Quick, casual, and careful. I'll cover."

Back in Cairo, at the actual palace, Walid's parents Rumi and Bhati were keeping things going for the king while he was away on the field trip, and they were benefiting from the assistance of Masoon, who had stayed behind for precisely that purpose. Some troubling rumors were coming their way from Tunisia, and Mafulla's uncle Reela had visited the palace twice in the past few hours to relay to Masoon and Walid's mother and father what he had been hearing from his various contacts.

One of the most surprising bits of information for Rumi and Bhati was that the new ambassador from Tunisia had been seen leaving town with his son, and with no official word to the palace concerning any trip he might be taking, or the length of time he would be away. This was information it was customary to make available to the palace in advance of any departure on the part of a high embassy official, and especially the ambassador himself. In fact, the custom was so strong among all the embassies that this was the first such contrary instance that anyone advising the palace had ever heard about. It was just not done. And since the Tunisian embassy had already been under grave suspicion concerning several unfortunate and even treacherous incidents around town in the recent past, the unexpected news was viewed as a potentially alarming development. Something had to be done to look into it, and soon.

Masoon immediately tasked an investigative team of four men to discover what the ambassador was doing. They left quickly to make inquiries at the embassy itself and with staff at the ambassador's residence, while simultaneously following up on the eyewitness leads that had brought Reela this news in the first place. They were to track the ambassador and his son, see where they were going, what they were doing, and why they were doing it. And they were granted the authority to bring them both back to the capital city for palace questioning about recent suspicions if it looked like they would otherwise not be returning soon on their own.

Masoon had just finished making some major new fortifications of the palace, its grounds, and the surrounding neighborhoods, mostly invisible to the casual glance, or even to careful observation. He was keenly alert to any possible avenue of attack and knew that some such event was most likely coming soon. More troops than ever before had been deployed in and around the palace, and near the city. With an ambassador under suspicion and having left the capital without warning, there was even a heightened alertness in Masoon's mind, and with other members of the government on site.

In less than two days, Omar Sassi and his son would arrive in Tripoli, Libya, just hours before Masoon's investigative team. Their intent would be to visit with Rasul Appolonium at Sea Watch and ask for some assistance. They, of course, had no idea what would actually await them at that location. And so they were in for a big surprise.

But Tripoli, Libya was not the only place where a surprise was most immediately about to happen. In Alexandria, at the Palace Hotel, a big shock was just around the corner. As Khalid led the group of students, now augmented not only by Layla but also by Hamid, Omari, Paki, and Amon, toward the dining room, loud laughter came from across the lobby. Several heads turned right to see what was going on. Mafulla took that as his opportunity to veer off about thirty feet to the left, as they were now halfway to the dining room. Within four seconds, he made it to the interior doorway where he had seen the man in white and he, like the man, quickly disappeared from view.

Within four more seconds, he reappeared with a very serious and even puzzled look. Walid happened to glance back at just that moment and Mafulla surreptitiously waved to him to come to the door. Khalid had just turned away from the students to point at some bright geometrical mural on the wall and talk about its history and artistic features, so Walid quickly walked toward where his friend stood. Set and Jabari both noticed his initial movement and saw Mafulla in the doorway motioning to Walid, but immediately turned their attention back to their teacher, thinking no more of it.

When the prince drew close, Mafulla grabbed his arm and said, "Come into this hallway. And look at this. You won't believe it." Walid passed through the doorway and, directed by his friend, squinted at the wall beyond it that was now being indicated. He got a little closer and felt a shiver run through his body. He immediately looked back at Mafulla, then glanced past him out the door to see Omari not more than twenty feet away, and walking briskly in his direction. Paki was at the rear of the group of students, now a good fifty feet from the doorway in question, and was looking right at his fellow palace guard.

"What is it, my friend?" Omari asked as he approached, now seeing the look on Walid's face, and yet remembering not to call him 'Prince' as he normally did, but to be more casual in the current circumstances.

"There was a mysterious man in white," Walid whispered in a low voice. "He was near the dock when we arrived and he was looking at us from a distance, in the shadows across the street, and then he disappeared. Now, Maffie just saw him in this doorway for a second and he vanished again. But look at what we've found."

Omari took a few more steps and turned in the direction that Walid had indicated. He peered intently at what the prince was now pointing toward on the left wall of the hallway. He said simply, "We have to tell Paki right away."

"I couldn't believe it when I first saw it," Mafulla said. "I had to look twice, and then a third time to be sure. But there it is."

"There it most definitely is," Walid concurred.

"Spooky," Mafulla said.

"Unsettling," Omari agreed in an equally low voice. He whispered quickly, "You should both come with me this instant. We have to get you back to Paki and Hamid right away. There are green ribbons at the next cluster of furniture, two in particular who've been watching you. Come now and move quickly." Omari's eyes darted about and he became inwardly attuned to all his senses and sensibilities as he lightly took Walid's arm and escorted him and his best friend out of the area where they had been standing. Paki had to be told about this, and immediately.

24

Out of the Blue

There are some things so completely unexpected that you have no idea at first what to make of them. But prudence dictates caution, and Omari's next words to Walid and Mafulla were: "Triple Double."

That instant, without any further thought whatsoever, Mafulla began to rehearse the doubles, or pairs of words, in his head: "Prepare, Perceive; Anticipate, Avoid; Concentrate, Control." A split second later, Walid was doing the same thing. Omari, by contrast, was not reminding himself of what he needed to do. He was just doing it. That was the simple result of who he was and where he was in his overall personal growth into the fullness of Phi. The Triple Double was just what he did at the first sight of what could signal serious trouble.

All of the Phi in Alexandria were scheduled to be in the lobby of the Palace Hotel that evening and were scattered around the various areas of that vast expanse, sitting or standing, and all appropriately well-dressed for the context, and most but not all were wearing small green ribbons. Omari knew that. And it was a large part of what made the sight they had just seen both mysterious and even a bit ominous at the same time.

As Khalid was leading his group into the dining room, steering the rest of them in before him, Omari got his attention, and with a smile disguising his concern, he said, "We'll be with you in just a minute. There's some quick business to attend to out here with Walid and Mafulla and then we'll catch up." Khalid smiled back and nodded to show that, whatever was going on, he was fine with their delay.

Omari then turned to Paki and, pulling him aside, said in a low voice, "Walid and Mafulla saw a strange man in white clothing back near the docks watching us arrive, from a distance and in the shadows. He then disappeared. Mafulla thought he saw him a minute ago in the doorway over there but before Walid could catch sight of him, he vanished again. Our younger friend decided to investigate, and saw something that completely surprised him. He called Walid to come see it and I followed, having noticed them both break off from the group."

"I saw you follow along. I was watching. What did you find?" Paki asked.

Omari said, "The sign of Phi. Someone drew the sign of Phi on the wall beside the door frame."

"So, it was the mystery man?"

"Most likely. There was no one else around when we got there."

"But … all the Phi of Alexandria are in the lobby wearing ribbons and being watchful over our group."

"Yes. That's what we believe."

"Who then was the elusive man?"

"We don't know. But by using the sign of Phi, he's likely either signifying to us that he is Phi, or that he knows some of us are."

Mafulla jumped in and said, "But why would he do something like that? I mean this, even about your second possibility: Why would he give us a signal that he knows some of us are Phi?"

"I have no idea," Omari admitted.

Then Paki said, "If he's unknown Phi and lurking about masking his presence, that could be a sign of danger to us, of some sort."

"How?" Mafulla asked.

"He could be working for an enemy and seeking to play some sort of nefarious game with us. It could be an opening move. Or, if he simply knows that some of us are Phi and has made this mark only to communicate this, then, even if he's a friend, that still could signal some sort of danger as well—something he's aware of and perhaps wanting to warn us about. I mean, why otherwise would he do it?"

"Yes," Omari agreed. "I was thinking the same thing."

"But what sort of danger, I have no idea," Paki added. "We need to tell Hamid right away, and Amon. The king should hear of it as well, as soon as we can get word to him. We don't know quite what it is that we're facing in this."

Walid spoke up and said, "But it might not be a problem or a sign of danger at all. It could be something else."

Omari replied, "True, but then why the stealth and the sudden strange disappearances?"

Walid nodded agreement and conceded, "That's a good point."

Omari then said, mainly to Paki, "Everyone goes on highest alert right now. But we don't alarm the group. We allow them a normal dinner. We tighten up our guard and engage in watchful waiting as we try to make more sense of what's just happened."

Paki said, "I agree."

Omari looked around the room and said, "Who's the senior Phi in Alexandria?"

Paki replied, "I believe it's the older man there who's sitting over by the piano."

"Good. Go greet him casually with a smile and ask him whether all his group is here and accounted for, or if there could be a member who's not officially involved in our little outing here."

"Good idea." Paki immediately walked across the lobby and up to an distinguished looking gentleman sitting near a grand piano that occupied its space magnificently, with its highly polished ebony black finish reflecting the lights of the room that sparkled off its surface. Omari, Walid, and Mafulla could soon see them talking.

Paki bent down to the man and was apparently speaking low to him. Then, the older gentleman slowly rose from his chair and stepped over to the piano bench, where he sat and played several single notes, a haunting combination, and then he began to coax more complex and strange melodies from the keyboard.

"Oh, my goodness," Omari said.

"What is it?" Walid immediately asked, showing concern. Mafulla quickly looked at Omari as well.

He replied with a look of intense interest, and almost of wonder on his face, "The first few notes the man just played, very slowly—F, G, G, A, B, D, G, E, F, were arranged in a mathematical series, what's called the Fibonacci Series, with the note F representing zero and each whole tone on the keyboard standing for a whole number, an integer, and the tones being mapped onto the series of integers."

"What?" Mafulla this time spoke in a voice of bewilderment, and he looked thoroughly confused.

Omari answered in a low voice but with a rushed pace of astonishment. He said: "F, the first note, the starting point, would stand for zero. G is one whole note up, so GG represented 1 and 1, and then the next whole note, A was 2, B was 3, D, the next note played, was 5 (C, which would map the number 4, was left out, since it's not in the series), and then we had G—8, E—13, and F again for 21. It's astonishing—really, amazing. Then, he began to play more quickly, and, I think, it's all Fibonacci, or at least it leads back to the series. When the speed increased, I got lost a bit."

"How in the world do you know all that?" Walid could not have been more astonished, himself.

"I ... it's just that I have an unusual mind, I think. I see mathematical relationships, and I have the gift of near perfect pitch, so I can hear notes as what they are, and ... and I've never heard the famous series captured in musical notes like this. It's equally strange and wonderful."

"What does it mean? What's he doing?" Walid looked at Omari and then back at the man.

"It's code."

"What?"

Omari said, "It must be a code for one or more of the other Phi from this area who are here tonight, maybe all of them. They must know what it means. He's likely warning them of the potential danger or mystery we've just come across, but in such a way that others won't know what's going on—apart from a haunting musical performance."

Walid could see some men and a few women around the room, here and there, turning toward the piano and paying close attention to the sounds. Then, ever so slightly, they began to alter their orientations on the room and to look about casually, watchfully bringing a new level of peak awareness to everything around them. A few moved closer to various doorways.

Paki came back across the room and said to Omari, "All known Phi are accounted for and present. And now they know to be on alert, apparently, from that very strange sounding piece of music."

"Good," Omari responded and turned to Walid, addressing him. "You and Mafulla can rejoin our group. I have to speak with Hamid and Amon. Hamid will likely want to be the one who sees the boss. I think Paki and I should look around for the mystery man right away. You two can enjoy your dinner and put all of this aside for the moment."

"Should I be in on the search, too?" Mafulla said. "I mean—I'm the only one who's seen him."

"I don't think so. You're here to be with your friends and learn more about Alexandria. You've described his attire and elusiveness. You should go participate in the dinner. Your absence would require too much explanation, and some details we can't share widely. The two of us can handle looking for the man."

"That sounds good to me," Walid said. "Are you fine with it, too, Maffie?"

"Yeah, it makes sense."

"One thing," Omari said. "Is he old or young?"

"It was hard to tell, but I'd say younger rather than older."

Omari said, "Ok. I have a feeling this guy knows how to find us, but I hope that we can now find him first, just to be safe."

Right before dark, a car had pulled up to the main gate of Sea Watch, in Tripoli. The two sides of the gate were open wide, so Ambassador Sassi drove slowly through it and up the long private road toward the main house. His son Karim was in the back seat, lightly napping. And on the passenger side of the front seat was Imar al-Baki, a highly placed Libyan official and long-time friend to Sassi. The ambassador had swung by his office and persuaded him to make the trip out to Sea Watch with him, in case any friendly intervention was needed with the former king. Since the Libyans were helping to provide such lavish accommodations for Appolonium and his entourage, the former king would be motivated to please or at least to accommodate the wishes of such a man as al-Baki.

Sassi shared with al-Baki the story he planned on telling the former king, both to show him where he might need help, and also just to rehearse the tale, which was of course being spun away from the full truth of the matter. The Libyan nodded his head and asked a few polite questions and seemed truly eager to be of help with the former king. As they pulled up, they could see that in the large parking area in front of the house there were two trucks and two cars, one of them quite elegant.

When Sassi got out of the automobile he had been driving, he actually stepped on a shell casing from the major gunfight that had taken place so recently, but it sank into the sand under his sandal and he didn't notice it. Farouk and Faraj had made their men police the area carefully and get rid of any evidence that might indicate what had just happened on the property. It was a good thing they had a lot of men at their disposal. Bullet riddled vehicles had to be moved to a garage out back, bodies had to be carried away, and several large bloodstains on the sand had to be shoveled up and removed in buckets. Hundreds of shells had also been picked up and discarded. The sand had been re-raked out front, and all seemed peaceful and quiet, although it was only the encroaching darkness that helped conceal quick repairs to the many bullet holes in the façade of the building, and across various walls. No one could have guessed at the violence that had just taken place here only several hours earlier. The new temporary residents realized that it would be best to keep all of it out of the sight of any Libyan officials who might stop by for a visit. With the right story about the missing monarch, everything could go smoothly for the short time they would need to remain here.

The two unexpected visitors and a newly awakened teenage boy all walked up to the main door and Sassi announced their presence loudly, using a heavy brass knocker in the middle of it. There was also a button off to the side, most likely attached to a bell. He pressed it as well and waited. And, at first, there was no response. "Well, I hope we haven't made this trip for nothing," he said.

"No, no, I'm sure they're here. They rarely venture out beyond the compound, from what I've heard," al-Baki said. "Plus, there are trucks and cars here. Someone is surely at home. But it's a big place. And they're not likely expecting anyone to stop by. We should be patient. Knock once more. At some point, a staff member will hear you."

Sassi did exactly that. He knocked loudly and pushed the button again. Finally, he heard footsteps. The door opened and a large man just stared at them for a couple of seconds and then said, "Yes?"

"We're here to see the true king."

"Oh, well, this is quick, and certainly a surprise. I assume you mean the true and future king of the nearby neighboring kingdom. Is he the one you seek?"

"Yes."

"Is he expecting you?"

"Well, no, I'm afraid not. But we come on urgent business that will be of great concern to him. I know him well. He's an old friend. Just please tell him that the Tunisian Ambassador to the kingdom of which you allude, Omar Sassi, is here to see him, with my son Karim and my good friend, the Libyan Director of Economic Affairs, His Excellence, Imar al-Baki."

"I'll do better than that. I'll take you to where he is."

"Oh, that would be so kind of you. We've had some long and hard travel to get here."

"Please, then, come in." The man held open the door and ushered the guests into the large entryway and across it, down a wide hall toward the back. The man stepped through a doorway and said in a strong clear voice, "The Tunisian Ambassador to Egypt, his son, and the Director of Economic Affairs for Libya are here to see the true and future king of Egypt."

The three visitors had stopped short of the doorway for a moment to allow themselves to be announced, and so couldn't see fully into the room yet, but they heard a voice laugh and say, "Good! Show them in, please." Their escort stood to the side and gestured for them to enter the wide doorway. Omar Sassi was the first through and saw, to his great shock, standing only fifteen feet away, the quite menacing Tau, who was, or at least had been, the head of security for Farouk al-Khoum.

"What?" was all that Sassi could say before Tau spoke with a rare smile on his face.

"The brothers are finishing up some business and will be with you momentarily." Sassi could now clearly see that across the large room, at the far end, both Farouk and Faraj were sitting in overstuffed armchairs and speaking with three other men who were perched on a sofa and a side chair. The ambassador could hardly think at all to process what he was seeing. This was the hideout and fortress for Rasul Appolonium, the former and future king of Egypt, provided for him by high-level officials in the Libyan government. But here instead were his greatest adversaries on earth, and the men Sassi most wanted to avoid at present. And they were receiving guests like this was their home. It was inconceivable. Sassi was completely confused and in a bit of a panic. He made himself take a few quiet and deep breaths to slow his racing heart.

Where was Rasul? What were these men doing here? It didn't make any sense. Had the two opposed forces formed an alliance? But how did they know in the first place that they were opposed forces that should join together? Maybe they didn't. It could be that one of them approached the other as an interested party, hoping they could work together and initially not realizing they were after the same thing. Perhaps, after talking, they all saw that they would be much stronger in league than apart for whatever pursuits they had in mind. Maybe they had indeed come to collaborate without either of the parties ever realizing that they had formerly been working for the same goal, in conflict with one another. Or perhaps they did understand that, but had moved beyond it. It was too unexpected, too confusing. The thoughts raced through Sassi's head.

A similar perplexed exercise of mental gymnastics was happening in the mind of the Libyan official. This situation, on the face of it, didn't make any sense at all—unless one leapt to a creative conclusion such as the ones that Omar was considering. As a result, al-Baki was having analogous thoughts to those bubbling through the stream of consciousness simultaneously being experienced by Sassi. The young Karim, of course, didn't realize the nature or incongruity of the situation, but intuitively sensed his father's anxiety right away. And yet, so far, everyone was acting casual, open, and friendly.

The three men who had been speaking with the al-Khoum brothers all rose together, seemed to do quick bows, and left through a side door. Farouk then waved the new group of visitors over to approach him. In response, they walked slowly across the room, with Omar's mind still spinning in near-panic mode and not knowing quite what to say, since, after all, he had come here convinced that Farouk had kidnapped or killed his men and he was planning to ask Rasul for assistance in stopping or even killing Farouk. He had prepared for awkward questions from Rasul about what he had been doing with the widely feared al-Khoum brothers, but had not anticipated even the possibility of what he was faced with here. He was in the surreal position of now approaching the one man he had been seeking to flee, and in the last place he ever would have expected to see him. Nothing made any sense at all.

Farouk spoke right away, looking at Omar. "What are you doing here, my old friend?"

"I need to talk to you."

"How did you know I would be found here, of all places?"

Sassi paused for a few seconds and said, "I have many sources, many eyes and ears on which I rely, directly or indirectly."

"Whose eyes and ears brought you here?"

Omar felt his throat tighten and his stomach go into free fall. But he showed none of this on his face. He replied, simply, "I have no idea."

"What?"

"I have no idea. My assistant back in Cairo, my chief of staff, simply told me that he had heard you would be here, and that I should come quickly. I was going to ask his sources for this surprising information, but he rushed me out, pleading for me to leave, telling me I had no time for further conversation, at the risk of my own life."

"Why would he say such things?"

"He had reason to believe that someone was kidnapping and killing my men, men from the embassy, and that I would be next. He was panicked and insisted that my son and I leave immediately to save our lives. He suggested that you would be able to help us."

"Who did he suggest was coming after you?"

"He didn't say."

"I find that hard to believe."

"He didn't know. I promise you, he just said that someone is killing our men and that we need help and protection. These were the men who were seeking to do the jobs you had given me. They were men on whom I was depending for my future and yours."

"I depend on no one for my future. I take care of my own future. And you should know that."

"Yes, I know, but you had asked certain things of me in that regard, and I was seeking to use the best resources I had in order to accomplish your wishes."

"They were directives, not wishes."

"I'm sorry. I know. My word choice wasn't good. We're all a bit tired. I mean simply to refer to the men who were in the process of enacting your directives."

It was making Karim very uneasy to hear all this for the first time, and to feel the nervousness of his father, a state of mind that Omar was working to hide well from the al-Khoum brothers and from his friend al-Baki—or at least he hoped he was concealing it.

"You don't look well," Farouk said.

"I don't feel my best, either. It's been a long time of travel to get here, and I'm apparently on the run for my life," Omar responded. Karim was shocked at these words and looked at his father now with a jolt of visceral fear in his gut.

Farouk replied, "I see. And, I'd like to know why you brought your friend, here, our Libyan guest."

"Well, when I heard you were here, there was no way I could know why. I thought you were going to be in Tunisia until the big events, and I had heard rumors that Rasul Appolonium had been making this place his home. You and I have a good working relationship, of course, but the former king I didn't know well at all, and so I asked my friend here to come along with me, in case I needed for him to plead my case also to Rasul. You know, since the Libyans were sheltering him and perhaps providing support, I thought that Imar might have leverage with him that I otherwise could not have—in case, the two of you were somehow working together now, which I would have had no way of knowing, but your reported presence here did surprise me and it necessitated my preparing for such a situation."

"How might Rasul be of help to you?"

"He still has many friends in Cairo. He might know someone who could help."

Farouk paused and said, "You speak many words, and I hear them, and take them all in. They are smooth and plausible. And so are you. But underneath, I detect agitation. The truth may be very different from what you're now seeking to have me believe."

"I would never lie to you," Sassi lied.

"I'm not a man to be lied to."

"I know. That's why I would never do it, or even consider it."

"But, sadly, I feel that you're engaged in precisely that, now."

"No, no, not at all. Why would I?"

"First of all, the fact that I'm here is a well-kept secret. I've had many men transported to this place for a specific reason, but the precise location of their destination and the purpose for which they were being brought here were carefully guarded until the very last minute. You say your assistant had word that we were here. But I can assure you that no one but a reliable few men knew we were coming to this exact place until mere hours before we arrived. And they would never talk of it." He stopped and said, "Unless, of course, you knew from Rasul or one of his men that we had been invited to visit here today. That's possible. One of them could have told you. But that would mean you were in prior contact with Rasul, despite what you've just said to me."

"No, no, I assure you. I've had no relationship at all with the former king, or with any of his men."

"Perhaps then, your chief of staff?"

"No one who is working for me, I can promise you. No one would have any reason to be in touch with Rasul."

"I see. Then, by the time that anyone else who might have

leaked word of our presence could have done so and communicated with anyone on the outside, thus sending a rumor out into the world, there would have been no possibility for it to have reached your assistant and brought you as quickly as you have showed up here after our own … arrival."

"Well, I'm sure …"

"Do you see what I mean?"

"But … I'm sure there's a suitable explanation."

"Yes, there's a simple explanation, quite simple. You're lying. You're a creative liar. You came here to see the man you believed to be staying here, Rasul Appolonium, and that's why you brought this other gentleman with you, to speak to him and perhaps to persuade him of something, or to do something for you."

"Well, yes, I believed Rasul was here, I don't deny that. I've said I knew it."

"But you also said you knew I was here."

"I had reason to think so, and it surprised me."

"But you could not have, you see, unless you were in communication with Rasul. That's my point."

"It must have been by telegraph that the information was conveyed, quickly, instantly."

"From where, exactly?"

"I have no idea. But from one of many possible places, of course. Tripoli is a modern city."

Farouk looked down at the floor and sighed. Then he looked back up. "I'm afraid the time of your usefulness to me is over."

Omar said, "No, no, no. I'm sorry that you say that or even think such a thing. It's unnecessary for you to feel that way, and I can assure you that I'm now in a position to be more useful to you than ever before. I have a new contact within the palace, a woman who has fallen under my influence and can give us inside information of all kinds that can't be obtained in any other way."

"Who is this woman?"

"I would prefer …"

"No, it's not at all a matter of your preferences at the present moment, or in any dealings with me."

"It's a lady named Hoda El-Bay."

"Who is she?"

"She's a teacher in the palace school and a very highly placed individual within the current regime, a close friend of the king, and a person with access to sensitive and important information that I'm going to have her provide me in assistance to your master plan."

"How do you know she'll give you such information?"

"I know the way a man knows about a woman."

Farouk looked at Karim and then back at Omar. "Good. I see. She'll be very useful to me, perhaps."

"With a certainty," Omar said.

"With a certainty," Farouk repeated, and then he looked over at his brother with a bit of an expression.

Faraj, who had been sitting quietly, chose this moment to speak. Addressing the ambassador, he said, "Would you like to see the former king now?"

"Well, yes, if he's here."

"He's in the garden, out back, having some quiet time. I can take you to where he is, all of you. I think we've talked enough, just among ourselves, don't you, brother?"

"Yes, Faraj. Thank you. Our guest has made a surprising and impressive argument. It's enough for now. Why don't you and Tau take our visitors out back to be with the king? It's a good time for them to join him, now that we've had this chat. I'll likely come out and check up on you all in a few minutes."

Looking at Omar, Farouk said with a big smile, "I thank you for the information and perspective you've provided me. We'll act on it right away. I hope you can forgive my harsh words and any other unpleasantness that you may have experienced because of my concerns. A man in my position can't be too careful at such a time as this."

"No offense taken, I can assure you," Sassi said.

"My brother and our friend Tau will take you to where the king is. And I'm sure you can stay here for as long as needed." Farouk waved in the direction of a back door, and Tau smiled and motioned for the three visitors to follow him and Faraj, who now also stood and gestured for them to precede him.

About a minute after they had left the room, give or take a few seconds, Farouk heard three quick gunshots in rapid succession, muffled but distinct, Pop! Pop! Pop! And he smiled, but this time, sincerely.

25

The Little Book

Dinner at the Palace Hotel was amazing. Once Walid and Mafulla had rejoined the group, they were shown to their chairs at a long table that had been created by pushing together several other tables, all covered with thick white linen tablecloths. Walid was seated next to Kissa, and Mafulla was directly across from him, next to Hasina. Khalid and Hoda knew what they were doing and cared about such things. They had arranged the guests perfectly, and put place cards with their names around the table.

When the boys got into the dining room and to the table, Bafur was entertaining the group with a monologue about his greatest meals, and his certainty that this dinner would rank up there with the best. He could be very funny about food and was getting lots of laughs from his classmates and the girls as he created lavish verbal descriptions of past repasts that had taken him to mystical heights.

"What was the one dish you couldn't stop eating until you were absolutely totally stuffed to the max?" Cabar asked him.

"Um, that would be a divine, delectable, unearthly, ethereal casserole I once had. It's called, 'Three Bean Casserole,' which I could never quite understand, since there seemed to be only two kinds of beans in it. But regardless and nonetheless, it was probably, of all the great things I've eaten in my life, the best ever—and I could not stop!"

"Made of beans?" Mafulla said before he had even sat down.

"Yes, two kinds in a wondrous brown sauce with meat, covered by a crunchy sourdough breaded crust and great savory melted cheese baked hard on top—altogether the best combination I've ever tasted."

"Beans." Mafulla repeated, with his eyebrows raised.

"Massive amounts," Bafur grinned.

"I suppose there were ... repercussions?" Mafulla ventured, pronouncing carefully his chosen term, as he sat.

Bafur grinned and everyone laughed. "Major repercussions," he admitted, to more laughter.

"Percussive repercussions, perforce, I'm persuaded," Mafulla said, over the laughter, and caused even more.

"Yes!" Bafur replied heartily, as he, too, laughed and said, "My enjoyment of that dish echoed and reverberated for hours."

"It was a dark and stormy night," Mafulla then narrated dramatically, gesturing with his right hand and looking up and down the table at the faces around him. "The thunder roared, the winds gusted, and camels fled for cover while people in surrounding kingdoms stopped and asked: What could this be—the storm of all storms? Or is it the roar of cannons in the distance? Or rather, perhaps, could it be the rumbles of a thousand wagons of war? Dogs sniffed the night air and howled."

Everyone at the table was chuckling as Mafulla went on. "A wise old man sitting outside his house in the cool of the evening, a former chef, in fact, alone knew what it was. He said, aloud, 'Ah, someone, somewhere, has overindulged on Three Bean Casserole, I might infer, that most famous dish ordinarily made of two types of beans—the third left out on purpose, I suspect, lest the earth itself could not bear the consequences and even the tides would be reversed.' Hours later, though, calm was restored across the land.

And peace ruled again over all. Though, the one remaining sign of that massive feat of gourmandizing and its implications was that, hours later, the sun arose in a thick and lingering haze. That, my friends, is the tale of Bafur and the Beans."

At the conclusion of Mafulla's extemporaneous remarks, everyone clapped, still laughing, and someone whistled loudly. Well, almost everyone clapped. Khalid and Hoda both had hands over their mouths so that no one could see their own embarrassed mirth in response to this major and grossly impolite silliness. "Dinner and a show," Walid turned and said to Kissa.

"Of course—you two are here," she replied and made eye contact with Hasina, who just shook her head while smiling.

Khalid then stood up, tapped his dinner knife on the side of a water glass, and got everyone's attention. He told them briefly what the dinner would involve, and gave a quick run-down of the next day's activities. He also implored them all to go to sleep as early as they could after dessert, emphasizing that they were going to have a very long and interesting day, at the end of which a train would take them back to Cairo, for a very late arrival and a sleepover at the palace.

"Tonight, you need your rest. I want your minds to be extra sharp tomorrow, as well as your senses," Khalid said. "There's much here to see and take in and understand. We'll all be richer for the new experience—but not if you go through the day exhausted and half asleep. I assure you that an early bedtime will purchase a wonderful day tomorrow. We'll be knocking on all doors at 5:45 AM for a 6 o'clock breakfast. That's early. I want you to be prepared and on time, because then, all the really interesting stuff begins! But for now, enjoy your dinner."

When he concluded his brief remarks and sat back down, a small army of waiters who had been standing by at the ready swooped over the table and set out the first course of their meal. All of the service staff simultaneously put the plates down at their assigned places in a perfectly orchestrated and expertly timed movement. And then, the feast began. Bafur, it should be said, was not disappointed.

While this was happening, the king was elsewhere in the hotel, just starting to have his own private dinner with a few of the most senior Alexandria area Phi. He was explaining to them all about recent developments and the threats to the kingdom that seemed to be looming on the horizon. He chose not to relay what had been done to try to steal The Book of Phi and the Ring of Phi, or to possess the Stone of Giza. Although he trusted these colleagues deeply, he knew that he could not take even the remote chance that someone would mention something to a friend or family member they thought to be trustworthy, who then might do the same, and so on, and somewhere in the chain of trust, someone less than fully cautious might gain access to information that it was crucial for the al-Khoum brothers not to know. When the stakes are so high, prudence must always reach higher. The king initially sketched out some recent events, like the attempt to assassinate the prince and his friends, and asked these trusted people what they might know or have heard that could help him prepare a solid and effective defensive strategy against anything yet to come. He also explained that he might be calling on some of them along the way to be of assistance. They in turn assured him of their loyalty to him and the kingdom and expressly offered to make available their talents, as Phi and otherwise, in his service.

Ali had the wisdom to listen more than talk throughout the entirety of his time with these remarkable individuals, and as a result, he learned more from what they said than he had even hoped he might. He understood great listening to be an art that, in its highest forms, must be cultivated assiduously. And this was an insight he had conveyed to Walid and Mafulla on more than one occasion.

Listening well is a spiritual discipline. And, paradoxically, it may require even more commitment and activity than speaking well. The skilled listener asks good questions, and follows up with even better ones. The great listener hears what's said, notices what's not, and takes in even the spaces between what's put into words. He or she pays attention to physical demeanor, facial expression, bodily movement, and the many delicacies involving tone of voice, along with matters of verbal inflection and even the pace of someone's speech. The most masterful practitioner of this art listens with nearly all the senses, both those we understand and even those that elude rational analysis, while still bringing us information.

The careful listener knows when to speak and when to remain silent, when to goad and when to wait patiently. A great listener can even embrace silence for its own riches. The master of this art does not try to dominate, but to respect the flow of conversation and revelation as it comes to him. He may steer it now and then, but just as often, he rides the current to see where it might take him. The careful listener is also self-critical and alert as to whether his own inclinations, beliefs, values, emotions, and needs—his inner interpretive filter—is biasing or distorting what he can take in and process. He never allows appearances to pass off, automatically, as realities.

The king was a skilled practitioner of all these things. And, as a result, by the end of the evening, he had learned a great deal, and the Phi who had shared the meal with him felt deeply appreciated and understood. Because of that, it was a needed bonding experience for all of them, and especially in light of what was yet to come.

They discussed many serious matters over the hours of their time together, but there was also great laughter at certain moments. Such Phi could relax completely in each other's company. There was no unhealthy competition among them, or any swirl of power plays to bolster big and easily bruised egos. They all, men and women, felt secure in themselves, knowing well who they were and enjoying each other's presence, even in such a time of threat. The fellowship of the mind that they shared allowed them fully to enjoy each other and their talk together. They knew that the world is packed with dangers and delights, and that the wise among us can make our way forward with a positive spirit, despite any challenges that might lie in wait for us up ahead on the path.

When the evening was over and the king said goodnight to all, they each felt a new sense of purpose and a corresponding personal commitment concerning their future together as firm supporters of all the good people in their kingdom. Then, Ali was able to go to bed a short time later with a great feeling of deep satisfaction in what he had been able to accomplish with these friends throughout the city.

Earlier on, before these members of Phi had their meal together, Hamid had been able to see the king privately for a couple of minutes and report on the odd developments downstairs. He received a few instructions to impart to Omari and Paki, and was thanked for his report. He then rejoined the group and had time to enjoy a quick version of dinner for himself.

After their own big meal, which was really a feast, Walid and Mafulla rode the elevator back up to their floor in the company of Kissa, Hasina, Cabar, Ara, and Layla. The girls were staying one level above the boys, so at the fifth floor stop they said goodnight to the prince and his friend, and the two boys got off and walked down the hall to their room. Once they had made it through the door, Walid collapsed on his bed right away. He took a deep breath and let it out and said, "I'm so full and tired at the same time I can't describe it."

"Yeah, me, too," Mafulla replied as he slid off his sandals and sat on the edge of his bed. "That food was unbelievable," he added.

"Definitely. And, thank goodness, there were not too many beans available," Walid said.

"Yeah, I was watching Bafur, and was prepared to wrestle any extra servings away from him—for the much greater good of us all, including the other hotel guests," Mafulla replied.

"So, speaking of other guests, what do you think about the mystery man in white?" Walid asked.

"I don't know." Mafulla lay down on his side, facing his friend. "I'm glad he didn't show up a third time. He was a little eerie."

"What do you mean?" Walid asked.

"I mean, he was just standing there by himself both times, staring at us."

"Was he looking at the group in general, or at us in particular?"

"I don't know. It was hard to tell. It seemed to me like it was just us, you and me, but I can't be sure."

"How old exactly do you think the guy is?"

"Not old, maybe early to mid twenties—maybe a little younger. I'd say he's younger than Paki or Omari or Amon. But he was always in some sort of shadow, so it was hard to tell. I could be wrong."

"I wish I knew what he was up to. What do you think about the Phi symbol written on the wall?"

"The circle was a little uneven, and the line was not exactly straight, but it was really not bad for freehand."

"No, crazy person—what do you think it meant?"

"Oh, I don't know what to think," Mafulla said. "He's got to be trying to signal us, but for what reason, I have no idea. And there's another thing. Why a drawing on the wall, rather than a note passed by a bellman, or just a simple conversation?"

"Yeah, good point."

"But at least from what he drew, I guess we can safely conclude he's not just some ordinary deranged guy or a common thief, or anything like that."

"I guess you're right." Walid was quiet for a few seconds. "But an extraordinary deranged guy is not out of consideration."

"True."

"Do you think we'll see him tomorrow?"

"Yeah, actually. I do."

"Are you worried at all about it?"

"No, not really. It seems Ok, strange enough, but Ok."

"Well, then, I suppose we can feel fine about going to sleep without running worst case scenarios through our heads. Knowing you, I'm sure you'd have a bad feeling if something was wrong, or any danger loomed."

"Yeah, so it seems."

"And you're sure you're not worried about anything in particular, or even pointedly concerned?" Walid asked.

"No, nothing other than the book that's been on my mind."

"The book."

"Yeah, the red book I've dreamed about."

"Oh. Ok, good. But if you have any wild dreams about anything at all tonight and change your mind about the danger element, remember to tell me."

"I will. No worries. See you in the morning, future philosopher-king." Mafulla rolled over and turned off the lamp that had been lighting their room.

"Yeah." Walid yawned and said, "See you later, cogitator."

They heard a few other doors open and close up and down the hallway, but just for the next ten minutes. Then the hotel grew very quiet. It was dark outside and so dark in the room it didn't take long for the boys to fall asleep.

The passage of time during sleep is exceedingly odd. Unless you dream and wake up to turn over or are otherwise disturbed, the entire night can run its course with no sense of the flow of moments at all. Some equivalent of a switch in your head flips at some point from on to off, and you're no longer a conscious participant in the ordinary world of space and time. Or maybe, it's less like a switch and more like a flame that gradually burns down. Your normal consciousness ebbs and slowly diminishes until—poof—it's gone like the last flicker from an old oil lamp whose tiny fire reduces down to nothing. What's interesting is that either you never quite experience that precise moment, that transition as such, or else you never remember it later. It's likely the former. Once the flame of consciousness grows small enough, then perhaps the special experience of self-conscious reflective awareness dissipates at the same moment as the flame, and so isn't there an instant after the cessation of it to take note of its passing. And what isn't noted can't be remembered.

Walid and Mafulla both slept deeply, but Mafulla eventually dreamed again of a library, a large library holding thousands of books—and once more, regular, modern books—and he could see on the floor under a shelf that one book had fallen and now lay there unnoticed until an old man bent down and picked it up. He examined it briefly and handed it to a young man who put it back on a shelf, and there it sat until it then fell back to the floor again hard with a loud thump.

"What was that?" Mafulla sat bolt upright in bed and felt a wave of alertness rush through his body.

"What?" Walid was roused from sleep as well.

"That noise."

"5:45, Time to get up! Everyone up!" A voice from the hallway announced. Then they heard a loud knock on the door across the hall, followed by the same declaration of the time and the next required actions.

"Oh, it must have been a knock on our door."

"My brain incorporated it into a dream."

"What was the dream?"

"A man was in a library, a big library. He had picked up a book off the floor, a regular book that was just lying there, almost under a shelf. He examined the cover and was opening it, and then looking into it and suddenly he gave it to a younger man, and he put it onto another shelf, in a different place, and it somehow dropped onto the floor again. The book hit the floor—Bam! I guess that was really the sound of the knock on our door."

Walid yawned and said, "Ok, then, that's creative enough. But like I said, I heard nothing. I dreamed nothing. There could have been cannon fire outside and I wouldn't have heard it."

"You would have heard Bafur."

"Yeah. No doubt. That's for sure. But we should really leave our poor friend alone."

"He should leave certain foods alone."

"Hey, like father, like son."

"Yeah, I guess you're right. Bashir's pretty legendary."

"He's truly notorious. And we will be, too, for being late, unless we get up right now and get down to breakfast."

"Ok. Are we supposed to pack up at this point?"

"Yeah, I think so, and take the bags downstairs."

The boys cleaned up, packed up, and got ready for their day, getting downstairs to the dining room, almost within the allotted fifteen minutes. But still, they were the last to arrive.

"Sorry, sorry we're late," Mafulla said, to the first group they encountered. "It takes Walid longer than most to tame his hair."

"Me? You're the one who was staring into the mirror for what had to be ten minutes!"

"Oh, that. It's completely existential, I assure you. I was just … examining my soul—a morning ritual to start the day. But I do glance over my outfit and the overall look, just in case, you know—really, just to make sure that nothing about my outward appearance will be too overwhelming for the citizens of this fair city who might not be accustomed to being dazzled so early in the day as we plan to be out and about. You know. Superior style brings responsibility."

That made four or five of his fellow students laugh or else roll their eyes and, just then, Khalid came up and herded them all into the dining room for a beautiful buffet breakfast, telling them that in thirty minutes or so they would leave together and venture forth to the site of the famous Library of Alexandria.

"I wonder if that was the library in my dream," Mafulla almost whispered to Walid as they were walking to the buffet table. And then he added, "It had to be."

"Maybe," Walid replied, "At least, symbolically. Since we're going there, and all."

"So, what does it mean?"

"Watch for falling books."

"But there aren't any books there any more, right? The library burned down, after all."

"Good point." Walid looked around and caught sight of his teacher and said in a louder voice, addressed to him, "Khalid! What's now on the site of the old library?"

"Not much. A memorial plaque, I think. But, close by, there are some shops, and two modern bookstores. So, books are still around."

"Thanks." Walid turned to Mafulla and said, "Ok, then. Just keep on the lookout for the mystery man, and watch for falling books from any high place today, I suppose."

Khalid asked all the boys to sit as a class at one table for breakfast, and Hoda did the same thing for the girls. They would all spend the rest of the day together, the teachers reasoned, and so it might be nice to have a few minutes for just each class to sit down and talk.

The boys began discussing right away the fact that Alexandria had once been the capital city, and someone wondered aloud whether the locals were jealous of Cairo being the capital now. Khalid reminded them that the years of Cleopatra in Alexandria holding court were a very long time in the past and that, likely, the Alexandrians had long ago fully adjusted to their altered and yet still exalted role in the kingdom. He said, "Schools here make field trips now and then to Cairo, so they seem completely reconciled to our place in kingdom governance. This city is great and important in many other ways."

That made sense. So they wouldn't have to anticipate angry and resentful locals wanting a restoration of governance and being just generally irritated to see kids from the palace school class in their midst. But then, really, Walid reminded everyone, no one knew of their palace connection except their security and several military men trusted by the king. So they all could walk the streets today without any worry. Or that, at least, was the conclusion generally drawn by the boys in their rambling conversation. The true dangers to come their way could be anticipated at this point by no one—and so the two boys who would face those dangers had no clue of what was waiting.

The girls were quizzing Hoda and Kissa on how it felt to be at the old stomping grounds of their illustrious ancestor, the Queen of the Nile. But Kissa reminded them that Grandma Cleo, as she called her, probably didn't do any stomping. She was, rather, reputed to glide. This got some smiles from the other girls and led into more talk of history and beauty and elegance generally, and then the beauty and elegance of the hotel they were all enjoying. Someone mentioned Paris. And someone else spoke of Italy, and especially, Milan. In what seemed to be no time at all, breakfast ended and Hoda helped guide them all out to waiting trucks where they loaded their bags and got ready for the brief ride to their first destination.

The visit to the presumed site of the famous library was initially not as exciting as most of them had hoped. There was almost nothing there to see. But Khalid did his best to paint a verbal picture of how things used to be. He was very dramatic about it all, and that made it more interesting. He described the dining room and meeting rooms of the library, and its gardens, as well as other gathering places where ancient scholars would meet and talk and come to new revelations and discoveries together. And he told them that history reports there to have been a prominent inscription above the shelves of scrolls in the library that said, "The Place for The Cure of The Soul."

"Very cool," Set remarked. But, despite their teacher's best efforts, the fact remained that looking at an empty space adorned by a lonely marker stone and an ancient plaque gets old pretty fast. And Khalid seemed to understand that. So he soon called for a break and gave them all exactly an hour to roam through the smaller shops within sight, along with the two modern bookstores whose presence seemed to commemorate the history of the written word here. He assured them that interesting things were likely to be found in those stores. And, who knows, he hinted, even an ancient manuscript could lurk in waiting on one of the shelves. You could stumble across almost anything in a city like Alexandria.

The nice thing about the shopping and browsing break was that the chaperones, escorts, and guards stayed outside each of the buildings in which the students were free to roam. After an interior sweep, the guards checked all external exits and secured the perimeter, but within that, they gave the students some space and a sense of freedom. It was a relief to be without the adults for a while, as nice as they all were, and as reassuring as their presence might be.

Kissa and Walid went right into one of the bookstores together, followed, of course, by Mafulla and Hasina. Some of the other kids walked into the same store, a place that was actually pretty big and stuffed with books, maps, and associated items. Others went first to the smaller nearby bookshop, a few wandered into various stores for clothing and local handmade goods, and three of the students got permission to just sit outside on some benches that offered a view of the water at a distance.

Walid always loved a bookstore. You never knew what you might find. Within five minutes, Kissa and Hasina had discovered three sections, side-by-side, that drew them like magnets, one on fashion and sewing and clothing patterns, one on food and cooking, and the other on movie stars and famous people. The owner must have known what many young women of the day would like, and had put these varied books close together on purpose. Walid and Mafulla, by contrast, started off with military and history books, and then told the girls they were going to wander off toward the back of the shop to see what was there. The girls were so mesmerized by what they were seeing that they were absolutely fine to split up for a while.

Walid found his way eventually to the far back right-hand corner of the store and pulled a book off the shelf that was about the oceans of the world, and he began to flip through it. Mafulla ended up in a section a few feet away, looking through a text about Crocodiles of the Nile, with illustrations. There was an adventure section and right beside it a philosophy selection. Interesting. Those two topics were normally thought of as worlds apart, but Walid and Mafulla both knew they could overlap considerably. When the prince first saw these two adjacent sections and noted their subjects, he thought to himself that he could spend all day right here.

Just then, a book ten feet away fell off a shelf and landed on the floor with a bang. Mafulla jumped a little and looked over and said, "No way." Walid quickly walked a few steps to where it had fallen and picked it up. He looked at the title: "Secret Societies of the World." He glanced around but didn't see anyone else close by.

"Hey, check this out," he said to Mafulla as his friend walked over, glancing at the shelves near him, as if to prepare for more falling objects. Walid held the book out to Mafulla, who took it and looked at it. The subject was by itself enough to get his attention on a new level. This could not be a mere coincidence.

The shelves of books closest to them were a good ten to twelve feet high in most places, and against the walls they were even higher. This particular bookshelf from which the volume had fallen was one of the ten-foot wooden units in the middle of the room, running maybe forty feet long or more and holding books on both sides. No one else seemed to be in this part of the store at the moment. There were plenty of shoppers up front, with the more popular sections full of recent novels and other stuff. There was poetry and some biography. But back here were mostly older and less frequently requested titles.

Walid found the space the book had been in before it had fallen, and something made him reach through the hole it had left between adjacent volumes and pull out the closest book on the other side of the shelf whose spine and title were facing away from him. It was a medium sized text, and when he lifted it toward him, he could see it was entitled "*Natural and Supernatural: The Universe Next Door.*"

Mafulla was glancing over a passage in the book on Secret Societies and Walid was now, within seconds, concentrating on the introduction to this very unusual book he had in his hands. They were both for the moment totally focused in on what they were reading, so neither heard the bare feet quickly and stealthily approaching them.

We know that, in ancient times, both the Egyptians and the Greeks went largely barefoot. Their gods and goddesses were likewise depicted in statuary, as well as in paintings, without any sort of footwear. But in modern days, very few people were to be seen out and about in these lands during daylight hours without shoes, except for the very poor, a few priests and nuns, and an occasional assassin whose work required the extreme quiet that only bare feet could provide.

A hand touched Walid's arm as a soft voice said, "Excuse me, are either of you, by any chance … Phi?" Mafulla, who was only a few feet away, turned and looked up quickly without otherwise moving. All his insides seemed to freeze where he stood. He could hardly think.

"It's you?" Walid said in a near whisper.

"Yes. I'm the one who's been following you."

"What do you want?" Walid asked, his body now tensed for action.

"It's important. I want to give you something," the young man said, "a book, if you're indeed who I think you are."

"Who do you think we are?" Walid again spoke.

"I think you're both Phi."

"How do you know about that?"

"My grandfather was Phi. And after his death a few years ago, I found in his things some journals and diaries where he had written about Phi. I saw a photograph of a man who's with you, an older man. I recognized him when you arrived at the docks, even though the picture was from many years ago and had faded."

Walid looked in the man's eyes and said, "Are you Phi?"

"No. Well, not officially, at least. But I have some of the power to know. It flares up in me only at crucial times. I really have no control over it. I've never been approached to be Phi, and I'm not known to any senior Phi as a possible candidate or anything—I mean, not as far as I'm aware. I don't really know any of them, either. That's why I'm approaching you, as younger men who would most likely be open to listen to me."

"How did you know where to find us?"

"I had a feeling yesterday that I should go down to the dock."

"Why?"

"I didn't know why. You'll understand, I think. But I've been hoping to meet a young Phi. I saw the older man and I recognized him and I was so surprised, and then I saw you. And I felt you might be Phi. So I followed you."

"You made the mark."

"Yes. I did. I just didn't know how else to get your attention in the right way."

"Why should we speak with you?"

"Because I'm the son of the son of your brother in Phi. I'm sort of in the Phi family."

"Ok. All right. Are you sure no one told you we were here, or even provided a hint?"

"I'm sure. If your visit is secret, I mean, if it's a secret that it's you as a Phi who are visiting, then you've not been compromised. I found out by accident, as most would say, or by need and intent, as I believe. I'm confident that, as Phi, you'll understand this."

Mafulla now stepped closer. "You're not dressed in white today."

"I had to be able to get in here without being recognized by anyone you might have told about me."

"What do you want to give us or tell us?" Walid asked.

The young man reached into a pocket. Mafulla tensed up for a second, but then relaxed. The stranger pulled out a small red book. It looked just like the one from Mafulla's dream. The stranger said, "The book I pushed to the floor and the one you found behind it are both titles you should read. I suggest you buy them today. I would get them for you if I could. But this is one you need not buy. It's very old. It belonged to my grandfather. He got it from his grandfather. It's something you may need soon. I have a strong feeling. And I give it to you freely." He handed the small book to Walid.

"It's the red book," Mafulla said. As Walid looked at the obviously old, formerly bright cover, Mafulla turned to their new friend and said, "I've had dreams about this book."

"Good. That's very good."

Walid asked, "What is it?"

The young man said, "I'm not completely sure. It's about another book, and also a ring and a stone."

Walid glanced over at Mafulla, who in turn, met his gaze. The prince said, "Really?"

"Yes. It apparently provides information about these three things. But it assumes that the reader already knows many other facts about the mysterious items."

"We know of the three things," Mafulla said.

"Good. Then you will be able to use this. And, at the end, there's an explanation of a code, a code of some sort that apparently can't otherwise be broken or interpreted. This book has the key to that code. Or, so it seems."

Walid felt his mouth go dry. His uncle had told him and Mafulla a lot about The Book of Phi, The Ring of Phi, and The Stone of Giza, and had explained that there were crucial passages in The Book of Phi, apparently the most advanced instructions on how to cultivate and use the most extreme Phi powers, and also important background information, that were in some sort of code or language that no one could decipher, and so it couldn't be read. The king believed that a key to this code must exist somewhere, but he had said that he had no idea where. Could this small book contain the vitally important key that no one in possession of The Book of Phi for at least two generations, and maybe more, had seen? If so, then, surely, it would be a source of immense power—maybe even beyond imagining. And as many other things did, it could be coming into their lives at just the right time.

Walid nodded his understanding. He said, "This will do great good in the right hands. But it would be truly terrible in the wrong ones."

"I know. Or, at least, it's what I felt. That's why I wanted to put it into yours. My grandfather told me once that it's a very old book that's been hidden away for the sake of safety. I wanted it to be even more safe, but also useful. I just felt like it was time."

"What's your name?"

"Ibrahim."

"Thank you, Ibrahim."

"You're most welcome."

"I'll make sure this gets to the right person immediately, one who will use it only for great good."

"Oh. Hi." Kissa had just walked up to get the boys and greeted the young man to whom Walid was talking.

"Oh! Kissa, I didn't see you. This is Ibrahim. He lives here and was just recommending some books to me and Mafulla."

"That's very nice of you," she said, looking at the stranger, who at this point was smiling.

"Ibrahim, this is my close friend, Kissa."

"It's good to meet you," he said.

"Likewise. We're enjoying your city."

"I'm glad."

Kissa turned back to Walid and said, "I'm afraid dad just stuck his head in the door and gave us all a five minute warning. We're supposed to be in the trucks then, for the next part of our tour."

"Ok, no problem. We'd better go up front then and buy these books." Walid turned again to Ibrahim and said, "It was nice to meet you. If you're ever in Cairo, go to the big public marketplace, find the Adi Shop, and tell them you want to see me, Walid, and Mafulla, my friend here, who's the son of the owner. You'll be given a royal welcome, I can assure you."

"I appreciate that. You're very kind," Ibrahim replied. "Take good care of your books."

"We'll be sure to."

"Bye, for now, and thanks again," Mafulla said as they all turned and walked up the aisle toward the front of the store, leaving their new friend at the edge of the Philosophy section, and right next to Adventure.

Kissa then looked back and said, "Goodbye, Ibrahim."

"Goodbye for now," he replied. And then he thought those last two words again.

"Where's Hasina?" Walid asked.

"Waiting for us up front. She and I found a couple of books, too." Kissa smiled.

"What are the subjects?"

"Um, I know this might sound strange, and they're very different topics, but we're going to share. She's getting one on French cooking, and we're both really interested in that."

"Yum," Mafulla replied. "I hope you two can cook something up for us."

"Yeah. We should," Kissa answered, and then added, "Or we could teach you how to cook something up for us."

"A much bigger challenge, I'm sure," Mafulla pointed out.

"We love challenges."

"And then Mafulla said to her, "What's the other book that you also mentioned?"

"Oh, yeah. I'm getting one on hand-to-hand combat, another shared interest of ours."

Walid laughed and said, "Really? French cooking and hand-to-hand combat? Those were in the same section?"

Mafulla suggested, "Maybe filed under Knives?"

Kissa laughed and said, "The combat book was actually in the sewing and knitting section, oddly enough."

"Very odd, indeed," Mafulla agreed.

She explained, "I think a prior shopper just put it down there and forgot it, and it looks really good. Of course, then again, maybe it was no accident that I found it where it was."

Walid asked, "What do you mean?"

"You can do more than you might think with knitting needles."

"I can imagine," he replied. "And this is just another great reminder that I'm glad you're my friend. I'd hate to get on the wrong side of a big knitting needle." They had arrived now at the front desk, where Hasina was waiting and Jabari was buying a book on magic tricks.

"You're actually going to do some magic?" Mafulla asked when he saw the title.

"Yeah, Manni's going to be my assistant," Jabari replied in almost a whisper. "But he doesn't know it yet. And don't say anything. He might want to get paid."

The little simian made a happy noise in Jabari's backpack and Mafulla bent over and looked at him and said, "Manni's such a good little monkey, yes he is." He then sort of chirped fast—the monkey, that is—and Mafulla laughed.

The girls bought their books first, and then Walid and Mafulla paid for theirs. The little red book given to them by Ibrahim was in Walid's pocket. All four of them walked out of the bookstore and turned toward where their trucks were parked. The prince saw

Hamid standing at the back of the nearest truck and said, "Hamid, good morning."

"Good morning, my friend."

"Do you know where my uncle is right now? I haven't seen him yet today."

The older man replied, "He had some business back at the hotel and said he'd join us a little later in the morning. Omari's also with him."

"Ok, good. Would you let me know when you see him, if you catch sight of him before I do?"

"Certainly. Is everything Ok?"

"Yeah, just fine, but I'd like to speak with him as soon as I can."

"I'll make sure to tell him and get you together."

Walid looked at the trucks and picked the closest one, where he could see Jabari and Set already seated in the back. Mafulla, Hasina, and Kissa climbed aboard with him, assisted by a friendly palace guard in civilian clothing who had accompanied them on the trip. When everyone was in the trucks and Khalid and Hoda had counted and then double-checked that all were present, they took off for the next historical site they were planning to visit. Alexandria was full of fascinating history, and they wanted to see all the top spots.

After a couple of minutes, Manni started growing a little agitated in the backpack. "I bet the little guy's hot in there," Set said. "It's a warm day. Maybe you should let him get some fresh air. Are the collar and leash on him?"

"Yeah, he's all secure," Jabari assured his friend.

"Ok, then if you want me to, I can undo the flap of the backpack, and you can reach in and get a good hold on the leash, and we can let him sit with us and maybe catch some breeze."

"Good idea," Jabari said. Since the pack was sitting on the bench between them, Set reached over and untied the flap covering the top of it. Jabari reached in, saying "Good monkey, Manni.

Why don't you come out for a while?" And that seemed to be just what Manni had wanted. He was calm and happy, at first just sitting on Jabari's lap, then walking carefully from lap to lap and visiting their friends, who all, of course, stroked his fur and spoke sweetly to him. He was a very popular fellow among all the students and, at any moment, could do something hilariously funny.

So it was no surprise when he saw Jabari's new book about magic with its colorful cover and grabbed it in both hands, then shook it up and down. That made everyone laugh.

"Very nice," Mafulla said. "I've wanted to shake a few books in my possession as well, now and then, and hard, but mostly school books, and especially our *Introduction to Greek*. But I guess it's all Greek to Manni."

Set commented, "I hear that. I've felt the same way, many times."

The little monkey chattered happily, spun around with Jabari's book, and then threw it down to the floor of the truck near Walid. "Manni!" Jabari said and laughed. "No throwing books!" He turned to the others and explained: "He must know that I'm going to put him to work helping with the tricks in that book."

Walid got up from his now bouncy seat and bent down to pick up the book of magic and give it back to Jabari. And, as he bent over, Manni ran around him to the side and somehow managed to get his little hand into the pocket where he felt the small red book, the key to the mysterious passages in The Book of Phi, and he slipped it out. Before anyone even noticed what he was doing, he leapt toward the back of the truck, to the outer limit of his leash, and he stopped, screeched, and then threw the book out into the road, which was crowded with people and traffic. Perhaps the most important book ever to be housed in Alexandria, a text whose papyrus form once survived the famous library fire by having been taken to a private home right before the conflagration happened now soared through the air and into the possibility of imminent destruction.

26

Ibrahim's Gift

"Oh, no!" Walid shouted as he turned and saw what had just happened. "No, no, no!" He watched in horror as the little red book arced out the back of the moving truck and into the street. The ancient key to The Book of Phi's otherwise indecipherable passages was quickly disappearing from view as the truck they were riding in continued on down the road.

"Jeepers!" Mafulla yelled, in total shock the instant he realized what was going on. Both of them were now up and moving quickly toward the back of the truck as the words left their mouths.

Set had no idea, of course, about the importance of what Manni had just tossed from the truck, but he could tell it mattered to Walid a lot, so he pounded on the wall of the truck cab and yelled toward the inside where the driver was. "Stop the truck!" And as he did so, he had a quick flashback of memory to the time when, on their last field trip, he had done the same thing, and to no avail. But this time, the drivers were all loyal, friendly soldiers, not kidnappers in disguise. However, the guard driving the truck still couldn't hear Set, or maybe did hear the knocks, but thought the kids were just goofing around. And then, before anyone could think, Walid had jumped from the back of the moving truck and Mafulla had followed him.

Fortunately, they were in fairly slow heavy traffic and the truck was rumbling forward at only a moderate speed. Stepping onto the back bumper, they were each able to jump down without getting hurt or hitting the pavement. They did have to dodge another truck behind them right away, a small commercial vehicle that was not a part of their transportation, and then they started running down the side of the street back to approximately where the book had been tossed out. Not thirty yards farther back, in the midst of a pedestrian crowd moving down the sidewalk, Walid saw a young boy, maybe eight or nine years old, bending over. When he straightened up, the prince could see that he had the old red book in his hands.

"Hey! Thank you! That's my book that was just dropped!" Walid shouted, with a big smile on his face. "I was hoping to find it! Thank you so much!"

In response, the boy looked up and seemed surprised, and then turned and took off running in the opposite direction with his find.

"Oh, no, oh, no, oh no," Mafulla said as they immediately gave chase. They were weaving around people and donkey carts and had almost lost sight of the boy. But Walid managed to catch a glimpse of him as he turned off the main street and into a nearby alley around the corner of a building.

"Over there! He's in that alley!" The prince called out to Mafulla and led the pursuit, running hard and closing in on where the boy must be by now. He had to retrieve the book.

Rounding the corner at full speed, Walid saw up ahead two rough looking young men of maybe eighteen or nineteen years old and an older man standing close together with them. The young boy was behind them now and was yelling to the others and pointing at Walid and Mafulla, "Those two are trying to hurt me and take my things! Stop them! Stop them!"

The two younger men spread their arms wide, as if to block the way forward, and began to move toward Walid and Mafulla, who had just dropped their pace to a walk. "No, no, no, we aren't going to hurt him or take any of his things, we just need the book, my red book, that he picked up from the street when it fell out of our truck." Walid was explaining the chase as one of the young men stepped closer and roughly grabbed his right arm with his own left hand, while producing and showing to Walid a four-inch knife with the other hand. This, of course, completely changed the situation.

As the threatening stranger was in the process of saying "Shut up," the second word never completely made it from his lips, while the knife was liberated from his hand and clattered onto the alleyway pavement. Walid doubled him over with a second quick strike, and he noisily collapsed to the ground with a loud grunt.

The other man had at this point produced his own blade and Mafulla said, "Don't even think about it. Put the knife down." But the guy then lunged at Walid, just to be stopped mid-movement by a flying kick administered with great precision by Mafulla. The prince had already put his first attacker to sleep with a fast neck hold, and was rising up when the second man, now on the ground but still in possession of his weapon, raised it like he was going to throw it at him. Mafulla was on it, though, and with a second kick sent the knife flying in another direction and then took the culprit down, immobilizing him as well.

At this point, and without a moment's pause, the older man was on them with a profane curse and what sounded like a loud growl. He was a large and heavy individual, and looked fairly fearsome, but the extensive Phi training of both boys had prepared them to see beyond such appearances and focus on the job at hand. And so, within about three seconds, they had their final attacker lying motionless on the pavement beside the others.

They both then looked around quickly. The boy was no longer in sight. He was gone. The street fight was just enough distraction for him to make his escape. That's how this operation worked. The boy with the book was one of three or four runners of about the same age who did this throughout the day for the men in the alley. They were all poor street kids who stole things of apparent value and ran, usually to this alley and for precisely this form of distraction and delay, though their protectors were always, otherwise, the ones left standing. The kids used the filter of the older men to get away with whatever they had taken. And they ran then to a nearby empty building where they would hide the goods they had taken: money, handbags, jewels, clothing, or food—whatever they could steal. The men would then sell the items and give the boys a small payment for their efforts, calling it "a piece of the action," and congratulating the boys for their work.

Walid and Mafulla ran the rest of the way down the alley and peered around the next corner of the building, but no one was in sight. "We can't let him get away with the book," Walid said. "You go left, I'll go right. Loop back around if you don't see him. Try to stay within shouting distance and, worst case, meet me back on the main street as soon as possible."

Mafulla took off running and so did Walid. This little red book could be crucial for the king's ability to face and defeat whatever challenges were coming from the al-Khoum brothers or the former king, or anyone else. It had come their way for a reason and now it had to be recovered. Walid then saw Mafulla come around the far corner of the next building. "There's no sign of him! None at all!" Mafulla yelled out.

"Let's hit the main street! Maybe he went there to get lost in the crowds," Walid shouted and turned a corner back in the direction of the broad, busy avenue where the chase had begun. But as he did so, he almost ran into another man moving toward him.

"Whoa! Ibrahim!"

"Are you chasing this one?" The man asked as the young boy struggled slightly behind him and wriggled hard to try to get free of his firm grip.

"What?"

"Let me go! Let me go!" The boy shouted and tried hard to shake out of Ibrahim's grasp, but to no avail.

"I think, perhaps, you should get your property back," Ibrahim said, and handed Walid the book that he had in his other hand. "It's too soon to be separated from it and it's not good for it to be in this one's possession."

"It's my book!" the boy said.

"How did you? Where did you come from?" Walid ignored the boy's protests and sputtered out these questions to his new acquaintance.

Just then, Mafulla got to them and said, "No way! Just no way at all!"

"Let go!" The boy yelled angrily.

"Silent!" Ibrahim glared at the boy, and gave him a hard shake, then turned back to Walid. "I was walking home from the store where we met and felt a strong inclination to go in a different direction than usual, so I came this way and I saw the boy running with the red book and, since he wasn't looking out for me, as just another face in the crowd, it was easy to apprehend him."

"That's amazing," Mafulla said.

Ibrahim continued, "I figured you two would be close by somewhere, so I moved quickly to find you. I had walked only for half a minute, and here you are."

"Oh, my goodness," Walid said. "Thank you so much. I was afraid I'd never see the book again."

"May I ask how it got into this young man's hands?"

The boy protested, "Somebody gave it to me!"

"Quiet!"

"Well, believe it or not, a pet monkey owned by another friend picked my pocket in the truck I was in and threw the book out of the open vehicle and into the street before I could stop him."

"Ah, yes, a story I hear quite often," Ibrahim said. And then he added, "What happened next?"

"We jumped from the truck really fast, but this kid had picked up the book before we could get to it. And he ran away, and then three big friends of his attacked us. We had to put them down back in the alleyway where they confronted us. And here we are."

"You lie! You're all liars!" The boy hissed out the words now.

Ibrahim ignored him and said to Walid, "That's quite an interesting sequence of events, to be sure. And I'm afraid that, in the process of what's happened, you've met some of our worst element here in the city. There are too many street thieves in recent days, and they use young boys such as this one as the snatch-and-grab resources for their crimes. It's a sad thing for us all to see."

Walid took a deep breath to calm and center himself. And then, regarding the boy more carefully, he said, "Look at me, please." The boy turned away and spit on the ground. Walid spoke again, anyway. He said, "This is the day your life changes."

"You can't make me do anything," the boy said, still looking away from Walid.

"I'm sorry that we had to hurt your friends, all three of them. I think this would be a good time for you to get away from them and find a new and better way to live."

The boy just scowled. Walid continued, very calmly, by saying, "I'm sorry. I should introduce myself. Maybe then you'll listen to me with a better attitude. I'm Walid Shabeezar, the Prince of Egypt, and sole heir to the throne of the kingdom, here from Cairo with some of my friends who go to school in the palace. We're visiting for the day."

Ibrahim looked very surprised and serious, and gazed at Walid, and then glanced over at Mafulla, who also appeared surprised, but nodded his head in confirmation of what had just been said.

The boy seemed stunned and stopped struggling and finally looked at Walid, who then went on to say, "You just took from me one of the most important books on earth. You stole from me, your prince, a member of the royal family ruling Egypt: your country—our country. The punishment for that traditionally is either immediate death, or life in prison from this day forward. But instead of that, I'm going to ask our friend Ibrahim here to give you the help you need to change your path and get away from the men who've been sending you to steal. You're better than them. You can be a good and great man, but not by stealing, and not by being around those men. Do you hear me?"

"How do I know you're a real prince? How do I know you're not just making this up and lying to me?" The boy spoke with much less aggression in his voice.

Just then, five soldiers led by Hamid, Paki, and Amon, all with weapons drawn, rounded the corner nearest them at a slow run, and Walid, as soon as he saw them, held up his hand for them to stop. They instantly obeyed his command and stood where they were.

He looked back at the boy and said, "Do you see? These are palace guards and soldiers in civilian clothing who have been sent to protect me. Look at their weapons. You just saw me raise my hand and they stopped immediately where they are."

"Yes."

"There are many more who would come if I needed them. Some of them are likely already taking the men in the alley to jail."

"I'm sorry," the boy said. "I believe you now. I didn't know you were the prince of my country. I'm sorry I took your book. But those men in the alley, they feed me and give me a place to sleep."

"You have no parents?"

"No. They're dead."

"No relatives?"

"I don't know."

"Ok. We'll make sure you have a chance at a better life. These soldiers, at least some of them, are from here in Alexandria. I'll have them take care of you and make sure you get a home and a school and a chance in life. My friend Ibrahim will check up on you and see to it that everything's Ok." Walid looked over at Ibrahim and he nodded, despite his surprise. The prince then motioned for Hamid to come over to the boy. "What's your name?" Walid asked him.

"Ben."

"Ben, this is Hamid, the head doctor in our military and one of the top leaders in the kingdom. He's a good and strong man. He'll introduce you to the Alexandrian soldiers and have them help you find a new home and a school, and new friends, and people to take care of you and feed you good food, much better and more tasty food than you have now, and they will help you to grow up well and have a great life. I can sense that you will use this opportunity properly."

Walid said a few things more to Hamid, explaining the situation that had just transpired, and mentioning only an important book of his that the boy had taken. Some soldiers were too close by for him to say more. He asked Hamid to place Ben into the protective custody of the local soldiers, and the doctor nodded and said, "Everything will be done quickly and in an appropriate way."

"Oh, and this is our new friend, our good new friend from a bookshop we just visited, Ibrahim, from here in Alexandria. He comes from a family known to many of our friends. He was just now of great help to us by intercepting the boy and retrieving the book. He's also our mystery man from the docks and the hotel, but is a good and benevolent individual, whose grandfather belonged to a very distinctive and ancient group because he had … special abilities."

"It's nice to meet you, Ibrahim," Hamid said with full understanding.

"Thank you, sir. It's my pleasure to meet you."

"Ibrahim will help be my eyes and ears in Alexandria and make sure Ben is well cared for and has everything he needs." Walid then looked at him and said, "Is that good with you?"

"Yes. It would be my honor, Prince."

Then Walid said in a voice of surprise, "I just realized that I never asked your family name."

"Hadad. My father was Mohammed Hadad. His father was Assur Hadad." At that name, Hamid showed a sudden spark of recognition and familiarity.

"Assur Hadad of Alexandria?"

"Yes."

"The military man?"

"That's my grandfather."

"I know of him and his greatness," Hamid said.

"Oh. You do?"

"Yes. May your family always be blessed, and your path in life be ever sure."

"I thank you, sir. It's a blessing to have met all of you this day."

"You were the blessing," Walid said. "Hamid, I'll explain it all later, but Ibrahim has done two great things for me and for the rest of us today."

Hamid smiled at the young man and nodded his approval. "You honor your family."

Ibrahim smiled back and bowed slightly. "It's my joy to make a contribution and be of service."

Walid spoke up and said, "Ibrahim, make sure that the men get all your contact information. I have a feeling that this is only the first of many days that we'll be seeing each other."

"Yes, Prince. That would be very good."

They spoke for a few more moments and Walid and Mafulla said their goodbyes to Ibrahim and Ben. Hamid then introduced them to the Alexandrian soldiers, they all quickly exchanged some information, and by mutual agreement, Ibrahim went away with Ben, to take him home at first and then to meet up with the soldiers later. They would then talk with him about his long-term situation and lodgings. Ibrahim however soon had the thought enter his heart that, perhaps, Ben was to stay with him and his mother and sister, not far away. He decided he would discuss this later on with the soldiers and see if it might work as a good solution to the situation.

Set, it turned out, had finally gotten the attention of the truck's driver and military guard by banging repeatedly on the back of the cab. They had pulled over, Set had jumped out, and the guard had gone around to the back to hear the whole story quickly told. He then took off in pursuit, after telling the driver to catch up with the other trucks and stop them, sending men to back him up in the search and assistance he'd be giving. He had looked around the area for a good three or four minutes before Hamid and the other soldiers arrived and met up with him. From then, they quickly found the criminals in the alleyway, along with their weapons, and took them into custody in case they were involved somehow in what was happening. And shorty after that, several of them came across Walid and Mafulla with Ibrahim and Ben.

One empty truck was waiting to take the prince, Mafulla, Hamid, and a few of the soldiers to meet up with the other vehicles, which were now already at their destination and being guarded by Paki, Amon, and several other military men assigned to the duty. It didn't take the truck long to get the boys back to their friends, who were now waiting for them before beginning the next tour.

When Walid and Mafulla rejoined everyone, they learned that Manni had been lectured extensively on the value of books, the importance of personal property, and the typical inadvisability of throwing things from moving trucks. Their prime primate friend seemed appropriately chastened, Jabari reported, and he then assured everyone that Manni would henceforth be kept on a very short leash in moving trucks, as well as on boats and trains. The list was clearly growing.

The big surprise was that Khalid and Hoda were now going to give the class a full tour of the sites where Cleopatra and Caesar were said to have lived and worked and developed their relationship. After greeting his friends and telling them that he had gotten his important book back, but with no further details, Walid took

Hamid aside and explained everything about the red book. Hamid in turn told him that the king would be joining the group any minute for a look at the Cleopatra story's main locales. And sure enough, he did show up only a few minutes later, accompanied by Omari and eager for a history lesson. Walid first made a beeline to him, and, taking him aside, told him all about Ibrahim and the red book and what had just happened. The king was stunned and greatly pleased to receive the book. He said he'd make sure that Ibrahim was amply rewarded and honored for his actions and, further, that young Ben would be well cared for and set firmly on a more suitable path in life.

The rest of the day was extremely interesting, without being quite so eventful. They toured several historical sites, Hoda gave some great short lectures, as did Khalid, and even Layla joined in on some historical aspects of what they were seeing, offering additional facts and insights that augmented everything their teachers had to say. It was a good day, a great field trip, and when they had finally made it to the train station for their late ride home, everyone was exhausted. Nearly all of them got some sleep on the train and by the time they rolled into the Cairo station, they had enjoyed enough nap time that they had no difficulty waking back up, getting their things, and then hopping once more into waiting trucks for the short ride to the palace where they'd all have a late-night sleepover—with the boys in one big room and the girls in another one, not far away. When they got to their assigned rooms, there were late snacks available and ample bedding for a comfortable campout on the thickly carpeted floors.

Ordinarily, a sleepover with all the students from each class close together, bunking on the floor of a palace room, would have led to talking long into the night, hijinks of various kinds, and who knows what else. But this evening, everyone was really tired from the trip. So within an hour of arrival, all of them were quiet, and no more than a few minutes later, everyone was asleep.

The king was in his sitting room with Hamid and Masoon, going over the small red book that Walid had given him. "I wish I had been able to go along on this trip," Masoon said.

"It was nice," Hamid answered. "Exciting at times, solidly educational, and what we brought back may be of unique and unparalleled value."

"This is amazing, and it's just what I've needed," The king said, as he looked over the first few pages of the little red book.

"What does it seem to cover?" Masoon asked.

"It looks like it's a commentary of sorts on The Book of Phi, or at least on the instructional parts of the book. And it also provides more background on The Ring of Phi and The Stone of Giza, including additional information about their powers, their uses, and their effects."

"Where do you think the book originated?" Hamid asked.

"Well, this printing, by the recorded date, was done nearly a hundred and twenty years ago, but there's no indication of how old it actually is, in terms of its contents, or who first wrote it."

"Do you think it's authentic and trustworthy?"

"Only a careful reading will tell. But if this young man Ibrahim is indeed the grandson of Assur Hadad, and if he got the book from his grandfather, who was an illustrious Phi, and he, in turn, from his grandfather, also Phi, it's almost certainly authentic."

Hamid said, "That makes sense."

Ali then added, "Whether what it says is true in every detail and worthy of our complete trust, we'll have to see."

The king's head butler, Kular, stuck his head into the room at this point and said, "I'm sorry to interrupt, Your Majesty, but will you and the gentlemen be wanting any refreshment this evening?"

"A pot of coffee and any nibbles that are easily available would be nice, the king said. Then, why don't you either go home, or else get some sleep here in the palace, my friend? I'm sorry to have kept you up so late tonight."

"No worries, Your Majesty. The stone still has its wonderful and unexpected effects, after all this time. I'm awake and have as much energy as might be needed. I'll get the coffee to you in just a few minutes, as soon as I can get it brewed."

When Kular had closed the door, the king said to his two friends, "I wanted you both here for a first reading of the book. I think the best procedure will be for me to read it aloud, and you can stop me for any commentary or questions, and at any time. I know that the key to the code will be of crucial importance to us, and whether I need your help with interpreting and applying it or not, I very much want your opinions as to whatever we discover with the use of the code, and especially in what those mysterious parts in The Book of Phi say about training and powers. However long I have on this earth, I know you'll likely help carry on when that time is over, and I want you to know as much as I do about all of this."

Masoon said, "I'm glad you called me to come and be here tonight. When do you plan on sharing the content of the book with Walid?"

"I'm not sure. I'll probably talk with him about it in the morning, and include Mafulla. Whether all of it is appropriate to share at this point with the two of them, at their age, we should be able to determine tonight. But my tendency is always towards complete transparency and sharing with the two of them, whenever it's at all possible and wise."

"It's a good policy," Hamid remarked.

"It is a great gift to us now to have been provided with this book in precisely the current circumstances. We may soon need the use of any new insights it can provide us."

"I think you're right, Majesty," Masoon said.

"Yes, I agree," Hamid seconded.

"Well, let's begin and see how far we can go."

27

A Sudden Storm

Two weeks had passed since the school trip to Alexandria. Walid and Mafulla had started some new and interesting Phi training to augment their normal sessions, as early as the afternoon of their first full day back. Kissa and Hasina also began a new form of training two days later, after the king had a chance to speak at length with both Hoda and Layla.

One of the strangest ongoing new lessons now being incorporated into their workouts was in the art of proprioception. Strictly speaking, proprioception is a sense like sight or smell, but it normally operates internally and registers only things about your own body's immediate location and orientation in space. The sense of proprioception is what tells you at any given moment where your arms and legs are, whether you're sitting or lying down, standing still or moving forward, or even turning in some way. It's highly developed in gymnasts, wrestlers, boxers, and practitioners of the various martial arts. There are a few top athletes in nearly every sport who seem to have a special acuteness in their proprioceptive sensibilities. And just as we can be taught to use our eyes better in art classes, our ears more discerningly in music lessons, our sense of touch more finely in pottery or woodworking, and our skills of taste and smell more discriminatingly in mastering the art of cooking, we can also learn more sensitive and accurate proprioception.

But going much farther than you might ever even imagine, the boys were now discovering how to use this sense beyond the confines of their own physical bodies and out into their immediately surrounding environment. This was all because of some things revealed with the use of the red book. They were told that due to the ultimate, overall, fundamental interconnectedness of everything in the universe, there is, in principle, no outer limit to the scope of our proprioceptive awareness. And yet, relatively few people have ever developed this perceptual ability to reach reliably outside the surface of their skin and beyond their most immediately apparent bodies. There have always been legends about great warriors and top masters of a few martial arts who seem to display this extreme of mastery, but there has been little publicly available confirmation of such stories. And, of course, the same is true of most deep and rare human abilities.

Since his own exposure to the red book, Masoon had been busy explaining to Walid and Mafulla how their many other Phi skills had prepared them well for doing exactly this—developing a more encompassing awareness of their surroundings that didn't depend on any of the other senses, but rather came directly and instantly, in virtue of being unmediated. And so then, aided by a growing belief that it was indeed possible, they were now making rapid progress in this strange and immensely useful capacity. It was all due to some profound and useful instructions in the little red book, as well as to passages within The Book of Phi that could now be deciphered.

There were also many other revelations in the red book that initially had astonished them and were now guiding their intensified training. One thing was evident from the contents of the small text: Our world is much stranger than our normal habits of thinking allow it to seem. It's only when we break through the walls of ordinary thought that we can access what's truly and fully available to us. Then, like a butterfly escaping its chrysalis, we can fly for the first time as we were intended to be able to soar. All the Phi training the boys had ever experienced had gradually moved their understanding in this direction, but the new insights of the red book were peeling back many deep layers of otherwise hidden assumptions and making new realities clearer to them in every lesson and on every day.

It was already the middle of summer. The palace school was on a year round, twelve-month schedule, with short breaks for vacation and rest throughout the year. One of those breaks was coming up soon. Some families traveled during the vacations, and others just enjoyed the kids being home. Walid and Mafulla typically spent their free time throughout these breaks on sports and fun reading and discovering more about the city. They'd go off to the marketplace when they could to visit the Adi shop, and drop by the Adi family home for a meal, and they'd continue exploring new parts of the capital. Of course, these ventures outside the palace grounds often brought them unsolicited new opportunities to keep their Golden Viper and Windstorm abilities well honed. But they never sought to prowl the city in search of crimes to stop or people to help. The publicity about the Viper and the Storm was still too great and made them keenly cautious about when and how they used their skills. But they always responded whenever they could see that they were truly needed in this way.

The king had guided both boys through a close reading of the red book in the days after their return from Alexandria. Having worked through it carefully himself, he knew that it would be important for them to take some time and stretch their experience of reading and discussing it over the entirety of a week, so that he could comment on what was being revealed and help them to interpret some of the more difficult parts, and then apply in their lives what they were learning. Since neither of them had ever read

The Book of Phi, due to their ages and still junior status in the society, there were some passages in the red book that were obscure and required the king's detailed explanations. But he wanted the boys to have full access to everything that was in this small compendium of carefully distilled insights, feeling somehow that they might be in need of it very soon.

In fact, it's no exaggeration to say that all the members of Phi in and around Cairo had been having strange feelings and unusually vivid dreams ever since the king and prince returned from Alexandria. No one could say exactly what he or she was sensing, and the dreams were all enigmatic, but there was clearly something unsettling in the air. And it generated more than a few serious conversations among normally scattered individuals in the fellowship of Phi.

Still, no one could know that a day of great difficulty and importance was soon to begin. It would come suddenly and with unanticipated forms of violence. Things were about to happen that forever would change life as they knew it, in the palace and around the city. But now, it was just barely dawn. Mafulla cracked open Walid's door and whispered, "Hey. Are you awake yet? Can I come in?"

Walid yawned big and replied, "Yeah. Sure. You're up already?"

"Bad dream," Mafulla said, as he walked in and quietly closed the door.

"Me, too," Walid responded.

"Oh yeah?"

"Yeah."

"What did you dream?"

"You first."

"Oh, Ok," Mafulla said. "Mine was simple, a big scary storm coming. But it wasn't so much the sights and sounds in the dream that bothered me as the feelings I had while I was seeing the storm on the way."

"Huh," Walid said. "I guess I had pretty much the same dream."

"Really?"

"Yeah. A big storm was on the way. And I had this deep, gut sense of how bad it could be."

"What do you think it means?"

"I'm pretty sure the dream is symbolic. I don't think nature is going to throw anything huge at us. It's not weather that threatens us right now. I feel like it's a human storm that's on the way."

"Yeah, me, too. I'm thinking … it must be the two al-Khoum brothers and their people, most likely."

"That makes sense. But, what about the former king—do you have any feeling that he'll be a part of it?" Walid knew how detailed Mafulla's dreams could be, and how uncannily accurate.

"No, no, I didn't see or sense anything about him."

"Ok."

"For some reason, he seems to be out of the picture."

"You think?"

"Yeah. I have no idea why, though," Mafulla added.

Walid swung his legs over the side of the bed, yawned again, sat up, and said, "By the way, did you hear that the Tunisian Ambassador has completely disappeared?"

"No. I hadn't heard that."

"They can't find him anywhere. He's not been heard from or seen since we got back from Alexandria. And his son's also missing."

"Karim the Dream?"

"Yeah."

"So, they both high-tailed it out of here," Mafulla mused.

"Nobody knows," Walid replied.

"I had a bad feeling about the two of them that went way beyond what happened at the party."

"Yeah, me too," Walid said. "But I could never really say why."

"Let's get some breakfast," Mafulla suggested. "You're going to need your strength. And I know I am."

Walid sighed and said, "Ok, give me a second." He stood the rest of the way up, stretched his arms above his head, wiggled his fingers, then put his hands as far behind his back as he could, bent over, straightened up, and shuffled over to where he could wash up. "Let me throw some water on my face and we'll go eat."

"Make sure to throw some extra on your hair in the back. It's a little too excited back there."

"Ha." Walid then yawned again, loudly.

Mafulla said, "You know, a mirror is sometimes your best-friend. Or, at least that's true in my own case."

"Mine's not like yours, gushing elaborate and effusive praises at me whenever I look into it."

"I would never have thought otherwise." Mafulla said this with a big grin and Walid just shook his head.

Within three or four minutes, they were walking down the hallway, but at a bit of a slower pace than usual. Entering the breakfast room much earlier than they normally did, they saw that Kular already had laid out many things for the morning meal. "The king must have come down and eaten here," Walid said.

"How do you know?"

"There's an empty plate with a few crumbs over there on the side table, and a coffee cup, and Kular has a lot out for this time of the morning. He can't have expected us, yet."

"Oh yeah, I hadn't noticed the cup and plate. And you make a good point," Mafulla said, as he reached for a plate of his own and began to put bread, cheese, and fruit on it. Walid went straight for the coffee and poured a full cup. Taking a big sip first, he then set the cup down and began to load some food onto his plate, as well.

"It's nice that the king wanders down here for his breakfast now and then," Mafulla commented.

"It is," Walid agreed. "Sometimes, it's clear he wants to talk to us first thing, but other times, it's maybe just because he knows food is usually here, and it's cozier than his big dining room."

"It's a change of pace, and all that. And, you know, he also sort of acknowledges us by his visits, even when we're still asleep. It's like our world is a part of his world."

"Yeah, that too."

Just then, Kular came into the room. He said, "Oh! Hello, Prince, and Mafulla. I checked your rooms just a moment ago and when no one answered my knocks, I supposed you might already be here at breakfast, although it's a bit early."

"We couldn't sleep," Mafulla said.

"Well, I'm glad you're already down here, because the king has asked to see you both in about fifteen minutes in his sitting room, if that's possible. This will give you time still to have a quick breakfast."

Walid said, "Do you have any idea why he wants to see us this early in the morning?"

"Not exactly, but it sounds like something big is happening or soon will be happening, and I think he wants to fill you in on it as quickly as possible."

"Really?"

"Yes. There's some sort of information that's just come to light. The king's with Masoon, Hamid, Naqid, your father, and Bancom right now, and there are a few other top officers of the military in the room, as well. There's a situation of some sort."

"Oh, Ok. Thanks, Kular. It must be important. We'll be there soon." Walid looked at his Reverso, which he had put on right before leaving his room as he always did. Fifteen minutes. He suddenly felt something tighten up inside him. It was almost like a twist of fear, a feeling that he'd never experienced in circumstances like this, with no imminent danger facing him. He also felt a touch of lightheadedness, but just a little, and then it cleared. The royal butler, of course, didn't notice any of that. He just did a slight bow and walked out the door.

"This sounds serious," Mafulla said.

"Yeah, maybe the storm is close." Walid took a deep breath.

"Well, we're very well prepared and we've been through a lot before," Mafulla reminded his friend.

Walid responded, "I'm sure we'll get through this, too, whatever it is. But I have to admit, I'm a little bit worried."

"It's natural, old friend," Mafulla said. We don't know what we're facing yet. The unknown can strangely come across as the greatest threat of all possible dangers and, at the same time, we know it almost always isn't that at all. It's just the blank screen on which our imaginations project their worst fears."

"You're right."

"And now we have the red book."

"True," Walid said, and then added, "That could make a very big difference, I think. My emotions just now sprang on me without being filtered through that new knowledge, and it really changes everything. It hasn't yet gotten from my head to my heart. So, I guess we should eat rather than worry."

"Yeah, but right now, I can barely taste anything," Mafulla admitted. "I mean, after hearing who's in with the king this early in the morning. Still, you're right. Let's finish up our breakfast."

The boys then sat in silence for more than a minute, eating quietly, each of them lost in thought or else in a realm apart from thought. Walid had a second cup of coffee and then looked at his watch. "We'd better get down there," he said, breaking the silence. "Don't you think?"

"Ok, just let me swig one more glass of juice," Mafulla replied, and did so. Then he put down his glass and said, "I'm ready for whatever lies in wait for us."

Walid let out a long sigh and said, "Me, too, I guess."

The boys walked together down the hall, entered Kular's reception area, and waited for him to appear. Coming out of a side room, he asked first whether they needed anything, and when they said no, he opened the king's door for them to go in.

Ali was just finishing with the session he was in. He held up an index finger to the boys as soon as they entered the room, and they knew to stop right inside the door and wait for a moment.

The king was bent over a map of some sort and was pointing here and there on it. Several top military officers were huddled around, carefully attending to his instructions. Masoon, Hamid, Naqid, Rumi, and Bancom were off to one side of the room at a distance, in a cluster of chairs that had been pulled together, and they were also at this point intensely engaged in conversation within their own huddle. Right beside them was a command center radio table, an operation that Bancom always set up in times of crisis so the king could have the most direct communication with his military leaders and officers in the field.

Walid just then heard his uncle say, "Right away, and with the greatest urgency," and the officers responded with various phrases like, "Yes, Majesty!" and "This minute!" and "Immediately!" They bowed and turned to leave, moving quickly across the room and through the doorway, all doing small bows of acknowledgment to Walid as they passed by.

The king then motioned the boys over and said, "Sit, my friends. There are some new developments."

"Is everything Ok?" Walid asked, already knowing the answer, as he and Mafulla sat down in their favorite chairs, both facing the king and feeling butterflies inside. Ali looked serious, but not worried.

"We've received word from Libya that the former illegitimate king of our nation, Rasul Appolonium, has been found dead in his compound in Tripoli, along with many of his men and advisors, including our own local crime nemesis, Ari Falma."

Walid spoke up, "That's a surprise for sure. But, in a sense, it's good news, isn't it—I mean, of a sort, and apart from the sadness that accompanies any early and unnecessary death. At least we won't have to worry about them any more. Any threat from them is gone."

"Well, there's more," the king said. "The new Tunisian ambassador to our kingdom, Omar Sassi, and his son Karim, along with an old friend of Sassi's, a high government official in Libya, have also been found dead in the compound—executed, all of them shot from behind."

"Oh, wow," Mafulla said.

"Why?" Walid asked.

"The Libyans were sheltering Rasul, we suspect, for lavish compensation and because of past favors. Not everyone in the Libyan government was involved, but certain elements, and a few of the Italians, who have a big presence in Tripoli. There are reports that the compound where he was staying was stormed by a group of what must have been mercenaries. And by the time the Libyan police got word of it and made their way to the place, a mansion named Sea Watch, where they discovered all the casualties, the perpetrators were gone. But they did find something in a thorough search of the house. There was a calendar and an expected visit had been recorded on it for when the terrible events likely took place. The former king had invited for tea … the al-Khoum brothers."

"So they turned on him and killed him and his men."

"Yes, and we suspect that the former king and his men had been planning to do the same to them, but the brothers came ready for battle, and apparently much better prepared than he."

"Do we know where they are now?"

"No, not exactly, but we strongly suspect that they're already on the way here."

"Now?" Mafulla said.

"Yes. They're moving on to the big target, having mobilized their men and eliminated what they considered to be all of the preliminary obstacles to their ultimate goals."

"But, you mean, right now? And even as we speak?" This certainly took Walid by surprise.

"It's most likely," the king responded. "There's some indication that they may have sent a small army of mercenaries into our territory already. Some scattered reports of sightings have just come in from the desert and from Alexandria. It seems that one or two groups may be traveling over land and another by water. Your new friend Ibrahim sent us word of the first suspicious activity at the docks in his part of Alexandria. It was confirmed by one of my generals."

"Ibrahim?"

"Yes, he was near the docks and saw something strange, a large number of men arriving, and could find no good explanation for what he was seeing. He said he had a feeling about it. He contacted us through his new military connections, by radio, late yesterday."

"How many men were spotted?" Walid asked.

"We're not sure. But we suspect perhaps a hundred or more, at least, taking into account all the reports that we've heard. It could be twice that, or three times. We have no better sense of it at present."

"Were they intercepted—the ones in Alexandria?"

"No, they were gone by the time we got word they had arrived."

"But we have a massive army that could crush two or three hundred men, or ten times that many."

"Yes. So they apparently intend, not a battle or a war with our entire military, but a surgical strike on us here in the palace. They're most likely coming here with a specific plan of attack. They mean to surprise us like they did the former king in Libya, but unlike in the case of the events there, they've already been compromised. Yet still, we should never underestimate Farouk and Faraj al-Khoum. They're smart and devious men, driven by an enormous ambition."

"What are we doing to prepare for them?"

"Several things. They likely plan to strike here so fast that there would be no time for our army to respond and come to our assistance, so we're quickly and quietly pre-positioning troops on palace grounds and in several surrounding areas, but in a way that's as hidden as possible. Masoon already did some work of moving men while we were in Alexandria, just as a general precaution that he felt was right, and his preliminary efforts have helped greatly in this."

"When do you think they'll make a move on us?"

"It could be a day or two. It could be no more than hours."

Something suddenly occurred to Walid. "Our school break doesn't start until two days from now. Within a couple of hours, the kids will all be coming in for classes, like normal."

"Yes," the king said. "We're sending out word to as many as possible that they should come in early today, if they can."

"Why?"

"We feel that they'll be safer here than in their homes."

"I don't understand. How could that be, if we're the target?"

"The palace is a bit like a fortress. Most homes are not. And many of the students live quite near the palace, in areas that could become very dangerous."

"Oh, that's right."

"We've also suggested to all their mothers and to any other relatives in their homes who don't work here that they should come and spend the day in with us. Their fathers all do work here, and most are already in for the day, thanks to our early messages. Your fellow classmates should be gathering in the school area by now, as well."

"What about my family?" Mafulla asked.

"They're receiving some special treatment. They've been moved to a safe place on the outskirts of town, within the past hour, and are well guarded. They're fine. No one's frightened. In fact, we've heard that your brother and sister are enjoying it almost like a vacation. There's a nice pool where they are now and plenty of room. Your parents, of course, asked about you and we've assured them that you're well protected. Your uncle will be here with us in the palace. He should be arriving within the hour, bringing us some more information that he's apparently received from his connections in the area."

The radio crackled to life, and the young operator began to write down a code that was coming through. He turned to Bancom and gave him the page. Bancom then read it over, spoke quickly to Masoon, Hamid, Naqid, and Rumi all at once, and within seconds he was presenting it to the king, as Masoon and Hamid left the room.

"You were right, Your Majesty. Teams Alpha and Beta have just seen, in each location we anticipated, perhaps as many as fifty men enter the buildings and presumably head for the tunnels."

The king said, "Make sure the tunnel teams got the message."

"Absolutely. Right away, Majesty." Bancom quickly turned back to the radio operator.

"What's going on?" Walid asked.

The king looked quite calm. He said, "The enemy's here already, a bit earlier than expected, or at least their advance units, and they're seeking to breech our security by entering the palace grounds through the two old underground tunnels, the one that comes into the basement, which of course we've long known about, and the one just recently discovered by Malik and Haji in the old outbuilding."

"I thought any attackers would make a frontal assault on the gates or try to go over the walls," Mafulla said.

"That would be too brazen, and too easily detected and repelled," the king said. "I suspected this was exactly what they would do, at least, initially. Farouk has long known of the tunnels, as you're aware, and may assume that we don't know of them, as hidden as they both are, and as recently as we've arrived. But there's one thing I should quickly tell you."

Just then, however, before the king could say another word, everyone heard a huge explosion that strangely sounded like a series of explosions in rapid succession, growing and merging together, and shaking the entire palace, rattling the windows, and causing even the marble floors to vibrate. A second such extended explosion then quickly followed and shook the floors and walls again, like an enormous earthquake.

Walid and Mafulla instinctively jumped up. They both said, at nearly the same time, “What’s that? What’s happening?”

28

The Elements of Attack

Naqid, the head of palace guards, and Walid's dad, Rumi, had instantly moved to the window and were peering down. "That was quite an explosion, Majesty," Bancom said.

"What's going on?" Walid asked again, with more than a touch of real worry in his voice.

The king sighed and answered, "The unfortunate but necessary demolition of our two ancient tunnels just took place."

"Why?" Walid was completely puzzled.

"First of all, for days, we've had many lookouts hidden within a mile or two of the palace. If they detected a number of suspicious men on foot, or unknown trucks moving toward the two areas where the old tunnels originate away from the palace, they'd been told to allow them to reach their destinations unhindered and to enter the two buildings. Once they had good evidence that the adversaries were down in the tunnels, our men had instructions to blow up both."

"Really?"

"Yes. We had explosions set all through each tunnel, along the tops and walls, powerful charges that would bring down a massive, totally crushing weight of earth on the intruders to stop them all at once and provide for their eternal resting place."

"Wow." Mafulla looked shocked.

The king continued, "The doors of the tunnels on our end had just been sealed with steel and concrete so they couldn't be penetrated. While the mercenaries were caught down below ground, we had to take the unfortunate path of eliminating their threat in an instant. I certainly regret and deplore the terrible loss of life, but their murderous intent had to be stopped, and this was the best way to do it quickly and safely, from our point of view, with no protracted battle in the city or on palace grounds, and no loss of life on the part of innocents, or on our side. I wish there had been another option."

"That's incredible," Mafulla said. "So … both of the tunnels are now … gone?"

"Along with those who had most immediately sought to exploit them for ill," the king replied.

"So, what happens now?" Walid asked.

"I'm afraid that's up to our opponents," the king said. "The next move is theirs. But we're already well positioned, and now we know that their action against us has begun. So we'll be on alert. Our eyes and ears are everywhere in the city."

"Will the al-Khoum brothers know of their sudden and complete failure in the tunnels?"

"There's no way to tell. If they don't know already, if they didn't have sentinels observing from a distance, but close enough that they could hear and feel the explosions, they'll still be likely to surmise it within an hour or so—the time they probably thought it would take their advance troops to get onto palace grounds, into the palace itself, to deal with us quickly. These were likely some of their most elite fighters, meant to penetrate our defenses by surprise and quickly take us out. When they get no report or signal of success, they'll most likely infer that we stopped their men."

"Wait," Walid suddenly said. "I just realized something. The explosions could have scared all our friends half to death, if they're already in the building like we are. Did Khalid and Hoda know about the explosions in advance, so they can reassure everyone?"

"Yes, they'd been forewarned earlier this morning."

"Oh! Great. Thanks."

"Yeah, that's good," Mafulla agreed.

Walid continued, "It made my heart jump just now to think what they all must have felt, otherwise. They would likely have guessed that we were the ones being bombed."

"I've had the teachers thoroughly briefed, and have even had Layla come in this morning with Hasina so that she could be on hand if we need her talents. She knew in advance, as well."

"That's a relief," Mafulla said.

Walid then asked, "Uncle, would it be possible for me and Maffie to go to the school area soon, just to be with our friends in case they somehow need us?"

"Yes, my boy, and actually, it might be safer for you to be in a different part of the palace, at a distance from me. Faraj is well aware of where this room is in the building. We don't yet know what to expect next, and it's important for the monarchy to survive this assault, whatever happens and however it plays out."

For some reason, it was not until the king had spoken those words that Walid fully grasped the seriousness of their situation in a deep and emotional way. But rather than frightening him, the realization just focused him, and strengthened his resolve. "Should we go there now, then?" Walid asked.

"Yes, and I'll have Omari walk with you," the king replied. "We'll also have Bancom set up a remote radio in your classroom for instant communication. That should be in place within twenty minutes or half an hour, at the latest."

"Good. Just let me know if you need us here and we'll rush back any time," Walid said, looking into the eyes of his uncle.

"I will. Be strong. Be safe," the king said, looking with great kindness, first at Walid, and then at Mafulla. "Watch out for each other today, as you always do. Use the full power of your minds. And remember your training."

"Yes, sir."

"Now, go be with your school friends. Your older friends here will be fine, as we carry on."

Across the palace, in Khalid's larger classroom, Hoda's class had joined the boys for the morning. The younger students in the palace school under the age of twelve and a few older siblings over the age of fifteen were in other rooms nearby with their own tutors or teachers in their wing of the palace. Parents who had come in just for the day were in a school kitchen and break room that was also close by. All the teachers, fortunately, had warned their students and the parents of a possible explosion and loud noise well before it happened, and so they were all prepared for it, but it was still a little scary when it actually took place in all its unexpected intensity.

Khalid and Hoda had both been briefed on the full nature of the threat that faced them all on this day. And they were explaining to their students the entire cast of characters involved, along with some of the history of recent palace intrigue, when Walid and Mafulla walked in. Everyone looked over at them. "Welcome, friends," Khalid said. "What can you tell us by way of updates?"

"You knew about the explosion."

"We were told that there might be one but not precisely what it would represent, or that it would be so impressive. We also weren't completely clear that there would be two or more. But we had enough warning not to be taken by total surprise, and that was good."

Walid stopped where he stood, looked at all the students, and explained. "Ok, here's what happened. The number one enemy of the kingdom, Farouk al-Khoum, apparently knew about two hidden underground tunnels that come into the palace grounds, and he knew this from his teenage years when he worked in the palace. He had a plan to use them some day. And today was the day. He wants to kill the king and, I guess, me so that he can be king.

He's worked all his life so far to create great wealth that could be used for that purpose. He's been living in Tunisia, apparently, and planning an assault on our monarchy. But he can't face our entire army, so he had to try to take out the leadership of the kingdom without fighting a broader battle. With that in mind just now, he sent about a hundred of his most highly trained fighters, mercenary soldiers under his pay, to sneak onto palace grounds and into the palace by using the two ancient tunnels."

Several of the students looked at each other. Haji said, "That's not good."

"Yeah, you're right." Walid continued his explanation. "The king anticipated this possibility, and had guards watching the buildings blocks away that hide the outer entrance areas of both tunnels. When they saw the men first enter the buildings, they gave a signal, and when they became certain that all of them were all the way in the tunnels, our men ignited preset charges to blow up both of the underground passageways and bury our murderous assailants under tons of rock, dirt, and sand. That way, they could be stopped without the problems that would result from huge gun battles in a city."

"Wow, so that was us stopping our enemies?" Malik said.

"Yes, and thanks to you and Haji, we knew of the second tunnel, one that they could have succeeded in using if you hadn't found it. So, because of you guys, we were able to stop them all and not just half the assault."

"Man, oh, man," Haji said. "How many of the attackers did you say there were?"

"Probably over a hundred." Walid replied.

"So, you guys really are heroes today, in absentia," Mafulla said, looking at Haji and Malik.

"In absentia?" Malik asked.

"Yeah, without even being there," Mafulla explained.

Now, Kissa spoke up and asked, "Will there be more attacks?"

"Most likely," Walid answered. "This was probably just the first of several, but the king has prepared in many ways for anything that might happen. He has elements of the military all throughout the palace grounds and in buildings across the entire neighborhood, reaching as far away as a mile or so from where we are. Many are even out in the open in plain clothes, pretending to be having coffee at cafes, working in shops, or going about daily business. But we have eyes and ears and guns everywhere today."

"Are we safe here?" Ara asked.

Walid responded, "We're certainly sitting in the main target for this guy, the palace, but because of the king's preparations, we're probably in the safest place in all of Cairo right now."

"It's still scary," Cabar said.

"Yeah," Bakat added, "We're all pretty freaked out about all this." Kit looked over at her and just nodded.

"It's good to be concerned, because that means you're alert. But there's no reason to be really scared."

"But in this room, we're pretty much defenseless," Set said.

"I think that's about to change," Walid replied. "When we were walking here just now, we were met by a palace guard who told our friend Omari, outside the door, that the king's sending some weapons to the room and he wants Omari to make sure everyone gets a quick lesson in their proper, safe, use, whenever the time is right."

"Really?" Jabari said.

"Yeah," Walid replied.

"This would be as good a time as any," Khalid suggested.

"Ok," Walid said. "I'll get Omari." He turned and walked back out the door, and within a few seconds four palace guards were bringing two large crates through the door. The men carried them over to the side of the room and put them down. Omari then followed them into the room.

"Thank you," he said to the other guards. "You can return to your post." And as the four of them left the room, he turned to the class and began with words of reassurance, explaining first that they might not have to use these weapons at all, but that the king wanted them available, just in case, and he was going to give the students a quick lesson in how they operate. He first asked if there was anyone in the class who had shot a rifle. Most of the boys raised their hands, and two of the girls, Kissa and Hasina. He then asked about handguns. Walid, Mafulla, Kissa, Hasina, Set, and Jabari raised their hands.

"Ok, I'll give some quick instructions first, and then let you hold one of the weapons. I'll ask those with experience to help me assist those of you who have none." Omari went over the basics of gun safety first, how to check whether it was loaded or unloaded, how to hold it when it was not in use, and then the way to put in its ammunition. He described a bit about the mechanics of firing, and then spoke about aim and the human side of shooting straight and true. He also mentioned the noise of firing and described the phenomenon of recoil. He said again, "Never point a gun at someone you don't plan to shoot. Keep the barrel down, otherwise. Up is second best. But never be careless about where it points. Accidents happen."

At that moment, another palace guard stuck his head through the door and said, "I'm sorry to interrupt, but we just received word that there's a fire downstairs in the far front reception room, and we've all been given a warning that we may have to evacuate within a few minutes and stay outside just long enough for the fire brigade to make sure the flames are out and all is clear."

Omari thanked the guard and said to the class, "Ok, then, given the uncertainties of the moment, I think I'll wrap up now as quickly as possible and ask you each to take a weapon with you, unloaded, if the order is in fact given to evacuate. You should also take some of the ammunition with you, as much as you can easily carry, on the outside chance that we may need it for protection. You can use your pockets or a bag to put it in. I see you have lots of book bags at your desks that can also be emptied out and used for this purpose. So, please begin with your preparations right away, in case we have to leave in the next few minutes."

A grave concern spread through the room and Khata said, "Do you really think we'll have to use these guns?"

Omari replied, "Right now, I don't expect so. I hope not, but we like to be ready for any remote contingencies in a situation like this."

The students began loading up the ammunition, as Omari had requested. And within three or four minutes, the other guard came back into the room. He said, "Sorry, everyone. We just got word that the fire is worse than we thought, and the palace fire marshal is asking that all non-essential people leave the building for just a bit, until we get the blaze contained and, hopefully, extinguished."

"Ok," Omari said and then turned again to the students. "This is a little rushed, but each of you who feels most comfortable with a rifle please take one, and anyone else pick up a handgun. Some may want to take both. Walid, Mafulla, help me get some of the ammo sorted out quickly and to the right people for the guns they have."

"We do have to go as soon as possible," the guard reminded them.

"I understand," Omari replied. "We'll need no more than a minute or so and we'll be right behind you."

Walid and Mafulla got busy taking some small boxes of bullets from the crate and putting them into the satchels and bags that most of the students had brought to class with their books. The boys all grabbed rifles, and a couple of them took handguns as well, while the girls mostly picked the smaller pistols in the crate. Khalid and Hoda and Layla helped them choose and then made their own quick selections.

At this point, out of their chairs and holding their guns, the students were all in quiet conversation with each other in various groups. Omari then directed everyone to follow him, and they began leaving the room and heading toward the nearest staircase, one that would take them all to the back side entrance of the palace. Walid walked up next to Kissa and gave her a touch on the arm. He whispered, "Don't worry. We're going to be safe."

She said, "I'm fine. Let's stay close, if we can."

Hasina came up to Mafulla at about the same time and he said to her, "Are you Ok?" She nodded and said, "Yeah, I'm focused, but some of the other girls are really scared, I can tell."

"It's amazing how much our training is helping me control the way I feel in the middle of all this," Mafulla said.

"Yeah, me, too," Hasina said. "And still, it's a little unsettling."

"You're right," Mafulla replied and then added, "But I think helping everybody else will actually help us settle down, too."

"I agree."

They walked down the hallway to the staircase, then down the long flight of stairs and toward the big open reception area that would take them to the main side door of the building. Mafulla got closer to the prince. "Walid, I just had a wild thought," he said in a low voice.

"What is it?" his friend asked.

"Farouk's men have come at us by earth, underground, and now maybe also by fire."

"You think?"

"It's too much of a coincidence, otherwise. We've never had a fire before and suddenly, today, of all days?"

"Ok," Walid said, "Maybe so. You could be right."

"But earth and fire—that means we should watch out next for air and water," Mafulla reasoned.

"What do you mean?"

"The Four Elements, remember? The king told you about them in the desert and then you passed on to me before Masoon brought them into our training. You know: Earth, Fire, Air, Water."

"But what made you think of them now?"

"Farouk was in … the group for a while, remember? He had early training and likely learned about them, and now he's maybe using them like he's used certain … mathematical things."

Walid said, "Ok. Earth and fire—the underground tunnels and the blaze downstairs." He looked impressed but also puzzled. He then said, "Next, water and air I guess. But, how?"

"I don't know."

"There were some earlier reports of men approaching up by the Nile in boats."

"Yeah, maybe that's it," Mafulla said. "That's the water, maybe."

"But, air? How could they come at us by air?" Walid asked.

"That gets me. I have no idea," Mafulla said just as they were approaching the side door of the palace as a group. "Surely, they don't have airplanes. Where would they take off and land?"

Walid's mind was working at lightning speed as they approached the downstairs rear side entrance for the palace. "Wait!" He suddenly yelled out to Omari, up front. "Don't go out the door!"

"What?" Omari turned and said, now no more than about five feet from the exit.

"Wait a second! No one leaves the building yet!" Walid yelled as he ran forward to where Omari stood.

"What is it, Prince?"

"Mafulla just had a thought. Farouk's men have come at us by earth, through the tunnels underground, and now maybe they've somehow started the fire."

"It's unlikely, but not impossible in the context," Omari said.

"Earth and fire. Those are two of The Four Elements. Next will be air and water."

"What do you mean?"

"They'll somehow come at us by air."

"How?"

Just then the palace guard who had come to get them opened the big outer door and said in a raised voice, "Prince Walid, Omari, I'm sorry, but, gentlemen, we need to continue our conversations outside." Walid looked up and out the door where he could see a few palace executives and staff members standing on the grounds in small clusters and talking.

"Ok," Omari said to him and then he turned back to Walid. "Give me a second to get the class out of the building and we'll explore this idea."

"But outside, we'll be in the open … air."

"Those who are already out there seem fine, and they're not being exposed to any smoke conveyed by the air in the palace," Omari said, looking around. "Toxic smoke from the fire can also be carried by the air outside, but a breeze seems to be blowing the other way."

"Ok." The people already outdoors in the fresh air did seem to be just fine, so Walid didn't protest at this point, but automatically yielded to Omari's reasoning and the ongoing sense of urgency conveyed by the guard who was still rushing them. Omari then turned toward the doorway again, took a few steps in its direction, and pushed open one of the two large wooden doors, He stood against it, propping it open for the students and teachers and he motioned everyone forward to it. The guard who was hurrying them held the other door open. The class then followed their lead and immediately began to go out through the double doors. But something nagged at Walid and he almost spoke up again. He felt a tiny battle of head and heart, as Omari's reasoning seemed sound, but there was something else.

Bafur was the first out, then Jabari, then Set. Ara and Cabar were next, with Malik and Haji right behind. But at that very second, they all barely heard muffled popping sounds in the distance and, up ahead on the grounds, farther from the building, two people who had been talking, two palace staff, instantly fell to the ground in a violent way, as if they had been shot. Then just a second later, a third person cried out, spun around, and dropped to the sand. Blood was visible.

"Snipers!" Omari yelled. "Back inside! There's danger!" He waved urgently to the few who were already outside and shouted once more, "Back here, quickly! Get inside! Run!"

"This is how they're coming at us by air, through the air," Mafulla shouted up to Omari. "Bullets through the air, raining down on us!"

Malik and Haji grabbed the arms of the girls and hustled them back to the door. Set and Jabari turned quickly and dashed back toward the doorway, but Bafur, who had been in front of them a few feet farther away, seemed to twist his ankle when he turned quickly, and he started limping, almost hopping back to the steps.

Omari was quickly scanning the windows of the buildings across the street from the wall around the palace grounds. He knew that, within minutes, kingdom soldiers would be on these snipers to stop them. But in the time until that happened, these enemy sharpshooters would have a wide-open aim at everyone who was standing outside the palace because of the fire. The thought crossed Omari's mind that there would be a lot more people outside the front doors and the far back doors in harm's way. The fact that they were at a side door, used typically only by the school's students, made their area less of a target zone. Who knew what was already going on outside the other exits? He realistically figured that there would be major casualties. But palace sharpshooters would trade volleys with these unseen snipers and nearby troops would soon surround them. He just knew that, in the meantime, he had to help keep the students safe.

Four rounds then hit the wall next to the door and above it. Ping, Ping, Ping, Ping! "Ow! Oh!" In the midst of his mad limping dash back to the door, Bafur suddenly collapsed on the marble steps right outside the threshold. Set, who was back barely inside the door and still close to it, heard his cry of pain, turned and saw him fall, and instinctively ran out again, staying low to get to him. He reached down, grabbed Bafur's shoulders and began to drag him toward the door, which was not an easy task. Omari had just seen what was happening a few feet away from him but before he could even move, a round hit Set and smashed him down to the steps as well.

Various voices yelled, "No!" "Bafur!" "Set!" When Jabari realized what had happened to his friends, he started saying, "Oh, no! No, no, no, no, no!" But he was next to Hoda at this point, and when he tried to move in their direction, she held on to him tightly.

"Stay right here," she insisted. "I need you here."

Walid and Mafulla practically dove out the door, right by Omari in the second he was turning to help, and frantically tried to get their friends pulled back into the building. Mafulla suddenly went down, falling flat, his face crammed into Bafur's back. A bullet whizzed past his ear and he heard it go by. If he hadn't fallen the instant he did, he would have been shot in the head. Walid jerked to his left a moment before he, too, heard a bullet pass close to his right ear. The two of them would have been dead on the steps in a pool of blood with their friends had they not responded to a vivid sense of what could have been nothing other than extended proprioception, with its uncanny awareness of the fast approaching proximity of those bullets and the looming intersection of the deadly projectiles with their bodies. The actions they took instantly saved their lives. Their training in this art, just like their different moves of the moment, had come in the nick of time.

But a sniper still had Walid in his scope. Omari, however, in his peripheral vision, had caught sight of a muzzle flash and, pulling out his own weapon, had quickly sent several rounds in that precise direction, suppressing the fire they had been taking and, unknown to him at the time, eliminating the sniper who had been locked in on Walid, putting a bullet straight into the man's forehead, the very instant he had decided to squeeze his trigger again, with Walid's head in the crosshairs. The German-made sniper rifle instead clattered to the floor and the lifeless body of the shooter collapsed silently where he had crouched behind a second floor window. And a great tragedy was averted.

Two other snipers who were nearby and hidden in an adjacent building suddenly experienced massive headaches and blurred vision. One dropped his weapon and grabbed the side of his head, howling at the sharp pain that coursed through his brain. He had inadvertently moved from a crouching position behind a window frame into a bent standing position as he gripped his head and lurched forward just inside that window. Within a second, a palace sharpshooter saw him move and took the opportunity that this afforded to end both his headache and his earthly sojourn.

Walid and Mafulla were able to take advantage of a temporary lull in the shooting to get their friends back inside the building, dragging them up the last two steps and across the threshold. They could already see blood on both of them and were focused on doing whatever they could to save them, if it was possible at this point. Suddenly, Rumi, Walid's dad, appeared at their side and said, "Let me take over here." He turned to the nearby senior palace guard and said, "Omari, put down your gun for a second and give me a hand. Walid, you and Mafulla can help in another way."

"How?" The prince answered.

"Take up your weapons and stand watch. I'm here now. And Omari has more training in trauma than you do at present. You're needed for something else. And, please, get farther from the door. Go back. Immediately."

The prince and Mafulla both had dropped their weapons when they ran out to get Set and Bafur. Now, they picked them back up and began quickly to load them as they moved backward, while hearing another volley of bullets hit near the doors, which Malik and the other palace guard were fast closing. Then, three sharp thuds sounded out loudly, shots that had hit the doors themselves, a split second after they were shut, rounds that otherwise would have come into the building and possibly have killed or wounded someone else.

"Everyone load your weapons!" Walid said loudly to all the students around him, and to the adults. "Move back from the doors and load your ammunition!"

Mafulla came up close to his best friend and said, "Earth, fire, air. We need to think: How will they attack through water? That's got to be the next thing that happens."

"Ok." Walid first thought again of boats on the Nile, but then said to himself that they couldn't come to the palace on water, and it's got to be immediate, somehow as the form or method of an attack. Then, he sought to make his mind a blank, which was not easy in the situation. But he was well practiced at this stage. He took a deep breath and let go of all emotion and thought. He breathed again, and a third time. A moment of calm coursed through him. The sounds around him faded. The emptiness he sought was becoming his. He was focused and completely open to new insight and truth.

He suddenly yelled out, "Malik! You and Haji help everyone with whatever they need! Mafulla, come with me!" Looking over at Hoda and Kissa, he shouted, "We'll be right back!" He took off running at full speed through the large reception hall and toward the main part of the palace where the fire was still burning. Without saying anything or asking a question, Mafulla was right behind him, at nearly a full out run, but all that he needed to keep up with his slightly slower friend.

"Water!" Walid yelled to Mafulla. "It's the fire trucks that will come through the Main Gate with water for the fire! I just hope … we're not too late!"

29

Chaos

Black smoke was pouring out of four large open windows along the first floor of the massive front right wall of the Golden Palace. Enemy snipers from nearby locations had already killed or seriously wounded nine people outside the main entrance of the building, hitting them after they had left the massive front doors to escape the fire, its smoke, and its deadly fumes. Dozens of others had made it out into the arrival courtyard and, when the shooting began, had taken cover behind anything that could protect them. Two diplomatic cars in the front drive were sheltering several people. A small wall and a granite monument were protecting others. Even a group of trees was saving a few lives. Palace guards had vigorously returned fire, once they realized what was happening and could locate some of the shooters. Nearby army units had been mobilized quickly and their advance reconnaissance and sharpshooting teams were now also identifying most of the sniper posts and working hard to neutralize them before the heartless mercenaries could inflict any more terrible damage.

The scene in front of the palace had been bad and getting worse for the first five or ten minutes, with unarmed people being shot and wounded or killed before many of those outside had figured out what was actually going on and where the bullets were originating. But by now, most unarmed staff had taken cover in some way and the kingdom forces engaging their adversaries were starting to prevail. However, in the back area, behind the vast structure housing the monarchy, things were not getting resolved quite as quickly. There were too many nearby buildings to check for sniper locations. And more of the overall resources available in this sector of the palace grounds initially had been devoted to the tunnel situation, where loyal troops had been busy making sure of their success in that effort, and so were otherwise occupied and at a distance from the many palace staff members who were standing outside when the shooting started.

As things were just beginning to calm down a bit out front, the main palace gates swung open wide to let in four fire trucks with sirens blaring, along with six ambulances that were following them close behind. Bringing up the rear were three large tan Egyptian Army trucks. The small palace fire brigade was already working hard to contain and extinguish the interior fire, but the blaze had been started by someone using gasoline, and so was difficult to defeat. The palace firemen who were outside welcomed the sight of the city's fire trucks pouring through the gate and coming to a stop right in front of the building. Palace guards also felt a sense of relief when they saw the military trucks barreling in as well.

As Walid and Mafulla got close to the front of the palace, still running through the main hallway, the smoke in the air became much worse. Walid ran up to a vase of cut flowers and, taking out the sand mask he always carried on him, dumped water from it onto the mask, and then held out the vase to Mafulla, who pulled out his mask for his friend to do the same to it. And now, with the wet masks on, they were a bit more protected from the thick smoke, at least for a little longer as they made their way forward.

Three firemen jumped out of the lead truck and pulled a hose toward the windows where the smoke was billowing out. A ladder was quickly put into place, the glass of the windows was smashed, and a stream of water was directed into the burning room. All of this, it quickly turned out, was no more than a bit of theater, meant to disguise what was going to happen next.

Two men from one of the other fire engines immediately ran into the front palace door with another long hose. But, unknown to anyone in the palace or to the king's fire brigade now shouting directions to their apparent colleagues, this hose was intended to pump huge amounts of gasoline onto the fire and throughout more of the rooms. Walid saw these two men in fire fighting outfits entering the front doors up ahead of them through the smoke and carrying a hose, not yet turned on. But something didn't feel right. He waved and yelled to them at the top of his voice, "Stop! Stop and stay where you are!" He could barely see one of them reaching down and pulling something from a pocket or bag. And then, from not much more than three or four feet behind his head, an explosion rang out that was nearly deafening in its intensity, and then another, a bit more muffled now than the first. The prince lunged downward into a crouching position.

Mafulla had known from the first moment that it was a gun being pulled, and had acted fast to shoot the assailant where he stood, and then the other false fireman, taking them both down to the ground before either of them could turn on their hose and douse the interior of the palace with more highly flammable gas. Walid could now detect its smell as they ran over to the downed men, guns held at the ready.

As this was happening, the ambulances and trucks that had just arrived were unloading dozens of disguised mercenaries onto the front grounds of the palace. They were all in stolen Egyptian military uniforms or emergency hospital ambulance garb. As a group of six to ten of them headed in the direction of the front door, Walid got close enough to the door from the inside that he could see what was going on. He saw them and quickly noticed the fact that the guys in medical clothing were, oddly, carrying guns and weapons of an unfamiliar appearance. He instinctively turned slightly to the side and shot into the tank of the fire truck where the long gas hose was connected. Three quick shots and it exploded in a giant fireball, killing instantly most of the mercenaries in the group headed for the door, and wounding the others badly. Because of the position of the truck and a quick scan around to make sure no palace staff or guards were near, Walid had been confident that this was the move to make.

He leaned up against the side of the wall now, sheltered from the doorway and the intense heat from the explosion's fireball, and reloaded his gun while coughing loudly. Mafulla had stepped into the doorway and let fly with four shots into another nearby truck and he had exactly the same result. A huge explosion took out another ten or twelve of the adversaries. One more truck remained with a gasoline filled water tank but, at this point, all the men trained in how to use it were either dead from the two nearby explosions or were quickly moving as far away from it as they could.

Mafulla was now suddenly doubled over, coughing from the smoke as bullets began to whiz by them on all sides. One knocked off a chunk of plaster near his head and imbedded itself deep in the wall. "We need to get out of here right away!" He coughed again and yelled at Walid, "Now! Now!"

"Ok" Walid said and also coughed loudly three times. His lungs were starting to burn. They turned and walked quickly back in the direction from which they had come, now almost constantly coughing and gasping for breath in all the thick smoke. But just as they were leaving the front entrance hall, three palace guards came up toward them from a side corridor. Walid yelled out, "Enemies are in disguise outside—those army and fire and medical uniforms are fake!" And the guards then ran forward to begin shooting out the door from crouched positions toward the melee of men and equipment in the front. One was prepared for anything and actually had with him a single hand grenade that he now ran and threw toward a cluster of the enemy soldiers. The blast that followed eliminated many more of them.

As this was happening, Walid led Mafulla up the nearest staircase to the residential floor. The smoke was still billowing. Through the thick choking haze, he could barely see Kular up ahead directing people around a corner and down the hall. They were walking quickly away from the residences and toward the far end of the floor. "Mom!" Walid shouted. "Mom!"

Bhati turned, stopped, and responded, "Walid! My son! Mafulla! Come quickly!" The boys followed her and Bancom, the king, Hamid, and Naqid, along with a few others down the wide hallway where the smoke was growing thinner with every few steps. Kular was right behind them as they all walked with a rapid stride toward clear air.

"Where are we going?" Walid said to Bancom, who was only a few feet away.

"To your classroom where I had men set up a radio command post earlier for your use, in case you needed it, but that was before the current chaos. We'll stop there and make an assessment."

The king was in conversation with Naqid as they walked down the hall. Naqid was assuring him that the palace guards had just been reinforced by a great number of regular Egyptian army who had come in the front gate and were now training their fire on the intruders all around that area of the palace. He estimated they should have that wave of the assault stopped soon. Unfortunately, not yet reported to Naqid was the fact that one of the stolen trucks that had followed the fire engines and ambulances through the gates had taken a side service road and disappeared around the back of the palace before the kingdom reinforcements arrived. Unknown to anyone in the palace or palace guard, except for three men at the side gate who were too busy defending themselves to report in, another authentic looking army truck had also entered that gate under the pretense of reinforcing the palace defense, just as the fire trucks had come through the front gates. So now, two trucks that were actually full of more enemy soldiers were meeting up near the palace side door, far from the current main focus of action. And this is the entrance where all the other students were gathered with their older guides.

Within minutes, the entire group following the king was in Khalid's classroom. Khalid and Hoda, though, were still downstairs with their students near the side door and awaiting further instructions. A newly sent guard had told them that the fire and smoke were not yet an imminent threat in that area of the palace, so they should maintain their position for the moment. He explained that it was still safer inside than outside in that part of the building. Khalid had asked about returning to the classroom, but had been told that it was better for a while longer to be near an exit, in case the fire and smoke situation should change for the worse, and the sniper problem was eliminated.

Unfortunately, that exit was also of course an entrance and was the door nearest to where the two stolen military trucks had just met. So far, all the king's preparations for any assault on the palace had been working about as well as could be hoped, aside from the initially unanticipated fire and sniper effectiveness. A part of the palace interior was burning and many good people, tragically, had been killed or injured, but no plan could have perfectly protected people and property against harm. The fire was still contained, the snipers were being stopped, and the royal family was safe—a net balance of preventing the very worst. But that was about to change.

Deception and misdirection had been the main tools used so far by the al-Khoum brothers. Preparation and flexibility had been the keys to the king's defenses. But the sheer speed of response had also been important. Rumi had gotten to the seriously injured Bafur and Set as quickly as he did because of an intuition Hamid had earlier that one of them should grab a medical emergency kit and go find the group of students, in case there was an imminent need. That's how Rumi had managed to arrive onsite just as the two boys were shot. He was able to examine their wounds less than a minute after they occurred and he had applied the best of field medicine to them both. But he could tell that his efforts were not working well enough. Bafur had lost consciousness on the steps and had not regained it. Set was struggling, fading in and out as Rumi worked on them both with Omari's help, as fast as he could. Hoda and Layla were also focused on the boys in prayer and powerful mental support, as were Kissa and Hasina, taking their minds temporarily off the sporadic sniper rounds and return shots they could still hear, now and then, outside.

Rumi's first job had been to figure out where the bullets had penetrated and what internal organs might have been damaged or compromised, while at the same time controlling and hopefully stopping the major blood loss from both boys. To free up Omari for another task, Layla came over to help with Bafur now, and Hoda quickly joined in an effort to assist with Set. They were certainly the guard's equals in this, thanks to their extensive Phi training for keeping people alive under battlefield conditions. But Rumi could tell that neither boy looked good at all. So he did what he now had to do. He brought the boys' bodies close enough together that their motionless hands could touch. Taking an object from his pocket, he placed it on Set's upturned palm and put Bafur's hand, palm down, on it as well, doing all that he could, in action as well as intention, to give it into their joint custody. It was now up to whatever power was in, or somehow worked through, The Stone of Giza to have its effect, in augmentation of all the first aid and medical procedures that Rumi and his colleagues had been performing on the two young boys lying motionless on the hard marble floor.

There was a loud bang against the door, not much more than

ten feet from where this desperate life-saving work was taking place. Now, seconds later, everyone heard another one. Something was hitting the door hard from the outside. Two palace guards ran up to Rumi and one of them, who was known well to him, spoke rapidly, "Doctor! You should fall back to a safe position! You have to be protected. We need your medical skills to remain available. We'll stay with the injured boys and get them to safety, nearby. Move away for just a couple of minutes until we see what's happening, and then you can rejoin them, when we can assure your protection and theirs. But for the moment, please, you and Omari lead the other students back and to cover! Ladies! You, too!"

There was a third loud boom. The massively thick door sounded like it was going to shatter off its hinges. Had it not been for that thunderous noise, getting worse each time, and the imminent threat it foreshadowed, Rumi would never have left Set and Bafur for even a moment. But he realized it would do them no good for their only chance at ongoing help to be shot within seconds. They'd likely not survive. And because the boys were already down and motionless, if they were alone for a few moments, they'd not likely be targets for any imminent intruders, in case there were any.

Rumi knew the students well enough to be able to help Omari lead them quickly and effectively in a time like this. In addition, he had just managed to stop Bafur's worst bleeding, while Hoda had subdued Set's, and so he was able to cover their wounds quickly. If he had to leave them for a minute in the care of others, this was the first instant he could even have considered it. So, expecting to get back to the injured boys within a very short time, he finally nodded his agreement and said, "Ok. We can move away."

At that signal, Omari, who was standing nearby, shouted to the guards to watch the boys as well as they could, and then waved over to two of the other students he knew and called out, "Malik! Haji! Help me get everyone across the room and in defensive positions! Prepare everyone to fire on the door when it opens!" He motioned to Rumi and they both moved backward and off to the side from where they were.

There was a mad dash across various parts of the large open space they were all in as the students and adults took cover where they could find it. They got behind columns, inside inner doorways, and onto a nearby stairway with four-foot sidewalls that offered some amount of solid protection. They were in their positions for no more than several seconds before a mighty crashing sound followed by a loud cracking of wood signaled the breaching of the door and a number of armed men in stolen Egyptian army uniforms stormed in, shooting. Initially confused for a moment by their appearance, Omari reacted in less than two seconds to their actions by ordering a salvo from the students and their guardians. He yelled, "They're enemies! Fire!" And all at once, including four palace guards who were there to back them up, twenty-two weapons suddenly fired at the intruders in a huge, ear-splitting barrage that cut down six of them instantly and took four others to the floor. The mercenaries were totally exposed in the large empty space they had entered with no cover at all, except for the few who weren't entirely in yet and were able to take shelter behind one of the fractured door panels that still stood almost upright.

Omari saw movement to his left and recognized Paki Alexander coming down an adjacent hall with what looked like eight to twelve men behind him. "Help at nine o'clock!" Omari yelled over the continued, scattered fire. "When they get in position and we can eliminate the attack, the stairway people go upstairs—fall back to the classroom!" He then looked toward the students behind the columns and in the two nearby rooms and called out, "When our friends start firing, that very second, run down the hallway here and take the first set of stairs to the second floor! And stay low!"

As the students on the stairway crept upward on their hands and knees, five palace guards came running down the stairs and crouched low at various points along the wall. The moment that

Paki's men get into position and started laying down a solid continuous blast of gunfire toward the door, the five guards on the stairs appeared over the wall and began firing as well. The students in all locations then made a break for it, along with Khalid, Hoda, and Layla—whose entire job now was to stay with them. In fact, Hoda and Layla ran a few steps from where they had been positioned to shoot, and then turned toward the outer door and caught a glimpse of more mercenaries who were waiting to come through that entrance. Both of them instantly shot from a low position and hit their marks before turning once more toward the nearby second staircase.

Cabar suddenly dropped her gun and it clattered to the floor. She stood, bent over and still and then started sobbing. Layla called out, "Are you hit? Are you Ok?"

"I'm scared and I tripped," she said.

"We're going to be all right," Layla reassured her. "Take a deep breath, and pick up your gun, and let's get upstairs."

"Ok," she replied in agreement, or at least acquiescence, as Layla took her arm to lead her back to safety.

During all this, Farouk al-Khoum and his brother Faraj were sitting in one of the two trucks that had pulled up near the side entrance where the battle was raging. Farouk reached over, touched the driver's arm, and said to him, "Take us now to the final location."

"No. Stop!" Faraj looked over at his brother with shock and disapproval and said, "What do you mean? We can't leave yet. We need to lead a regrouping effort. Our men are all being cut down."

"They're serving their purpose," Farouk said. "And their full wages will never leave our pockets."

"They're soldiers!" Faraj said, taking tremendous offense at his brother's words.

"They're pawns," Farouk replied. "Their fight here is now their business and not ours, and you know it. They're keeping the entire palace guard busy so we can slip around to the loading dock, where our vital actions will begin. Remember the plan!"

"We can help them and we should!"

"No! Keep your focus! As I've told you, we have to go right to the spot that's going to be the most lightly guarded, especially now in the midst of the fight. And the back service stairway located there is our best path to the king's residence. Now's the time to use it."

Faraj was furious, but for the moment said nothing more in reply. His brother had never revealed before that his plan was for the soldiers to serve merely as a distraction and die. His own idea was for them to penetrate the expected weak defenses at the side entrance and approach the royal residence from a second angle. Now, Farouk was asserting his authority and changing the plan, or else revealing what his take on the plan had always been. He clearly had no respect for anyone and cared about no one except himself. But Faraj deep down really already knew this, and it was a piece of knowledge that had kept his inner fire of resentment burning for years.

"Don't just sit there and sulk! Prepare yourself!" Farouk barked out. He turned again to the driver and said, "Now! Take us!" The truck engine revved and then lurched, and they began to roll toward their destination.

"These men are brave and they fight for you!" Faraj couldn't hold back any longer.

"Yes, many men who fight wars are brave. But men who start wars are bold. And those who win wars are shrewd. You know that. We have our own purposes. If they die for us, then they die. And either they live again, as their religions teach, or they don't and will have no more suffering, so why fret about their fate? They were born to die, and many are simply doing that today. We're not increasing at all the number of deaths in the world."

Faraj seethed. He said, "You're so arrogantly glib."

"No, I'm simply right."

"You care more about words than people. That's why you have power. The greedy and the gullible believe you. But you don't sway me. I see things as they are."

Farouk retorted, "I make things as they are. Now, we'll do as we've agreed, or the consequences will fall on your head."

Their driver steered the truck around the back corner of the palace and up to the loading dock. Farouk and Faraj then quickly got out of it, along with the driver and two other well-trained bodyguards, all of them in official Egyptian army uniforms. Farouk did a simple wave of acknowledgment to the two palace guards who immediately appeared at the entrance.

"Who are you?" One of the palace guards shouted toward Farouk. "What do you bring us?"

"We bring plans, new tactics for turning back this assault," Farouk shouted over the sounds of gunfire coming from the middle distance as he approached the men. He showed them what looked to be a map and explained, looking from one face to the other, "Now that we've provided ample reinforcement on every side of the building, we need all the palace guards to redeploy to be closer to the king. I have a diagram of what we need. I'll show you." His words made sense. The two guards nodded their understanding. Farouk and the other men walked up the stairs next to the dock and he began to unfold the map as they approached the guards and they all went together through the door there and into a small room. Faraj lingered on the edge of the dock near the stairs to keep an eye open.

Farouk said to the guards, "Here, I can lay out the plan and your part in it." He bent over a nearby small table to spread the map out, and when the guards had also drawn near and bent over to look at it, his men quickly attacked them from behind, dropped them on the spot, and then pulled their bodies out of sight.

Bancom was upstairs on the radio in Khalid's classroom, getting status reports for the king. The muffled sounds of gunfire and occasional muted explosions could be heard in the distance. But the classroom was far away from all the current action and there was an eerie sense of something almost like calm in the atmosphere within those walls, although Walid could feel his heart beat strongly, and seemingly throughout his whole body. Mafulla was having the same experience, and had just stopped coughing from all the smoke he had inhaled downstairs near the fire.

Amon suddenly appeared in the doorway of the classroom and said, "The students are all falling back from downstairs to this area. Omari and Rumi are leading them. Paki's there and providing covering fire for them with a contingent of palace guards. What's the safest place for the students to go right now, while you're here?"

Hamid answered, "The library. Have them go to the back of the library and stay ready for any possible intrusion. I think that's where they'll be the safest."

"Hamid!" Walid said. He had just that very moment suddenly come to a thundering realization that not only surprised him but even shocked him to the core. Hamid turned around toward him, and the prince said, "Where's Masoon?"

There was a moment of silence. Mafulla was dumbstruck to hear his friend ask this question that, strangely, had not even entered his mind in the middle of all the frantic activity they had just been through. But it was now the question of all questions. Where is Masoon, indeed? The top military man in the kingdom, the legendary warrior and second most senior Phi in the area had not been seen or heard from during all this attack on the palace and the people he was sworn to protect. How could it be? Mafulla's perplexity, like Walid's at the moment, was mixed with anxiety and even a touch of fear, shading into dread.

Hamid replied with no expression, "He's not here."

"What?" Walid said.

"Orders of the king."

This made no sense at all to either Walid or Mafulla. Why would the king order Masoon to be away from the palace at a time like this when he would be greatly needed? It couldn't be to preserve the monarchy. He wasn't in the royal lineage. What could be happening?

On the first floor of the building, at the side door entrance that had been defended earlier by the students with Rumi and Omari, the palace guard had now fought off all incoming intruders, and they decided it was time to fall back to a better position of ambush in case still others would seek to enter that door. But then, one of the guards who had been left nearby to watch over the injured boys during the fighting noticed Set slightly move his left arm and then a leg.

"The boy! He's alive and moving!"

"I thought they were both dead," a nearby guard replied.

"No, no, I just saw him move a little bit. We have to get him. Come with me."

"Yes, Ok, but we have to be very quick, before more of the enemy might charge in!"

The guards moved across the short open space that now separated them from the bodies of the two boys. One grabbed Set and the other took hold of Bafur, putting them over their shoulders with great effort and not noticing the stone that one guard's foot accidentally kicked across the floor toward the doorway. There was still gunfire outside close by and so they hurried toward a place of safety with the boys.

Set groaned. The guard carrying him said, "We're getting you to a safe place. Doctor Rumi is upstairs hoping, I'm sure, to come back and check on you, but it's much safer to take you to him now."

"Ba," Set tried to say Bafur's name but could not.

"Don't use your energy speaking. Stay quiet and still."

The men carried the boys up the long staircase and, just as they got to the top, they heard several mercenaries enter the door once more, shooting into the entry hall before they crossed the threshold of the building. But this time there was, unexpectedly, no immediate resistance. The palace guards who had fallen back to an ambush position did not yet return fire. They would wait until this party was deeper into the hall with no quick way out, and then cut them down from two directions. Six men had entered the building and were still firing, now seemingly at random. One of them happened to notice the large emerald that lay in a shadow right next to the door. He reached down and picked it up and looked at it closely, then put it into his pocket and said to the man beside him, "I just found something I should take to our leaders, to the al-Khoums. It looks like it might be of great value. They need to have it. They could give us a reward."

"Whatever it is, keep it for yourself, idiot," the other man said. "You can't count on rewards from them!" The men momentarily stopped firing and crept forward in the unanticipated quiet, looking around them and seeing nothing. The thought crossed their minds that the palace guard must have retreated to safety under the withering assault of those who had come before them through the large doors, many of whom nonetheless now lay dead around the hallway.

The finder of the stone whispered back loudly to his companion, "I understand, but what I've found is better to turn over immediately. It's the right thing to do. They'd kill me if they discovered I took it, or even if I left it here after finding it. Someone may have seen me pick it up. I'll dash out with it and give it to them quickly. I'll be right back."

The other man just grunted and said, "Whatever you do—just hurry. We'll need all our guns for the next stage of this."

The man with the stone wasn't overly concerned about a reward. And his prime motivation was not even a fear of their leaders. He had just been looking for a reason not to go farther into the palace and be shot like so many others who had preceded him this day, and whose bodies were now sprawled all around, dead or dying. This jewel was the excuse he'd been seeking. But he might indeed be offered a reward, anyway. If, however, he was sent back into the palace without one, then at least his true reward would be that the men ahead of him would most likely by then have taken the hostile fire awaiting them and him, had he continued on now and not used the gem as an excuse. This way, he might live another day. He thought of himself as at least improving his chances.

But when this soldier with the stone returned to the place outside where the two trucks had been, one of them was gone. There was a badly wounded man leaning against one of the remaining truck's front tires. The man with the stone asked him, "Where are the brothers?"

"They took off that way," the wounded man said, pointing.

"What do you mean?"

"They took off, around back!"

The soldier with the emerald hesitated a moment and then started to trot along the access road, gun in one hand and gem now in the other. He scanned the side of the building and all its windows for palace guard sharpshooters. But they were all otherwise occupied for the moment and he made it around the corner of the building safely, and then to a point where the truck he sought finally came into sight.

Farouk and his men had just killed the palace guards inside the building at the small table fifteen or twenty feet away from the loading dock. Faraj still stood out on the dock and kept watch, for the moment, pondering anew his own role in all this. He continued to seethe inside with a growing fury toward his brother.

The soldier jogging up raised his hand, waved, and approached him, climbing the steps to where he stood. "Mr. al-Khoum! I've found an emerald, a large precious gem that I thought you might want."

Faraj eyed him and then looked at what he held out in his hand. He said, "Yes, give it to me. What's your name?"

"Ahmed Barsook," he replied, "from Morocco."

"I'll offer you a good reward for this at the end of the day. For now, stand watch here, so I can go with my brother upstairs. Shoot any enemy who approaches."

"Yes, sir. Gladly, sir! And I thank you." The man realized that he was being given what might likely be a much safer task than storming into the side entry to the palace. His desperate plan was working. In a sense, he had a great reward already. Anything else would be extra.

Faraj looked at the jewel for a moment and marveled at how much it resembled The Stone of Giza that he was already carrying in his pocket. That arrangement was a result of the great compromise of the day—Farouk would carry The Ring of Phi and Faraj would possess what they had just recently come to believe was the famous Stone of Giza. Of course, they didn't know that both the items they had been protecting and depending on were fakes.

So Faraj had what he thought was the authentic Stone of Giza in a pocket already. But this identical looking emerald appeared in the light even more beautiful. Could it just be the light? Or is it possible that there are two such stones? Or was this one of the synthetic replicas that had been created recently with no flaws or cloudiness? These thoughts immediately all ran through his mind. He put the new stone into another pocket and turned to join his brother and the others before they made their way upstairs.

"What did that man want?" Farouk grunted out as Faraj approached. He had caught a glimpse of the mercenary talking with his brother.

"Never mind. It's of no concern. He gave me a quick report and now he's helping us here. He's taking the watch position on the dock so I can be freed up for more important things."

"There's nothing more important that you can do," Farouk said, adding, "except at this point to stay out of my way."

Faraj was completely incensed at the arrogance of his brother. He shot back, "Watch yourself and your words, brother. I've had about enough of your foolish drivel today."

"Foolish drivel? You control your mouth, you leech," Farouk nearly hissed. 'I've carried you this far on my back. Don't make me throw you down now, just short of the goal."

It was all Faraj could do not to shoot his brother on the spot and rid himself of all the needless aggravation that poured forth from his overweening haughtiness. A sense of almost uncontrollable rage was building up in him. The stone in his pocket was having its customary effect and bringing forth, as well as magnifying, the emotions and attitudes he normally tried to hide. If the older Farouk had not been blinded by his own insolence, he would have detected that his brother was no longer to any extent under his influence, if indeed he ever had been. And this could mean trouble.

Upstairs in the classroom, Walid looked stunned at what he had just heard. He said to Hamid, "I don't understand. Why has the king sent Masoon somewhere else today, of all days? We desperately need him here."

"He's on a special mission," Hamid explained, as he got up close to the prince and lowered his voice. "He's leading a small group of senior members of our society to eliminate any major threat that exists outside the palace grounds right now. We had word earlier that a large group of armed men and vehicles had been gathering across town at a distance. We think they were positioning themselves to be Farouk's final wave of attack, and Masoon's mission is to remove the possibility that they ever make it here."

"Oh, Ok. Good. That makes sense. I was puzzled. How many men does he have with him?"

"Five."

"How many is he up against?"

"There are likely dozens—maybe as many as a hundred, but probably no more."

"Good. Then, I'm not worried for him," Walid said and smiled.

Hamid returned his expression. "It is good," he said, simply.

Mafulla had been listening to all this. "Wait." He looked puzzled. "Where's Uncle Reela? He was supposed to be here."

"Oh! I'm so, so sorry, my friend. In all the turmoil and commotion, I forgot to tell you." Hamid turned and said these words with a very serious and concerned look on his face. He took a deep breath and prepared to report the very bad news that he had not yet conveyed. He then first put a hand on Mafulla's shoulder and said, "Shortly after Reela arrived was when the front part of the building was first evacuated. He was near the door at the time and was sent back into the front courtyard. I'm afraid he was shot by a sniper."

30

A Stone's Throw

"Oh, no," Mafulla responded to Hamid's words, stunned to the core, his mouth suddenly dry and a light dizziness clouding his thoughts.

Hamid quickly added, "But your uncle wasn't killed. He's one of the lucky ones. He's being treated in the palace infirmary with several others. He was wounded, but not seriously, by a sniper out front and he managed to get safely back into the building."

"What a relief! You scared me half to death," Mafulla said.

"I must have. I didn't mean to. A thousand apologies—my mind's on too many things at once and I should have given you the good news first. He'll be all right," Hamid said. "He was just deeply grazed on his arm at the shoulder. It's a fairly superficial wound. I saw him myself right afterwards and made sure he was Ok."

"Oh, good."

"He was very blessed to avoid much worse, and the fate of so many today."

"Should I run down and check on him?"

"No, not now. You're better off here for the moment. It's actually better in many ways for you to be here. And I can assure you—Reela will be fine. I actually expect him to join us soon. The medics in the infirmary know where we are and have instructions to escort him here when they have a free moment."

In the library, Kissa was feeling a sense of high agitation. "Mom," she said to Hoda, "I can't stand it any more. We're just stuck here waiting. We should be doing something. I shouldn't be sitting here."

"I was feeling exactly the same way," Hoda whispered back in a low voice. "I think we're going to be needed soon."

"What can we do?"

"I'll ask Layla if she can stay with the students and allow us to take some action. I've been feeling like we should check on your brothers."

"That's a good idea."

Hoda got up and walked over to Layla and spoke with her quietly for a few seconds. Layla was nodding her agreement to whatever was being said. Hoda then came back to where Kissa was sitting with a gun across her lap. "It's fine. I asked her also about Hasina going with us. But she wants her to stay here for now, and I can't blame her."

"Yeah, I understand."

"I said Ok, that we'd go find our boys and be back in no more than a few minutes."

"Where do you think Baqid and Shumar are right now—in the kitchen still?" Kissa asked.

"Shumar once told me that they can use the large pantry in the kitchen area as a safe room. It has thick walls and a secure door that was designed so it can be locked from the inside. I bet that when they heard the gunfire, the head chef insisted they all get in there and wait it out. He's a sensible and cautious man."

"You're right," Kissa said. "So, Ok, I'm ready," she added as she lay down the rifle she had been holding and stood up and tucked a pistol into her belt. "Lead the way." Hoda then walked quickly between the long bookshelves and over to the door, followed by her daughter, and then she slowed and approached the doorway more cautiously.

Walid's dad, Rumi, had left the students a few minutes earlier to go check on Bafur and Set and, on his way, he happened to meet the guards carrying them upstairs. He quickly asked about the boys, heard what the men had to say, and led them down to the infirmary where more crucial medications were available and where the two seriously wounded young men could rest more comfortably. As they walked down the hall, at a distance now from the library, Rumi asked one of the guards, "Where's the stone they had? The emerald?"

The man just looked puzzled. "What stone is that?"

"The stone these boys had their hands on while they were lying together on the floor," Rumi answered.

"I didn't see a stone of any sort," the first man said.

"Neither did I," the other guard offered. "We just picked the boys up as quickly as we could once we noticed some movement, and I saw nothing else."

Rumi said, "As soon as we get these boys to safety, you must go back to where their bodies were lying and look all around there for a large green stone, an emerald. It's very important that you bring it to me. I can't explain now, but their health and the health of many others today may depend on this."

"But it's still an active environment, with hostile fire possible at any moment."

"I understand. So take precautions, but do whatever you can to return to where the boys were and look for the stone. It's of the greatest and most crucial importance."

They both nodded, despite the fact that they really didn't understand why they were being told to do this and, as soon as they had laid the boys down on infirmary beds, they turned to leave. Reela Adi happened to see them across the room and stood up and said, "Wait for a moment. Can you take me to the king?"

"I'm sorry. We're on orders right now and can't do anything else," one of them replied.

But Rumi overheard the exchange and looked up from Set, whose breathing now was more normal. He said to the guard, "It's Ok. The king is in the main classroom down the hall. You can escort our friend there on your way downstairs. But do be quick about it, and then you have to go find the stone and bring it straight to me."

Back down the hallway a distance, and right outside the library door, Hoda had paused for a moment. Kissa said, "What is it?"

"I'm not sure. Maybe nothing. I just wanted to stop and listen for a second."

Kissa nodded and gave her a moment more, then said, "What's the best way from here to the kitchen?"

Hoda replied, "There are service stairs, but I have a strange feeling about them. There's also a dumbwaiter that goes straight down into the kitchen."

"A dumbwaiter?" Kissa looked puzzled.

"It's the small elevator that transports food from the kitchen straight up here, where it can then be taken over to the royal residence areas or anywhere else, like the classrooms."

"Oh, that's what the thing's called. I've seen it. It's how the food gets up here still hot."

"Yes. We can both squeeze into it, I think, and it will be safer than we might be on the stairs. Plus, we'll arrive in the kitchen itself, whose outer doors have likely been locked from the inside for protection."

"Oh, I hadn't thought of that."

"And then we can go straight to the pantry door and knock and identify ourselves so that we can get our boys out of there and to what I hope will be an even safer place."

The two ladies walked briskly down a hallway. Gunfire could still be heard downstairs and the slightest trace of smoke could be smelled in the air around them. The dumbwaiter's door slid open quietly, and Hoda got inside with her knees up to give Kissa plenty of room for doing the same. Once both of them were in, Hoda closed the door as much as she could and reached around to push the down button. There was a metallic noise and a slight jolt and they began moving slowly downward. As soon as they got beyond the opening and into the lower shaft, it grew totally dark. Kissa closed her eyes, almost as if pretending that the darkness was her choice. Hoda remained alert in all possible ways. After what seemed like a long descent, but one that could not have taken more than twenty or thirty seconds, they were at the bottom. Now Hoda wedged open the outer door, slid it fully up and, looking all around, got out of the device without making a sound. Kissa followed her lead and did the same.

Hoda had been right. The outer doors of the kitchen were closed and locked. The inner storage area off to one side within the kitchen was also closed and most likely locked from the inside. That's where the boys would be. She approached the door and knocked on it. She put her mouth up close to the edge of the door and cupped her hands to form almost a complete seal between her face and the crack of the door. "Hoda El-Bay, looking for Shumar and Baqid. Hoda and Kissa here in the kitchen."

She kept her ear close to the door now and could hear the muffled sound of someone inside saying, "What? What was that?"

She cupped her hands again and said, "Hoda El-Bay, looking for Shumar and Baqid."

There was silence for a few seconds. She could then hear a latch inside and the door cracked open the smallest bit. "Mom?" Shumar said.

"Shh. Open up," she whispered.

The door opened to reveal about eight members of the kitchen staff standing or sitting in the large pantry. Hoda nodded toward Shumar's boss. "Chef, I need my boys for a bit. Can they come with me?"

"Is it safe now?"

"No. Not yet. You should stay where you are until someone you trust brings word that all's clear. But at the moment, I need to take Shumar and Baqid with me, if you don't mind."

"Certainly, as you wish. I don't think anyone will need our food service any time soon."

Hoda smiled at that and said, "Actually, if the boys could bring some water with them, we're going upstairs to where the students are safely tucked away from the lunacy of the current attack."

"Sure. No problem. But what's going on outside at this point?" The chef asked this with a look of great concern.

"There have been waves of assault on the palace, but we're repelling all the attackers and will soon have the upper hand entirely," she replied. "For now, though, you and the others should continue to stay in here where it's safe." She turned to her sons and said, "Boys, grab water enough for twenty or more for the next couple of hours, and any easy snacks that will provide some nutrition for the students in hiding, and come with me. We need to go. Chef, if you would, please follow us to the outer door and relock it when we leave."

Everyone did as she asked and, within a minute, Hoda, the two boys, and Kissa were on the move down a nearby hallway, at a distance from the service stairs and toward another staircase. Hoda was a few feet ahead of everyone. She came to an intersection with another hallway and looked around the corner in both directions before turning right. But just a second or two later, and not more than fifteen feet behind her, someone else rounded a corner and entered the hall.

A low-pitched voice said, "Stop right where you are!" Farouk had sent one of his bodyguards to check out nearby hallways for adversaries before they slipped up the service stairs to the second floor. He didn't want to be caught from behind in a difficult and exposed position. And he was still waiting for the last wave of attackers to descend on the palace any minute now, before he made his crucial move to the second floor. The bodyguard's job was to make sure that all was clear around them, and there would be no unpleasant surprises.

The instant that Hoda heard the man's voice, she stopped. Shumar, Baqid, and Kissa were still in the adjacent hall, and also stopped where they stood, out of sight. They immediately pressed themselves up against a wall to try to prevent being seen. But Hoda was trapped. Kissa thought quickly. If she reversed course for ten seconds, very quietly, she could take a different route to the hall where her mom was and come up behind the man who had appeared behind her. She motioned for her brothers to stay put and slipped off her sandals, pointing to them.

Kissa then moved quickly and silently down the hallway in reverse, taking a turn into an intersecting hall and another turn and then, from behind, she saw the man confronting her mother, now thirty feet away from her, up ahead. She began to creep forward slowly and still without a sound. The man had just said to Hoda. "Egyptian military. Turn around slowly." She did as he ordered and looked right at him. He said, "Oh, my! What's a beautiful lady like you doing carrying a gun out in the open during a fierce fight and time of siege?"

"I don't know," she responded in a near whisper, and with a tone of sincere and perplexed innocence. "A man just gave it to me and said, 'Protect yourself.' But now, I'm not sure how, or from what."

"What man said that to you? Where is he?"

Hoda just put her hand to her throat and grimaced and made a choking sound, then bent her head down. The man was thoroughly puzzled at her action and stared at her, trying to make sense of what had just happened. Is she choking? Would he have to save her? He took a small step forward and was about to speak. But, before he could say or do anything else, and at that signal, Kissa silently whipped off her belt in a crouch, putting her pistol down gently and, jumping up and lunging ahead, wrapped the belt fast around the man's neck, and jerked it tight in the same movement. He dropped his gun to the floor in the instinctive urge to get both hands up to his throat to defend himself. And that was all it took for Hoda to pull out a knife and throw it hard into his chest. A quiet grunt was all the sound that he could make before he collapsed and expired on the spot.

"Mom," Kissa said in a loud whisper, "How did you know he's not real military?"

"His uniform. All the attackers are wearing genuine Egyptian army uniforms, but the version seen only on men in the western desert brigade, none of whom have been summoned here. It's slightly different in color and markings from the other uniforms."

"Oh."

"And if you'll check his weapon, you'll notice it's not from our military. It's not Egyptian issue."

"I see," Kissa whispered.

Hoda then turned and called softly down the nearby adjacent hallway, "Shumar! Baqid! Come quickly!" They crept out of their hiding place and gave Kissa back her sandals, and then with quiet whispers of concern followed their mother in the direction of a close staircase.

Seeing an armed palace guard approach, Hoda signaled to him and said in a low voice, "Take my sons to the library upstairs. We'll follow shortly."

"Mom, are you sure it's safe for you to stay down here?" Baqid looked very concerned.

"No, but I am sure there's something I should do. So, go now with this man and we'll join you later. Layla will give you weapons. Help watch over the students. That's your job now. Go!"

As the boys followed the guard a bit farther down the hall and up the stairway that had been their destination on this floor, Hoda said to Kissa, "I have strong feelings about the back service stairs. We need to check them."

The two guards who had been sent by Rumi back downstairs to

look for the stone had already arrived at the hallway nearest to the first floor side entrance where the stone had last been seen. Seven palace guards were tending to some enemies who had been shot in the ambush that had been planned for any further incoming mercenaries. Five dead or severely injured men lay on the floor in pools of blood.

A thought occurred to one of the guards who had been told to find the stone. He saw an enemy soldier nearly doubled up and groaning in pain but conscious. He bent over and asked him, "Did you see on the floor near the door you entered an emerald, a large green stone? You need to answer me."

"No."

"Did anyone see such a thing?"

"Ask your dog," the man said and groaned.

"We can help you live or let you die right here on this floor. Did anyone see a large valuable stone?"

The man grimaced and then said, "Maybe one of the others."

"What did he do with it?"

The man groaned again loudly and replied, "I don't know. It could be what you're talking about. Whatever it was, he found something he said was valuable looking and he took it to the generals."

"Where?"

"Outside."

"Where in particular?"

"They were in a truck. That's all I know."

The guard who was doing the questioning said to his colleague, "We need to get some of our men to go with us outside." He agreed and asked the others who among them could go. Four volunteered. So the six of them jogged down to the side door, carefully looked out, saw that no other action was taking place nearby, and headed straight for a lone truck. A man was dead next to the right front wheel. Two more men were dead inside. There was no one who looked like a general, and no sign of a stone.

The palace guards did a thorough search of the truck's interior and of the mercenaries' uniforms, and this went on for more than five minutes, as they looked around as thoroughly and quickly as they could. And for all their trouble, they found nothing. But tire tracks then showed them that there had been another vehicle. So all six men followed the tracks in the direction they went, around the side and then along the back of the large building.

Hoda returned to the body of the man she had dealt with, and together she and Kissa pulled the still warm corpse down the hall and around the corner into the side hallway where he would be less likely seen by any of his confederates who might be in the area. She then led Kissa around back toward the kitchen area again and down some other hallways. They silently approached the open area just inside the dock and near the back service stairs to the second floor.

Hoda stopped Kissa and looked around the corner, hearing low voices not far away. There she saw Farouk and Faraj al-Khoum just a few feet from each other, both with their backs to her. Farouk was maybe six feet in front of Faraj and was talking to two other men. Faraj was looking off to the side, toward the dock. Not even knowing why she was doing it, she took something from her pocket that the king had earlier given her and quietly tossed it toward Farouk's feet, on the side where his brother stood, and then immediately hid again.

There was a loud clatter of the object on the floor, and then silence for two seconds. Suddenly, there was a loud whispered voice. "What are you doing, you klutzy, stupid moron?"

"What?"

"The Stone! Did you drop it or throw it, or what?"

"I did nothing."

"Well, here it is! You somehow dropped it, you careless idiot! I should never have given it to you in the first place!"

Faraj quickly felt his pockets. "I dropped nothing, you sack of camel dung!" A lifetime's worth of insults and deep anger exploded inside his head. He dug into his right pocket and spit out the word, "Here!" and threw his stone at Farouk—the one he had carried all day. Then he dug into another pocket and said, "And here!" and threw the other emerald at him, the one he had just obtained, hitting Farouk a second time with this additional stone that also, like the one before it, now clattered to the floor. "You can pick them up and eat them and choke on them all, you stupid, arrogant fool!"

Farouk had thrown up his arms in a defensive way and looked to see what had hit him. He was shocked almost beyond words and said, in something like a whispered shout, "What are you doing? Have you lost your mind? Are you deranged?"

"You're the one who's sick and totally deranged!"

Farouk was stunned. "What are all these stones? Where did you get all these stones?"

"Shut up! Just shut up, you piece of trash! Shut your mouth or I'll cram your precious stones down your throat!"

"You can't talk to me like that!"

"I can talk to you however I want! And you can have your magical stone. I don't need it, because I won't be the one injured today!" He pulled out a knife and pointed it at his brother. I think it's time to see if your legendary gem helps at all."

"You're a dead man," Farouk nearly shouted, as Faraj moved to lunge toward him with the knife, but a loud gunshot rang out and Faraj dropped to the floor with a stunned expression. Farouk's bodyguard had pulled out a revolver quietly and with little sign of motion while the brothers had been arguing. He had always thought it would come to something like this. And he had been trained and paid by Farouk, not his brother. He knew where his loyalty should be.

The other bodyguard with them, however, had been recruited, trained, and paid by Faraj, and so his immediate instinct was to take down the shooter, as he now raised his own weapon. But knowing he was outnumbered by Farouk and the other man, he held his gun on Faraj for the moment, merely for show, as he desperately tried to think of what to do until his close colleague returned, another man hired by Faraj who had left earlier to do a sweep of the nearby halls. He knew also that Farouk's final assault was scheduled to begin any minute and that this was no time to be seen attacking the elder al-Khoum brother, who in everyone else's eyes was the ultimate leader.

But he also knew that the gunshot itself had created an even additional problem. Someone had likely heard it and would be bringing men into the area, looking for the reason and source of the sound. Even with the likely imminent return of his friend, Faraj's chief bodyguard knew that the four of them could hardly face a larger number before they were suitably in place with their plan. But that confrontation might happen any second now, because of the noise. And the best trained of them all had just been shot in the gut, by all appearances. He was on his hands and knees, knife hand on the floor, and so the exact location of his wound couldn't be seen.

Before anyone could move or react further, Hoda and Kissa stepped out from where they had been hiding, with guns aimed at the two clearly armed men, and Hoda yelled, "No one moves! We'll kill two of you before any of you can pull a trigger!"

"If you fire a single shot, even one," Farouk said in a threatening voice, "everyone you love will die in the next instant."

"You're lying," Hoda replied. "You're bluffing like the desperate trapped man that you are."

"I've prepared for this day. Your friends and family will all have painful and instant deaths if you shoot anyone here."

"Put down your weapons," Hoda said to the two bodyguards. "Put them down this second."

"No! They will do nothing of the kind," Farouk replied. "I've just had my brother shot. I'll have your loved ones slaughtered in an instant."

"You can do nothing now," Hoda said.

"One shout from any of us and they're gone," Farouk said. "You can't kill all three of us before one can shout. No one's that good, not even if you're Phi. I swear to you that one of us will bring down this building and the wrath of the ages on all within it if you touch any of us with a bullet or knife or anything else. Put down your weapons! And bring me the king now! This is between him and me! Bring him now and save your loved ones, all of them. There's no other way."

Hoda didn't know what to do. He was surely bluffing, one voice in her said, but he couldn't have let himself get into such a vulnerable position with no way out, as smart and devious as he is, another voice countered. She also felt the force of his words in her soul, but fought that force. And then she did something that surprised her, and Kissa, as well.

31

The Confrontation

HODA SAID, "KISSA, GO GET THE KING."

"Are you … sure?"

"Yes. Do it, please. If anyone makes a move, the one with the big words is the first dead man. You know I can hear a trigger move, from even a great distance. I can feel it in my soul. I'm Senior Phi beyond anything this man knows or can imagine." She spoke with supreme confidence and said this in a voice loud enough for all the men to hear. It's safe to say that her deep genuine confidence, projected in her tone and words, eroded theirs instantly, which was her intended effect. She changed the odds with everything she did. That was part of what it meant to be Senior Phi. Her gun slightly moved to point directly at the head of Farouk al-Khoum.

"I have a riddle," Hoda said. "Kissa, how many Senior Phi does it take to light a candle, or snuff one out?"

"I have the answer," Kissa said, without moving her gun. "About the same number it takes to obliterate an armed group of men like these."

"You're right. And I think these men understand what we're saying. So you can go and get the king. As you know, I'm the only one here who is guaranteed to be fine."

There was a pause and then Farouk said, "Bring no one else, just the king." And Kissa disappeared without a sound.

"May I turn slightly to see the one who speaks to me? Farouk politely asked.

"You may," Hoda replied.

"Thank you."

Farouk then turned slowly and gently in Hoda's direction, and what he saw instantly sent a terrible chill deep within his soul, but he managed to hide his reaction. He had heard of an extremely beautiful woman who was Senior Phi, and that she was as legendary as anyone had ever been. She was almost mythical. Rumors had described her as one of the most dangerous human beings alive—at least, to any adversary. Farouk knew that he must play this game at his very best. He had learned everything he could about the king. But this one was almost entirely a mystery, and that made her even more dangerous.

"I know who you are," he said, simply.

"Good," she replied, just as simply. But then she added, "Your knowledge, though, inevitably falls short."

"Perhaps. But I hope you know who I am," he replied.

"I know exactly who you are and what you are, inside and out," she said. And there was a pause, while he took this in and pondered it.

"Despite all appearances, I have the upper hand," he said.

"That's your illusion, which is unfortunate for you," she replied. "It's mostly illusions that bring men down."

"There are many fierce warriors who are about to descend on this place," he said.

"No. Those men are now dead and will never see this place," she responded. He tried to stare into her eyes, but there was a power there that would not allow him to, any more than he could stare into the sun. He grew silent and felt a wave of concern. Then he smiled. At that same moment, Faraj groaned and collapsed fully onto the floor where he now did not move.

Upstairs in the classroom where the king had established his temporary command post, he had been speaking privately to Reela Adi only for a couple of minutes before Kissa came up and into the door with her urgent message for him. He immediately ended his talk with Reela and gave her his undivided attention. She provided a brief explanation of the situation downstairs and the apparent need for him to accompany her back down, right away. Farouk was making threats that, in light of the fire that had apparently been set by someone with access to the palace, had at least some degree of credibility, however small. They were in a position where they needed to heed this one demand of his, just to give them more time to figure out whether he was bluffing or his threats were real. One bag of dynamite had been intercepted, earlier. But there might have been more. Everyone could be in much more danger than they realized. Kissa needed to return with the king, and with him alone, quickly. She urged that several guards at the same time be sent around their part of the palace, to search for any explosives that might be hidden away. But she again stressed the need to return immediately with the king.

Walid listened to her and then vigorously protested. But Ali touched his arm gently and reassured him that he believed it was the thing that needed to be done in that moment. Still, the prince worried aloud about Kissa. She said, "I'll be fine. I don't even need this gun. I have mom and she's ready for anything. And I'll have the king with me. There's no greater protection than that. Plus, you know how well we've all been trained."

"But it's driving me crazy that, at a time like this, and with you under such a threat, I can't be down there with you!" Walid said.

"It's important that I return just with the king," she replied with a firm kindness and a total confidence and conviction in what she was saying. Something inside Walid now told him that he was supposed to yield, despite all his agitated feelings to the contrary. He knew that he should let Kissa go and follow through on this unexpected mission without his help. He then felt a momentary sense of peace about it, once he had yielded to the idea, even though he still didn't like it.

"Ok," Walid said. "Ok. But what should I do?"

Kissa said, "Stand ready to be the king, if it should come to that. There's nothing else we need right now."

"She's right," Ali said. "As hard as it is, stay here, monitor the radio with Bancom, and join with Hamid in making any difficult decisions from this command post, you and Mafulla. Reela can also be of good counsel. We need you here in my place while I'm downstairs. Plus, there are many innocent people in rooms off this hallway who might need your presence here."

Walid took a deep breath. "I'm just not accustomed to being on the sidelines."

"You're not on the sidelines. You're in the game still and in a place where you're most needed now, despite the appearance of temporary quiet. You've done more than enough already today downstairs, as a true hero—you and Mafulla, both of you. But you must be here in case more such heroism is needed."

"Ok," he said as he let a deep breath out. "Ok. Be safe, Uncle."

"You, too, my boy," Ali replied.

"Be safe, Kissa."

"I will, Walid. Stay strong and safe, and I'll see you soon," Kissa said. She then left the room with the king to go face in person his chief enemy of all, a turn of events that no one would have expected.

Back downstairs, everyone had stood still after Faraj collapsed, as they listened to him struggle to take in a breath, and then they couldn't hear him breathe any more. Maybe another three or four minutes passed, perhaps as many as five, during which time only sporadic and muffled gunfire could be heard at a distance.

Suddenly, a voice called out from around a corner down the hall, "Kissa here again, now approaching with only the king." Everyone tensed slightly, except for Hoda. No one knew what would happen next. Kissa walked silently into view again with her gun drawn and held exactly as it had been when she left, pointed at one of the bodyguards. Three seconds behind her, King Ali came forth to join the group as requested, apparently alone and unarmed.

"Your Majesty," Farouk said, with sarcasm dripping from his voice. "It's so good to see you."

"What do you want?" the king asked, with no particular tone in his, and with no distinct expression across his face.

"I want to save the lives of many by inviting you to capitulate and vacate your throne now before any more have to die. Agree to this and you can escort your defenders and associates safely from the palace into permanent exile."

"Your expression of concern for the lives of many surprises me," the king said. "But I must decline your invitation."

"My men could shoot you now, on the spot. Your two women here can't stop them both." His voice dripped with insult, as if it were he who truly had the upper hand.

"They won't shoot me and lose their lives in this hall for nothing. What would they gain? They wouldn't enjoy even a minute more of this world and its many glories. Of course, my friends here would first eliminate just one of them, and also you, and then the other. So what would it benefit you? But you know that. And, even if these men could somehow kill me, a task much more difficult than they or you realize, and you somehow miraculously escaped the inevitable response of my 'two women,' as you call these warriors, my extraordinary nephew would rule the kingdom from that instant forward and defeat your sadly misled men. The palace would be cleaned of all your tragically wasted blood before the end of this day."

"Don't speak to me of my blood when you should be considering your own and how you can keep it within your veins for another hour."

The king smiled and said, "A small dog can bark viciously at a lion. But there is no benefit in the bark."

Farouk inwardly flashed with rage at the comparison and, mixed with his visceral fear of Hoda, this emotion interfered with his clarity of mind. For the first time, he was unsure of his next move. But just that second, the soldier who had found the emerald and given it to Faraj and who had been left to watch the dock appeared from around the corner with his gun held high and pointed right at Kissa.

"General!" he said to Farouk, as he saw Faraj lying on the floor. "I have the young woman in my sights and will shoot her to eliminate her gun and change the odds here in our favor." The king, hearing this, knew that Kissa didn't yet have the full degree of power to reliably evade a gunshot that he and Hoda possessed, despite once recently having managed such a feat. It was not yet strong enough in her. He couldn't take the chance. And so, he instinctively put his hand into his pocket. And additionally, at that same moment, well aware that he could and likely would be shot in response to this young soldier's action, Farouk also put his hand into his own pocket.

Hoda realized she would have to swing around to shoot this newly arrived enemy soldier and that, if she waited for his trigger sound, she might not be able to make the turn and get off her shot in time to stop his own. She knew Kissa had avoided a bullet before, but not in a situation like this where there would immediately be others that she might not be able to escape, even if she evaded the first one. And Hoda, by taking out this gunman on her left, would not likely then be able to stop both bodyguards in front of her, in such relative close quarters. There was little room to move. They were all now in such close proximity. She knew she couldn't wait any further to act, but if she took the needed preemptive action to stop this new man, she would most likely set off a barrage of gunfire from the others that would be hard or perhaps impossible for her daughter to dodge. It was a terrible dilemma. And there was now little time to think.

Hoda was still balanced on the fine edge of what action to take when she and the king and Farouk all heard or at least sensed the same thing at the same time—the reckless soldier who had no idea who all these people might be was already pulling the trigger to shoot and kill Kissa. The man was too far away and too awkwardly positioned for them to be able to stop him any other way that would be safe, and the king was unarmed with anything but his own physical and spiritual force and The Ring of Phi. It was an implement of power he would likely never have used for himself—to secure his own safety or life. But for sweet, smart, wonderful Kissa, the love of Walid, and a young woman who could be so important for the kingdom in years to come, he could do nothing other than slip a finger into it at the first intuition that this trigger would be pulled. He then instantly turned the inner band of it with his thumb at the least first sound of the deed being done so that, before the hammer of the gun could rise and strike and the bullet could fly, the legend of the ring would be, then and there, put to the ultimate test.

But in the split second prior to that moment, Ali also sensed that Farouk al-Khoum was doing exactly the same thing, putting on and twisting the ring that he had in his own pocket, the fake ring that the king had tricked Faraj into taking when he had poisoned Kular and demanded the kingdom's most secret treasures in return for an antidote that would save the good man's life. But of course, Faraj and Farouk didn't know that The Book of Phi they took that day as their ransom was a counterfeited substitute, or that The Ring of Phi in the same box was a fake, or that The Stone of Giza that came with it was a synthetic duplicate of the real one and thus without any power.

So, the very moment that the king turned the inner band of the real Ring of Phi, Farouk al-Khoum had also turned the inner band of the replica with the firm belief that whatever he would experience in the next moment to escape the situation or defeat his adversary would be entirely his own doing. But, as the course of events actually developed, what happened next made no sense to him at all. It was something he never could have expected.

Across town, Masoon had encountered his own situation that no one would have expected. The al-Khoum brothers had a small army of mercenaries preparing for a final assault on the palace, and their positioning in a widely scattered staging area was the strangest thing that Masoon and his small group of Phi had ever seen. It took keen attention and some careful thought to realize what was going on.

The enemy soldiers were arrayed in two parks and several vacant lots separated by old buildings in accordance with the Fibonacci Series of numbers. This was not at first, of course, obvious at all. Masoon initially saw no one in a place where he had expected men, and then spotted just a single mercenary on guard duty alone, and at a distance another solitary sentinel, then in a separate location not far from them, he saw two armed men talking together, and in a different nearby place, there were three. He didn't initially notice the pattern, as strange and unexpected as it was.

Further reconnaissance revealed a cluster of five men off by themselves, and then other groupings of eight and thirteen. By that point, Masoon had caught on to what was being done. He knew that the next groups he came across would likely contain twenty-one, thirty-four, and fifty-five men, respectively—in all, one hundred and forty two additional mercenaries dispersed around an area maybe two miles square. Some were on foot, others were mounted on horses, several were in trucks, and others were in automobiles—all armed and awaiting their signals. But not many of them were within the sight of others. They were separated for safety and to keep their numbers from being obvious, as well as for Farouk's own falsely mystical reasons. Designated messengers would move about and alert them all when it was time to make their move on the palace.

There was no conceivable military justification for this mathematical organization of assembling and preparing the men. It had to be the sad delusion of a disturbed mind to think that aping the hidden structures of nature in this particular way would access some form of esoteric power. It was the sort of strange superstition that can arise from any lust for control over others. And all it did was spread these men out and make them more vulnerable. In each location, as a result, Masoon knew exactly how many adversaries he would face, and thus he could be sure of when their threat had been eliminated.

With his small group of powerful compatriots, he had two things that these many men did not have. He had with him nothing but Phi, and he had the crucial element of surprise. In addition, he and his group had also positioned themselves deliberately in a way that did make sense, given what they faced. They first used quick, stealthy, and nearly silent hand-to-hand combat techniques to take down the lone individuals and smaller groupings of men. Then employing a lethal combination of apparently supernatural aim and speed with arrows, and finally with sharpshooting and explosives delivered in different and precisely effective ways, they managed within less than thirty minutes to eliminate the entire spread-out and scattered array of hired soldiers, none of whom could escape to play any role in the planned assault on the palace. Farouk had wrongly assumed that all the king's resources would be in and around the palace, and so had his men, who were now totally surprised and overcome.

The confrontation was dispersed and episodic, but it took much less time than the king's men had anticipated. It was one of those situations where apparently every move was on point, every defensive act from the other side was overcome with ease, and a focused divide and conquer strategy accomplished what it so often does and ruled the day. This all played out in a part of the city where there were a lot of old warehouses and lots of empty space, with not many civilians to be seen. So the Phi left the field of battle as it was and made haste to return to the king.

Masoon was now on his way back to the palace with all his men, only one of whom had been lightly wounded, and they were already in sight of the palace walls when Farouk al-Khoum and King Ali simultaneously twisted the beaded platinum inner bands of their white gold rings and entered the strange and capacious space between moments whose hidden existence we might suspect, but that we rarely experience except in such times of great danger or trauma.

It's one of the many paradoxes in this world: A catastrophe that opens such an unexpected space in time is a gateway to an inner oasis of peace that can't even be imagined by anyone who is not in the midst of the disaster—or, at least, not by anyone who hasn't visited such a spiritual place before. And the king had, by different means, been a frequent guest in this normally hidden domain, this extra dimension of expansive being. But even he was quite surprised at exactly what happened next.

He found himself sitting on the warm sand of a high dune in the middle of the desert. It was early morning, but the sun was already beginning its daily arc across the sky. A light breeze drifted across the land. In front of him were the last red embers of what had been a small fire, apparently started before dawn, as breakfast fires most often are, out in the desert. Across the smoldering embers sat the figure of Farouk al-Khoum.

The first thought that appeared in al-Khoum's mind as he emerged from a temporary faint and an unexpectedly thick dizziness, and now found himself in a radically new setting, was that he had managed to use his legendary ring safely, and that he had somehow produced this result, whatever it was. He felt a wave or surge of a sense of power well up within him, but encompassing that sense and also constraining it was a profound state of perplexity at where he was and what was going on. He was sitting, and his head was slightly turned down. He first saw the embers of the fire. He felt the warm sand and air. And then he suddenly noticed, right in front of him and also seated, his enemy, Ali.

He thought to stand up, but could not. He went to raise his arm, and it wouldn't respond. There was no heavy leaden resistance. There was just nothing. With inner panic, he realized that there was no feeling of muscle control of any kind in him. He could no longer blink an eye. He was seated, but somehow also paralyzed, as if frozen in place. He could think and sense and feel his own emotions in the moment, but he couldn't move. He fought a deep primal fear that arose in him instantly at this realization, and he struggled mightily to put it out of his heart. He had to stay strong and somehow gain control of himself.

He tried to focus on the outer situation. Maybe this sense of paralysis is temporary, due to the change of scene, or the travel, or whatever had brought them to where they were at the moment—no longer in the palace, no longer with other people, no longer anywhere familiar. Perhaps his mind and body just needed to adjust for a moment and all would be fine. The king was not moving, either. It might be that the first man to move would then defeat his enemy here, wherever they were. And he had the ring, so the first move should be his.

These thoughts were soon interrupted. He somehow heard the king speak. But the man's mouth did not move. And it was not the tone and timber of a normal voice at all. It was as if words from the king, and clearly from this source, were appearing in his mind. The words were, "You're in a special place."

Farouk tried to answer but his vocal chords and tongue and mouth would not work. His thoughts alone could respond. He said in his mind, and so asked in the only way he could, "Where am I?"

"You are where you need to be now." The answer was quick.

"What is this place?"

"It is a between place."

"A what?"

"A between place."

"I don't understand."

"You can see down the dune behind me, I would venture. There is an oasis, a beautiful place of rest and restoration, peace and power."

"How do you know that?"

"I just do. And behind you, not too far away, there is a storm—a painful, tumultuous storm churning up a blast of sharp projectiles and destroying everything in its path. I can see it well. And I tell you this. You must now choose your next destination: the oasis or the storm."

"What do you mean? I brought us here. I make the rules."

"You brought us here, yes. But you don't make the rules. These rules are not made. They just are."

"What's happening?"

"You're being given a chance, one last chance to choose your path, to pick your place—in the oasis, or in the storm."

The king's lips were not moving. His arms and legs were motionless as well. He was sitting still, unmoving and unmoved. His eyes were locked in on Farouk's eyes. Farouk could feel the penetration of them into his soul. He tried to turn the tables and become the actor, the agent, and the force at work in this moment, but could not.

The voice spoke again. "You've spent your life in the outer edges of the storm. You've been blown like a paper in the wind by greed, envy, pride, ambition, resentment, callousness, anger, and hatred. There's been no peace in your soul. The power of lust and endless desire has nearly extinguished any shadow or shred of love."

"I love nothing. I have no love."

"That's not true, or you would not be here now. You would not have a choice remaining to you."

"What do you mean?"

"You must confront the storm that's already inside you and choose. You will now give yourself to it fully and finally, and then enter the destruction of a greater tempest, or you will leave it for the wonderful oasis that awaits you."

"Did I bring us here through the ring?"

"You certainly brought us here through your actions, and a ring was involved."

"So I have the power."

"You have no power here and now, except to choose your final path. And you need to choose without delay."

"You're an old fool and speak without knowledge."

"You must release your hatred and your addiction, or you're doomed. What do you most deeply want?"

"I want you dead."

"I want you transformed."

"Why?"

"Yes, why, indeed? You must wonder."

"I don't understand."

"Your father—the bare, remaining shadow of his spirit pleads for you."

"You know nothing of my father."

"I do. And I know more."

"What do you think you know?"

"Your mother wants the oasis for you."

"You can't speak of my mother! What could you know of her?"

"I know that she's here, close by, down the dune and near the pool in the trees where she finally chose to be. I know that from her heart she wants you to make the choice to join her. I can hear her say 'Farrie,' in a voice of great love."

Farouk felt something clench up inside him. Confusion muddled his thought. "I brought myself here to save myself!"

"I brought you here for that same reason."

"I have ..." the words stopped. Before he could think anything else, images began to appear in Farouk's mind, and yet more real than the mere fleeting mental images of a daydream. They began in his childhood and flashed vividly, and as fully three dimensional as if he was there, in each place and with each person again. And these experiences came and lingered and went, showing him every significant event and influence and opportunity and choice in his life, at once and yet in order—in full and with feeling, with real depth, but as if taking no time, while yet using all the time that was needed. He tried not to feel even a twinge of grief, or guilt, or loss, or regret. He fought the various emotions that were welling up in him. But they came surrounded with a power of acceptance and affirmation for his soul like nothing he had ever experienced. And it gave rise to a strange longing. There was a Yes beneath the howling and persistent and habitual No that he had always directed at such feelings. The Yes began to wear away at the No. But he resisted. He sought to be what he thought of as strong. And then the voice came once more.

"I'm telling you. You have a choice: the oasis or the storm."

"I have the power to choose my own fate," Farouk formed this thought with insistence.

"Yes you do." The answer came back.

"The power is mine."

"The only true power comes through a certain release."

"But."

"You must let go of the storm. You must release all that's counterfeit in order to gain all that's real. You give up most of what you know, and then you'll receive much more than you can imagine. Hear all the voices that now call out to you. Feel what's in the deepest place of your heart. Choose now. But choose well."

Farouk then heard his mother's voice faintly but clearly. And he hurt. He hurt deeply. It was an inner anguish. He didn't want to feel a pain like that. He couldn't allow himself to experience such a wrenching hurt—not for a moment more. And he reacted.

That instant, Farouk was back in the palace, as if no time had elapsed, but he was now, as he opened his eyes, somehow moving between the soldier and the girl. The bullet that had been fired ripped into his neck and took him down. Kissa was spared. Hoda then took out the shooter just as six palace guards appeared, guns drawn, and the two bodyguards yelled out in self-protection. The first shouted, "Stop! I surrender!" and dropped his weapon to the ground while kneeling quickly, followed by the other saying and doing much the same. Farouk's body now lay on the floor not far from Faraj, to the complete and utter shock of everyone there, except the king.

32

Two Are Better Than One

"There's an old proverb," the king said, projecting his voice well throughout the large room. "Two are better than one; because they share a good reward for their labor. And, if one falls, the other will help up his fellow. But woe to him who is alone when he falls; for he has no one to lift him up." As he spoke these words, he was standing at the center of the long head table in the banquet hall where he had first addressed his followers on the day they initially took control of The Golden Palace and the future of the kingdom.

"Please raise your glasses!" He spoke to the large gathered assembly of diners, as he lifted up his own. And all did as he requested.

"I'm proud to be your king, deeply so, and Walid feels the same way about being your prince. But now, he will be more than just a prince to me and to you. Two are better than one. So, from this day on, we'll begin to rule in new ways, henceforth, increasingly together. Allow me then to offer a toast for this new regime: To a new reign of two!"

Many present repeated his words of toast and said, "Here, here!" and "May it be so!" The king sipped from his glass, and with a crescendo of clinking glass around the room, all others then sipped from theirs as well.

Masoon then stood with his glass raised and shouted, "To the King and Prince!"

There was a responding roar of voices as everyone in the great hall replied heartily, "To the King and Prince!"

Masoon then followed with the loud and hopeful call, "May they live long and prosper!"

All present repeated the words. "May they live long and prosper!" The king gestured in appreciation with his glass and looked over at Walid with a small salute, and then sipped again from it. And everyone followed his lead, while stomping feet and pounding their free hands on the tables in a joyous sound of acclamation.

Then, as the noise subsided, the king began to speak once more. "Thank you, my friends and companions in the fellowship of the mind and the work of the kingdom. Thank you for helping us through the very difficult time we've just endured. Thank you for your bravery and loyalty and your unending energies in service to our ideals. There is an oasis within the heart of each of us that has helped us to face the storms that have come our way, and to prevail, and then to be healed and refreshed, and restored."

Ali paused for a moment and said, "Please raise your glass again, and a prayer, for those good people we've lost. They were brave and loving and worked as hard as any of us for what they believed in and treasured. They're not with us now in body, but in spirit they'll always remain. Their work here is done, and they now refresh themselves at the great oasis that's meant for all of us ultimately to enjoy."

He paused for a moment and looked around the room, and then continued. "We'll carry on for them until, one day, we join them in their peaceful and glad enjoyment of the warm sand and cool water and refreshing breezes that still await us." The king paused once more and then said, "To our departed friends!" And he sipped from his glass, as murmurs of the repeated phrase swept around the vast hall, and all in attendance drank in honor of their friends.

The king then waited for another moment, and went on. "We

have seen much in recent days and have learned much. And we do well to remember always that what we understand about this complex and beautiful and often dangerous world of ours is small compared to what we do not yet see. So we walk humbly in the light of what we do know, while dreaming nobly of spreading that light and vastly increasing the reach of its circle." He stood in momentary silence again for the thought to linger in the room. And then he continued once more.

"We have had a chance, in what we just lived through, to be reminded of how the schemes and games of misguided greed have often allowed deeply damaged, corrupt individuals to gain wealth and power for a time, and at the expense of many innocent lives. But we've also seen once more that these apparent victories are always eventually reversed and that, in the short time they last, they are in each and every case a terrible blight on all who bear their awful consequences. We've been reminded, as well, of the true sources for enduring achievement in the world, and of the foundations on which we seek to build our future together: the power of love, the quest for justice, the guidance of wisdom, the light of goodness, and the great and vital joys of real friendship."

There were sounds of agreement all around the room. The king then said, "I thank you from the bottom of my heart for living these things and bringing them all into the service of our kingdom. Please enjoy this dinner in honor of our fallen companions, and in recognition and appreciation for each of you and your great efforts for your fellow citizens in the months and days past, and for the many years that are to come!" The king then exclaimed, "Long live our land!" And, taking another big swig from his glass, he then returned to his seat.

A chorus of the phrase, "Long live our land!" echoed throughout the hall. There was then a fearsome stomping of feet and clapping of hands and roaring of voices throughout the hall that reached a thunderous crescendo and then subsided, giving way to various scattered shouts of affirmation, laughter, and the sounds of many lively conversations starting up again around the tables in the room.

"My goodness," Shamilar Adi said, "I've never been at such a dinner as this!" From their table near the front of the great hall, they had felt surrounded by the mighty sounds of approval and swept up on a huge wave of positive affirmation.

"It's wonderful!" Shapur added. Sammi and Sasha just had their hands over their ears and were making faces.

At the double long head table set up on risers in front of the room, along with the king sat Masoon, Hamid, Rumi, Bhati, Reela, Walid, Mafulla, Hoda, Khalid, Kissa, Hasina, Layla, Set, and Bafur—all heroes in various ways on the great day of siege, now some weeks past. Set and Bafur were still pretty patched up, and Bafur said he was glad at least that he didn't have to miss the meal, which made everyone around him laugh. He could barely stand or even sit down unassisted at this point, still, but he was thrilled to be alive and to have heard from both Rumi and Hamid that he would eventually make a full, one hundred percent recovery from his wounds. The king had retrieved The Stone of Giza from the scene of the great confrontation and had put it into Bafur's possession—with a tremendous effect already, given the severity of his injuries. King Ali had told Walid privately that, soon, Bafur would be in the best shape of his life, and would likely surprise everyone. Ali also intimated that he had given special assistance to their friend Set in other ways, as well, and that he would soon be at his physical best ever.

Set was already in better shape, but still in moderate pain, and yet nothing could keep him from feeling more pride than suffering as a result of what had happened and the role he had spontaneously been able to play. What we do when we don't have time to think, but just act on our instincts, says a lot about our character and who we are. He had acted to save his friends with no thought for his own safety. There were scars on both boys that would, over the years, fade, but would nonetheless remain just visible enough to testify for the rest of their lives to what they had done, endured, and survived. They both now knew in a different way what they could take and how they could rebound and, in a strange but intelligible sense, it gave them both more confidence and greater courage for the days to come.

In the early hours and days after the assault on the palace was over, Hasina initially had felt a great deal of guilt and regret that she couldn't have helped out more in the center of the action. But her mother convinced her that the job of watching out for her friends who didn't have the advantage of Phi training had been of crucial importance. She should feel great pride, not regret, in having been asked to do it, and then in having done it well. Sometimes, small things can make a big difference in the grand scheme of this world.

At many times during the siege, a word from Hasina had comforted her classmates beyond their ability to describe. And by the time of the big dinner, she was beaming with pride in everyone who had played a role in the defense of what they believed in, as well as in the protection of the people around them who meant so much. Mafulla and Walid had initially felt a little bit like Hasina did. But the king was able to convince them that they had played a huge role in turning back the attackers, watching over their peers, and then helping to run the temporary headquarters of the palace defenses while the king was on the errand that helped finally end it all.

The Kingdom Daily News was running headline after headline about the king and the prince and Mafulla, as well as praising many other members of the monarchy for their defense of the palace, the city, the kingdom, and the rule of law in those recent difficult hours. An even greater level of regard for both the king and prince had spread throughout the kingdom in the days since then, as rumors of almost supernatural military abilities and powers floated around everywhere. There were also whispered accounts all over town that the famous crime fighters, the Viper and the Storm, had personally been involved in defeating these recent enemies of the kingdom. The paper even printed on the front page a widespread speculation that these superheroes of the city had been called into action by the king himself. The common conviction overall was that, due to many different heroes in the city, good had prevailed and the future now promised wonderful things ahead.

The king had privately told Walid and Mafulla about his use of The Ring of Phi, and what seemed to have happened as a result, as best he understood it, and as much as he could put it into words. They were naturally astonished at his report and reported to him in turn some of their stranger experiences during the battle for the palace. They said they were deeply reassured that the lessons they had been taught over the previous year, when put to the ultimate test, had proved themselves over and over throughout these recently trying events. Every challenge is an opportunity, the king then reminded them. And the power of the mind is great. Aligned with love and goodness, the mind at its best can overcome and create and prevail beyond anything we initially might imagine.

Two days after the palace attacks, Walid had worked up the nerve to speak to Kissa more explicitly about his hopes and desires for a future together with her. She responded that she felt the exact same things as he was expressing, and was equally committed to him. Mafulla and Hasina also had experienced a similar conversation, but had said nothing about it yet to anyone else. The trauma they all had faced somehow had opened them up to the revelations and promises that might not otherwise have been uttered aloud and so explicitly for perhaps years to come.

There was something deep that was bonding these four together powerfully, and variously, two by two, but each pairing of them in similar and also subtly different ways. Walid and Mafulla felt joined by destiny, as if they were brothers. And Kissa and Hasina experienced the same sense of kinship beyond normal ties. They were family in a profound and real sense. The fact that Walid and Kissa, and then Mafulla and Hasina, felt themselves walking the same path together was also something special and wonderful beyond what any of them could yet fully realize.

But this didn't mean that they wouldn't be tested and further challenged in many ways throughout the days to come. That's the nature of our world. It's universally how our journeys unfold. We're here to be examined and refined and taught and grown and molded into the best of what we can be. And that often involves hardship and struggle. But as the king had said, when one falls down, there will be someone to pick him up, as long as souls united stay together and fight for each other and what they believe and know.

As they sat at the head table during dinner, much of this was running through each of their minds. Walid then looked around and caught the eye of Ibrahim, who had come to Cairo just for the occasion and now gave him a small salute. The book he provided had guided the king and Masoon and Hamid and the boys in more ways than they ever could have guessed, and had crucially prepared them for the trials they survived. It would help them through much more as well.

Ibrahim saw Walid's gesture and smiled big and saluted back. Mafulla caught a glimpse as well and turned to Walid and lifted his own juice glass over to clink on the edge of Walid's. He said, "To new friends and new books. May they long continue to come into our lives."

"Yes, indeed," Walid replied with a big smile. "That's well wished and well said."

APPENDIX

The Diary of Walid Shabeezar
Wisdom Under Fire

I've noticed something strange. I'm not really good about keeping this journal, or diary, every day. But the days I do write in it, I feel more satisfied when I'm ready to fall asleep. And I always benefit from the writing and thinking. It clears my head. And I learn. When I read later what I've written, I often understand even more. So, why don't I do this every day? I'll try. Uncle Ali says that if you live life with eyes wide open and pay attention, you can learn something new every day. I'm ready. And maybe I'll take more notes along the way.

∆ ∆ ∆

Some mysteries you can explain. Others, you just have to live.

Never overlook the opportunity of coincidence. Every coincidence is a door that needs to be opened. More surprises may be inside.

It's not always easy to draw a line between what we choose and what happens to us apart from our choice. But, in the end, we can always choose how to react. And that shows the high value of choice.

Daily choices are crucial. And no choice is unimportant. They all add up to create so much of the life we live.

There may be certain circumstances of my birth that offer a key to the future. That's probably true for each of us. Some of us concentrate on overcoming the situation through which we entered the world. Others focus on making the most of it. But it always marks us and is important for our later self-understanding. How this works is not going to be clear at every point of life. It has to unfold. We just need to be aware of it. I got this insight from Uncle Ali, and I had to write it down before I forgot how he said it.

Every one of us is specially marked in some way and for some great contribution to the world, however large or small it might seem.

You don't have to please everyone or impress everyone. You just have to be the best you can be. Then, the right people will be pleased and impressed. But even that's not your job.

∆ ∆ ∆

We'll never know everything we'd like to know, as long as we're alive in this world. There are always things yet to be revealed.

True friends care more about each other than any benefits the friendship might bring. Most people don't seem to understand that and treat their friends almost like employees, or servants, with the attitude, "Are you doing for me all that I want and need?" And that's the wrong question to ask. Turn it around.

A friend can take the sting out of stress, and make uncertainty easier.

The idea of competition is interesting. Does it always pit one person against another? Is there supposed to be a loser? That's how it seems on the surface, but maybe in fact real competition is all about personal growth and working to get better. Anything else by the name is either just a game for fun, or else a waste of time.

Those who cheat at a game show they don't understand the proper role of games, and those who cheat in life reveal a bigger confusion.

∆ ∆ ∆

Happiness is all about contentment, fulfillment, and enjoyment. And that just means accepting your present, growing properly toward your future, and living each day with pleasure and love.

True happiness isn't just about how you feel, but how you are. It's both subjective and objective. We need to remember that there are two sides of the coin.

On good days, nearly everything seems better. On bad days, nearly everything seems worse. But real wisdom means not being swayed by how things seem. It requires calm reflection on how things are.

Ask good questions. Then ask more. Be active, open, and curious.

Funny people make life better—but not the cynically disdainful or the sarcastically corrosive. Put-down comments can be hilarious in the moment. But they can then act like a poison on the soul. So, beware of bad funny. Happy and kind funny is ideally what you want.

A laugh is always a sign of who you are. What you laugh at tells a story. Those who can't laugh at all miss a lot. Those who laugh at the wrong things are missing even more.

Nothing can improve your day like a clever friend. Aristotle was right to think that wit is a virtue, or a source of strength for living. Masoon taught me that. He can be really funny, although he looks very serious.

Anxiety and irritability prevent happiness. Kissa told me her class discussed this connection. We let both of those things enter our lives too often. They never help us. They're not our friends.

Another insight that Kissa shared: Lazy is incompatible with happy, despite any appearances to the contrary. Happiness is the good fruit of an active life well lived.

∆ ∆ ∆

Talents attract opportunities. They're like magnets. But this doesn't mean that the opportunities will be easy to find, simple to recognize, or straightforward in their results, when taken. We need to work hard to spot them and use them well. But they will appear.

Destiny keeps tabs on us and knows where we are. Fortune can find us when it needs to. We should keep that in mind.

A new path of action can be right for you even if you don't know at first exactly where it will lead. Follow your heart. Take the first step.

Danger can be different things for different people, and yet, in some of its forms, it's the same for all. Training and preparation deflect danger. And the Triple Double is always key. Remember: Prepare and Perceive; Anticipate and Avoid; Concentrate and Control. It's a universal toolkit for dealing with trouble.

Helping people is a reward in itself. We're wired deep for each other.

△ △ △

Kindness is something that, in even small doses, can have big results.

Harshness is something that, in even a glancing blow, can do great harm.

Full attention is a tremendous gift to give another person.

Inattention and indifference wound us, and others.

We were born to care, and to need care. We should cultivate caring connections wherever we can.

The more we give, the more we get. But we all know that. Yet, we often forget and seek the effect without the proper cause. Be in all things a giver. Then you'll be amazed at what you receive.

Every life is a doorway into the mysteries and depths of existence.

Every person bears witness to something vital. Give it a voice.

In each soul, the unique meets the universal.

When we treasure people more and live with kindness, we flourish.

△ △ △

Beauty is a beacon for the good and the bad. It brings with it great responsibility. It's a form of power. And so the principle of the two powers applies. It can be used to help or harm. It's up to us.

Character understands context. Those who are oblivious to context in the pursuit of their own desires ultimately destroy themselves.

Propriety isn't just about constraints or limits, but about proper power and right action in the world.

Praise can be genuine or it can have an agenda. The wise person isn't manipulated by its use, and doesn't employ it for such purposes.

There's an old expression: "All that glitters is not gold." Value and appearance can be quite different. Those who lose their heads to illusion lose their footing in the world.

Proper self-esteem is a shield against illusion. Live your true self and you won't be misled by false promises.

Confidence without arrogance conquers much, while arrogance alienates many.

△ △ △

An early rise can bring a surprise. The freshness of a new day often has secrets to share that the glare of busy action may later hide.

Start each day with clarity, compassion, and hope.

Most people have depths we don't suspect. And yet relatively few cultivate that depth sufficiently and grow it into something truly extraordinary.

Negative emotions can block important perceptions. You may have to clear your heart to open your mind and see the truth.

△ △ △

Any position of public responsibility attracts friends and enemies.

Clever adversaries will strike when and where you least expect it.

Even impossible looking problems can often be solved by thought and courage—but they may also require the help of a friend.

The power of the mind is never to be neglected. We should seek to develop an ongoing awareness of the potential scope for its use.

We can have a clear conception of what we want and a focused concentration of the mind on how to get it, but without a strong inner confidence, we can't often succeed in the quest. This is back to Uncle Ali's 7 Conditions of Success: Conception, Confidence, Concentration,

Consistency, Commitment, Character, and a Capacity to Enjoy the Process. It's amazing how useful it is to remind myself of these seven things, and how effective they seem to be when used deliberately.

∆ ∆ ∆

A person out of balance, obsessed, and addicted can do great harm.

A person who is balanced, focused, and free can do great good.

Proper ambition, like so much else in life, is a midpoint of aspiration that falls somewhere between excess and deficiency. There's a too much and a too little. Most people understand that too little can be a bad thing. Few seem to realize that too much can be even worse.

Ambition is a great example of the two powers—for good and ill.

A wise older person who has been farther down life's path can teach us so much that we need to know for the journey that we, too, will make.

It's good to be around older people and younger people, too. At each age, we have a distinctive experience of life. We can learn a lot from different ages and stages. I love Mafulla's little brother and sister. They remind me of so much that I might otherwise forget.

The charisma of eccentricity can be of great power. But beware of those who use it as a key to unlock any door, without sufficiently caring whose door it is, or where it might lead.

∆ ∆ ∆

Questions or ideas that come to mind seemingly out of the blue, with no prompting or context, may be signs of something important. Don't reject them too quickly as not making sense. Pursue them as you can, and you might discover something new.

Be ever a blessing, never a curse to this world where you're a guest.

The imagination is a great power that can bring gain or pain. Again, it's all in how we use it.

Many opportunities are open for only a limited time. Too much analysis, deliberation, or hesitation will allow them to vanish.

Nothing is better than wise action when the time is right.

The more you know yourself, the more quickly you'll recognize the opportunities that are right for you. And then, the more you recognize your proper opportunities, the more you'll know yourself.

Maffie had a funny idea for a tombstone: "Mafulla Adi—Currently Unavailable." I hope he'll continue to be available for a very long time.

Life will bring us some wonderful people and take some away. We need a peaceful acceptance of both gain and loss in this phase of the journey. The present world is simply a stage along the way.

∆ ∆ ∆

We fear death. But it may come, when its time is right, with calm and confidence and peace. Most endings are also beginnings. Death may be the ultimate example of both.

I was so sorry to learn that we lost Mr. Kaza. It's a big thing for Mafulla and his family. But I know Shamilar and Shapur understand the wheel of life and how it turns.

There are wonderful things in common between the innocence at the beginning of our journey and the enlightenment we hope to achieve before its end. An ample measure of wonder and acceptance is a part of the overlap.

We need hands open enough to receive in gladness and release in peace.

The more I come to understand the attitudes of humility and nobility, the more I see their crucial importance for a powerful and positive life.

Kissa told me of the interesting discussion her class had about the souls of books. Sometimes, when I read, I feel like another soul is touching mine. Is it always the author, or perhaps even sometimes the spirit of the book?

Can a character in a book have a soul? I hope so! I'd like to think of my favorite characters in books as fellow souls in the world.

△ △ △

Those who are prepared and aware flourish. Those who aren't, don't.

Take seriously your intuitions. We can know what to do before having any clue why.

Our world calls for a strange dynamic balance of boldness and caution, and both are equally important.

Sometimes, I feel a weight of responsibility and then someone close to me steps up and shows that I never have to shoulder it alone. That's one of the many great things about having the right people as friends.

△ △ △

Malik and Haji found the mysterious second tunnel today! And enemies of the kingdom were already using it. Curiosity saved the day. The guys showed how this vital quality leads to important discoveries. I'm glad they got to be heroes. They deserve it.

The curious end up in interesting places. They tend to have the best adventures.

Cultivate a healthy curiosity at all times. Pursue knowledge well.

Maffie and I also helped catch a guy today who was in the palace and up to no good. We were observant, saw something suspicious, and took action. And it paid off. We also acted wisely and trapped the guy with plenty of backup in the room. Uncle Ali noted that aspect of our actions. We're learning.

Being brave doesn't always mean bearing risk alone. Prudence and courage best walk together.

△ △ △

Intellectual argument at its best is just a reasoned presentation of ideas. It's an exploration with the intent to find truth, often through what Khalid calls a process of at least tentative advocacy. It's not an exercise in ego. The best arguments and intellectual discoveries come from a place of humility as well as nobility.

I believe there's a deep purpose in things, but not that everything is determined in advance. I believe in free will, but also that we're often a lot less free than we think. And yet again, there are other times when we have a lot more freedom than we ever might imagine.

Life is full of mysteries. The world overflows with surprises. And the deepest truths often stay just beyond our normal sight.

Khalid not long ago talked about Aristotle's list of the virtues, or the personal strengths we can bring to any situation. I've always liked the fact that he included wit as one. But just today, watching Mafulla perform one of his impromptu routines for some of the girls, I came to appreciate it in a new way. It can really bring people together and create positive energy. Way to go, Aristotle. And, yes, of course: our very own Mafustotle.

∆ ∆ ∆

There's something special about water, something beautiful and soothing and peaceful. But there's great danger, too. It's another example, for sure, of The Double Power Principle.

When Jabari fell into the river today, many brave people acted instantly. They didn't deliberate. They just did what had to be done. That's how courage is. When a desperate need appears, the courageous person acts quickly, and with a focused concentration.

Jabari told a strange story about what he experienced underwater. There was a light. The king said he visited the source. This just reminded me that the reality in which we live is more complex and interesting than we normally think.

There is a lot more to life than is evident on the surface of things.

The source of all may be no distance away from us whatsoever. There could be a sense in which it's in us, or, more likely, somehow, that we're in it. Or it could be that both these things are, paradoxically, true. We live and breathe in it and through it and because of it.

There may be a point where with, in, and am come together.

Sometimes, every second counts. And that's probably true more often than we think.

There are no empty moments. We help fill them up. But the question is: Do we fill them well?

A wasted moment is one that's full of unrealized positive possibility.

The next moment you have is truly yours. Use it well.

∆ ∆ ∆

Leaders don't watch from a distance. They jump in and lead from up close.

No one can live a good life without knowledge, and the practical wisdom to use it well.

The work most worth doing is work from the heart. If you can't put your heart in it, then do what you can to take yourself out of it.

My first sight of the Mediterranean Sea happened today. It was awesome!

Are there many oceans, or one? The philosophical problem of unity and diversity can be seen in many ways.

Not everything has to be compared to something else. Things are what they are and can be appreciated for their own uniqueness.

"The ocean is the greatest of all bodies of water, because it's lower than all the rest: They pour themselves into it." That's deep wisdom from the Chinese classic, the Tao Te Ching.

The ocean is a model for any leader. It's great because it's low. Its nobility is linked with its humility. Because of its lowliness, other sources pour fourth and make it great.

The best leader is the servant of all. And ultimately, as the great leader guides all followers wisely and well, those followers can make the leader and themselves greater by pouring forth the best of their knowledge and energy.

△ △ △

No one of us is the center of the universe, although it's strangely natural to think so. We each need an emotional Copernican Revolution, displacing us, in our own view, from the center. That will allow us to do greater things with others.

If a new exercise isn't comfortable, lots of people stop doing it. But with exercise, the goal isn't comfort—it's results. That's almost a parable for life. We often have to look at the means in terms of their ends. We need to evaluate things properly.

One of the most important skills in life is the ability to listen. Listening is an art and a spiritual discipline to be cultivated.

Deep listening is one of our most neglected life skills.

△ △ △

Most people rush to judgment about most things most of the time. Don't do it. Don't rush to judgment. Take your time.

One of the most important human qualities is openness.

Be open. Embrace positive possibility. There's always a next adventure.

We're here to help other people, as well as to develop our own talents. And so we should be open to any opportunity to do so, however unlikely sometimes the path might seem.

Growth is a key to life. It's all about good and healthy growth. Think about this.

△△△

There is an old expression, "Truth is stranger than fiction." The real world is indeed much more novel than any novel. Most of the strangeness of our days is hidden to our normal understanding. The best fiction just reminds us how odd and wonderful and endlessly challenging it all is.

You would never know the most important things about an orange or a lemon if you just looked at their surfaces. You have to open them up, and then you can come to know them in a completely different way. The same is true of many situations and many people. The same is also true of life itself.

We start off thinking that surfaces show us what things are. We end up realizing that they more often hide what things really are.

We typically use only a tiny fraction of the power of awareness that's available to us. Awareness is well worth cultivating and growing.

△△△

Leadership is about preparation, planning, and quick adaptation.

We live in a world of uncertainty. The leader is a person who can keep calm and guide others forward with reasonable confidence in the face of the unknown.

A powerful philosophy of life brings confidence and encourages creativity.

In watching the king and Masoon and Hamid, I've come to realize something important about how they manage to be so brave in the face of challenges. They always seem to do the right things. And these things are simple to identify. There are, universally, five steps to courage: (1) Prepare for the challenge, (2) Surround yourself with support, (3) Engage in positive self-talk, (4) Focus on what's at stake, and then, (5) Take appropriate action. We should all do these things when dealing with difficulty and challenge.

Have people in your life that you can really believe in, and everything else is easier.

Where there's life, there's hope. Transformation is always possible. In choice is power. In choice lies the best culmination of destiny.

If there were only one rule in life, this might be it: Choose wisely.

But if the rule had to be abbreviated even more, it might end up being this: Love.

Acknowledgments

Writing the story arc from the prologue to this series, *The Oasis Within*, through Volume One, *The Golden Palace*, and Volume Two, *The Stone of Giza*, through Book Three, *The Viper and the Storm*, and this book, *The King and Prince*, as well as in the other completed volumes of the series yet to be published, has been the most enjoyable intellectual and perhaps spiritual experience of my life. As I've mentioned before, some time in February 2011, right after breakfast, an unexpected movie started playing in my head. I saw, as vividly as you can imagine, a boy and an older man, sitting under a palm tree in desert oasis, talking. I couldn't believe how much I enjoyed even the first few bits of their conversation. I ran upstairs to my study and began to type up what I had just seen and heard, as fast as I could. I wrote about ten pages. The next day, the same thing happened, and I wrote another ten pages or so. I had no idea what all this was. I had never had such a compelling imaginative experience as I was suddenly enjoying with this little movie in my head.

About a week later, I woke up and again right after breakfast I mentally "saw" a book cover and a title for *The Oasis Within*. I realized then for the first time that what I had been seeing and writing down was supposed to be a book. And so I regularly made myself available at the keyboard almost every day, in case the movie was going to play some more. And it did. For fourteen months, initially, and then for five years, on most days, I saw more sequential clips of the film, and wrote down the dialogue I heard and descriptions of what I saw as well as I could. On occasion, the film would not play for a day, or two, or three. And then it would start up again, at any time and at any place. I was once in a resort hotel pool in Scottsdale, Arizona, the day before I was scheduled to give a talk, thinking that the first book was finished, and suddenly the movie started up and I had to leap out of the water, run into the nearby spa, and get a pen and lots of paper. New chapters then flowed onto page after page as I sat in a chair poolside and scribbled as fast as I could.

On May 25, 2012, the current installment of the story, this book, *The King and Prince* was done in its complete rough draft, two days before the eighth birthday of my wonderful granddaughter, Grayson Teague Morris. And so, Gracie, I dedicate this book to you!

I want to thank again everyone who has encouraged me in this amazing endeavor, including many of the people in my business audiences who have heard about it, and all the people who workout with me nearly every day in the gym. They've been listening to blow-by-blow accounts of the writing process between bench press grunts and biceps curls. My main workout partner Don Sharp gave me needed encouragement on the days the movie wouldn't play in my head and I worried about whether I was going to actually have to make up stuff to pull all the puzzle pieces together. I never did, and he encouraged me to have the patience to wait until the next turns and twists of the tale revealed their secrets so that I could just write down what I saw. Another member of the Sports Center Crew, Tom Ryder, early on suggested a summary of insights to end each book, and as a result, we have the diary appendix for each one. I'm also very grateful to my wife Mary, who asked me to read a chapter or two or three aloud to her at night while they were being written, and that process helped me immensely in catching typos and making small edits, and even understanding better the overall flow of the story.

Once again I've benefited from the fine work of my friends Ed Hearn and Bruce May in their expert line editing. And I want to thank Sara Morris for her always great cover design and Abigail Chiaramonte for all other book design matters. Thanks also to you readers who keep me going with your great comments!

J. K. Rowling's Harry Potter stories first piqued my love for the coming-of-age tale. My repeated readings of her books prepared the soil deep in me for a thorough receptivity once the movie of these events began playing in my own heart and mind. I never said to myself, "I think I'll write a coming-of-age story set in Egypt in 1934." It just happened. But when it came, I was ready. And it never felt like I was making a single decision concerning what would happen next. My job was just to watch the show and write it all down. I hope this transcription is good enough to help you see much of what I've seen, in what's been for me the experience of a lifetime.

The three dogs Lexie, Ollie, and Abbey gave me frequent opportunities for fun breaks throughout the days of my writing. I'm grateful for that. Then Lexie moved on to the next big adventure. I hope we're reunited some day and can pick up where we left off. And I'd love one day for Walid to have a dog. Wouldn't you? I hope it happens. But of course, I don't feel like it's up to me.

I also want to thank you who are reading this for picking the book up and looking it over. I even more deeply thank you if you've chosen to live a while with the characters and their story. Spread the word. Your friends may also enjoy the journey recounted in these pages. May something in it resonate deeply with you and then open up some doors for your own best adventures in this world. And then let me know what you think. I'd love to hear.

Tom Morris
Wilmington, NC

Afterword

Beyond *The King and Prince*

First, there was *The Oasis Within,* a short tale about a series of deep conversations and surprising events that took place as a group of men and camels crossed the desert in Egypt in 1934. It's a prologue to the series of longer novels I never saw coming. Then there was *The Golden Palace*, the official Book One to the series of subsequent stories about a group of remarkable individuals collectively entitled:

Walid and the Mysteries of Phi

Next came *The Stone of Giza*. Then it was *The Viper and the Storm.* This is the official series Book Four. If you've read the prologue, *The Oasis Within*, or you've enjoyed *The Golden Palace*, The *Stone of Giza*, and *The Viper and The Storm*, you'll likely love all the books to come, which together present a sprawling epic account of action, adventure, and ideas set in and around a reimagined Cairo, Egypt in 1934 and 1935, with a few sojourns farther abroad. They all contain tales about life, death, meaning, love, friendship, the deepest secrets behind everyday events, and the extraordinary power of a well-focused mind. The events they relate will eventually interact with such classics as Plato's *Republic*, *The Epic of Gilgamesh*, *Beowulf*, *Frankenstein*, and *Moby Dick*, among many other classic and seminal texts. With unexpected humor and continual intrigue, you'll gradually discover in these books the outlines of a powerful worldview and a profound practical philosophy of life.

To find out more, visit **www.TomVMorris.com/novels** or go to **www.TheOasisWithin.com.**

All these books are available for large group purchases at special discounts. To find out more, contact the author through his oldest and most reliable email, **TomVMorris@aol.com** or his website. Tom is also available to speak with book groups via email, Skype, or any other means that would help in the discussion of these stories.

About the Author

Tom Morris is one of the most active philosophers and public speakers in the world. A native of North Carolina, he's a graduate of The University of North Carolina (Chapel Hill), where he was a Morehead-Cain Scholar, and he holds a Ph.D. in both Philosophy and Religious Studies from Yale University. For fifteen years, he served as a Professor of Philosophy at the University of Notre Dame, where he was one of their most popular teachers. You can find him online now anytime at **www.TomVMorris.com.**

Tom has been honored with the University of North Carolina's Distinguished Young Alumnus Award, as well as with honorary doctorates in recognition of his work. He has been a George A. and Eliza Gardner Howard Foundation Fellow, through Brown University, and a Fellow with the National Endowment for the Humanities.

Tom is also the author of over twenty-two pioneering books. His twelfth book, *True Success: A New Philosophy of Excellence,* launched him into an ongoing adventure as a philosopher working and speaking throughout the world. His audiences have included a great many of the Fortune 500 companies and dozens of the largest national and international trade associations. His work has been mentioned, commented on, or covered by NBC, ABC, CNN, CNBC, NPR, and in most major newspapers and news magazines. He's also the author of the highly acclaimed books *If Aristotle Ran General Motors, Philosophy for Dummies, The Art of Achievement, The Stoic Art of Living, Twisdom, Superheroes and Philosophy*, and *If Harry Potter Ran General Electric: Leadership Wisdom from the World of the Wizards*, as well as many others. Tom's newest nonfiction book is a revelation of the deep philosophy behind the success of Steve Jobs. It's called *Socrates in Silicon Valley*. His most recent books include the philosophical prologue to the current series, *The Oasis Within*, and the subsequent books, *The Golden Palace, The Stone of Giza*, and *The Viper and The Storm*, as well as the current volume. He just may be the world's happiest philosopher.

Φ

www.ingramcontent.com/pod-product-compliance
Lightning Source LLC
Chambersburg PA
CBHW020616310726
48979CB00008B/1513/J

* 9 7 8 0 9 9 9 3 5 2 4 4 1 *